FIFE CULTURAL TRUST

D0582943

Velvet

FIFE COUNCIL	
96663	
PETERS	29-Mar-2016
TF	£6.99
TEEN	FIFE

Velvet

TEMPLE WEST

Swoon Reads   New York

A Swoon Reads Book
An imprint of Macmillan Publishers Limited

First published 2015 by Macmillan Children's Books
an imprint of Pan Macmillan
a division of Macmillan Publishers International Limited
20 New Wharf Road, London N1 9RR
Associated companies throughout the world
www.panmacmillan.com

ISBN 978-1-4472-9042-1

Copyright © Temple West 2015

The right of Temple West to be identified as the
author of this work has been asserted by her in accordance with the
Copyright, Designs and Patents Act 1988.

All rights reserved. No part of this publication may be
reproduced, stored in or introduced into a retrieval system, or
transmitted, in any form or by any means (electronic, mechanical,
photocopying, recording or otherwise), without the prior written
permission of the publisher. Any person who does any unauthorized
act in relation to this publication may be liable to criminal
prosecution and civil claims for damages.

1 3 5 7 9 8 6 4 2

A CIP catalogue record for this book is available from
the British Library.

Book design by Ashley Halsey
Printed and bound by CPI Group (UK) Ltd, Croydon CR0 4YY

This book is sold subject to the condition that it shall not,
by way of trade or otherwise, be lent, resold, hired out,
or otherwise circulated without the publisher's prior consent
in any form of binding or cover other than that in which
it is published and without a similar condition including this
condition being imposed on the subsequent purchaser.

TWO SIDES OF HELL

THEY SPENT WEEKS KILLING EACH OTHER. NOW SOLDIERS FROM BOTH SIDES OF THE FALKLANDS WAR TELL THEIR STORY

VINCENT BRAMLEY

Rathmines Library
157 Lr. Rathmines Road
Dublin 6

JOHN BLAKE

Published by John Blake Publishing Ltd,
3 Bramber Court, 2 Bramber Road,
London W14 9PB, England

www.johnblakebooks.com

www.facebook.com/johnblakebooks 🔲
twitter.com/jblakebooks 🔳

This edition published in 2009

ISBN: 978-1-84454-821-7

All rights reserved. No part of this publication may be reproduced,
stored in a retrieval system, or transmitted in any form or by any means,
without the prior permission in writing of the publisher, nor be otherwise
circulated in any form of binding or cover other than that in which it is
published and without a similar condition including this condition
being imposed on the subsequent purchaser.

British Library Cataloguing-in-Publication Data:

A catalogue record for this book is available from the British Library.

Design by www.envydesign.co.uk

Printed in Great Britain by CPI Group (UK) Ltd

© Text copyright Vincent Bramley, 2009

The right of Vincent Bramley to be identified as the author of this work
has been asserted by him in accordance with the Copyright, Designs and
Patents Act 1988.

Papers used by John Blake Publishing are natural, recyclable products
made from wood grown in sustainable forests. The manufacturing processes
conform to the environmental regulations of the country of origin.

Every attempt has been made to contact the relevant copyright-holders,
but some were unobtainable. We would be grateful if the appropriate people
could contact us.

For my daughters Beth and Meg,
and for all our children

Contents

Introduction

THIS BOOK began life between April and June 1982, when I and thousands of other ordinary soldiers, British and Argentinian, met on the battlefields of the Falkland Islands. War is something we British have been used to for centuries. By contrast, Argentina is a relatively young nation and in its much shorter history it has fought few wars, suffering more from internal conflict than external.

The Falklands war, by comparison with the two world wars and many much smaller conflicts, was a small-scale affair, but it was a war nevertheless. What is significant is that it was an undeclared war, the politicians preferring to use the word 'campaign'. Calling it this does not alter the fact that hundreds of soldiers lost their lives and hundreds were wounded. And, as at the end of most much larger wars, a political regime collapsed – the military junta of General Galtieri.

Some years ago I asked myself who the real winners of the war were. Was it the Falkland Islanders? They have their freedom again, but their life is hardly the same as it was before 1982. Or was it the British government? The Conservative Party undoubtedly won a second term in power largely through Britain's military success, after which a wave of patriotism and a renewed sense of national unity temporarily swept aside the country's economic troubles.

Or were the victorious soldiers the winners? The soldier receives a medal and returns, often with difficulty, to peacetime life. He also has the sense of having done the job he is paid to do: to fight. But I believe that, in addition, he has the knowledge that he has served democracy, and in my view it is justified to fight in its defence as we did. Therefore it is ironic that, during a war waged against the suppression of democratic freedoms, those freedoms should be abused at home. The Falklands war was a heavily censored war – and a war that was heavily stage-managed through the media. Not only did faceless bureaucrats in the Ministry of Defence (MoD) monitor very carefully the British press coverage, but, as I noticed as soon as I returned home, the war was publicized in such a way as to appear completely clear-cut.

At the time I could easily imagine the ordinary man or woman thinking: ah well, this business down in the Falklands doesn't seem to have been too bad. And yet, with the perspective of time, it seems that the public weren't totally hoodwinked by MoD censorship. For they donated millions of pounds to the relatives of the dead and injured. And that is what makes me feel proud to be IBritish. For me, winning the war is secondary to that feeling.

But while the public cared, the government clearly did not, as is evident from the stories of some of the soldiers interviewed for this book. The nearest the ordinary citizen can hope to get to knowing the truth is to be related to a soldier who served in the Falklands, or perhaps even over a pint in a pub, with a veteran who chooses to reveal what the MoD wished to conceal.

For a number of years now I have studied military history, and this interest brings me to the question of who writes the history of our wars. Usually it is either a professional historian, a politician, a journalist cashing in as soon as possible after a conflict, or a general writing his memoirs, in which he explains how he won the war. They will not have been in the thick of the battle. But if any of them has, by all means let him tell you the facts.

The result of this 'expertise' is that the reader is left not much wiser about what soldiers are like or what actually happens in battle. The book you are about to read will, I hope, dispel some of this mystery, and present more than a few hard facts. The public lack of understanding of soldiering is something I see even more clearly now that I am back in civilian life. I am not saying that all the blame lies on the public's side, for as often as not when a civilian meets a career soldier there is mutual misunderstanding.

We have looked at how history is presented to us, and that is one of the main reasons for public ignorance of military matters. But the soldier himself is steeped in a culture that blinkers him to life outside the forces. He will talk with a sparkle in his eyes of the comradeship and deep friendship he finds in the Army, and of the structure the regiment gives to everything he does. A soldier fights not for Queen and country but for those friends he loves and respects, and secondly for himself.

By this time the civilian is thinking to himself that this guy must be from Mars, or that he has been totally brainwashed. I can tell you that brainwashed he is not. What is talking is comradeship and a sense of discipline that is instilled in him from the day he becomes a soldier. Now, discipline is something that both sides should agree on, given its ever-faster erosion by a tide of crime and lack of respect for person and property.

What form does military discipline take and what are its results? The British Army is famous throughout the world for its discipline. The civilian knows that much, but what is less well known is that an important element that sustains it is elitismelitism. Not the elitismelitism of the officer class, but the pride that regiments take in their own superiority. Each member of a body of fighting men is disciplined to preserve that sense of superiority – not, of course just to brag about it, but to demonstrate it by actions within the commonly agreed code of conduct.

One of the great strengths of the Army is its cap-badge rivalry, its inter-unit competition. In the Parachute Regiment we refer to other regiments as 'craphats'. The Royal Marines, although part of the Royal Navy, are also craphats, or 'cabbageheads', both names coming from the colour of their headgear. In general, anyone not in a red beret is a 'hat'. Senior officers at the MoD are 'heavy hats'.

It is rivalry – nothing more, nothing less. Other units have names for us which I couldn't possibly dignify by repeating here. However, I believe, like many of my comrades, that far too much emphasis was placed on cap-badge rivalry during the Falklands war. The blame for that lies firmly in the lap of certain senior figures who should have known better. As one of my former comrades says: 'There are good hats. And there are very brave hats. The Parachute Regiment would not exist or be capable of carrying out all its tasks if it was not for the hats in support.'

In fact the main obstacle in the path of today's Parachute Regiment is senior members of the Army and the Ministry of Defence. They have never liked the elitism of units like the Paras, particularly in peacetime, and this attack on constructive rivalry affects many parts of the military machine. But when a war breaks out the faceless officials of the MoD suddenly start begging for military success and they want elitism without delay if it means securing their own jobs.

In the present, probably short, period of peace these same mandarins are striking in another way at the very heart of professional fighting units like the Parachute Regiment. They have dreamed up a redundancy programme under which excellent soldiers are leaving a dwindling band of their comrades to fight a welter of red tape. The result is that the morale of those in the ranks is being sapped. But it is more serious still when we remember that it were not many decades ago that a British prime minister stepped off a plane bearing a piece of paper and spoke of 'peace in our time'. The sad thing is that those officials in grey suits argue more passionately about the removal of a tea and coffee machine from the corridors of the MoD than about the disappearance of yet another superbly trained body of fighting men.

In 1991 my first book, *Excursion to Hell*, was published. It was my own personal perspective on the Falklands war, and in particular the battle for Mount Longdon. My aim was to give the view of the ordinary soldier, but the government did not want to know the facts of warfare as I and others like me saw it. It was not the sort of book a senior military commander would have written, one that would have been thoroughly vetted by the Ministry of Defence. But the fact is, it did not escape official attention, for fifteen months after its publication they initiated a police inquiry conducted by Scotland Yard.

I could write a whole book on this painful episode, but what stands out is the tacky way the government handled the affair. The unmistakable message was that only they can call the shots in such matters. However, I believe firmly that the ordinary soldier has the right, just like a general or a politician, to publish his account of that, or any other, war. I object to bureaucrats distorting the facts, contradicting the experience of those who were there.

Military writers often glorify war. This book is not about glory. It is simply about individuals thrown together in war. My aim has been to write it in such a way that its message is clear to every reader, from the high-ranking civil servant to the ordinary man who has no understanding of military matters. Nor is this book an apolitical study. I ask you to put aside your opinions about the political rights and wrongs of the Falklands and read it as an account, largely in their own words, of soldiers of both sides who fought in that war. It is about their lives before, during and after the Falklands: how they came to find themselves on those bleak islands, what they experienced in battle and what happened to them and their families afterwards.

In June 1993 I travelled to the Argentinian capital, Buenos Aires, for the first time, in the company of two ex-members of the 3rd Battalion, Parachute Regiment, and representatives of the newspaper *Today*. There, in a backstreet hotel, we met on camera two Argentinian veterans of Mount Longdon. The aim of our visit was to show that the soldiers of two formerly warring nations could meet amicably without governmental interference or prompting. It took place at a sensitive time, for an inquiry into alleged war crimes by British soldiers was currently in progress.

It was while talking with my interpreter that I glimpsed the possibility of a book based on frank discussions between myself and both Argentinian and British Falklands veterans. The unstinting help of Patricia Sarano, of the Argentinian television company Channel 11, was to prove invaluable. I gave her a list of questions for other Longdon veterans.

These men she tracked down and interviewed informally, faxing the transcripts to me back in England. Three months later the synopsis of this book was approved by the publisher.

It was now that my real work began. My research clearly had to extend beyond talking to four or five ex-soldiers. To make things more difficult, as a result of the police inquiry my name was being splashed across the national newspapers every few weeks, so that it became harder to get Paras I had fought alongside to come forward.

Nevertheless, between October and December 1993 I interviewed five ex-members of 3 Para at great length, noting down every relevant detail of their personal lives. And I spent hours each day pinpointing their exact movements during the battle for Longdon. Over Christmas, after long, hard negotiations with friends in the know, I persuaded a twenty-four-year-old Argentinian living in England to assist me in my research in Argentina. Meetings took place in locations chosen to ensure confidentiality, primarily to prevent either the British or the Argentinian press from getting wind of the planned second trip. This may all sound overdramatic, but during that period certain members of the press were taking every step to probe into my life and hinder me. It is something I shall not forgive. To hell with them!

I first met Diego Kovadloff through a brief interview I gave to an Argentinian magazine. His impeccable English, his intelligence and his sense of humour forged a friendship between us at once. This young man, fourteen at the time of the Falklands war, was to become a vital link in the chain of production of this book, as his interpreting skills were essential to me. After numerous telephone calls to Argentina we had gained the agreement of a number of Longdon vets to meet us in their own homes.

On 18 January 1994, after flying via Switzerland and Brazil, we arrived in Buenos Aires to complete my research. I was nervous as I stepped off the plane and I was acutely aware that, knowing no Spanish, I had to rely totally on Diego for what would be a very emotional exchange for both sides. Also, I knew that if just one reporter knew I was there, not only would six months' work be destroyed, but our Argentinians would be unlikely to assist me. This was all the more probable because they are understandably reserved as far as the Falklands war is concerned.

How would I react to meeting the soldiers who had played a part in killing my friends? On the other hand, how would they feel seeing their former enemy? Would they focus on the politics of the war? Would they embroider the truth, or just downright lie? A thousand questions raced through my mind as we drove to a secret address in the Argentinian capital. After all, as far as I know, no one has written a book like this, where the author fought the very people he later interviews.

Buenos Aires has a strong European feel to it, inevitably mainly Spanish although the influence of Italy and Britain is also marked, particularly in the architecture. Cafés and newspaper kiosks lining every main street also gave it a continental European character. But what struck me immediately was the way the people drive. Where possible, they race at high speed along roads with few road signs and then bunch up like racing drivers at the lights, with perhaps eight cars straddling a road meant for four or five.

Impatient drivers revving up and sounding their horns at the lights are not unheard of in Britain, but they are more like the norm in Buenos Aires. In the suburbs the lights are often ignored completely, and driving along those roads I felt like I was at the wheel of a dodgem car at a fairground. The state of repair of the roads hardly makes for a smooth ride either. After experiencing this and the frantic driving of the locals, I've not complained about our roads once since being back in England.

On the whole I found the people of Buenos Aires honest and polite, and the service in restaurants and cafés prompt and friendly. I was learning about a race of people I had been conditioned to think of as overexcitable and quick-tempered. Our cultures are undeniably different in many ways, but I soon felt relaxed in this lively, round-the-clock city.

However, in the suburbs of Buenos Aires I saw the stark poverty in which very many of the city's populace live. They do not have the safety-net of unemployment benefit like Britain's, and receive next to nothing from the state. It was a common sight to see street vendors as young as six standing on street corners or threading their way between cars waiting at traffic lights. The poverty I saw made me realize how, relatively speaking, everyone is materially comfortable in Britain. We have deprivation in our inner cities, but nothing to compare with what I saw.

Most of the people living in the suburbs, where I was to interview the Longdon veterans, live in single-storey bungalows consisting of a living room and kitchen in one, one or two bedrooms and a bathroom. They are small compared with the average two-storey terraced house in Britain. Normally a large table dominates the living room, where there is usually also a TV. The occupants sit and talk for hours around this table in a time-honoured tradition of family life.

The Argentinians pride themselves on eating well, particularly steak and barbecued food. After coffee it is the normal practice to sip a tea called maté from a pot with a spout. It reminded me of the American Indians passing round the peace pipe. The first time I was offered maté I thought it was a drug in liquid form, like hash oil. Nevertheless I liked it.

The Argentinians I was to interview all lived in Lanus or Bandfield, twenty minutes' drive from the centre of Buenos Aires. They had belonged to the 7th Mechanized Regiment, an infantry unit, and had been conscripted from the same area, unlike the British Army, in which men from all over the country serve together. We have a voluntary army with a professional structure, whereas the Argentinians operate a system of conscription.

At birth every Argentinian citizen is given a national identity document which has to be renewed when the holder reaches sixteen. For males this renewal entails inclusion in a 'class' based on year of birth. In May of each year a conscription lottery is broadcast on the television and radio and printed in the newspapers. The numbers published refer to males who have reached the age of nineteen: it was mainly Class of 62 that served in the Falklands war. Young men whose last three digits on their identity documents correspond with the lottery numbers must present themselves for a medical examination in their local military district. Since a percentage will be exempted from service on medical grounds, more men than are needed are called up.

This sounds complicated to us who have a voluntary system, but it works. A further feature is that, by law, all conscripts working at the time of their call-up have their jobs left open for them and 75 per cent of their wage is payable during military service.

Because Argentina has not experienced war on our level, it has no firmly established aftermath programme for its soldiers. The government failed to respond adequately to the needs of those suffering physical and mental injury as a result of the Falklands war. Despite the difference between our countries, this will strike a familiar chord in many British veterans of the campaign.

The Argentinians do have veterans' groups, although over the past twelve years the movement has become split. Some groups regard their position as largely a political issue, and make their views felt, while others aim to quietly rehabilitate one another in group discussions. I am well aware that some Argentinian veterans wouldn't dream of sitting down to talk with me, an Englishman. That is why I had to secure the interviews before leaving Britain.

For fourteen consecutive days after our arrival in Buenos Aires, often working sixteen or eighteen hours a day, Diego and I interviewed my former enemy. With each individual I met I was unsure of how I would be received. But what I witnessed in every home has changed my outlook completely. As one soldier to another, we acknowledged our shared experiences, and each man wanted the public to know his story – just like my comrades from 3 Para. I was greeted in every home I went to with a sincere handshake, a hug and, most moving of all, a friendly smile. Not once did I come across suspicion or even lack of courtesy.

Food was always provided, along with beer to smooth the proceedings. Other members of the family sat in on most of the meetings, in many cases hearing their relative's war experiences for the first time. They were all eager to learn about the British way of life, my friends and our military system. One of the veterans said to me: 'This is a weird experience. Never did I think an English former enemy would come here into my neighbourhood and my home, but the funny thing is, it's going to be an Englishman that's going to tell our story! Nobody has really bothered to listen to us. Because we lost, everyone ignores us. After all, I did have many friends killed. It still hurts today.'

After meeting men like this, and feeling their genuine

warmth alongside the sadness of their memories, I realized that every veteran I spoke to would, regardless of the language barrier, fit in socially in a British pub on a Saturday night. And for me that was an important discovery.

I must now thank all the people who have supported and helped me over the two years it has taken to research and write this book. Without Patricia Sarano's contribution you would not be reading this book today. The same goes for Diego Kovadloff, whose excellent interpretation and translation, support and humour have been of immeasurable value. I would like to thank Jorge Altieri, who worked tirelessly to establish contact with his former colleagues for me, and Edgardo Esteban, who assisted with professional confidentiality in the case of further contacts. Thanks to the Argentinian family who accommodated me while I was researching in their country. They have asked to remain anonymous. Thanks also to Chuchu and Juan, two civilians who wined and dined me at all hours during my brief periods of free time.

Many thanks to Julie Adams and Steve Tebbutt. (Thanks for the photocopier.) To all the staff at Bloomsbury, particularly David Reynolds and Nigel Newton, who had faith in this project. To Richard Dawes, whose professional help and advice over the years has made him a valued friend. And special thanks to Alastair McQueen, who as my editor navigated his way through my manuscript and who has guided me away from the press harassment which has been an unpleasant feature of my life for nearly two years.

I want to thank my friends who have stuck by me during this most difficult period, in particular Paul Read and Martyn Benson. Also my parents, Fred and Pam, my brother Russell and my Uncle Brian, whose support for me throughout my life has never wavered. And particularly warm thanks to my wife, Karon, who has suffered long and hard with me. She and all my family have proved pillars of strength.

I offer this book to the memory of all who lost their lives in the Falklands, British and Argentinian alike. They cannot tell their story.

AT THE GOING DOWN OF THE SUN AND IN THE MORNING
WE WILL REMEMBER THEM

Vincent Bramley

Aldershot, July 1994

Part 1
Friends and Foes

1

SANTIAGO GAUTO drew deeply on his cigarette, making the red end glare fiercely. He held the smoke, then blew it up towards the ceiling. For a moment he paused, then he began to relax, and I was glad I had come here to this modest little house near Buenos Aires to meet a man my comrades and I had been trying to kill almost twelve years before.

He had greeted me at the door with a welcoming smile and a friendly handshake, then showed Diego, my interpreter, and me into his kitchen cum living-room. We sat round the table and he looked me in the eye and said: 'This is my home, Vincent. It is yours, too. Please.' Then he passed me a cool beer from the fridge, saying: 'Let's have a beer together. It's an honour to meet one of my former enemies.'

'Salud!' We raised our bottles of beer and I handed him an English cigarette and together we smoked and drank our beer and began to talk. We had both been a little nervous and, deep down, wary about this meeting. But now the ice was broken, we had overcome the first hurdle, and the chat was flowing, particularly about why I had come to see him.

Leabharlanna Poibli Chathair Bhaile Átha Cliath
Dublin City Public Libraries

We were both as curious about each other as any soldiers from opposite sides when they meet so long after a battle.

For a moment that great smile flashed again and then he said seriously: 'It is a brave thing you do, brave of you to come here alone, so far, to be surrounded by people who – even though it is all a long time ago now – could still want to harm you because you are English. I appreciate what you have done, what you are doing. Believe me, it is a brave thing and a big thing you do here today. I am proud of being chosen by you, Vincent. Maybe it is one of those beautiful chances in life... Someone picked me out, gave you my name and now we meet. Yes, it is brave, brave for both of us to meet.'

Watching me with deep, dark, puzzled eyes from behind the curtain which served as a door was Mayra, a classic picture of beauty and childhood innocence, bewildered by the strangers and the language they spoke to her father.

Sensing her confusion, Santiago said: 'Mayra, come to Papa.'

Diego talked quietly and calmly to his seven-year-old daughter and I turned to watch his lips as he translated the conversation. 'Don't be afraid, Mayra,' he said. 'This man Vincent has come from another country, a country many miles away. Many years ago, before you were born, he and I were enemies. We tried to kill each other for what we both believed was right. Don't worry – now we are at peace. Now we are about to become good friends.'

I looked at Diego as I stubbed out another cigarette. His eyes had filled with tears. I turned to the little girl as she moved from her father, came towards me and climbed on to my lap. She, too, was crying, tears rolling down her little face. Then she kissed me on the cheek and hugged me.

'Papa respects you. We are all friends now, yes?'

'Yes,' I said, wiping her tears away in just the same way as

I do for my own daughters when they are afraid or upset.

The room was quiet for a while, all of us deep in our own thoughts: me, the intelligent, big-hearted hospitable man who was my enemy, and Diego, who was too young to have had to endure the craziness of those events on the Falkland Islands so long ago, which to those who were there seem like just last week or even yesterday. This man, who was once my enemy, showers me with the hospitality and respect unique to soldiers who have fought each other, who have given of their all and who now accept that the war is over and that we should be friends.

He stubbed out the English cigarette and said: 'Good fags, Vince.' And the silence was broken. 'You know, I started smoking when I was fourteen and I still can't make my mind up whether it's a habit or for company!'

We laughed and his eyes swept the room. 'I was born here, on a table in this very room at four o'clock in the afternoon on 4 May 1962, the youngest of a family of four brothers and a sister. The woman who delivered me was called the local midwife, but she wasn't really a midwife, just a tough old woman from the neighbourhood. Unlike a lot of people my parents are true Argentinian. My mother's father was a chief from the Guarani tribe from Corrientes, a province in the north-east of the country. When I was four or five he came to visit, to see me, his latest grandson. He had a big gaucho knife in his waistband, but he refused to sleep in the house. He slept outside because he thought the roof might fall in on his head. He was from a different culture, as were my parents, and times were different then. Hard times. But when you see what is happening in the world today it makes you wonder if things weren't better then.

'When I was five my parents split up and my mother was left with the five of us. It was hard for her, on her own having to fend for us, but we survived. You have to, don't you? My childhood was tough, but I have no complaints. It was tough for all the other kids in this area. Under the circumstances I was happy. I wasn't brilliant at school, but I passed through primary school and then left in the third year of secondary school. I was at school with Beto – Jorge Altieri – another veteran of the Mount Longdon battle. We knew each other because we lived in the same neighbourhood.

'I got a job in a printer's and was soon earning more money than my mother, even though she was working in three houses, looking after a couple of blind kids in one place, cleaning another and caring for an old lady in the third. My sister left home and one of my brothers got married. Another went off to the south of the country to work as a mechanic. I was able to save some money by this time. Every weekend I would go to the discos in my best clothes. I loved boots: Texan-style cowboy boots. I remember buying my first pair, the unforgettable feeling of getting something you had saved for.'

Just before his nineteenth birthday Santiago received his summons to do national service and thus had his first experience of the chaos and confusion which reigned in the Argentinian Army at the time.

'There were too many of us. I, along with four others, was surplus to requirements, so they put us on a plane and sent us to Puerto Deseado, Santa Cruz, in the south. They didn't want us either so within seven hours we were back on a plane to La Plata to report to the 7th Regiment, which was my district regiment anyway.'

He was sent for induction training in San Miguel del Monte and it was his tough upbringing which saw him through, particularly the 'dancing', or what is called 'beasting' in the British Army.

'In San Miguel the instructors told us it would rain every day, but it didn't and they were really disappointed that the weather held until the very last day. We learned basic soldiering, marching, saluting, fieldcraft and, of course, we had 'dancing' – everywhere, every time, dancing. I became good friends with a guy called Dario. We became solid mates; the sort of friendship you make in rough times.

'At one time Dario was laid up for twenty-five days in a tent very ill with a swollen testicle. He couldn't move and he wasn't able to walk to the cookhouse for his food. I said I would take food to him. The corporal made me dance all the way every time, making me crawl; run, anything, all the time screaming in my ear: 'Come on, you fucking faggot, take the food.' It was exhausting, I was flat out, and they kept dancing me just because I wanted to take food to a mate.

'Another day I was being danced by a corporal for no reason at all when an officer asked him why. He said it was because I had been rude. The officer asked for witnesses and the whole company backed me up. The corporal spent fifteen days under arrest. At least one of our officers had a sense of decency. He went by the book, yeah?'

At the end of their first forty-five days of initial training. Santiago was one of a small group regarded as the best in the intake. He was rewarded with five days' leave. So, too, was his pal Dario Gonzales, who, despite his injuries, had made the grade. Santiago was sent as a batman to a lieutenant, and Dario to a captain. For a while it was relaxing, sometimes playing chess with the officers and occasionally beating them at it.

Santiago was intrigued to discover that almost every man in the company had the same blood group. Was that the way they decided on a military formation? He supposed it made things simpler for the medics if everybody was the same should they go to war.

Thirty of them were selected to form a commando group within the company. Extra training followed and the days of chess with the officers were over.

'We had instruction at night in all weathers. It was fucking freezing in winter. We were taught how to make and plant booby-traps, we did lots of extra shooting and had to strip and assemble weapons while blindfold. They even taught us how to stop an electric train, which was fuck-all use to us. Maybe one day I'll go to the station and stop one!

'I was still looking after my officer. He was a collector of weapons and I used to have to go to his home to clean his guns. I'll always remember he had a beautiful original Luger. We also had to do a lot of training for a running competition which we won and they gave us medals.

'One time Brigadier General Joffre, who commanded X Brigade and was also Land Forces Commander in the Malvinas, came to visit us and see something at the nearby theatre. All thirty of us were ordered to escort him and guard him. We all lost our leave to look after him. Arseholes.

'On the whole, though, I had a good time. We were a good group with a good attitude and we behaved ourselves and got on with it. We got more leave than the rest and because of our behaviour I got an early discharge. I was out on 23 December, in time for Christmas, and on the way home I was the happiest man around.'

Santiago did what many young men then liked to do as soon as they got away from the clutches of authority. He grew his hair. He was back in his old job at the printworks and happy. He had done what his country demanded of him.

But four months later he was back in the barber's chair on an Army base, his treasured locks on the floor, his tooled cowboy boots replaced by Army-issue ones. Santiago had been recalled and was back in the 7th Regiment. No matter what the future held, his mother, at least, would be OK. Under the law his employers were obliged to pay his wages to her while he was called up. (It was only when he returned from the war that he discovered they hadn't sent her a solitary peso.)

'We left for El Palomar for a flight to the Malvinas. The streets along the way were full of people waving and cheering. It was all very patriotic. Some guys got carried away with it all. But some other guys were thinking other things. I remember asking myself: Where the fuck are we going? What for?'

I met Jorge Altieri on my first visit to Argentina, in June 1993, eleven years after the Falklands. I had gone there with Denzil Connick and Dominic Gray, two of my comrades from 3 Para, and Alastair McQueen of the London newspaper *Today,* who had covered the Falklands war for the *Daily Mirror,* and Ken Lennox, another *Mirror* veteran who was now the chief photographer on *Today.* The *Today* team was with us to cover the first meeting of veterans of the battle for Mount Longdon. That was all we had gone to do: to meet, shake hands, and talk to each other of our experiences.

However, after meeting Jorge and another veteran, ex-Corporal Oscar Carrizo, everything changed. The meetings with these guys laid the foundation for this book. I only spoke to them for a short time through Patricia Surano and Daniel Fresco, two researchers for Argentina's Channel 11 television network. The information from these brief, off-camera chats hit me like a thunderbolt. These men had stories to tell. Their war, too, was a terrible one.

I left Patricia a list of questions and she tracked down four more veterans and sent me their answers and a taste of their experiences. The more Patricia dug, the more enthralled I became and it was on her research that I based the original synopsis for this book.

Six months later I was on the streets of Lanus, just outside Buenos Aires, with Diego at the height of the rush hour to meet Jorge, this time away from the cameras and the reporters with their prying questions. He had worked tirelessly contacting other veterans of Longdon, and now he greeted me like a long-lost friend and led us through a maze of backstreets to his home for a meal with his wife and parents.

In many ways Jorge's home is a shrine, a living memorial to his days as a soldier. The blue and white flag of Argentina stands proudly against a wall. There are certificates, souvenirs and replica weapons hanging on the walls. Grapevines form a canopy over the table in the backyard.

After the meal the others watched and listened quietly as Jorge and I pored over photographs and maps of Mount Longdon, pinpointing our respective positions on that fateful day in June 1982. Jorge's polite manner to me, his former enemy, put me at ease and we both relaxed completely as the evening wore on. From time to time he would smile warmly at me across the table and as he told me his life story in his soft voice I couldn't help thinking of this man as a friend. At the same time I felt great sympathy for him because his account of the war itself reminded me of the stories of some of my own comrades.

The son of an Italian immigrant mother, Jorge told me: 'These streets round here, these streets of the Monte Chingolo Estate, are my streets. These are the streets where I grew up, where I played. My mother was married before, to a policeman who was killed in the line of duty. When she marred my father she had two sons, my brothers. I have good, loving parents and brothers.

'Like thousands of other kids from this area I went

through primary school, but dropped out of secondary school after my first year. I just wasn't interested. I did a short course at technical school studying radio and TV. My real love in life was martial arts. I discovered the joys of the techniques when I was fifteen or sixteen. My brother, Miguel, and I went to see all the Bruce Lee films. They just fascinated me. I was in a club, the Bandfield Club, and practised judo three times a week for two hours. Lots of other kids came to try it out, but they gave up. I stuck with it and then Chan Do Kwan, another martial art, which I did on Mondays, Wednesdays and Fridays. In the end I was in the gym training six days a week. I won a judo competition at the Universidad de Belgrano. I was a blue belt at Chan Do Kwan and orange-belt standard at judo as well as being secretary of the judo club. I loved it. I was about to start a job as an instructor in self-defence for the police in our area, but then my number was called and I had to go to do my duty as a conscript.

'I could have got out of it because I was born with a nasal problem and I could have proved to them that it had left me with a breathing difficulty, but I wanted to go in. I even fancied my chances of becoming a regular and maybe even ending up a corporal or sergeant.

'I remember we all gathered to be taken to the 7th Regiment camp, expecting to go on trucks, but they made us walk. And when we got there they told us: "You're conscript soldiers. You left your balls outside. Inside, we command everything, so don't play the cock here.'

'They gave us all green fatigues and our civvies went into a locker. I knew not to take good clothes – I went in old ones. If you take your best clothes they get nicked. Then they divided us up by height and sent us to different companies. I was sent to B Company.

'My name, Altieri, caused me problems straight away. A

corporal called Rios thought I was a relative of General Galtieri. He just wouldn't have it that my name was different. So because of my name I got my first dancing lesson.

'I was issued with a FAL 7.62mm rifle. Other guys were given FAPs – light machine-guns – and others got PAMs [sub-machine guns]. The main emphasis in shooting practice was making every bullet count. I was also shown how to use a bazooka, how to make and lay booby-traps, and how to navigate at night, and we went on helicopter drills, night and day attacks and ambushes. Although we got the basics of soldiering, we still spent most of the time 'dancing'. B Company was known as the 'dancing company' by everyone else in the regiment.

'At six o'clock every morning we would parade in front of the national flag, salute it, do close order saluting of each other, get danced everywhere, dig 'foxholes' or field latrines just to fill in the time. We were never given any proper tests and even on the shooting ranges we had different weapons each time so we never had a weapon we could zero properly and call it a personal weapon. It seemed a continuous punishment of running, crawling, digging and guard duty – and dancing.

'Even after our forty-five days' initial training in San Miguel del Monte the dancing continued. We were never left alone. From dawn to dusk it was dance, dance, dance. We even had to dance to the toilets. Then they decided to make B Company a special commando within the regiment. We were the 'dancing commando'.

'On 9 March 1982 I was discharged. My conscription was over and I was going to take up the job with the police. I was going to lead a normal life. I was going to be a normal civvy. I screamed: 'I'll never come back here again. Yeah!'

'I was just relaxing back into the civilian way of life when, on 30 March 1982, there was a demonstration in the

Plaza de Mayo, right by Government House in Buenos Aires. A guy called Dalmiro Flores was killed, shot by plain-clothes police. I'll never forget it, because three days later the Malvinas were captured. I was happy we had recovered what I believed was rightfully ours, but I couldn't help thinking that Galtieri had ordered the taking of the islands to save his position in power because the population was rising against him after the shooting.

'Rumours soon began to circulate that Class of 62 – my conscript intake – would be recalled. I was in bed at 6 a.m. when the local policeman came round with my call-up papers for war. My mother said: 'No, don't go. I'll hide you in a neighbour's cellar.'

'I told her: "I would much rather die defending the nation than be shot on our doorstep as a coward. I want to go."

. 'At 11 o'clock my father and brother took me to La Plaza to our regiment. Outside it was a madhouse, with guys screaming 'Los vamos a reventar!' ['We're going to thrash them'] and 'Viva Argentina, viva Argentina!' Those of us recalled gathered on one side outside the camp. I remember seeing 'El Ruso', the Russian, and 'El Abuelo' [the grandfather], so called because he was thirty years old. He was studying law and had asthma, but he still ended up in the Malvinas.

'I remember thinking: These are fools. They're not thinking what can happen.

'Then the gates opened and we were greeted with the usual bollocking and shouting. We had to put our names down for a State life insurance. A guy called Massad dealt with that. Ironically he was to get killed over there.

'That night, after they had assigned us to our company lines, we were all just fucking about, playing around, throwing bread at each other. Nobody was taking it seriously. That's how it went for a few days.

'Then, Class of 63 – the conscript intake after our year – returned to the regiment from their basic training. They just grabbed their weapons off them and gave them to us. You should have seen them, all dirty and rusty. They had been doing the rounds of the training units for the last four or five years. We had to strip them down and clean them thoroughly. Some of the new conscripts – remember they had just forty-five days' training under their belts – were then drafted in with us to fill in some of the gaps in the regiment. Some of them were given new weapons, but I can also remember some really old Mauser rifles, dating back to 1909, being carried by some of the men for sniping. They were really out of date for modern warfare.

'Next we got our green fatigues. That was on 13 April. Then they gave us all a pair of trainers. Trainers! I suppose they thought we could do a lot of gymnastics in the Malvinas!

'Different parties of soldiers were leaving the camp at different times. Nobody had told us anything, but we just guessed we were heading for the Malvinas. As we stepped on to the buses to leave, the officers told us our relatives were at the gates and we were to shout '*Viva Argentina*' as we left so that they could see we were happy to go.

'We were taken to El Palomar and waited and waited to board a Boeing 707 for a flight to Rio Gallegos in the south. For many of us it was our first time in the air. We thought it would be like it is in the commercials and joked about the service we would get from the flight attendants. There were no flight attendants. There weren't even any seats for us. Only the officers and NCOs were given seats. The rest of us had to sit on our kit on the floor. We were all there crammed in together. Then the plane took off. I can still see it now - bodies, kit, weapons, everything flying all over the place. It was just like being on a crowded bus when the driver suddenly hits the brakes.

'At Rio Gallegos there was another long delay – twenty-four hours this time. Apparently the delay was because a plane had gone off the short runway in the Malvinas. So we actually set off for the Malvinas on 15 April.

Kevin Connery was a soldier's son. His father, Frank, spent twenty-five years in the Royal Engineers, serving in the sort of places the Army liked to use on the recruiting posters – and some they didn't – raising his large Catholic family of three boys and five girls with his wife Winifred. Kevin was born in Southampton in April 1957 and was soon a seasoned traveller as the family followed Frank on his postings in Turkey, Malaya and Singapore. Kevin's earliest memories are of Gilman Barracks, Singapore, with its swimming pool which helped the lively five-year-old burn off his near-boundless energy and cool off after playing in the tropical sun. It was also the place where he had his first brush with death.

He contracted malaria and remembers his fear and confusion as his grieving family gathered at his bedside, crying and praying for him. He was not expected to live. But there was a streak of determination running through the sickly mite, a determination to live, a resolve to enjoy more days in the sun at the pool in Gilman Barracks.

Kevin fought the disease – 'I suppose God had destined me for better things' – and recovered. It was a long haul, but he made it. Just as he did, his whole life was turned upside down again by the sudden death of his beloved mother. Some of his sisters were by this time in their teens and like every big family they drew together to give each other strength.

Young Kevin continued his schooling in Singapore and began to develop a passion for rugby, one of the great loves of his father's life too. But nothing is for ever in the Army.

Frank's time was nearly up and he was posted to Marchwood in Hampshire to finish his service. He quickly settled down to life in England again. There was to be no more upheaval, no more moving every few years, and Frank quickly found himself a job. Kevin's four elder sisters and eldest brother had married and left home and Frank looked after young Kevin, Sean and Kathleen.

Kevin became the 'potman' at the local British Legion, collecting the empty glasses and returning them to the bar, earning pocket money and embarking on a new journey, this time of knowledge. He was fascinated by the yarns the old soldiers told as they sank their pints. He was absolutely enthralled by their tales.

At the age of eleven Kevin went to the local secondary school – 'its name was Hardley and we nicknamed it "Hardley educational"' – where he spent five unhappy years, being bullied and playing truant.

'I was skinny, puny and thoroughly bullied. I had sandpaper rubbed over my face and my hands burned on the Bunsen burners. I was kicked and pushed and punched and in the end was frightened of my own shadow.'

He allowed the bullying and the truancy to overshadow his natural intelligence and ability, he now realizes. But despite it all he left school at the age of sixteen with five O levels and two CSEs. He was going to do what he had always wanted to do: join the Army. He had first applied when he was fourteen and had been told he would be welcome in the Royal Engineers, his father's old regiment. Kevin wasn't sure, and although he knew all the old soldiers' stories, he had still not decided what type of soldiering he preferred. But he made his mind up after attending a two-day course at the Youth Selection Centre at Brookwood, near Camberley, Surrey.

'I saw a poster of a Paratrooper landing ready for action.

I knew right away that was going to be me. My brother Sean had already joined 1 Para and he had broken his back. My family was against me joining, but I had made my mind up. I was adamant, 100 per cent adamant. Sean being a Para had nothing to do with my choice.'

Kevin went to the depot as a 'crow', a boy soldier. Like everyone else he faced P Company, the rigorous, week-long training for Parachute Regiment selection which sees more men quit than pass. Most of those who drop out do so because they just cannot hack it or decide it is not for them or that they want to try some other type of soldiering with a non-airborne regiment. They become what Paras call 'craphats', or 'hats' for short. There was no danger of Kevin being consigned – or consigning himself – to the ranks of the hats. Today he remembers the training 'as a long but worthwhile torture'.

It was also a journey of discovery for him, a long, hard, painful road which saw a wretched little fellow become a self-confident, professional military man.

'When I arrived I was a kid with no aggression whatsoever – only a puny, picked-on kid. The only violence I had ever used was on the rugby field in tackles, not fighting. The very day I joined, my squad was marched into the gym for a spot of "milling" – a crude form of boxing – under the platoon sergeant, Frank Pye. God, was he a hard bastard!

'I sat on the bench awaiting my turn to go into the centre. I was shitting myself. The whole thing was scaring the shit out of me. I was shaking with fear knowing I was certain to be beaten up. I knew I was going to get beaten up because I always got beaten up. Nothing has ever frightened me so much. I went into the ring to fight a guy called Nick Newbold, who was the same build as me, and he proceeded as I knew he would – to punch almighty fuck out of me.

Then Frank Pye stepped in. He dragged me to the corner of the gym.

'To the day I die I shall always remember his eyes. He looked into mine, deep into mine, deep inside me. He read my life story there and then on the spot. He had a big face, a big man's face, and he said: "Go in there and fight all the people who ever bullied you and all the people who ever put pressure on you. Go in there and just fight, just let it go, son."

'I went back into that ring and, do you know, it took three adults to pull me off him. I fought with such aggression - it just seemed to seep out of every pore in my body. Frankie pulled me to one side again and said, simply: "You'll do."'

That moment of controlled aggression changed young Kevin Connery. He was determined he would pass the course. Frank Pye, a legendary Parachute Regiment NCO, had turned a boy into a man.

Kevin joined the ranks of 3 Para – with the distinctive green DZ flash on the arm of his parachute smock – in 1978 in Germany. By this time he was completely dedicated to the battalion and the regiment, to his comrades, and to the traditions of professionalism and bravery he was required to respect and uphold. Kevin Connery, just like the rest of us, was a Paratrooper from the soles of his feet to the top of his head. All he needed was the chance to prove himself.

As Britain seethed over the invasion of the Falklands the men of 3 Para were leaving their base in Tidworth, Hampshire, for Easter leave. Kevin had already beaten them to it. He was on honeymoon with his bride in Switzerland. As British Rail staff hurriedly scribbled notices to post at all mainline stations saying 'All 3 Para personnel return to barracks immediately', Kevin was blissfully unaware of all the drama. He was more concerned with doing what honeymooners do and talking to his wife about their future life together to be concerned about what was happening in the world outside.

As officers and NCOs set about the task of getting the battalion ready for war, groups of excited soldiers dropped everything and poured back to camp. Other teams were tracking down the soldiers who had missed the recall. Some, they knew, would bitch and moan, but there wasn't a man among them who would want to miss out on the chance of a good scrap. Not even Kevin. When he was found he immediately began his preparations to return to his unit, a decision which shocked his bride, but no one else who knew him. Newly married man or not, it was: 'Sorry, darling, we've got to bin the rest of the honeymoon.' To be fair to Kevin he wasn't exactly over the moon about the recall as he had the same first thoughts as many of his mates: that this was just the 'brass' saying 'hurry up and wait' yet again. He still half believed this to be the case as he kissed his wife goodbye and, heavily loaded down with kit, negotiated the steep gangway of the giant P&O cruise liner SS *Canberra*.

It was five years since that day when Kevin had first seen the poster of the Paratrooper. Now, as he stood on the deck, he was one. Lean, fit, and with his blond hair cropped and barely visible beneath his red beret, he was ready for anything. He had served in Germany and Canada, but his only operational soldiering had been in Northern Ireland. This was what he had joined for – if it happened. For a little voice deep down inside was still telling him that this was just like the 'phoney war' of 1939. Everyone was walking round armed to the teeth and saying: 'We'll get there, then nothing will happen.'

Christ, he thought, why doesn't some bastard just make his mind up and either let us get on with it or tell us to piss off back home. As the *Canberra* steamed away from Ascension Island, that dust-covered volcanic furnace right in the middle of the Atlantic, 'some bastard' had made his mind up. We were going to war. Kevin watched as the great white ship, hemmed in on all sides by other civilian merchantmen and a protective cordon of 'grey funnel liners', the warships of the Royal Navy, confidently negotiated the ever-heavier South Atlantic swell. Every day it became colder and the days shorter. A Royal Navy frigate gave a demonstration of its fire-power. Navy and RAF Harriers streaked past, displaying the hardware fastened under their wings. It was all meant to boost morale.

Hercules transporters – from which Kevin had jumped many times and which had been nicknamed 'Fat Alberts' by the RAF – lumbered overhead, parachuting mail and more supplies to the fleet. This was when it dawned on him that something big was on and he was definitely going to be a part of it.

It caused him to ponder what lay ahead, and a great swirl of emotions engulfed him. Misgivings and nagging doubts began to eat away at his confidence and excitement. He wasn't the only man aboard the ship to suffer those thoughts. Most kept them to themselves. They were professional soldiers, for Christ's sake.

He prayed to himself: 'What happens if I'm not the Paratrooper the training has programmed me to be? Jesus, what if I become a coward? Oh, God, I don't want to be a coward in front of my mates.' As the ship sailed ever southwards, Kevin, like many of the Paras, could no longer accept the luxury of his surroundings.

The training, the programming, the traditions of how Paratroopers prepare for battle, were automatically taking over. They no longer needed the cinema – except for lectures – the well-appointed bars or the comfortable restaurant. They had served their purpose, but they were not needed for men preparing to go into battle. Paratroopers didn't need this sort of thing any more. It was 'hat' kit. They didn't need to go to war by bloody boat, either. That was for the Marines. He had always believed that if a war had happened in his time he would have parachuted into action, just like the soldier in the recruiting poster, to establish a bridgehead and hold it until the hats caught up and came to hold the line while the Paras fought through yet again to establish another forward area, while the enemy reeled from the onslaught as the 'Red Devils', as Hitler had named the Paras, did what they were conceived to do. It seemed undignified, somehow, to be going to war in a landing-craft which looked like a fucking floating rubbish skip.

Like most Paratroopers, Kevin didn't like Marines. As far as he was concerned, they were just another collection of bloody hats and the sooner he was away from them and fighting the Argies the better. But it was a manoeuvre constantly practised by the Marines which, he maintains to this day, was the scariest thing he had ever had to do since that fateful day when he stepped into that boxing ring back in Aldershot.

The exercise is called cross-decking: stepping from a ship into a landing craft to get to another ship. And the Navy, in their wisdom, decided to carry out this manoeuvre in the middle of the night, in the middle of the Atlantic. Laden like a pack mule, Kevin joined the long line of Paras waiting to step from the wallowing ship into the dementedly bobbing landing-craft pitching under his feet for the short journey into the dock of the overcrowded assault ship HMS *Intrepid*. He still shivers as he recalls that step from the door of the *Canberra*, over the glassy black bottomless ocean below to the slippery steel bulwark of the diesel-belching landing-craft as 'just about the limit of testing one's nerves'. Once you've forced a Para to do that someone will have to pay. So there'd better be a war and it won't be hard to guess who is going to be the winner! You don't force Paras to behave like hats and expect to get away with it.

2

IT WAS TWO o'clock in the morning and we had just scoffed a huge barbecue in Felix Barreto's garden. It's like a compound, with a big concrete wall and picket fence to deter the prying eyes of those still prowling the rutted, bone-jarring streets outside. For three hours we had cruised the alleyways which pass for streets in the sprawling, menacing barrio, or shanty town, which surrounds Felix's home. Thank God we had an off-road vehicle because a normal car wouldn't have negotiated ruts and bumps which made tank tracks seem as smooth as billiard-tables. We were feeling uneasy in this alien place, watched by silent eyes as groups of young men scavenged for discarded plastic bottles to sell for a few coins. We were watched, as all strangers are watched here, with cold, blank stares. Back home it would probably be as near as dammit a no-go area at night. There were no names on the houses or the streets. Eventually someone pointed out a track which could lead us to Felix. Half an hour after midnight we found him, sitting patiently with his wife and son, showing no sign of irritation at our lateness. He welcomed us warmly and we sighed with relief – me, Diego and Longdon veteran Antonio Belmonte. At last we felt safe.

I smiled to myself, thinking: twelve years ago I was trying to kill this guy; tonight I'm grateful to be feeling safe in his home. Sensing my unease, Felix said: 'This neighbourhood looks after its own. You know, nobody steals from each other round here. Doors can be left open. Crime is almost nil... '

When you look at Felix you can understand why. This is a hard area. A place where hard men live. And you believe him when he says: 'I've had to fight all my life, with my fists or with words, just to survive. Outsiders don't understand what it is like to have to fight to survive all your life, from the moment you are old enough to sit up and take notice.'

This man with thick, dark, wavy hair and a fierce black moustache is one of those people you respect automatically. His piercing blue eyes never waver as he talks, in a quiet voice, about the lot he has been dealt in life. And you know that if you get on the wrong side of him you do so at your peril. His upbringing, like that of many soldiers in many armies throughout the world, was a harsh one.

Felix Barreto was born on 31 March 1962, the first of six children of a father of Italian descent and a Paraguayan mother. Four sisters arrived between him and his little brother. Soon afterwards his father left the family home in Resistencia, in the northern province of Chaco.

'All I can remember is having to work to survive. We all had to. My mother was left with six kids and there is no such thing here as unemployment benefit. If you are unemployed you've had it. We lived in poverty and the only way out of it was to work. I started work at the age of eight, selling newspapers and fruit on street corners and delivering bread while still going to school. Every penny went towards supporting the family. My schooling was OK – I was even top of my class.

'Life in the barrios is hard. I never had a proper toy in my life, not even a football. I grew up in the same shanty town as the great footballer Maradona. I knew him. We kicked a ball about together, but it wasn't footballs which ruled this place – it was guns. It was a violent place and if you didn't stand up for yourself you didn't survive. My mother was strict with me and I thank her for it now, although at the time I resented her punishments, such as being kept in when everyone else was out on the streets playing or working. There were certain people I wasn't allowed to associate with. It was her strictness which meant I escaped the guns. You'd see kids of eleven with guns planning robberies and the police couldn't even get into this place after them. I was punchy even then. I took no crap from anyone. If you didn't fight people walked all over you, but I didn't steal. That is one of my merits: I have never stolen anything from anyone.

'When I was about twelve I came south to live near Buenos Aires to get better work with more money. I got labouring work on building sites, which was really hard for a kid of my age. I was determined to better myself and my family. Then I got work in a factory, making shoes. It was a big factory and the machines made so much noise you could hardly think, let alone work. It was called the Delgado factory and I worked there every morning. In the afternoons I worked in a plastic workshop. I used to sleep on the floor there. Then I feared I would lose the job if I was caught so I slept out in the open in one of the squares in Buenos Aires. Some of my workmates saw me and realized I was having a rough time, so they spoke to the boss and the owner said I could sleep in the factory until I got my wages at the end of the first month. As soon as I got my wages I went and rented a small house then went for my mother, little brother and sisters.

'My mother got work as a *mucama* [maid] in a clinic and in family homes. But we weren't getting on. Mother had tremendous pressures on her. I was back at school as well as working, but the system was different in Buenos Aires. What we had done in the second year up north they didn't do until the sixth year. I was having to do everything all over again. I was having quarrels and fights almost daily. There was no reason for the rowing. I was hot-blooded and it was second nature for me to fight, but I don't know why I did it so much. Anyway, they kicked me out of school. There were more rows at home so I left. I never went back, not until the day before I was sent to the Malvinas.

'I rented a room in a small *pensión* near Bandfield, in Lanus, and managed to support myself.. I organized my life. I met my wife-to-be then, when I was just fourteen, and we've been together ever since. On Saturdays and Sundays we went out dancing in the discos and it was back to work on Monday with no sleep. I did my own washing, ironing, cooking and cleaning. I have always kept myself and my place spotless. I settled into a rhythm, working hard in the shoe and plastic factories and dancing at weekends. At sixteen I was hanging around with guys twice my age. They taught me how to survive on the streets. One of my friends had a truck and taught me how to drive it. I did deliveries for him in my spare time.

'I got my call-up papers when I was nineteen. I wasn't annoyed about it because it was something which had to be done. I looked on the bright side – it could have its advantages! By law I had to receive seventy-five per cent of my wages from work and my job had to be kept open for me. So off I went to the Army.

'I felt sure I would like the Army, but straight away I

discovered that the system was very unjust. I accept that military systems are all about discipline, but we were treated badly right from the start. They had this thing about superiority. I mean, they wanted us to bow to the guys with rank. All that sort of thing simply wasn't me. I've never bowed to anyone. They really wanted to humiliate us. We were called Class of 62 because that was the year we were born.

'I was having run-ins with a corporal who had taken a dislike to me. One day I wanted to phone my girlfriend during our lunch break. The corporal started throwing a fit. He was going to "dance" me: press-ups, sit-ups, jumping on the spot, etc. I had had enough of his continual harassment and dancing. So I refused to dance for him. I told him I wasn't going to do it any more. I was going to fight him. Then an officer who had been passing got involved. He told the corporal he was wrong and danced him. He was furious, but you can imagine things didn't get any better for me after that.

'But I found a way to get even. Every time we went to the canteen I would get a burger and a Coke on the corporal's chit and falsify his signature. Ha! I can't remember how many burgers and Cokes I had before they caught me. I was obviously heading for the *calabozo* [jail] and that was after they had danced me. What a dance. They danced me all day long, but I avoided jail because we were scheduled to go on a big exercise the next day and they wanted every man there.

'But just when I thought I had done my punishment they came for me. There was this corporal and a Lieutenant Baldini. They took me to the shower room and hung me over the shower pipes with handcuffs. I can't remember how long they left me hanging there, but afterwards Baldini said I'd go nowhere in his army. Deep down I had wanted to stay in the Army after conscription, but now I could see no future in it for me.

'You know, looking back on it now, Baldini was wrong. He was a military man through and through and a good one, but as a person he was useless. He wasn't interested in relationships with his soldiers or treating them decently.

'In March 1982 Class of 63 was arriving at the barracks and I had four days left to do – and the Malvinas were taken. I sensed right away that I wasn't going to be discharged. With just two days of my time remaining 1 was sent out to help round up the guys who had been discharged. They didn't tell us anything-it was all uncertainty. We weren't told if we were going to the Malvinas or if we were going to cover for a regiment in the south which had already been sent. It seemed more likely we would be covering for another regiment, guarding their camp and the like, because even though they had issued us with all the gear to travel we still had our old training weapons. We couldn't be going to war with them, could we?

'I dashed home to my bedsit and gathered all my belongings together and took them to my mother's house for safe keeping. It was the first time I had been home for years, but I didn't tell her anything. I really didn't know anything.

'Back at barracks the feeling grew that we were going to guard a camp down south. We boarded a Hercules C-130 at Rio Gallegos and took off, but we were turned back because of bad weather. It was only then that we found out we had been flying to the Malvinas. If the weather hadn't forced us back we wouldn't have known where we were going until we landed:'

To Dominic Gray, life was a challenge to endure and to enjoy-right from the moment the midwife smacked his backside when he came into the world on 12 October 1960, in Brighton, West Sussex. Dom's father, Peter, was an engineer and a dealer in Harley-Davidson motorbikes. As Britain shrugged off the last of the austerity brought about by the Second World War people were able to afford cars. Motorbikes were becoming less popular, so dealing in expensive imported American machines was a hard business.

Peter, who had been a prisoner of the Germans in occupied Jersey in the Channel Islands, was thirty when he met the girl who was to be Dom's mother, and married her when she was just eighteen. It was a match on which the gods did not smile kindly. Dom arrived in a world where his dad was working every hour he could to sell and repair the motorbikes and where his mother wanted more than rock 'n' roll, motorbikes and being cooped up with a demanding baby in a small flat above the workshop. The marriage was rocky. Dom's mum started to go out on the town at night, and he remembers arguments and loud, violent rows. Even the birth of his brother, Daniel, failed to heal the scarred union. 'One day she just upped and left. I've never seen her since,' Dom recalls.

Dom and baby Daniel went to stay with their maternal grandmother. She had a drink problem and Peter believed the boys were being mistreated. They moved to London to stay with their Aunt Barbara for six months before Peter decided to move them to his sister Joan's care in northern France, where Joan had married a Frenchman called Jean. Peter was doing a lot of business there and would be able to visit his boys more regularly.

'I was very happy with Auntie Barbara, but France was idyllic,' Dom says. 'Daniel and I were there for four or five years and we started to go to school there. We learned French. It became our first language. The happiest days of my life were living with Aunt Joan. The house was by woods and a big lake and near a farm. When we were told dad was coming to visit, Daniel and I would dash to a bench beside the road and listen for the roar of his motorbike. I can still hear that roar as he came round the bends to this day. The joy of seeing him was indescribable. It made me feel like I was part of a family again.'

But Dom's joy was short-lived. His father decided he should return to England 'for a short holiday'. In reality he wanted his elder son to be educated in England and the boys were parted. Daniel was to stay in France.

'Joan would never have agreed to allow me to go to England if she had known the full story. She would never have willingly allowed us to be split. She had virtually adopted us as her own. I had never been away from Daniel before. I missed him – it was if we were one person, we were bonded so close. I stayed in a terraced house in London Street, Worthing, with my father's parents. I was totally bewildered. Uncle Jean took me to my grandparents' house, then left. I sat in the corner of the room totally confused and bewildered. I had thought I was being taken back to France to Daniel and Joan. But I was left there, with new keepers, and speaking French.'

His grandmother, although in her seventies, had love aplenty for the bright-eyed but sad little boy. She had Victorian values and a very keen sense of duty towards her little grandson. Dom quickly became very fond of her, but the pain of the separation from his younger brother was still eating away at his insides. He managed to see Daniel again at holiday times, but they were growing apart as they were raised by different, but very kind people, in different environments.

Dom's parents eventually divorced in the mid-1960s and it was then he made the first of several court appearances. This one was to decide where he and Daniel should live, in whose care they should be placed. His father won custody of the boys, with whom he had been abandoned. Soon he would remarry and have two more children. Dom saw him only at weekends as he built another thriving business in Second World War vehicles.

Peter's collection became one of the biggest in England and the business began to make him fairly well off, if not rich. In addition, it soon kindled an interest in things military for young Dom, especially as he now travelled with his father at weekends to shows and saw the collectors there, dressed in their Second World War uniforms and creating their make-believe world. Dom enjoyed these adventures with his dad as any boy would. He missed him when he wasn't around, but his devoted grandparents provided a good home and emotional stability for him.

Like everything else in Dom's life it was all too good to last. His grandfather, Bill, died and his grandmother was now too old to cope with the boy on her own. She went off to live in London and Peter moved his new wife and family into Gran's house.

'At first it was great, but the novelty of being allowed beans on toast whenever I liked instead of proper food and being allowed to stay up late to watch TV – things Gran would never have allowed – soon wore off. Things were going rapidly downhill between my stepmother and me. I was at secondary school and I didn't realize at first that she knew dad was so successful he was really going places. Her plans were made and there was no place for me in those plans. As far as she was concerned the only family going places with him was her own family and not the previous one.'

Things went from bad to worse. Returning from school, Dom would find there were no meals for him. He fought and squabbled daily with his stepbrother and stepsister. His father was always working and when he came home he heard only one side of the story.

'I was a teenager by this time and teenagers don't really talk to adults about their problems. I started hanging round with kids who, I thought, were similar to me. Not bad, just adventurous. I became a burglar, breaking into shops and selling the goods. I worked on my own. I would nick cars and bikes. I was eventually caught and it was the perfect lever for my stepmother to be rid of me.'

Dom was put in court and faced a sentence in a detention centre, but West Sussex County Council's Social Services Department was pursuing a new policy aimed at keeping thirteen- and fourteen-year olds out of detention. He was fostered with a couple who were former social workers and who ran a small bed-and-breakfast hotel. He left his troubles behind him. He knew he had to keep his nose clean because one wrong step would see him back in court and the detention order enforced. He knew, too, his chances of joining the Army were slim and any more trouble would put the kibosh on them completely.

'I left school at sixteen and went to work on the local building sites. I grafted, really grafted, and stayed out of trouble as much as I could. I went to the recruiting office to suss out how I could join the Army, but my conviction was against me. When my review came up I went back to court and everyone agreed, police, social workers, foster parents, everyone, that joining the Army was the best solution.'

So the slightly built, not very tall, teenager fighting the world and 'the system' every day of his life took himself off to the local recruiting office in Worthing, and saw the same poster that Kevin had seen on the wall of his local recruiting office, as soon as he walked through the door, showing a Paratrooper landing ready for action. That's for me, Dom told himself. But he reckoned wrong. The recruiting sergeant took one look at the teenager before him and soon disabused him of any notion of becoming a Para. He'd seen too many Paras in his time and this little fellow had as much chance of becoming one as the time-served sergeant had of walking in space. He was too short, too skinny and too underweight.

For Dom it was just another challenge. He had decided he would be a Para and that old bastard wouldn't stand in his way. After all he had been outwitting people like him – pillars of the system – all his short life. The answer was simple. He visited his doctor, who put him on a special diet to help him gain weight. What he lacked in physique, he more than made up for in determination. And determination is what every man who wants to be a Paratrooper has to have by the barrow-load. Dom Gray has determination by the lorry-load.

As he left the courtroom for the recruiting office he could sense the relief of the local police and welfare agencies. Hopefully, they had seen the last of him. Let the little bastard go off and get up to his tricks in the Army and they would sort him out. They won't take any shit from him. Dom, with his mat of thick, dark hair and ever-twinkling eyes, was genuinely more high-spirited than bad, someone who had taken too many knocks in such a short life, a little fellow who needed a channel for his limitless energy and aggression, a kid who needed the 'family' the Army had provided for thousands of youngsters like him down the centuries.

The dreaded P Company was just the thing for a lad like Dom. It would knacker him, teach him, give him a sense of achievement, a sense of direction and – equally important – a feeling of belonging. Dominic Michael Gray was going to be a Paratrooper come hell or high water and bollocks to the recruiting sergeant. He was only an old hat anyway, a Fusilier with a hackle on his beret which looked like a fucking ugly budgie.

By the time the Falklands drama erupted in April 1982

Dom was twenty-one and had four years' hard soldiering under his belt. He had served in Germany, Canada, Northern Ireland and Oman, that secretive and backward desert sultanate in the Middle East where the SAS had fought a bitter little war against communist insurgents. They had taken the battle to the Moscow-trained terrorists and, using their own tactics, had beaten them. Not only had communism through the barrel of a Kalashnikov been stopped in its tracks; it had also been sent into full, undignified retreat. The Paras at that time were being courted by the SAS, most of whom had begun their soldiering careers at Aldershot. They wanted the Paras as their ever-ready backup, men used to moving at a moment's notice, soldiers discreet enough to simply vanish from their barracks in Britain and pop up again on the faraway battlefield, men used to operating unsupported far behind enemy lines in small groups or larger formations, men who could easily adapt to any hostile situation, and men who relished the prospect of a good scrap, the opportunity to put into practice everything they had been trained to do. In other words, soldiers they knew were as professional as them and in whom they could place their trust.

As Dom and his mates in B Company lined the decks of the *Canberra* watching the bustle of last-minute loading, he struggled to take it all in. Here they were being swept along on the massive tidal wave of publicity. The TV cameras, the photographers, the reporters all there to see them off – it was all a far cry from the way Paras had been brought up to go to war, slipping away quietly from some secluded, sealed-off airfield. As he watched the dockers load stores and kept out of the way of senior NCOs and their apoplectic rages, he became impatient to be under way. He wanted to get there, to get to grips with the enemy before some silly bastard called it all off. This was going to be his big chance, a once-in-a-lifetime opportunity to prove his soldiering ability, his big chance to show the knocking bastards back home who had written him off as another bad lot that when men had to stand up and be counted he would be among them, not skulking in the corner of a boozer with a copy of the *Sun* and cheering when the news came on TV.

A much-liked lad, Dom had acquired a lot of skill. He had worked closely and hard with the rest of the company in training and was desperately keen to see how well they could do together in the real thing. He had never thought the British Army would fight a conventional war in his time and this was an opportunity too good to be thrown away. After all there were hats doing twenty-two years who would never see action, never even serve in Northern Ireland.

As the *Canberra* slipped down Southampton Water, Dom was alone in the crowd with his personal thoughts. He had managed to say a fond farewell to his dad – whom he still adored – in the departure lounge. He had climbed back on board as the military bands prepared to play them off. Despite the publicity he was proud to be British and soon, God willing, he would prove just how good the modern generation of Paratroopers was, just how entitled they were to carry the mantle of their glorious predecessors. He would prove to his friends, his nation and to himself that he was one of Britain's finest.

Yet even as he sailed off to war Dom couldn't help but reflect how things could have been different for him if he had been allowed to stay in France with his Aunt Joan and brother. It is a thought which still haunts him, because in 1990 – eight years after the Falklands – Daniel was found murdered in a backstreet in Paris and since then Dom has always wondered whether, if they had been left together, his younger brother would have died so tragically.

On the long voyage south the training schedule was at

times hectic, but it didn't sap all the energy which coursed through Dom and his mates. They soon planned unofficial extensions to their military training – 'special missions'.

'A few of us would ambush Marines on the ship for a good punch-up. We were pissed off with all the hassle we were getting from them, so we gave them some back. Although we were supposed to be on the same side the rivalry between us was intense. (I remember after the war a few of us were talking about them and we decided that their toms [private soldiers] were not unlike us in their professional outlook, but their top brass were complete arseholes.)

'But at that time they were fair game. Our corporal, Stewart McLaughlin, was a real hard Scouser. He was anti everything non-Para. His word was law. He was all Para through and through, straight out of a war comic. The ultimate warrior. He didn't stand any messing or any fuss. You either did what he said and you did it immediately and properly, or you suffered. That was it: instant punishment on the spot. We respected him and felt at ease being led by him, but sometimes it was all a bit too much.

'So, one night, we decided to give him some of his own medicine. We decided we would ambush him and give him a going-over. We told him we had beer in our cabin, which was illegal, and he took the bait. We were a very close-knit bunch because that was the way Stewart wanted it. We were his toms and nobody else could fuck us about or pick on us. All we wanted to do was point out in the way he would best understand that the toms had rights and should be able to voice an opinion at times. Anyway, he arrived and we jumped him. He sorted the lot of us out. We all finished up with bloody noses, fat lips and black eyes. I had two black eyes for weeks. Stewart really enjoyed himself punching the crap out of us. But, in true Para style, he was proud of us because we had given him a work-out.

'We prowled the *Canberra* together in search of beer with Stewart, as befits a corporal, in command. One night we were in one of the crew bars on the *Canberra* – a place which was out of bounds to us – when one of the crew started to get stroppy with us and, in particular, Stewart. It was a silly thing to do and Stewart responded by 'lumping' him and then attempting to force him out through a porthole. This caused a fairly serious shoulder injury to the guy and the MPs were called and we were nicked. We were all marched in before the CO on disciplinary charges.

'I'll always remember being marched in front of him and the shock when my eyes took in the luxury of his cabin. I couldn't believe his spacious living quarters compared with our cramped accommodation below. I was still eyeing up his cabin when we all got hit with a £200 fine and extra duties. The fine didn't bother any of us because we were going to war and if we weren't around at the end of it we wouldn't have to pay. It was as simple as that, but the extra duties did hurt.

'We then cross-decked to the *Intrepid* and were crammed into the corridors and bulkheads. The ship was jammed solid with sailors and soldiers absolutely jam-packed with Paras and Marines all awaiting the green light to go, and then they told us to report to the galley to begin our extra duties punishment. There we were, all rammed and ammoed up, cleaning the dixies they carted the food around in. We all had our sleeves rolled up and were scrubbing away – and there was some scrubbing because of the number of people on board. There was pile after pile of pots and pans and dixies. Stewart had flames coming out of his nostrils. What made us even madder was being told to go to the hotplates and start serving breakfasts to the fucking Marines. That really was taking the piss. Anyone who gave us a look or made a stupid comment had piping hot beans ladled over their hands.

'We were still cleaning dixies and serving food as the *Intrepid* sailed into Falkland Sound for the landings. We dashed straight from the galley to the landing-craft. I have a sneaking suspicion that the top brass delayed the landings to make sure we had cleaned all the dixies... '

I climbed from our car to greet Germán Chamorro. This meeting was to be different from the others in that, like me, Germán was an ex-Para. He had been in control of a 120mm mortar and artillery on Mount Longdon, and I knew his onslaught had proved a hellish experience for 3 Para during the battle. His handshake was firm and he gave me a reassuringly warm smile as I said hello.

We all went quietly into his house and as we settled down around the kitchen table there was a slight nervousness in the air. Diego relieved the tension by getting Germán to speak of his apprehension about meeting a British soldier after the war. This made him feel relaxed enough to grin at me and admit: 'You know, the English language has given me some bad memories, but this project that you're doing is good. After all, it's the common soldier that always suffers, not the government officials.' Within five minutes we were all laughing – largely because this stocky, jovial man has a wonderful sense of humour, ironically very much like that of my close friend Denzil Connick.

Germán always knew he would be involved in a war. He had always been fascinated by soldiers, war and the history of conflict. It was, he believed, his destiny, ever since the days when he had played soldiers in the streets of Adrogue, the Buenos Aires suburb where he grew up with his parents and three sisters. His parents emigrated from Paraguay, where his father had learned his trade as a builder. Work in Argentina was plentiful and he was able to provide his growing family with a good lifestyle.

In those days Adrogue was a good neighbourhood and the young Chamorros were well off compared with many other kids of their generation. Germán, born on 12 August 1962, returned to the area after the Falklands war and lived there until four years ago. He had been to primary school locally and enjoyed it, rushing home afterwards to play soccer or cops-and-robbers or soldiers on the safe streets. But secondary school was different.

'It was difficult,' he recalls. 'Very difficult. I even failed break time! Eventually my parents gave me an ultimatum: "Study – or work."

'I chose the easy one: work. Earning my own money really suited me. I was a teenager and the world for me was all discos, clubs, drinking and women. I tried re-education at one stage – you can do that here – because I regretted leaving school at fourteen. I worked on the building sites with my father for a time then became an odd-job boy for one of my elder sisters. I did that right up until I was called up for the Army. Times have changed a lot in Argentina since those days.

'Do you know, when we went to discos sometimes we were absolutely shit-scared if there was a razia – a police raid. It was a real risk being there, because if drugs or something like that were found you could become an NN [missing person, one of the "Disappeared Ones"] and just for being there you got an automatic two months in jail. Sometimes, when I look around the streets today, I miss the strict order that ruled in those days. We still had a good time and I remember the parties to celebrate when Argentina won the World Cup in 1978.

'My call-up came in August 1980 and I went to La Plata and volunteered for the Parachute Regiment. I was sent to Córdoba in the north central province. There were about fifty of us lined up for a medical and they gave us all an injection with the same needle. There was no AIDS about then. Because I was going for the Paras the service was longer. My friends all thought I was mad losing up to two years of my life to the Army. I went to the 4th Artillery Parachute Regiment near La Calera and straight away I knew I was into something different. I knew then I was away from my home and family.

'Suddenly, at the age of nineteen, I am just a piece of crap, a nobody. It was the hard discipline that hit me: eat, sleep, fart only when the military tell you. That first week of induction was a big shock to the system. Two hundred of us were posted within the regiment. I was sent to C Battery, which was broken down into two companies. My boss was Lieutenant Suárez and he was a good officer and was to prove it later. He had golden balls.

'Training was "dancing" from the start. Reveille was at 5 a.m. and dress in a minute flat. In our dormitory huts things were so cramped half of us dressed while the others washed and then we changed over. Then it was inspection followed by a dance around for three or four hours, marching, saluting, running, anything. Basically, they were just fucking us around. For forty-five days I had this and what I missed most was home. Apart from five days on the ranges and weapons training it was always the same. The food was bad – and I mean bad. There were no tables and we all sat back to back to eat. I remember red insects floating in my food. Tasty! Everyone had the shits, all sitting there on the latrines in a row without any toilet paper. I lost six or seven kilos there.

'Some guys deserted. Those who were caught went to the *calabozo*. After our forty-five days of basic training I could march, salute and shoot. They gave us four days' leave, but my first day was spent travelling home and my last day travelling back, so I spent the other two days eating, sleeping and drinking as much as I could. My haircut made me stand out from everybody else.

'On my return I had to do another forty-five days of parachute and continuation training. Two mates of mine deserted while on leave. We always had to stand in formation for raising the flag in the morning, then they gave us a pep talk. The parachute training area was two kilometres from our barracks and we had to run there and back every day with our helmets on. We did all our ground exercises and one day they brought out a Hercules C-130, the traditional parachuting aircraft. Three days before our first actual jump we all boarded in jumping order and the plane went round and round the field without actually taking off, but we all had to fall out the doors and roll on the field as if we were actually parachuting.

'I'll always remember my first jump. Every Para does. There I am in the aircraft with my balls up to my throat with thinking about it. We're ordered to get ready, hook up, double-check equipment, tap the helmet of the guy in front to signal everything is OK. We are all standing there staring at the red light, knowing that seconds later it will go green and we're going to go. My heart was doing overtime; I could hear it pounding inside me. Suddenly it's "green on" and guys are disappearing out the doors. I'm shuffling to the door. I get there and find myself pushing against the dispatcher's arm. He's holding me back. "What the fuck," I scream at him.

'It turns out I'm the last one out and we've overshot the DZ [drop zone]. Everyone is going to think I've lost my bottle. I pleaded with the Air Force sergeant. Here I was, all hyped up and ready to jump, and this bastard has stopped me. On the next pass I got out, falling for three seconds in the slipstream and then I'm in another world: peace, a real sense of peace, just floating down. Unreal.

'We have a tradition after your first successful jump in

which you choose a godfather and everyone baptizes you with cider and flour. I'm a fairly chubby guy so they nicknamed me Yogi Bear. I chose Lieutenant Suárez as my godfather. Once you have done three jumps you get your red beret at a ceremony. I did ten!

'At the end of this forty-five days of training we are only two thirds of the way through. Normal conscripts do a total of about forty-five days. Because we are Para-artillery we do ninety. But we got fifteen days' leave before the heavy artillery training and then it was working with howitzers and mortars. As soon as we had done that we went on manoeuvres, firing shells and moving from position to position with the guns, just like they do in a real war, to deal with the enemy changing position.

'Everything was going well until I accidentally dropped my rifle on our gunpowder bags in a ditch. Apart from feeling like an arsehole, I lost my next leave and was danced by being forced to crawl through thistle and thorn bushes. I was confined to barracks while the rest of them went on leave. I was really pissed off, I can tell you.

'After all that they made me a clerk in charge of the leave and guard-duty rosters. It wasn't a bad number and I soon had a good trade going in bribes for changing duties. Everyone hated the 2-4 a.m. duty. A guy nicknamed Dracula used to bribe me with cigarettes and food to cook the duty book. Cigarettes are currency and I could exchange them for anything I wanted. That's the way it goes, isn't it? Looking back, it wasn't a bad number.

'From time to time we had to do a *razia*, patrolling the streets near the barracks. It was hard, boring work. At that time in 1981 the terrorists just weren't around any more – they had gone to ground. We were out, fully armed, in the local square, stopping cars and checking on the drivers and occupants. Sometimes we'd demand a few fags. If a bird was driving we'd irritate the locals – the *Cordobezes*, we'd call them – by chatting up their women. The rest of our patrol was spent killing time and doing fuck all.

'We had a guy on attachment to us, a big tough commando from 601 Regiment. One day in the office I forgot to introduce myself – "Parachute soldier Class of 62 Chamorro" – when I was looking for the regiment's orders. He danced me around his office and then told me to carry on. As soon as my back was turned he sneaked up behind me and put a knife to my throat, saying: "Never drop your guard, soldier. Always be alert."

'The bastard ran away during the fighting at Darwin. Ha! There was a story doing the rounds about him at the time that he had killed and gutted a snake and made his soldiers eat it, telling them that when at war a soldier must eat what he can find. Now that is a cruel irony when you bear in mind what happened to us later for trying to eat what we could find on the Malvinas.

'They began to discharge my intake just before Christmas 1981. Sixty guys went and I was awaiting my turn. Then, on 22 December, orders came through for a parachute jump. Nobody wanted to do it. Lieutenant Suárez was going mad. We jumped from a Fokker on the 23rd and then he began dancing us. He said anyone who fell would stay in camp for Christmas. We crawled through thistle bushes, through mud, ran, jumped – you name it and we did it. I was one of ten guys left on their feet, all covered in dirt and dust. In the end, he gave us two days' leave.

'Leave was precious and didn't come round often enough. One time some of us scored with some girls on a train and arranged to meet them another time. We had to slip out of camp and hitch a ride to their place. We went absent for three days, but my sergeant was delighted we had got our ends away and fined me a coffee and three croissants.

'Another time the MPs spotted us on a train. We had no leave papers, so we got off at the next station. They chased and chased us. You have to remember that the bastards got a bounty of more leave for every absentee they caught. Anyway, some people hid us in their house and then some Japanese tourists gave us a lift into Buenos Aires in their camper.

'At the beginning of 1982 we did absolutely fuck all as we waited for discharge. Class of 63, our replacements, began arriving in February. I was told I would be discharged on 30 March, so I went home on leave before returning to the regiment on the 30th. On that day there was a big *quilombo* [disturbance] in the capital. It was a clear symbol of the unrest which was growing in the country. The Central Union of Workers had organized a protest rally against the government. One of the demonstrators, Dalmiro Flores, was shot dead by the police. I wasn't really aware of this.

'Next day, 31 March, I'm still in camp and still in the Army. I went to see my boss and he gave me another eighteen days' leave. I went back home, where it was quiet and peaceful.

'Suddenly, about 6 a.m. next morning, my father has the radio on and we hear: *'Hemos recuperado Las Malvinas.'* ['We have recovered the Malvinas']. Then there was marching music. Things didn't add up until I began to realize the government had ordered the action to divert people's thoughts from the unrest at home.

'Then a friend rings up and tells my mother there is a Para company on the Malvinas and he thinks I am there. I talk to him. I didn't know anything about the Malvinas. I can hear my parents swearing in the background: *'milicos de mierda'* ['fucking military'] and for the next eighteen days the house was a place of madness with me saying I knew I was going to be sent there and my parents telling me to shut up.

'My mother was angry because she had lived through the revolution in Paraguay. She knew what war was. "This is madness – they are going to kill you;" she would tell me. We were glued to the television and radio watching the communiqués. I rang my regiment and they told me no orders had been received. On the 18th, when I should have reported back, I stayed on at home for a big barbecue. Eventually I decided to go back to sort out my discharge. At the railway terminus I met some guys who had deserted. They knew that the regiment would actually be going to the Malvinas within a week. I decided to ring home and tell my family. My mother began to cry: she wanted me to desert. But I knew this was my destiny.

'When I get back to the camp I meet some other guys who are also late back. A first lieutenant calls us into his office and starts to give us a serious bollocking. "You're a bunch of deserters, bad soldiers, the country is at war etc, etc." He rages that the officers and NCOs have already gone and I start to laugh. "Chamorro, what are you laughing at," he screams. "You are the first to go. Go. Go now. Fuck off!"'

And so, like many others, Germán Chamorro began his journey to destiny.

3

DENZIL CONNICK is a Welshman and proud of it. He was born in Tredegar in 1956, the eldest of four sons of Ernie Connick, a hard-working miner, and his wife Carol. Denzil played happily with the other miners' children, and as they grew up together he was forever winding them up with his practical jokes and incredibly tall stories.

While Denzil was still a child the changes which began to shake the world in the 1960s began to find their way to South Wales, where, far below ground, his father toiled at the coalface. Ernie sensed the wind of change and shrewdly switched jobs to another industry which formed another part of the economic backbone of Wales: steel. He moved Carol and the four boys up the road to Chepstow, just on the Welsh side of the Severn Bridge, and worked hard until his retirement.

It was this down-to-earth working-class background which fashioned young Denzil. It taught him to face adversity with courage, to meet life's challenges head on, to work hard and to try even harder and 'to never let the bastards grind you down'. He was fifteen at the beginning of the 1970s and had decided he wanted to join the RAF. However, his academic record fell short of the nine CSEs the RAF demanded for his trade, so he decided on the Parachute Regiment. It seemed the next best thing!

The whole family turned out on the platform of Newport Station to see young Denzil off on the long journey to Aldershot, the traditional home of the British Army, and of its toughest unit, the Paras.

At just fifteen and a half Denzil Connick joined the other school leavers on the first great adventure of his young life on that day in 1972 when he joined Junior Para. For eighteen months he underwent the rigorous and often brutal training needed to win the coveted red beret and prized blue wings of a Paratrooper, one of the finest breed of soldiers Britain could produce.

In January 1974, his chest bursting with pride, his Welsh heart flooded with emotion, his head in the clouds but his feet firmly marching on the ground, Denzil and the boys of 400 Platoon became the men of the Parachute Regiment. He'd made it.

By the time the Falklands emergency began Denzil was already a seasoned soldier, a lance-corporal who had become what the Army calls 'a trusted and reliable asset to his battalion'. He was a radio operator with the anti-tank platoon in Support Company, the old sweats of the battalion. He had become a popular character with the officers and men and was famous for his singing, which had cheered many a heart – and upset many a landlord – in pubs in Aldershot and everywhere else in the world 3 Para served. As a pal says: 'If the lads were bored, you could count on Denzil to have everyone singing by closing time.'

In April 1982, when the battalion embarked for the Falklands, Denzil had served ten years in the ranks. He was one of the few junior soldiers who had experienced being shot at for real. He had also been able to shoot back. It happened in Northern Ireland, where he had already done three tours of duty. Here was a man who knew the exhilaration and fear of action, who had faced the stark reality of kill or be killed, who had seen a comrade mortally wounded and who knew that the truth of the battlefield was much different from the bar-room bravado of the young, inexperienced toms thirsting for action.

Six years earlier he had been helicoptered into Crossmaglen, south Armagh, the heart of what the media loved to call 'Bandit Country', an area where the security forces had seemed to have given up aggressive action in favour of containment. It was an area the IRA dominated, filtering across the border from Co. Monaghan, which thrusts up like a huge club from the Republic into the soft underbelly of Ulster. The local IRA boyos paraded the streets of Crossmaglen and the lonely lanes surrounding it quite openly, picking likely ambush sites and forcing the British Army and the RUC to enter and leave the base by helicopter.

The men of 3 Para were to change this. Denzil flew in with the rest of 2 Platoon, A Company. And soon they were out looking for the Provo gunmen, faces blackened with camouflage cream, bergens full of kit on their backs, weapons loaded and ready, and putting themselves on offer.

They didn't have long to wait for their first contact, which came with a savage suddenness as the four-man patrol of paratroopers crossed open ground near Drumacaval right beside the ill-defined border. Four Provisional IRA gunmen started firing at them with an American Second World War Garand semi-automatic rifle, firing armour-piercing bullets, and three Armalite rifles.

'They opened up from a small copse two to three hundred

metres away, catching us fifty metres from the nearest cover, a drystone wall,' Denzil recalls. 'There was a hail of bullets coming at us, but we managed to gain the cover of the wall after a hectic dash. That was when we discovered they were using armour-piercing rounds... because they punched their way through the wall we were sheltering behind.

'The only reason none of us was hit was because they opened up on us too early. If they had just waited they could have got us, but we quickly spotted their four firing positions. Kev, our patrol commander, gave us a fire order. We didn't need to be told twice. Kev, Geordie Melling and Geordie Snowdon and me blasted back at them. I reckon we each fired forty or fifty rounds back at them. Our fire control orders were good, and we had practised, and it worked. We fired and moved and fired and moved and soon they stopped firing. We advanced on them and got into the copse. During the fire-fight Geordie Snowdon's rifle was actually hit by a bullet which rendered it useless. But we still got on top of the bastards.

'We found their firing positions in the copse with the spent cartridge cases on the ground and we found blood. We knew we had hit at least one – if not killing him, wounding him. We could see their getaway car driving off, but because it was on the other side of the border we couldn't "hot-pursuit" them or shoot at the car because they weren't shooting at us from it.

'We radioed in, then had a reorganization and debrief and waited for a chopper to arrive with an ammunition resupply and a new weapon for Geordie. Then we carried on with the patrol for another two days.'

As well as gunmen targeting them from across the border, soldiers in south Armagh are also at risk from what the senior officer level in the security forces in Northern Ireland refer to as IEDs, Improvised Explosive Devices. To the man in the street and the soldier on the ground they are bombs or booby-traps, and the Provos had laid so many in this area that it was littered with them. They were just lying there, hidden and waiting to be activated by remote control.

These are nasty weapons designed by cowards and used in a cowardly fashion. The soldiers were always wary of them, always on the lookout for the tell-tale signs, always seeking a likely detonation point. Many a Paratrooper and craphat would dearly have loved to have had the opportunity to get his hands on one of the bombmakers, tie him to his handiwork and set it off underneath him.

Although Denzil had been both frightened and exhilarated by his baptism under fire, he began to realize that he was quietly confident about confronting the faceless terrorists who haunted his battalion's operational area. The brief but fierce contact had concentrated his mind, and now he was ever alert to the lurking dangers, his senses honed to an incredible sharpness. In later analysis of the action he realized he had gone through everything he had been taught about reaction. He had done it automatically: weapon drills, target location and identification and returning fire. It worked and it showed that the discipline and training drilled into him since he joined the regiment was second to none. And deep in his inner self was the glow of contentment that when the crunch had come he had not failed. He had not let himself down under fire, nor had he failed his three comrades. All four of them had responded to the challenge as they had been trained.

In south Armagh danger is ever-present. Every minute of every hour of every day a soldier is there he is in danger. Later in the tour of duty the same patrol was positioned round a landing zone for a helicopter. It was a good spot for a rendezvous and the Paras thought it had not been used for some time. They had been taught not to be predictable or to betray an observable pattern in their patrols.

'We didn't know at the time, but it had been well used. I remember the occasion well. We were all spread out in defensive positions about a hundred yards apart along a hedgerow. A bomb had been planted, but obviously we didn't know. As the patrol radio operator I was the furthest away. Suddenly there was this huge bang and Geordie Snowdon took the force of the blast. He was barely alive, but we managed to resuscitate him. He slipped into a coma. In hospital they put him on a life-support machine. He was bad and we all knew it. He was in a coma for two weeks. His parents were at his bedside. Eventually they gave permission for the machine to be turned off and our Geordie died. He never regained consciousness.'

The death of Geordie Snowdon hurt and angered his patrol. Long into the night, they went over the ambush again and again. They thirsted for the chance to avenge Geordie: and when it came, Sod's Law took over.

'We had a contact with an IRA sniper shooting at us from just on or just over the border – it doesn't matter. But we got him in our sights and our GPMG [General Purpose Machine Gun] gunner was lined up on him. All the time we had been complaining about the condition of the link ammunition we had been issued for the gun. It was old and bent. We were really browned off about it and when the gunner, Ian Long, opened up, the bloody thing only fired one round. Every time we had asked for replacement ammo we had been ignored. Now we were really pissed off with everyone ourselves. Of course, as soon as this happened they gave us new ammo. A lot of good it did us then.'

To Denzil, the authorities' response to the question of the

ammunition was a perfect example of their approach, both political and military, to dealing with the running sore that is Northern Ireland.

'It's too namby-pamby. They say we can't be too aggressive and that we should adopt a hearts-and-minds policy. The IRA have never relented, never given an inch, never reacted to our nice behaviour and I doubt if they ever will. The Army should be allowed to patrol much more aggressively.

'You never forget some of the sights I have seen. I remember another of the lads being blown up. I remember them putting what was left of him in polythene bags before they put him into a body bag. Maybe if the politicians saw this sort of sight they might change their minds. It is the soldiers on the ground who pay the price for the shiny-assed Whitehall penny-pinchers.'

Six years on, Denzil, like many of his comrades, freely admitted he didn't know much about the Falklands or even where they really were. 'They sound a bit Scottish to me,' he would say in his distinctive Welsh accent with the ever-present twinkle in his eye. You couldn't be sure if he was being serious or not. Denzil was no thick soldier.

The whole idea of going to war – a full-scale shooting war with normal rules, not the yellow-card-governed, kid-glove stuff of Ulster – didn't worry him at first because he simply didn't believe it would happen. It just seemed like yet another exercise. It had to be. After all, who ever heard of Paratroopers going to war on a luxury liner? Who ever heard of Paratroopers being seen off by hundreds of relatives with the band blasting out the regimental march, 'The Ride of the Valkyries'? Someone was taking the piss, surely?

Paratroopers normally slip away 'to some secluded airfield in the dead of night and drop on to the battlefield before the enemy even knows he's left camp. But if that was what the bosses wanted, who was he, a lance-corporal, to argue?

As the *Canberra* slipped her moorings and was gently coaxed out into the middle of the Solent shipping lanes by the bustling tugs for the long journey south on that Good Friday night, Denzil decided he would settle in for a little pampering and enjoy the luxuries on offer. He joined his mates in the bar assigned to the junior ranks of 3 Para. Being Denzil, he soon got to know many people, and soon re-established contact with an old schoolfriend, Greg Quigley, a *Canberra* crewman. And what could have been more natural than for Denzil and his old mate to reminisce about their youth over a gallon or two.

They regaled each other and everyone else in the drinking school with their escapades, particularly about the days they bunked off school together. They would meet in the crew bar, away from the gaze of the officers and senior NCOs, where the hospitality of Greg's fellow crewmen knew no bounds. But being there was against the military rules and out of bounds for Denzil and every other soldier on the gigantic ship. To this day Denzil doesn't accept that he was doing anything wrong. As far as he is concerned his only 'crime' was in being caught.

On the first occasion the commanding officer gave him a warning, on the second he was fined £300. He couldn't believe such a heavy fine – a fortnight's wages – for such a minor misdemeanour. However, he returned to 3 Para's bar at the stem of the ship, overlooking one of the swimming pools, to sup the regulation two cans per man every evening until he received orders that the Battalion was, in fact, going to land on the islands.

We had been sitting round Luis Leccese's table, in his spacious and attractively furnished flat, for at least three hours, chatting and eating our way through a memorable dinner. The talk was interesting and light-hearted, relaxed and friendly. Luis was not only keen to learn about the British Paras, but was also very curious about Britain and how we live. Would he be welcome in our homes, like I was in his? That evening, his whole attitude, like that of each of the other Argentinians I met, made me rethink what so many of us in Britain have been led to believe about Luis's fellow-countrymen. They're not hot-headed, rude or impetuous. In short, every one of the veterans I interviewed was a perfect ambassador for his country.

Alberto Carbone, another Mount Longdon veteran, and long-time friend of Luis, was there, too. There was lots of laughter as they poked fun at each other, the sort of banter you come across in any English pub when mates meet up for a few beers on a Saturday night.

We studied battlefield maps and photographs together, and Luis pinpointed the position he occupied on Mount Longdon on one of the maps I had brought with me. Then, when I showed him pictures of prisoners of war and asked if he knew any of them, he almost froze with shock. His eyes filled with tears, and, pointing to the haunted face of one of the POWs, he said: 'Me.' There he was, sitting among a group of captured Argentinians, a sad figure of a man, only nineteen or twenty years old. Everyone was silent as he asked: 'My God, did I really look like that?'

There was a powerful feeling in the room – you could feel it, almost taste it – as Luis passed the picture to his wife and the memories came flooding back to all of us. Now, after twelve years, he was looking deep into a painful past. He drew long and hard on his Marlboro, exhaled the blue-grey smoke, and let the emotion of the moment ebb.

We were in Bandfield, a twenty-minute drive from the centre of Buenos Aires with its smart boulevards, bumper-to-bumper traffic, bustling pavement cafés and non-stop wailing of ambulance sirens. It is not what you expect a

South American city to be – it is more European, more Italian than Spanish.

Like many Argentinians, Luis is from Italian stock. Both his parents are Italian, and arrived in Buenos Aires after the Second World War.

'My father is from northern Italy, but I don't know much about his background there because he never talks about it. I know he was in the Second World War, but he has never said what he did or even whose side he was on. I have four brothers, the eldest of whom was born in Italy, but he came here as a baby. We didn't have a deprived upbringing, but we certainly weren't well off. Yes, there were times when we had to go without, but so did nearly everybody else in this area. This is where I grew up, this is where I played as a child, in these streets round here.

'After I had been at school a while I became a real handful. To be honest, I developed into a right oaf. I used to skip school more than I attended because it was too much like hard work. There was a gang of us and we used to laze round the streets all day. Even when I did go to school I would get out on the street as soon as possible, skipping homework and even meals. Despite it all I didn't have to repeat anything at school. I don't know how I managed that. When the time came for secondary school I found it really hard and that was when I was caught out by my lack of work at primary school. I went instead to technical school for a year to study *comercial de noche* – bookkeeping and accountancy – and as soon as that was over I left school. I was fourteen.

'My parents laid down the law: if I wasn't prepared to go to school then I'd better get out and work. I worked with my middle brother in his shoe shop until it went bust. Then he opened a small factory making kitchen worktops and I joined him there for a year. My eldest brother also had a small factory making clothes and next I went to work for him. Life was good... I was fifteen, earning money and still living at home and able to buy my own clothes and still have enough left over to go to the local discos.

'We spoke a mixture of Spanish and Italian. Father was a true Italian, but as time went on he learned to speak castellano [Castilian Spanish]. In March 1981 I was called to Colimba. I wasn't exactly mad about doing my military service, but if I had to do it then do it I would. It was the only way to look at it.

'I remember we had to do two medicals. The first I can't remember a thing about, but the second, well, I was put into a room, we were all put into a room, loads of us, and we were then told to strip naked and then they made us open up our rear so they could inspect us. They looked right up our backsides. The medical man then came and told me to stand up straight and he looked at my feet. Then he made me show him the soles of my feet and do turns and more turns and then he walked away. Back he comes with a much higher-ranking medical officer and I did the same for him and the pair of them stood there humming and hawing and the senior one said: "Send him anyway."

'You see, I have flat feet and should have failed the Army medical there and then. But I was in and they gave me inoculations, a uniform, kitbag, boots and a rifle and put me on a bus with all the others for the journey to San Miguel del Monte. The two months I spent there on basic training felt more like six. I can honestly say the instruction I received there was the most stupid I have ever heard or experienced in my entire life.

'We used to be up at 6 a.m., wash and parade and then go into the field for training. One exercise we had to do called target identification, which had us kneeling or lying on the ground using our thumbs or fists up before our eyes to try to locate where an enemy was sniping at us, still makes me giggle. It always seemed to me that by the time I had gone through all this stupid thumb and fist business I'd be fucking dead.

'Night training was just the same as orienteering, copping messages left at checkpoints. We would also have to stand facing a partner saluting and shouting... Jesus, you felt like a bunch of complete arseholes standing there shouting and saluting each other. It was unbelievable nonsense. Another piece of bullshit they made us do was called area cleaning. This was bullshit of the highest order. We would form a line and walk across a field holding a blanket, collecting everything to make it tidy, even the smallest twig. That fucking field was clean enough to eat off by the time we'd finished with it.

'After a month of this crap we went for shooting lessons. The range was basic and so was the instruction. They taught us how to hold the weapon, how to breathe when shooting, and then the target would pop up and we would go ping! Once we had done that we would advance towards the target firing from the waist. That was all we learned: how to fire a rifle and 9mm pistol. I wasn't to fire a weapon again for a year... and then it was to be in a war.

'Towards the end of this training period they began to ask us what we knew and what we could do, like driving or working as a mechanic or any trade. I could drive, so I was sent to the vehicle depot. Anyone who couldn't do anything the Army regarded as useful stayed in the infantry. They spent the rest of their time guarding everything and jumping around like arseholes.

'The "dirty war" which spread fear throughout our country was coming to an end at that time. There appeared to be less tension about. A lot of guys were going AWOL, just disappearing when on guard duty. When the corporals went to inspect the guard positions all they would find would be a guy's helmet and rifle. The guy himself had vanished, never to be seen again.

'It wasn't hard to see why guys went. We were supposed to be paid a monthly wage, but they always found ways of getting our money, fining us for so-called lost kit and other stupid things. If I was lucky I would finish up with about fifty pesos at the end of the month. The regiment had several exercises during the year, but I missed all the firing because I was in the Service Company, looking after and driving the trucks. When they went on exercise I was used to drive the food to them in a truck.

'By March 1982 the next conscripts were arriving and we were waiting for them to fill our places so we could go home. I remember I was really looking forward to Civvy Street. I had just a week left to do when they told us to prepare for something. They didn't tell us what it was, but I had a suspicion it was to be the Malvinas.

'One minute I'm sitting there dreaming of freedom and home and the next I've drawn my rifle – the same one I've only ever fired once – and I'm on a Boeing 707 with no seats, flying out across the South Atlantic to the Malvinas. I couldn't take it all in. I never dreamt for a moment I would ever be fighting in a real war.'

Jerry Phillips comes from a background shared by thousands of other British soldiers, the ever-on-the-move Service family. His dad, Michael, was a highly skilled RAF technician whose work was maintaining the flight simulators in which the jet-jockeys of the Air Force kept up the skills needed for flying the multimillion-pound planes with their sophisticated systems and hardware. Jerry was born in Singapore, where his father, then a corporal, was stationed. Every couple of years the Phillips family was on the move, with a posting back to Britain and then back to exotic Singapore again.

Young Jerry loved Singapore and the lifestyle, boosting his pocket money by prowling the jungle fringes collecting brilliantly coloured butterflies and tropical fish, which he sold to American servicemen on leave from the carnage of Vietnam. Later he branched out, catching snakes and reptiles, which he sold to the locals, who used the skins to make handbags and wallets for the tourists. At school, too, things were going well. By the time he was eight, young Jerry was such a good runner that he won a place in the Singapore Schools' Junior Team.

The earliest drama Jerry can recall was when a poisonous snake chased his big sister. As she ran for her life Jerry leapt into action with a stick and clubbed it to death. 'I'll always remember that bloody snake,' he says. 'It would have killed my sister with one bite. It was my first frightening experience in life.'

His next followed quite quickly when, in 1968, just before he was nine, his parents' marriage broke down. For a time Jerry's life fell apart. Peggie Phillips and her four kids were now just surplus baggage as far as the RAF was concerned and they were shipped back to Britain to a rundown Second World War camp where broken families were temporarily housed. Life was hard for Peggie and her brood, and the RAF didn't care. Soon, they were on the move again, this time to Ilfracombe, in Devon, where Peggie had a friend who let her and the children crowd into a one-bedroom flat. For a further two years they lived on top of each other until Peggie got a job as a school dinner lady.

'Life was still hard,' recalls Jerry. 'Dinner ladies are very poorly paid and she had us four kids to support. We couldn't compete with the other kids at school with their new bikes and smart clothes.'

To compensate, Jerry took on a poorly paid paper round, before discovering that thieving paid better. At night he would slip off, do a burglary and then sell the proceeds.

Living in Devon also sparked another passion in Jerry: sea fishing. Sometimes he would spend all night fishing in Ilfracombe Bay – an activity frowned upon by the local social services department. 'Time and again the nosy bastards summoned us to their offices and said I was disorderly because I chose to fish all night. I never skipped school to go fishing. Their attitude really annoyed me.'

By the time he was fifteen Jerry had had enough of life in Devon and decided to join the Army. The Parachute Regiment was the place for him, he decided, because another of his hobbies was making model soldiers and he liked the ones of the Paras! He sailed through the tests at the local recruiting office and was sent to the reception centre at Sutton Coldfield, Warwickshire. Shortly after arriving he was interviewed by another recruiting officer, who had seen his test results and tried to persuade him to join another arm of the service.

'My mind was made up even more firmly as the interview began because a Para officer walked past. There was something different about him. The red beret was the first thing to catch my eye, but it was the way he walked: so confident, so macho. Give the recruiting officer his due: he tried for over an hour to get me to change my mind, but it was made up.'

Jerry returned home to await the summons to Browning Barracks, Aldershot, to join the Paras. When it came he packed his belongings – including some stolen goods – into a holdall and set off. He had just arrived at the camp and was being allocated his accommodation when the police arrived and arrested him. A court sent him to a detention centre and he did five weeks' 'hard labour' on a farm. Again his life was in ruins, but, like many a veteran fallen on hard times, he insists: 'The Parachute Regiment is the toughest, but the most forgiving unit in the British Army.'

As soon as he had served his sentence the Paras accepted him back. It had all happened before he joined and as far as they were concerned he had repaid his debt to society. Now he was about to risk his life for his country and if he was prepared to do that he could hold his head up.

In 1975, at the age of sixteen, he joined the Junior Parachute Regiment, the toughest junior soldiering in Britain. 'For eighteen months I had the shit kicked out of me. They trained me and made me into a professional soldier. They won because I wanted to be won.'

He was sent to 2 Platoon, A Company, 3 Para, based in Osnabruck, West Germany, and realized right away that the hard training in Junior Para was only a preparation for life with the seniors at battalion level.

'It was a hard, hard, hard way of life. Those guys in my first platoon were hard bastards and, being a 'crow', I was always being picked on for the dirty jobs. That's the way it is. It happens to everybody. But I couldn't imagine that the so-called hardest prisons could hold harder men than the ones I was serving with. I remember reflecting back on my life... In Singapore we had had two servants, then no father, then poverty and now this. Jesus. But I'll tell you something: 3 Para gave me a family back. At first I was a loner, but I soon made friends and established very strong bonds with other guys who came from a similar back ground to me.

'The next two years just flew by. Militarily, the training was hard because that is the only way to be professional: train hard and fight hard. Paras always train hard and fight even bloody harder because that's the way we are. Socially, it was different. Jesus, did we have some scraps with the craphats in any pub or disco anywhere in Germany we could find them. Some had balls and scrapped back, good hard fist fights nearly every weekend. The Paras trained me correctly – play hard, work hard – and moulded me. The only thing they have failed to do is mould the rest of the world yet, but hopefully that will come!'

During this time Jerry also did a tour of duty in Northern Ireland, but because he was still seventeen he was not allowed to patrol the streets until he was eighteen. When he was allowed out on to the hostile streets he found the whole thing frustrating and boring. A lot of the work was ineffective because of what he regarded as flaws in the command structure. Remember, Jerry Phillips had been marked down right from the beginning as a bright boy and the recruiting officers had wanted to steer him away from the infantry towards what they regarded as 'more brain-taxing' soldiering. The only way to change things was to go for promotion.

Back in Osnabruck, Jerry's platoon commander singled out the young soldier for a promotion course which he passed at the same time as he swept the board in every race he entered during the battalion's sports week. Then he was sent on a physical training instructors' course which, again, he passed and was posted to D Company, the specialist long-range patrolling and behind-enemy lines surveillance experts. This was the big league, the company where only the best and most experienced soldiers served. Jerry was thrilled, learning new skills and having more freedom to develop his own techniques. At nineteen he was a full corporal, one of the youngest around, a tribute to his old platoon commander's vision. More courses followed, all ending in passes, including one of the most demanding of all, the LRRP (Long Range Reconnaissance Patrol) course in Germany run by the SAS. Here special forces soldiers from all of NATO come to test their skills. To Jerry Phillips and every other Para who ever attended the course the others were all there to be beaten: Paras come second to no one. He was quietly taken aside by a man in the distinctive sand-coloured beret with its coveted winged-dagger badge and told to go for SAS selection as soon as possible. He was the type of soldier they wanted.

Jerry was proud he had been approached to join the 'Ultimate Soldiers', but another Northern Ireland tour was on the cards, with a chance of some action, and that had to come first. At the end of 1981 he applied to go on SAS selection and was accepted. All he had to do now was wait for a slot on the first available course. To while away the time he went on a sniper course at Warminster in Wiltshire, the home of the School of Infantry, and regarded by many as the finest sniper course in the world. Some of the finest marksmen in the British Army form the instruction cadre and pass on the skills, learned over many years, of concealment, movement, marksmanship and target identification. As soon as Jerry became familiar with the L-42 bolt-action 7.62mm sniper rifle it became a part of him. Every time he squeezed the trigger the target fell or had a hole in it. He drank in everything they had to teach him, every little hint a man must absorb to be a professional sniper. He passed, of course, and returned to the battalion, now based in Tidworth, to await the next challenge: SAS selection.

But it wasn't to be. General Galtieri saw to that by invading the Falklands.

'I couldn't believe it,' Jerry says. 'I had just travelled all the way from Tidworth to Cambridge, where my mum had settled, to see her for Easter when there was a news flash on TV and film showing the notice-boards at the stations saying all 3 Para personnel had to return to camp. I managed to get a lift, travelling most of the night, and when I got back the atmosphere was so unreal, so quiet. There were just a couple of guys walking about. There was no war-in-the-air feeling or any of the hurry-up-and-wait syndrome.'

As the *Canberra* slipped her moorings in Southampton, Jerry had a deep inner glow. He couldn't help but feel that for once in his life he was in the right job, in the right place at the right time. As for everyone else aboard, it was his first experience of sailing to war and the dedicated, professional soldier in him didn't like a lot of what was going on around him.

'The routine on the ship wasn't like anything I would have expected and there was too much bickering. Units were bickering over who was in charge and there was bickering in almost every company, platoon and section over training, over equipment and over personnel. Senior personnel in our own company picked the people they wanted and it finished up, as far as I'm concerned, a divided company. Allocated weapons were changed around. I loved the GPMG, and that was taken from me because of battalion shortages. I was really pissed off no end about that, but I did accept that as I was one of the few trained snipers in the battalion I could undertake that role. We had what I labelled senior call-signs and junior call-signs and I was one of the latter.

'We had been briefed that our objective on landing was to be Port San Carlos. As D Company our role would be long-range patrols deep into enemy territory, observation posts and standing-listening patrols, all sending intelligence back to battalion HQ. We would report all enemy positions and movements back. But because of the earlier carve-up it was the senior call-signs who got to work closely with the SAS while the rest of us junior call-signs were left back with the battalion. By this time we had cross-decked from the *Canberra* to HMS *Intrepid*, where the SAS were based, but just before the landings the SAS lost more than twenty men when a helicopter crashed into the sea. It was the most men they had ever lost at one time.

'Many of the men killed were to have been working with 3 Para – and some were ex-Paras – so our senior call-signs filled the gaps in our area. As we had been left back I just settled down on *Intrepid* to wait for the "green on".'

I interviewed the other Argentinians for this book in January 1994, but it was in June the previous year that I had met Oscar Carrizo. I was in Buenos Aires with Dom Gray and Denzil Connick to attend a press conference set up by Argentina's magazine *Gente* and the television company Channel 11., and Britain's *Today* newspaper. The aim of the event was to show that, despite an ongoing Scotland Yard investigation into alleged actions by British soldiers during the Falklands campaign, Argentinian and British veterans of the war could come together in friendship.

A giant of a man, six foot four tall, Oscar was a corporal but, unlike the other Argentinian soldiers in this book, was a regular soldier. He was nervous when we first met at the conference, but soon warmed as our conversation, conducted through an interpreter, progressed and we swapped photographs of the war. I was to listen to his story for an hour, away from the cameras and the lights, in the lobby of the hotel and then over a meal.

Oscar was born on 7 May 1960 and spent his twenty-second birthday on the Falklands as his country revelled in the euphoria that followed the occupation of the Islas Malvinas, the soggy cluster of wind-lashed islands housing a collection of sheep farmers and kelpers who seemed to spend their entire lives swathed in layers of woolly sweaters, bobble hats and wellies to defy the biting winds. His country had long regarded the Falklands as part of Argentina, and Oscar, one of five children of an oil worker, was as proud as any man that the blue and white flag of Argentina was now flying over Government House in Port Stanley.

At the age of seventeen he had waved goodbye to his parents, two brothers and two sisters, and turned his back on the modest family home in Mendoza, one of his country's southern provinces snuggled in the Andes.

'I always wanted to be a regular soldier in the Army. I was married in 1981 and my son was born in March 1982. Everything was good. I was a father and a corporal and I was excited about going home to see my son and my wife. But as soon as the Malvinas became ours all our units had their leave stopped. So, on 13 April 1982, I travelled with my unit, the 7th Infantry Regiment, to Rio Gallegos... and then straight to the Falklands.

'All I know is that as a regular soldier I was proud to be on the islands fighting for my country and our flag. I sent a telegram to my wife in Buenos Aires and one to my parents in Mendoza. No one back home knew I had gone until they saw the stamp of the Malvinas on the envelopes.'

4

AS DIEGO and I drew up in our car, Antonio Belmonte greeted us immediately from his gate, his eyes kind, his smile genuine. The whole look of the man, mature and calm, put me at my ease before I even shook hands with him.

Inside the house the rooms were cool, huge overhead fans wafting a gentle breeze around the table at which we sat down to eat and talk. Antonio explained that he is a first-generation Argentinian son of Italian parents who scrimped and saved to raise their fares to cross the Atlantic to escape the devastation which scarred Europe at the end of the last war. His father was a soldier in Mussolini's army which invaded Albania and Greece as part of the Axis forces, then collapsed in the face of the Allied invasion of southern Europe. The Italians' Nazi allies gave them a simple choice: fight alongside us – or go to labour camps. There was another alternative for some, which Antonio's father chose: fight with the Allies to rid Italy of the Nazis. But he was captured and sent to a prison camp. Soon after the war he married, but found it hard to settle in post-war Italy, so he decided to go to Argentina in search of a better life for his bride and young son. A year later they joined him and for the next twelve years they worked and slaved for that life. The family began to grow: first, in 1961, came a daughter and then, a year later, Antonio was born.

He grew up in a typical loving Italian family. His parents mingled well with their Argentinian neighbours in Lanus and had learned the language. By sacrificing the chance to increase their family beyond two children in the early years, they had built a firm foundation for a good home life for them. Unlike many immigrant families in many countries, they didn't cling to the old ways, so Antonio grew up feeling like an Argentinian, proud of his country of birth. He is proud, too, of his father who laboured long hours in a soap factory, spending his spare time playing with his kids and telling young Antonio stories of his earlier life and of his experiences during the Second World War.

The conversation turned to the Falklands and I showed Antonio photographs of Argentinian POWs, hoping to jog his memory. Seizing on one shot of an Argentinian soldier being searched by a member of 3 Para, he said: 'I'm ninety per cent sure that's me. I remember that happening to me.' Antonio's story began to unfold.

'You know, when I was in the Malvinas, on Mount Longdon, waiting for the war to start, I used to think of my parents. I would be sitting there in the wet and rain and the cold wind. I would be hungry and I would think particularly of my father. It's like I was in telepathic communication with him. I would sit waiting for the war, wondering how I would perform, and remember his war stories. That was the only knowledge I had of war. We were a tight, united family and the three of us were smothered in love by our parents. Our childhood was happy, very happy. We could not have wished for better parents.

'They brought us up to appreciate the simple things in life. That is why I say I am a simple man, I'm not soft in the head or a simpleton, but I don't demand too much either. At school I was a bit slow, but my mother got me extra tuition and I passed my exams. I dropped out of school after my fourth year at technical college and then conscription came. I was happy to go because I knew everything was well at home. Unlike a lot of the other lads who were called up I had no worries about my family.

'I passed the medicals and then they gave us the Army haircut and the shouting began. They seemed to think all the shouting would get us in the military mood and turn us into soldiers. I was sent to San Miguel del Monte like everyone else who joined the 7th Regiment and I wrote to my parents so that they could keep in touch with my whereabouts. On the bus to the training camp I thought to myself that this wouldn't be too bad because it was camping, you know, sitting around relaxing and enjoying yourself! It was nothing like that. They danced us, made us jump up and down, shouted, made us crawl here and there and punished us if they thought we were not paying attention. They made us sweat a lot, I can tell you.

'We were taught the basics, and I mean the very basics, of soldiering. Then we returned to the regiment, which I found very boring. Terribly dull. I know some of the people fancied soldiering as a career, but I thought the whole thing was a bore. Sometimes I found myself doing some soldiering in the morning, or being given instruction, but as far as I can remember the afternoons were all about cleaning the place. The barracks was cramped and there were about 900 of us all getting in each other's way.

'They also had a system where conscripts with certain trades – painters, electricians, builders and the like – were sent outside to help on civilian projects such as repairing and decorating schools. For some reason they sent me to work on a school and I missed a lot of training, particularly the big manoeuvres, because of it. On one occasion a big exercise was coming up which I very much wanted to attend, but the headmistress of the school told our authorities she wanted her work finished and we were ordered to stay and do it and miss the exercise.

'Time was dragging and I felt I was being sold as a slave to outside civilian interests. As the time of my discharge, 30 March 1982, approached, the days dragged even more. I began to feel I would never be free. I was totally unaware of any problems between my country and the British and then they told us that some problems had arisen at a military compound called Campo de Mayo and that we may have to guard it for two weeks.

'I remember popping into the canteen to grab a Coke and found we had taken the Malvinas. There, on the television in the canteen, were our soldiers walking about the Malvinas. A great group of us just stood there, drinking from our cans, and watching it all on television.

'Over the Easter period my family came to the 7th Regiment's camp because they were worried that I hadn't come home and that I still hadn't received my discharge. When they got there I had gone, moved on to Campo de Mayo. I was as confused as them. Nothing was happening and there was nothing going on around us to indicate we were going to war.

'Suddenly, at 4 a.m., our barracks doors crashed open and an officer told us to get our kit together and get on the buses outside. They weren't Army buses, but from a private company. Some of the lads who had been discharged a month earlier were back and others from the new intake – who had just done their four weeks' basic training – were there too.

'An officer stepped on to our bus and said: "Soldiers, tomorrow we will meet in the Malvinas."

'That was how I knew I was going to war. I didn't even get a chance to tell my family.'

Tony Gregory had endured more than his share of misfortune in his early life. Born in London in March 1960, he was never to know his father. He was never to know the love a father has for his son, or the real warmth of family life, until he joined his brothers-in-arms in the Parachute Regiment.

'I know my mother, but not my father. He was, apparently, a waste of rations who drank too much. When I was six months old my brother Steve and I were put in care in Dr Barnardo's by our mother. We were looked, after by a couple called Margaret and Irvine Harvey, who were house parents. I was with them for four years and they wanted to adopt me, but my mother wouldn't allow it. The Village was one of Dr Barnardo's homes, and I think there were about 600 kids there, mainly poor blacks and poor white kids who had been totally abandoned and never knew their parents. I was to stay in Barnardo's for the next sixteen years. I spent most of my life in the orphanage. I was thoroughly institutionalized. But I did see my mother one Sunday a month.'

The impressions of his boyhood are still vividly etched in Tony's memory. Even now, almost twenty years on, it takes no effort for him to see the home in his mind's eye. He remembers the big wall surrounding the forbidding house, the name of the headmaster, a retired colonel who ran it with all the strictness and discipline of a Victorian authoritarian. The children slept in dormitories. Young Tony suspected the regime was not dissimilar to that of a Borstal, where tearaways were sent for punishment. He had done nothing wrong except to be born. Boys caught talking after lights out in the dormitories were punished by being made to sit for hours in cold, draughty corridors in their pyjamas.

He remembers, too, the woman who was supposed to look after them and who took great delight in humiliating her wretched charges. 'Her favourite punishment was to make us strip until we were almost naked and let the girls watch. I hated her. For seven years she was with us. She was always a bitch.'

It was a harsh regime. Their pocket money was sixpence a week in old money: two and a half pence in today's money. Everything was regimented; done to a schedule: eating, sleeping, playing, schooling. They were not allowed beyond the wall and referred to people outside as 'outsiders'. Nearly all the other children were orphans.

'I suppose I was an exception because I did have a mother, but at that time she was only my mother because of nature. I never had the feel of a mother's arms around me.'

The wretched children's whole existence was contained within the orphanage walls. They knew little or nothing of the outside world. They were not allowed out and those who did slip out for a look around found that the local police had the power to hold them until a superior from the home eventually called to collect them to return them for punishment. Occasionally they would be taken to the seaside, and Tony remembers sitting open-mouthed and gawping at all the people, all the normal people going about their normal everyday business. He couldn't take it all in. He also recalled seeing the ships steaming past as they headed far beyond the horizon, and the fascination and wonderment of it all.

Early in the 1970s Tony's life began to change a little for the better. New legislation meant orphanage children were allowed to attend outside schools. He was eleven and can still remember going to school as if it was yesterday. Poorly dressed and with only his dinner money in his pocket, he enrolled at Fairlop Boys' School in Barkingside, Essex. It was a whole new world for the boys from the institution, a new world where they met kids who seemed to them to have everything a boy could want: parents, bikes, money and decent clothes. But the Barnardo's boys also had to run the gauntlet of their better-off fellows. For some of the other pupils ridiculed and hounded them in that particularly cruel way only youngsters are capable of, inflicting hurt deep in their souls, constantly wounding them with their cruel jibes.

The whole sorry situation was bound to come to a head. Tony found it very difficult to settle, impossible to adapt to his new surroundings. The conflict festered deep down for two years. Despite it all he still attended school, refusing to play truant, or to walk away from it. When he was thirteen he started to answer back – with his fists. Anyone taking the piss out of Tony Gregory, his clothes or his background, had to face his full fury. Inevitably he regularly ended up on the headmaster's study carpet. He had taken enough, had endured more humiliation than most of us face in a lifetime, had lived with the knowledge that he was different for long enough, had tramped the streets to and from school feeling people were pointing at him as if he were a freak.

His outrage made him a scrapper, a tough nut. He shaved his head like a skinhead and joined a gang, dishing out violence to any other gang who crossed his path. He went to youth clubs looking for punch-ups, and stalked the streets afterwards in search of 'bovver'. Fuelled by his bitter resentment at the hand life had dealt him, he was fast heading off the rails, fast becoming a tearaway. It was only by sheer chance that he had not finished up in the hands of the police. He realized his standard of education was about three years below that of his contemporaries and this made him feel even more of an outcast, even more frustrated.

Anyone who tried telling Tony Gregory that life had its ups and downs received a disbelieving sneer. There were no ups in Tony's life until Bill Sardinson took him aside for a 'get-a-grip-of-yourself' lecture after a careers talk. Tony told the astonished teacher: 'I want to join the Navy.' It had been his secret, dearest wish ever since his first excursion to the seaside when he had seen the ships all those years ago.

Bill Sardinson confirmed that his standard of education was too low, but said that he would talk to the Royal Navy careers officer, who was a friend. The officer provided the targets Tony had to aim for and another teacher spent six months giving him extra tuition during recreation times. Tony sat the Navy entrance examination and failed it miserably. But the effort put in by his teachers impressed him. He was aware that people had tried to help him, that they had believed in him. At last he had something to be grateful for, something he still remembers with pride. And although he failed the exam his standard of literacy improved beyond recognition. He could now read and write.

In the orphanage there was a system whereby couples worked as house parents, looking after groups of the children. One couple, Ken and Anne Cox, looked after Tony between the ages of twelve and sixteen. 'They helped me as much as possible,' he says. But he was still a kid from nowhere and going nowhere fast. He became a soccer thug, joining the London Reds – a band of so-called Manchester United supporters who lived in the south of England – and was in the thick of the action with rival supporters anywhere he could find it. He took on part-time jobs to fund his football hooliganism. He sold the *Evening Standard* on a street corner and ran errands and did some labouring for local builders. As his last year at school approached he persuaded the school authorities to allow him to have three days a week off so that he could work for a local builder. It was a situation which suited the authorities and Tony alike as they both knew full well he would pass no exams. The builder paid him £5 a day to do the donkey work and it kept him out of trouble. At sixteen he was able to leave school and a social worker was assigned to him to prepare him for leaving the home and going off into the big outside world. Officially, the institution had a say in the boys' lives until they were twenty-one, but in reality it also wanted to see the back of them.

The boys were discovering discos and girls and yearning for their freedom. If Tony wasn't back by ten o'clock at night he would have to rouse the duty house parents and this would result in a punishment such as being refused permission to go out for a time. One day, after a row, he left the home with all his belongings in a small bag. He managed to contact his brother, Steve, who gave him a room in a house he was sharing. The builder for whom he had been working gave him a full-time job and paid him £25 a week. Out of his wages he had to pay £18 for his room, leaving him only £7 for food and everything else he needed. Steve moved out and Tony was alone in the world.

'My brother told me a guy called Peter would collect the rent money, but I hardly ever saw him. He, too, disappeared. I was scared, really scared, because I was living on my own in this house without any contact with anyone. I didn't even know whose house it was or who was supposed to get the rent. Then, one day, these four really heavy guys crashed in. They were looking for this Pete. They didn't harm me, but it frightened me. I got in touch with my social worker, who eventually found the owner and said she would come to see me. I cleaned that house from top to bottom. I wanted to impress her so she would know I could look after her house properly.

'I had put my rent money aside. Saved it so it was all there. She arrived, never saying hello or anything. She just told me to get out there and then. She was an absolute cow. I couldn't believe it; neither could my social worker. He said I would be homeless, but she couldn't care less. That was it: I was on the streets. The social worker found me a place in a hostel for the mentally disturbed. It was the only place they could put me. Jesus.

'Eventually a friend's parents offered me a place in their home and I got away from that dump. They treated me really well and for two years I was really happy with them. It was something I had never experienced. Then they decided to move to another area. They offered to take me with them, but I was happy in my job and didn't want to leave it so I moved into bedsits. I just kept moving from bedsit to bedsit.

'One day I had a bit of luck. I was on a bus going to work and met a girl I knew called Lin. We were chatting and I asked her if she knew anyone who was looking for a lodger. A couple of days later I saw her again on the bus and she said her mum, Diana, would put me up. I moved in with them and their family. It was good. I found happiness at last. I shall be grateful to them for ever. I lived there right up until I joined the Army.

'I was in my local pub in Ilford one Friday when five lads who were on leave from 1 Para came in. I knew one of them, Lawrie Wells. They were really enjoying themselves, singing and generally performing. There was something about them, they were really solid mates. I tagged along with them for the weekend and when I went back to work on Monday on the building site my mind was just about made up. I started to question the older blokes who had served in the Army to try to get a feel for it. I knew I was going to go for it and within a few weeks I walked into the recruiting office in Forest Gate and met a Para sergeant there. I later found out he was Dex Allan, who also served in the Falklands.

'At that time I hadn't a clue what the Paras were about, but having met those guys I wanted to be one. I just had this gut feeling that this was going to be my big chance in life. It was going to be my big chance to achieve something. I had to sit an entrance examination and, do you know, I passed it. I was totally stunned. All through my life I had never passed anything. I still hadn't a clue what the Paras were about, but that didn't matter now. This was my big chance. I wasn't going to miss it. Do you know that on building sites I was shit-scared of climbing ladders? It never dawned on me I was joining an outfit which would require me to jump out of an aircraft!

'I went to Sutton Coldfield for three days and passed all the tests. Wow! I was on my way. I was accepted into the Parachute Regiment and joined 463 Platoon at Browning Barracks, Aldershot, in 1980.

'Because I had lived in dormitories most of my life I adapted very quickly to barracks life. I could cook, iron, wash, sew and everything else. These were basics of life to me, but I was surprised at how many lads couldn't do this. The physical side of the training was very tough going, but I felt I belonged for the first time in my life. When the day came for the passing-out parade I was really proud. Nobody ever thought I'd make it in life and I had. I'd proved them all wrong. My mother turned up with my stepdad. It turned out he had been a glider pilot who was wounded at Arnhem in the Second World War.

'I had opted for 3 Para because the mates I had made in

training were going there and I went off to join them in Northern Ireland just after Christmas leave. I flew to Belfast and was met by Paras in plain clothes, but carrying loaded weapons. It was a real shock to the system. We drove to Keady, in Co. Armagh, where I was joining 7 Platoon, C Company. I was the only one from our intake to go to Keady. Our quarters were in the police station and it was a cramped shithole. I was shown a bunk in a Portakabin-type building. It was cramped and overcrowded. Everyone was out on patrol and I waited nervously for them to return, then I went to bed. At three o'clock in the morning they returned, dragged me out of bed and ordered me to clean their weapons. Being a 'crow', I was expected to do all the dirty jobs. I had expected it. I got 'rubber-dicked' [tricked] a lot simply because, as a crow, I didn't know the score in battalion life. It is standard procedure in the Paras to be given all the naff jobs until you are accepted by the rest of the platoon. You're there as a gofer. On the other hand they did look after me out on patrol. They taught me everything, particularly the section corporals. I did town patrols, border patrols and duties on sentry in the sangars guarding the camp. The lads made sure I was shown the ropes on the professional side and the corporals watched over everything. They encouraged me all the way.

'Over the next five months of the tour I settled into battalion life. I was learning and, after two months, I belonged. That was when I knew I had been accepted. One day we were out on a border patrol. It was my twenty-first birthday and I had told no one. Back at camp they found out and gave me a special birthday treat: no more rubber dicks. They said: 'No one should be dicked on his birthday.'

'I was getting on well with just about everybody in my section and platoon. After Northern Ireland we had a social life as well and we all stuck together. We worked hard.

Between April and August 1981 we were constantly training. I can remember feeling thoroughly hacked off about having to go to Canada on another big exercise, but once we got there I thoroughly enjoyed it. We did everything over there: live firing, section, platoon and battalion attacks, escape and evasion and forced marches everywhere. By the end of 1981 I am proud to say that 3 Para were one of the most highly trained units in the British Army.

'At the beginning of 1982 the battalion was on Spearhead – twenty-four-hour stand-by-kit packed ready to move anywhere in the world trouble erupted. Anywhere the government wanted to send a fighting unit we would go. We also did a lot of cross-training: Rifle Company lads learning how to use mortars, sustained-fire machine-guns and anti-tank weapons.

'I managed to get on a mini course for snipers at Warminster, using the L-42 sniper rifle. I can clearly remember coming back to the camp at Tidworth one Friday evening in April. Normally, on Friday evenings, the camp would be deserted. We were all in the back of a lorry and it stopped at the guardroom and we could hear the guard talking about the Argies invading some place called the Falkland Island [sic]. None of us had a clue where it was. We were told to go to our rooms and await orders.

'Looking from my window I could see the parade square. It was a real beehive of activity. Helicopters were buzzing in and out, lorries were toing and froing and there were lads running about all over the place. Eventually we got orders to check our kit in readiness for a move to war. I didn't believe it. I honestly thought it was a wind-up, a great big, brilliant rubber dick. It wasn't...

'This was going to be the real thing. All over the country members of 3 Para were being recalled. It was the first call back to barracks since the Suez crisis of the 1950s. Well, the flak and flap was something different over the next couple of days. Pack, then unpack. We're going, no we're not. On the bus, off the bus. We zeroed our weapons up on the ranges.

'It was all very exciting, but I'm not ashamed to say I felt something weird coming over me. I did not join the Army to go to war. I know that sounds stupid. I know that is why we are there and what we are there for. The nearest I ever expected to get to any sort of war was Northern Ireland and that had been a quiet tour. I had joined the Army for quite different reasons, I suppose. But there was no going back now. I was a Paratrooper and I was going to do my duty.

'The main topic of conversation among all of us was what we'd be like under fire. Everyone seemed to be out to prove to himself and his mates just how good he would be. Personally, I just wasn't tuned in to all of that. Perhaps it was shock, I'll never know, but that is honestly how I felt. I was scared, nervous, but was prepared to fight with my mates in 7 Platoon, C Company. Believe it or not, I was one of the oldest "toms" in my platoon. I was twenty-two. That's not very old, is it? But most toms in our battalion in the Falklands were aged between seventeen and twenty. We've heard a lot about the Argentinian soldiers being so young, but the truth is there wasn't very much difference at all, hardly any in ages. I was one of the more mature toms simply because of the way I had had to live my earlier life. I matured quicker. I had to. I know, too, that it has been what they call human nature over hundreds of years to fight and to kill, but I couldn't help thinking there was something sad about it all. Don't get me wrong: I will defend right from wrong just like any other man, just like any other Paratrooper.

'By the time we began leaving Tidworth for the *Canberra*

in Southampton, I was mentally shaping up to war. I fell in with the rest and was swept along with all the others on the wave of patriotism and pomp. When we got to Southampton I knew we were going to be shit on by the Marines. It was going to be their show. I predicted, quite rightly, that most of 3 Para would be billeted below the water-line, where just one torpedo strike could drown the lot of us. We were given a four-berth cabin which was so small only two men could stand to unpack while the other two lay on their bunks out of the way. All we could unpack was our personal washing and shaving kit. Our weapons and webbing had to be kept locked in the cabins at all times and we couldn't help laughing when we were told we had to wear trainers in case our boots caused any damage to the decks.

'As we sailed from Southampton I saw my mother and stepfather on the quayside, waving. We sailed on the evening tide with the ship lit up as if she was going on another world cruise. The bands were playing and everyone was waving Union Jacks. The atmosphere was electric. It was a moment to feel proud to be British. As the ship sailed out of reach of the cheering and noise I was standing against a deck rail. I looked around me and could see some of the lads standing with their heads bowed. There was a quiet, eerie silence then. It fell over all of us. It was as if all of us were thinking at the same time: Christ, we really are going to war.

'Within days we noticed how the Marines seemed to be getting the best of everything. They were first to scoff, which meant the best choices were gone when we got to the hotplate. They had the first sittings in the cinema and the best bars on the ship. Things were simmering and I could see it was all heading for a big fight. I remember thinking we were all supposed to be on the same side. I knew there was always going to be rivalry between us, but not to this extent. Some of the Marines were a good bunch, but it was the top brass and their attitude which I blame for a lot of the friction. Mixing was frowned upon and a lot of damage was done. I don't think it has ever really been properly repaired.'

Despite all this bad feeling, Tony and his platoon knuckled down to serious training. It increased in intensity as each day dawned. There was no messing about as lessons learned throughout their Army careers were gone over again and again, drills became automatic, second nature, as the joking vanished and everyone focused on their objective: to fight a war and come home again unscathed.

'We had a period of really intense training at Ascension Island and when the ship sailed from there going south we were all hyped up and wanting to fight. The biggest morale-booster for us was the arrival of 2 Para on another ship, the *Norland*. At least now we had a sister battalion nearby, two Para battalions together. It was going to be a Para war: no stopping at any red lights. The only thing pissing us off now was all the political shenanigans with the United Nations and the American Secretary of State, Al Haig, on his diplomatic shuttle around the world, slowing the momentum. We tried not to let it affect us. And as we sailed through the Roaring Forties we knew it was a goer. Intelligence started to flow in to the ship. Our medics trained hard and assured us that if anything happened to us we would be in good hands. That was another morale-booster after the news of the sinking of the *Belgrano* and HMS *Sheffield*.

'I still remember the atmosphere and the faces of the other guys in the bar on the night the ship was piped silent so they could tell us of the disaster of the *Sheffield* being attacked. You could see in the eyes of everyone that this was a no-going-back situation. There was a real scary silence over the room. We even took lifeboat drill seriously next day.'

The audacity of the Argentinian Air Force pilots, with their deadly French-built Exocet anti-ship missiles, had also concentrated the minds of the Royal Navy and Task Force brass. The *Canberra* was big, very big, and she was carrying the bulk of the British assault force. She was a prime target and something would have to be done. So, in the middle of the night, everyone was roused from their beds because it had been decided to lessen the effects on the Task Force should the *Canberra* be hit by an Exocet or 'tin-fished' by a torpedo from an enemy submarine.

The men of 3 Para would cross-deck to HMS *Intrepid* and the men of 40 Commando, Royal Marines, would also move to *Intrepid,* the command centre for the forthcoming landings. This would all be done in the middle of the night in the heaving South Atlantic.

'We were all ammoed up and being called forward to cross-deck. We had trained for it at Ascension, but that was in reasonably calm, warm water in daylight. Now, in the middle of the night, it was a frightening experience. One by one we took our turn, standing holding on to the rail at a door on the lower deck of the *Canberra*, waiting for the landing-craft to rise up on a wave, then step on board. If you missed you would have sunk like a brick or been crushed between ship and landing-craft. We all made it.

'On *Intrepid* I found a space in one of the corridors like everybody else. I was the section machine-gunner and had 700 rounds of linked ammunition around me. I knew my orders and just settled down to wait. That's the soldier's game: waiting. When the notice to move came my nerves were settled, but I couldn't help laughing when I saw the guy who was dishing out the grenades. He was sat on a grenade box, smoking and priming them. He'd just ask, "How many, mate?" and then chuck them into your hands. All the rules and regulations had gone out the window. I smiled again as I stepped into the landing-craft... it was all OK.

Alberto Carbone had sat quietly through my talk with his old friend Luis Leccese, occasionally reminding him, with a friendly laugh; of their escapades. The pair of them reminded me of a couple of street-wise wheeler-dealers, alert, aware and always ready to look after each other.

When I interviewed him, Alberto began by insisting that he was just an ordinary guy: 'I could tell you my life story in one minute flat.' But then he added: 'I reckon lots of people, looking back at their lives, could say: "I've nothing to tell" – perhaps I would have said that. I was just like the guy next door... But the Malvinas war has taught me a lot about life... '

Alberto is a second-generation Argentinian, born, as were his parents, near Buenos Aires, his grandparents having emigrated from Italy. Going back to his early life, he explained that he was a rebellious, high-spirited youngster, regularly in trouble at school. But, despite warnings about his behaviour, he managed to get through primary school, passing all his exams.

Secondary school was different. He was booted out after the first year when an ink bomb he threw from a classroom window smashed on the head of a passer-by. 'It was some old geezer just walking past. It didn't help after the other bother I had been in,' he reflects with a grin.

Alberto had been in trouble before for bombarding the school caretakers with stink bombs and refusing to wear the correct uniform. His father decided to send him to night school and during the summer holidays an aunt who was also a teacher was drafted in to give him extra lessons. The new regime worked and he managed to absorb most of what he was taught. It also suited him, leaving him free most of the day to roam the streets and get into more mischief.

'I'll always remember this Italian mother coming to our house to complain about what she called my unruly behaviour. She was always moaning that she wanted me locked up for beating up her kid. I wasn't a bully, but he and the other Italian kids always rubbed me up the wrong way and there was only one way to put them in their place. That's all I did. I used to work on Saturdays and Sundays to get money so I could go to discos on Friday nights. At the discos you met girls. I'd go out with one for a while and then see another I fancied better and change. We all lived in blocks of flats and I remember one young girl who lived in our block, very pretty, who always nodded and smiled at me. But she was only about fourteen or fifteen, so I left her alone. Too young. I was eighteen and had my eyes on others.

'After leaving school I had a variety of jobs. I started off as a panel beater, got bored with that and went to a chicken slaughterhouse. Then I tried my hand at making pullovers in a clothing factory, but that didn't suit so I became an ice-cream man. That job I enjoyed and stuck with it for three years. I had no real responsibilities except for a period of two or three months when my father lost his job and I was the sole breadwinner for our house. All in all we weren't poor, but we weren't well off either.

'It was shortly after I noticed the young girl in our block that I was called up for my conscription and I put her out of my mind. I had other things to think about. I wasn't too keen on the year's soldiering facing me, but I knew it would be very hard to beat the system, so I decided to get on with it and get the best I could out of it. As everyone else says, the first sixty days are not good, but at the end of it I landed myself a great number compared with what the rest of the lads had to put up with.

'I became a military-ambulance driver. I ate in the hospital canteen, which served better food than the regimental cookhouse, and I slept in a good bed with clean sheets in a hut. All I had to do was assist the medics and drive them about. I was out of the camp, away from the regiment and its discipline every day. All I had to do was behave myself and I had a very cushy existence. The only other thing I had to do was guard duty. Everything has to be guarded. My whole life in the Army was a waste of time and guard duty was the biggest waste of all. It must be the most boring task of soldiering.

'Normally I just guarded the vehicles when it was my turn to do it. One night, however, they sent me on a duty with the regiment... a serious guard duty. It was so boring I left my rifle in its case and decided to get my head down for a while, but I overslept and the next thing I know is one of the corporals is standing over me, shouting. Next thing I can't find my rifle because he's hidden it and now it looks like I've lost it. I'm in big trouble, a lot of very big trouble. Losing your weapon is a serious offence and I didn't know he had hidden it.

'I was sentenced "to the flag". That meant I had to spend two days standing rigidly to attention, staring straight at our national flag on its pole near the regimental prison. The only time I wasn't there was when they danced me off at meal times or if any of the other prisoners had visitors. They didn't want the visitors to see me standing staring up at the flag so they would bang me into a dungeon until the visitors had gone. That was the only time I fucked up during conscription and it taught me a lesson the hard way. I hate to think what they would have done to me if I really had lost my rifle.

'Halfway through my service there was a really big exercise involving the 10th Brigade. I don't know what the top brass had in mind at the time – whether it was a rehearsal for the Malvinas or not – but it was big. There were at least 10,000 troops involved and I had to drive a vehicle with a big cannon on it. I couldn't find the exercise area at first, then I got lost trying to find the regiment and then I got lost trying to find my company. I got there in the end and they sent me off to get a truck fitted out with a field kitchen and drive that around delivering food to the infantry. When I got to the front line all the big guns were firing and the heat was unbelievable. They were holding this exercise in a desert. If it was a practice for the Malvinas they were holding it in a very strange place!

'The infantry soldiers were in a very bad way. They were in a dreadful state from hunger and thirst. They were so bad with thirst they even tried to get the water from the radiator of my truck. I'll never forget the dreadful state they were in.

'About a week before my discharge I was told, for some reason or another, that I had to go back into training with the new intake. Just a refresher, they said. This was March 1982 and the only training I wanted to do was for my return to civilian life. The Malvinas had now been taken and we thought we were going to guard the camp of a regiment which had been sent there. We hadn't been told anything about going to war. We didn't even know what a war was. That may sound naïve, but we had never really been taught anything about war.

'When we found out we were going to the islands we still didn't believe we were going to a war. We were heading for the Malvinas, sure, and that was OK by me and the rest of us, but it was probably just another big exercise.

'Surely they would have told us if we were going to war... '

Part 2
Walking, Waiting, Suffering

1

D OM WAS fuming. This was what they had sailed 8000 miles to do and he had just spent the last few hours on extra duties, washing dixies in the galley and serving breakfast to the bloody Marines. As far as he was concerned they were all 'boat people' of the most pathetic kind.

Psychologically he had been all saddled up and raring to go from the time their training on Ascension Island had finished. His rifle was in perfect condition and the magazine of twenty rounds clicked home. His face was smeared with camouflage cream and his webbing, although heavy, was bearable as it enveloped his waist and shoulders. He was carrying as much ammunition as he could get his hands on.

Like the rest of the Paras, Dom became agitated as the landings got under way. 'Typical,' he muttered to himself. 'Typical. The brass have fucked up yet again.'

They had been promised they would land in the dark. That was the way Paras went to war – at night, scaring the enemy shitless, suddenly appearing among the bastards. They definitely did not go in broad daylight unless it was absolutely unavoidable and they did not go to war in a bloody rubbish skip of a Royal Marines landing-craft sticking out like a bulldog's bollocks as the finest target for miles around. He was fuming. So was his entire section.

Here they were, squeezed together like sardines, not even knowing if the enemy were dug in and waiting for them on the beach. Would it be like the D-Day films he had seen where hundreds of other Allied soldiers were chopped down as soon as they stepped from the landing-craft or blown to smithereens by artillery and rockets before even getting a chance to close with the enemy? From what he had seen of them the belching little rubbish skips they were using in May 1982 had changed little from those used in June 1944.

Enemy were known to be in an observation post on Fanning Head with a clear view of the landing beaches of San Carlos Water. What if they had their range and had big guns up there? The Navy had bombarded them during the night, but, unfortunately for the Navy, that had had to stop when the only gun on the only ship they sent to do the job seized up. The Argentinians' job was to call in artillery and air strikes, he assumed.

He knew if it had been Paras up there this lot in the water would have died where they were, particularly in daylight. There was no way any bastard would have lived long enough to get sand on the soles of his boots. It was said the SAS had been sent to finish the job, to drive them away or zap them where they stood. Fair enough. But had they?

The whole thing was turning into a pantomime. And if this was what it was like at the beginning, what was it going to be like when they got ashore? Dom didn't have long to wait for an answer to his unspoken question. The troops braced themselves for the craft to grind on to the beach – then the charge ashore, then... nothing. Sweet FA. The ramp of the landing-craft refused to go down. Now they were really in the shit. All it needed was one bomb, or one lucky artillery shell, and they would all be fish food. But the uneasiness was soon replaced by cold fury and the Paras took matters into their own hands, or rather feet, and began booting the ramp door down.

They had been promised a dry landing, stepping from the landing craft straight on to the beach. The SBS, the Special Boat Squadron, another group of hats the Marines believed were equal to the SAS, had checked the beach and sworn the landing-craft could easily beach there. Well they couldn't, and Dom, being a short-arse, didn't fancy jumping off the ramp into the water to try to wade ashore. He didn't want to drown, sinking like a brick laden with kit, before getting a chance to fight. But the order was given to go and off they went, waist deep in the freezing water and on to a beach the Argies had long deserted – if they had ever been there in the first place. The cold water made him gasp and froze his bollocks to hazel nuts. He couldn't believe that at last they had got one thing right: they had been promised an unopposed landing and that they had got.

Dom is absolutely convinced that if the enemy had been waiting he would never have got off the landing-craft, let alone set foot on the beach. Later he discovered there had been forty Argentinian soldiers at Port San Carlos, the Paras' landing site, and they had bugged out as the landings began. They could have caused mayhem if they had chosen to hold their ground. It would have been a different story if 3 Para had been there. Definitely. There would have been a lot of mourning back in Argentina that day.

Felix Barreto looked down on the scattered islands his country had for so long claimed as their own as the four-engined Hercules C-130 banked and locked on to its final approach for landing. Minutes later, as the tailgate whined open and he stepped on to the Malvinas for the first time, he was engulfed by the feeling that he was going to be in a war. Soldiers were everywhere. Defences were being built at the airport and batteries of anti-aircraft guns and missiles installed. Heavily fortified positions were being built to cover just about every conceivable line of approach.

'Just for a very short time, as I picked up my heavy weapon and luggage, I thought the English would not dare come this far,' admits Felix. 'But when I saw the defences I knew then we were preparing for war. You could feel it in the air.

'Major Carrizo, our company commander, gave us some orders and we started to walk towards Puerto Argentino [Port Stanley]. I couldn't make out where we were supposed to be going. We just picked up all our kit and started to walk. We were laden like pack mules, but you could sense there was going to be a war. It was there all around us, it was everywhere. You couldn't escape it. We had arrived at 10 a.m. and moved out shortly afterwards. At 5 p.m. we were still walking. It was hard work because of what I was carrying. We didn't march through Stanley – we trudged through it. I was surprised, however, when we were ordered to keep on marching, right through the town. I had expected to be allowed to rest, even to be told to stay there for the night for sleep. Nobody seemed to know what to do about us or to care. Major Carrizo handed over command to a lieutenant and he seemed more interested in hitting us to make us go faster than in leading us. There was no organization by our own people. We were exhausted, we had not been given any rest, we hadn't been fed and suddenly here we are marching in a cold climate, a climate we are not used to.

'I couldn't take much more. I said to the officer: "You'll get nowhere hitting us." Then I sat down. I'd had enough.

I didn't want to get up again because I was so cold. I was so stiff. I felt as if we had walked thirty kilometres. We were conscripts and no one wanted to know about us. We were being badly treated. I knew I was there to fight, to go to war, but this wasn't what I expected preparation for battle to be like.

'Before we took the Malvinas I knew absolutely nothing about the place. The way the military told us about the islands filled us with pride and strength, as if the English had stolen them from us and we were there to defend something that was rightfully ours. Because of this I felt deep inside me a love of that land, a love... I don't know... a love of it even more than of my own home. Inside me, when I had arrived, I had been very proud to be there.

'Now, as I sat in the cold, I was angry. I felt anger at the empty trucks everywhere, at the helicopters buzzing about. Why were we having to carry such heavy loads when empty trucks were passing us all the time? If the trucks couldn't carry us surely they could carry our kit? We dumped all our heavy kit in a pile and carried on with just our weapons and rucksacks.

'We marched on through the capital and finally reached the old English barracks at Moody Brook. It was in a mess, but I was glad of the halt. My back was killing me, really hurting, and I was glad of the chance to get a rest. I was really starving by then, aching with hunger. The officers told us we would be sleeping here for the night, but they refused to give us any food. It had been a long, long day and at the end of it we were refused food. Inside it was dark, no lights, just soldiers sleeping anywhere they could. They were all over the place and I was tripping over them. The only place I could find to sleep was on top of a coil of barbed wire.'

Next morning, tired, aching and still hungry, the

wretched conscripts struggled back into their equipment.

'We moved into the hills and things started to get even worse. We had never been in terrain like this before. Combined with the wind, the rain and the cold, the terrain made the march a killer. We went up and down and round and around and then we ended up on this place called Mount Longdon. At the time I didn't know it was Longdon because I'd not seen a map. None of us had. I never saw a map the whole time I was in the Malvinas. Not one miserable map.

'When we got there this corporal, who wasn't a bad guy, and I started to build a position and a shelter. We had to sleep back to back with only our rucksacks over us for warmth. Remember, we had left our other kit behind on the march. We shivered through three or four nights like that until a chopper turned up and threw all our kit out on to the wet mountain. No sooner had we started to make things better for ourselves than a signal arrived ordering us off the mountain and back to Moody Brook. That really pissed me off because after just one night at Moody Brook they sent us back up the fucking mountain. Talk about yo-yos!

'This time we had to carry all the mortars, 90mm cannons, ammunition, everything, and we had to carry it right up on to the summits. It was hard, very hard. A friend and I kept on encouraging each other to carry on. We felt we would never see home again. What with the weather and daily routine, we just became resigned to our fate. We wrote farewell letters home to our girlfriends and just settled down as best we could to wait. I was never scared – just resigned to my fate. Eventually I was given a firm base, like a rearguard, about 800 metres from the rest of the company. Lieutenant Baldini and the rest of B Company were way up top above me. I really felt sorry for the corporal who was with me, poor guy. He wasn't infantry at all. He was a storeman and hadn't the slightest clue about living in the field. He also had a heart condition and he really suffered. They evacuated him just fifteen days before the war ended.

'Conditions on the mountain were appalling. Hygiene was a disgrace. We had no toilets, no field latrines. We simply crouched among the rocks and emptied ourselves. As far as water was concerned, we drew it from a small pond. We broke the ice and then drank from it. I was only able to wash four times in sixty-six days. I was stinking and it upset me because I have always been scrupulously clean.

'My weapons were also in a dreadful condition. I never knew if they would work when the time came. I had a rifle and, in my position, a .50-cal machine-gun, but I was never allowed to test-fire them. That is still niggling me to this very day. We could not guarantee that our weapons would perform when the time came and we couldn't point this out to our officers because they would take it as criticism and jail us. They would think we were questioning their orders.

'At night we did two hours on sentry and two hours off. During the day snipers covered us. On top of all this food was virtually non-existent. I never got anything that was better than bad or awful... and that was when I got some. Let me explain. Sometimes we got coloured water with a couple of pasta lumps in it. That was it! That was what they issued to soldiers sent to fight a war.

'Because I was out on my own manning the gun, food was a major problem. When and if it did reach me it was cold and complete shit. We were cold and I was hungry all the time. We all felt that we had been deserted to fend for ourselves on that mountain. Now, I'm a survivor. I have been one all my life. I wasn't going to starve to death for anyone, no way. I was hungry and the cold and the wind and the rain was making it worse. A man's body needs good hot food. The rancho [field kitchen], when it came, only dished up dirty water. Absolute shit. I began to slip away with a few others into Port Stanley, first of all to see if I could get some clean drinking water. The craving for clean water was overpowering. I would leave my mate in our position so it wouldn't look abandoned. Officers rarely came to check, so I could run down into Stanley. I would make my way to a warehouse and join the line of soldiers unloading lorries and containers and then steal what I wanted, then run all the way back again. Nobody down in Stanley knew who I was and I was able to steal cheese, soup and sweet potatoes. We began taking it in turns to go into town to forage. We never left our position unguarded in case someone stole our supplies. We had to look after ourselves. Do you know, no one ever questioned the willing volunteers who turned up to help them unload the trucks, but it was all too good to last...

'One day an officer – I had never seen him before – turned up and asked me where I was from. I hadn't taken my weapon with me and he began hitting me. Hard. Real punches. I covered myself against his blows and began thinking of a way out. I didn't want to be hanging round because I was in big trouble. I made a run for it, but I hadn't gone far when I heard him cock his weapon and shout: 'Halt or I'll shoot', so I stopped dead in my tracks. He started punching me again and kept on punching for a while. Then he made me sit down. He was beside himself with excitement and nerves. He had me kept under guard all day, right up to 6 p.m. Then he marched me back up on to Longdon at gunpoint at the head of the group and back to our positions, so that he could humiliate me further.

'Then he ordered me to lie on the ground and tied me down. I was lying there, spread-eagled and staked to the ground, wondering what was going to happen. I thought I was going to be shot. I was really depressed and frightened and cold and hungry. All I had wanted was some food. I don't know how long I could have been left there if it hadn't been for a sergeant, who was disgusted at this, cutting me free. I was really cold and wet and distressed. The sergeant was very angry at my treatment. So was I after my release and I wanted to go and confront the officer, but I didn't know who he was or where he came from and by this time he had vanished. About a week or so later I heard he had been wounded somehow and had been evacuated back to Argentina. I was glad. It was as if he had been cursed for what he had done to me and I was very happy about it. He deserved everything he got.

'I had just got over that when this other officer turns up and he's got a thing about shaving every day. Can you fucking believe it? Water is scarce enough even though we're in one of the wettest places in the world and I'm not about to waste what little clean drinking water I have on shaving. So he basically gave me the message that if I didn't shave he'd take me behind the rocks and shoot me. I still didn't shave, but I did trim my beard. We didn't often see officers. They left us to fend for ourselves.

'However, I remember another occasion when another officer arrived. He was quiet and polite. He asked me very quietly on a couple of occasions if I would hunt for a sheep, but I wasn't sure. He asked our major and he said if I did he would put me in a war crimes court martial! But the idea was planted in my mind so I went out hunting and got one. I found the officer and gave it to him. He took his share and gave me the rest and there was no problem.

'Even up on the mountain I was bartering. As I said before, it was a way of life to me and I am a survivor. I always had to sew my own clothes when they were damaged, so when the lads up on the mountain needed theirs repaired I did it and they paid me in hot drinks or by doing some of my sentry duties.

'Next thing the bombardment started, normally between 22.00 hours and midnight. I never thought the English would come, because the weather was so bad. How could they possibly land? My position was fabulous. I was proud of my bunker. The .50-cal was perfectly positioned and the ammunition was out of the way, but ready to hand for when it was needed. The bunker was camouflaged and on two levels and held two people comfortably. It was a metre deep, with a tent on top and then a metal sheet with peat, stones and rocks to add to the camouflage and protection. Inside we had our weapons loaded and pointing at the entrance. In the walls we dug more holes for machine-gun ammunition, rifle magazines and cigarettes. I even made a little light which ran on cooker fuel and it never leaked or flooded. Inside we felt secure, well protected. Apart from a direct hit by a shell or a bomb, we should be safe.

'In the days leading up to the battle I was joined by First Sergeant López. Our position was about 300 metres from A Company and C Company. One night I wasn't sleeping properly. I would wake at the slightest noise. Communications within the regiment were not very good and the wind was blowing straight towards us. I suddenly saw some figures coming towards us and told López. We fired a couple of rounds in their direction and then I could hear orders being screamed at us to stop firing. It was a corporal from C Company doing the shouting.

'First thing next morning I was taken to C Company's command post. They wanted to hit me and stake me out. I said: "If you're not going to tell me who you are when you're walking about at night in my killing ground then I'm going to shoot you." They were furious, but López had opened fire as well, so they didn't stake me out. But if he hadn't been with me I would have been punished.

'As the days passed the bombardment on our positions grew. We hadn't even been told that the English had landed or that they had taken Darwin and Goose Green. But once the British had taken those objectives the shelling increased on Longdon. The English gunners were very good. They knew where to aim most of the time. They seemed to be particularly interested in a radar position we had near B Company – my own company – lines. For a week they seemed to settle into a routine of shelling and it was a case of sleep when you could.

'All the time the weather was worsening – by mid-June it was biting winds, rain, snow, sleet, added to our chronic food shortages. I was wearing two shirts, a jacket, long underpants and wrapping my feet in sheepskin inside my boots. Our officers still weren't telling us anything, if we were about to be attacked or even how close or far away the English were.'

Tony Gregory was still OK as he made his way to the front of the landing-craft. That's where the machine-gunners were positioned for landing because it was where they could lay down maximum fire-power on any waiting enemy. With him went Paul Read, his number two, whose job it was to feed the snaking links of gleaming ammunition into the hungry weapon. As Tony prepared to sweep the beach before leading his section ashore he was aware of how quiet the lads had become in the landing-craft behind him as they sheltered from the icy wind. Their main concern wasn't having to fight their way ashore, but getting their feet wet on such a cold day.

Several of them left the Royal Marine coxswain in absolutely no doubt about who would be the first man to die that day if so much as a drop of cold water penetrated their boots.

'The one thing I cannot accept about the landing was the idiot order for all of us to carry two mortar bombs. We had enough weight already. We were loaded to the hilt. I'll never understand that. All the way in I was muttering to myself: "This is it. This is it." My heart was pounding. Fanning Head was being engaged in battle and I was ready to fight. I had confidence in my weapon and I knew I could hold my own. Once we cleared the beach we were to head for our objective, Settlement Rock, right up on a hill overlooking what was to become "Bomb Alley".'

The coxswain had clearly taken the grim threats seriously: he dropped the ramp just a foot from the beach!

'Brilliant, absolutely brilliant, no wet feet, and I'm off and running straight up the beach. My GPMG has 100 rounds on it. I'm going... Jesus, the sweat... the weight... but I'm going and there's no one shooting at us... we're OK... I'm down... we're doing a fire-and-manoeuvre... still no incoming fire... up... up... up again... run... keep on going... there's the objective... yes, we're going to reach it OK... sweat... Jesus, the bloody sweat... it's running from me head to me toes... I'm bollocked... we've made it.

'You know something? None of the enemy stayed to fight with us!

'Our daily routine on Settlement Rock was to make sure the Port San Carlos bridgehead was secure from any Argentinian counter attack. We had to protect the guys bringing the supplies of ammunition and other equipment which we needed for the break-out. Our battalion was spread out inland and the Navy covered the sea to our rear. The main threat at this time was from the air, with formations of three or four aircraft at a time bombing and strafing the shipping. However, we dominated the ground to our front with continuous fighting patrols just in case they sent troops to test us.

'We would patrol out through the right arc of our company formations and re-enter our own company lines through the left arc. It was standard procedure.

'One day we were in our own positions looking out over our arcs of fire when we spotted a formation of men walking about. They were about 800 metres away and bang in our killing ground. We reported instantly to our company headquarters and the signallers relayed it to the battalion. We asked if we had any friendly forces out in the area and the reply came back as negative.

'We watched this body of men in our killing zone. We watched their every move. They could only be Argentinian Special Forces prodding our defences. A signal was given to engage them. We opened up with mortar and machine-gun fire. Quite a few rounds had been fired before an urgent order came through to cease fire immediately. All the gunners fired. I reckon at least fifty rounds were fired by our platoon. The rest of the gunners were blazing away. We waited and watched. There was a lot of shouting going on and medics running out, but we still watched and waited.

'About an hour went by before we were told we had actually been firing at our own men. A patrol from A Company had strayed into our arc of fire. We felt sick, totally gutted, pissed off – you name it, we felt it. Thank God no one was killed, but two of the lads were badly wounded and they are still suffering to this day. Someone, somewhere, had really cocked up. The incident brought morale plunging down. Who can you blame? At the end of the day, no one. It was a tragic accident and, unfortunately, the sort of accident which happens in war. But I often think about the wounded lads and wonder how they feel about it.

'Soon afterwards we received our orders to move to a

place called Teal Inlet. As we were moving out we got the news that 2 Para had secured Goose Green, but had taken casualties. It was then, and only then, that I fully realized that despite the air raids and the "blue on blue" [accidental clash between forces fighting on the same side] we were actually fighting a war. I knew, too, that we would be next... but where?'

When the 'green on' came, Jerry Phillips, like every other professional corporal, was ready. His L-42 sniper rifle was cradled protectively in the crook of his arm. His ghillie suit – the special camouflage outfit all snipers wore and which looked like a jumble of rags – was carefully stowed in his back-breaking bergen. He had worn it once before on this voyage: when he shuffled round the decks of the *Canberra* while it rode at anchor off Ascension Island to be photographed by Tom Smith, the *Daily Express* photographer who was to accompany the battalion throughout the campaign. Smith's film was sent back by satellite transmitter and Jerry's picture appeared in newspapers and magazines all over the world. But at this particular moment in time the world didn't know what Jerry Phillips was doing.

A fully loaded magazine had been clicked on to the rifle he had patiently zeroed before leaving England. Together with young Dickie Absolon, another sniper, he had carefully checked the weapon again while on the ships. In his pockets and pouches he carried the top-of-the-range 'green spot' ammunition manufactured specifically for snipers. Grenades topped off his load of personal munitions.

Jerry was impatient to be off. The landings had been delayed long enough. What was supposed to have been a night-time landing was now taking place in broad daylight. It wasn't on. Paras were creatures of the night, that was when they were at their most effective. They did most of their training at night, parachuting at night then tabbing across country and appearing out of the dark in the midst of their enemy, scaring the living shit out of them. On exercises they had caused mayhem in craphat lines, clinically and silently taking out their sentries, then 'killing' the hats as they festered in their doss-bags. That's what they should be doing to the enemy, but this time doing it for real.

As he climbed into the landing-craft he was quietly confident. He already knew his orders. He would take his four-man patrol ashore with B Company, working closely with another patrol led by a lad nicknamed 'Six Foot'. As soon as they landed they were to tab out from the beach to Cushy Mountain, ten miles away, looking for enemy positions and activity.

The landing-craft seemed to take for ever as it chugged across the cold water towards the tiny settlement of Port San Carlos. Fanning Head, the feature which commanded the landing sites, was taking a pounding. The Argentinian spotters there were under intense bombardment from a Royal .Navy warship. The SAS were also attacking them from the land, pouring machine-gun and grenade fire into their positions.

The sight pissed Jerry off no end. With every ounce of his being he wanted to be a part of it instead of being wedged in this bloody landing-craft like a sardine in a mess tin. The journey seemed to be taking for ever and as his frustration grew so, too, did the pain in his back, shoulders, and everywhere else from the appalling weight of the equipment he was carrying.

'I had 159 lb on my back, plus my webbing, plus my weapon, plus what I had in my pockets, plus the fucking mortar bombs we had to carry ashore. It hurt. Jesus, did it hurt. It got to the point where I was hoping that if the

Argies were waiting for us to land they would shoot me first because the amount of kit I was carrying was murder anyway. It felt as if I had another body strapped to me.'

Any thoughts of allowing the enemy to kill him soon evaporated as the landing-craft at last neared the beach. The old deep-down spirit began taking over, spurring him on. He had seen people killed before as a youngster in Singapore. He had seen the public hangings there and those shocking sights had made him determined that he would not finish up like that. He certainly wasn't going to give any Argie the chance to snuff him out. But given the chance he would gladly have hanged the Royal Marine coxswain of the landing-craft who ran aground fifteen feet from the water's edge, forcing the soldiers to wade ashore through three feet of ice-cold water.

'That was all we needed at the beginning of a campaign. Some guys' feet never warmed up or dried out again. They got trench foot and that caused mayhem in the ranks. It took a heavier toll of us in the campaign than bullets or shells. It was a basic mistake not getting us closer to the beach. Other than that, the landing itself was nothing to write home about, nothing like the movies. There was no enemy there waiting for us. They had bugged out.'

But on their withdrawal, the Argentinians had drawn blood. They had shot down a British helicopter, killing the crew. As the soldiers squelched round the settlement Jerry saw the bodies lying on the shore. As far as he was concerned the war had begun in earnest.

'The local farmer told us they had been machine-gunned in the water as they tried to swim ashore. I felt for them. You can forget cap-badge rivalry, these guys were British soldiers, English the same as us. It brought home a feeling of "know your enemy" to all of us. If this was the way they played at war then we could play by those rules as well. We took off after them and spent all day chasing them. The terrain was dreadful and the going was hard. After just two kilometres we had slowed down to a plod. The terrain was like the worst parts of the Highlands of Scotland. We couldn't tab fast with 150 lb on our backs. By this time we had joined up with Six Foot and he became section commander. I took over as lead scout.

'By nightfall we were still after them. We were patrolling deeper and deeper into enemy territory and I could hear them in the dark. At one stage I was about to open up on them, but I wasn't 100 per cent sure they were Argies. Then I heard them moving about. It was something about their movements which removed any doubts I had. There was this nagging sixth sense which also told me not to fire – a little something. I began to feel they knew we were there, too, and where we were. I know I made the right decision because we later discovered there were about forty of them and they heavily outnumbered us. We lost contact with them and set off for Cushy Mountain. It was important to set up our OP [observation post] before first light. We dug into the side of a slope for camouflage and overhead protection from bombs and mortars. Nobody could have seen our position, even from a couple of feet.

'Before dawn a real heavy mist enveloped us. I lost Six Foot, who was only fifteen feet away to my left, and I lost my sentry, too. We couldn't use torches to search for each other and we couldn't start shouting. We were deep in enemy territory, remember. I started crawling about and found my sentry with his machine-gun and brought him in closer, about eight feet from the position. I sent one of the other guys to relieve him and he got lost. In seconds. This was really embarrassing, I can tell you. Then the guy who had been relieved came in from a totally different direction and nearly got himself shot. Instead of shooting him I punched him out of sheer frustration. Things were going from bad to worse. My lads were new to D Company, but that was no excuse for these stupid basic mistakes. They were, after all, Paratroopers and should not have been behaving like hats in training. The more mistakes they made the more punchy I became. If any of the other soldiers found out about the way they had been fucking about we would have been laughed out of the battalion. But my punchiness was making them wary of me and if this went on we wouldn't be able to work together.

'But as the fog cleared and we were able to take bearings we confirmed we were in the right position. Things calmed down and I worked out a stag [guard duty] routine when we got a signal to return to battalion headquarters as the Argies were supposed to be counter-attacking. We broke position, compromising ourselves in the process, and deployed in an all-round defence. We waited and we waited and we waited. For more than an hour we lay there waiting for the enemy to come towards us. We never saw one. We managed to mark out on the map a possible DZ we thought enemy Paras might use and another one which could be used if they decided to reinforce us with 1 Para, who were still stationed in Northern Ireland.

'Eventually we began tabbing out towards our own lines. It was only then we found the reason for the panic, a blue on blue. C Company had shot up a patrol from A Company, thinking they were Argies, wounding some of them quite badly.'

Antonio Belmonte's confusion at the manner in which he was ordered to the Falklands was compounded even further when he stepped from the Boeing 747 jumbo jet at the staging post of Rio Gallegos in southern Argentina. As the troops milled around in the general confusion of the move

Antonio was taken aside, shown a radio, and told he would now become a radio operator. He spent the two days waiting, trying to learn how to use it. It all seemed crazy to him. Everything was crazy. Even though the journey from El Palomar to Rio Gallegos was his first time on an aircraft he knew there was something strange about it because there were no seats on the plane! The soldiers were squeezed in and told to sit on their kit.

'Despite it all, morale was good after take-off. Some of the lads got carried away by it all and they sang and sang. Maybe it was to try to forget what they were heading for. But others were singing, too, about kicking the British out. I was just thinking. I knew I was going to the Malvinas, but I still didn't believe there would be a war. I still honestly believed a political solution would be found sooner or later.

'After the 747 they put us on a smaller plane and our kit went on another one. An hour before landing an officer told us that we should collect our kit as soon as possible and be prepared for an eight to ten kilometre march at the other end. It was daylight when we landed. I wasn't in the mood for such a march, particularly as I now had the radio as well as my other kit to carry. We formed into columns for the march to Port Stanley and within a short time it was obvious we were struggling. My legs wobbled under the weight on my back. I couldn't go on, so I sat beside the road with a soldier called Alberto Petrucelli. He wasn't a bad guy. [He was to die on Longdon.]

'But somebody had to help me. An Argentinian truck came by, empty, but the driver wouldn't assist me. Then, of all ironies, an English kelper stopped and gave me a lift. I was sitting beside him, following another truck carrying all our officers. He dropped me off between the post office and Government House, which was our rendezvous point in Port Stanley. I waved goodbye and thanked him. Straight away one of our officers came over and started ripping into me. He insulted me in every way possible for using my initiative. After all, the officers had had a lift, so why couldn't we?

'I waited for the rest of the company to arrive. I was looking around this Stanley place and I began thinking and began to feel a bit... well, I felt we were going to suffer. The company arrived, worn out after carrying all that kit. We formed up again and they showed us a map with the position we were to head for. It was called Longdon.

'We were tired and weary with all the travelling and the marching. Off we headed into the mountains. We were simply not prepared for the climate or the terrain. The cold was knifing into me like a frost. We had done marches in our country, but there was nothing we had ever experienced like this place. Major Carrizo led the way up. All the vehicles stayed in Stanley.

'Major Carrizo was in charge of B Company and NCOs commanded the sections. [Argentinian army sections are similar in size to British infantry platoons.] Then the corporals commanded ten soldier groupings. However, I was under First Lieutenant Nairotti, who was attached to us from the Comando en Jefe. We reached the mountain and the start of a horrendous endurance test I never want to repeat. The wind and the cold and damp climate started causing problems right away. We didn't have the proper clothing for the area at that time of the year. We had no waterproofs, so when you got wet you stayed wet. The only way to dry clothing was to wear it in your sleeping bag and hope your body heat dried it. I wore two sets of clothing nearly all the time. If only they had told us where we were going and what the land and climate was like, then we could have prepared ourselves for it. Although, at that time, the weather was our major problem it wasn't our only one.

We spent the first night in a tent and next day our next immediate problem presented itself: the little folding shovels they issued us with were useless for digging in with.

'Each rifleman had four magazines of twenty rounds and I also had a 9mm pistol and two magazines of ten rounds. Each section had a spare box of ammo. It was made of wood so we broke the boxes up and lit fires to try to keep warm and dry our clothing. The ammunition was old, not the sort of stuff you'd expect to be issued with to fight a war. The ammunition, out of its box, soon rusted up. We spent sixty-six days up there preparing and not once did they bring up more ammo or any cleaning kits for any of the weapons. We had to make do as best we could.

'They had brought the artillery guns in by helicopter, but not the ammunition or medium and heavy machine-guns. We had to go back down the hill and keep manhandling all that stuff up to the positions. They had put us up in a position about 200 metres from the bowl area, a feature formed by a dip along the summit, and up there food soon became a major problem. At first we were fed from the mobile *rancho* twice a day. A bucket was brought round the positions. All it contained was warm black water which tasted, smelled and looked like kerosene or varnish. There was no sugar, no biscuits, nothing. Our so-called main meal consisted of hot water with cabbage sailing in it. We all started to deteriorate very quickly.

'Things were bad, so the soldiers decided they would go for the sheep. They began slaughtering them until the officers stepped in and said that if we did it we had to send them to the *rancho* so that everyone could have an equal share. Fine by us, so we sent the sheep to the *rancho* but little or nothing came back up the hill. Where was it going? Somebody somewhere was getting it.

'In the end I began to go to Stanley each day to get food,

getting back about dark and hopefully picking up the password for that night in case I was shot by our own sentries. In Stanley I used to disguise myself and join the soldiers working in the food depots, then I would fill my pockets – especially my trousers which were big and baggy – and smuggle the food back up to my friends on the mountain. Do you know how bad it was, the hunger? Do you know what it was like to go down into Stanley and see containers and warehouses stuffed with it, with everything you could possibly want, and not know why it didn't reach the men up on the mountains? A couple of times they sent a few small tins of meat and a few biscuits, but that was meant to feed a whole company of men. Even those meagre supplies were interfered with by the soldiers delivering them. If I managed to get a tin up on the mountain I used to think it was a miracle. And out of that I would try to save a little – even though I was starving to death – just in case it was even longer before the next delivery. It was all about personal survival, that's how fucking bad it was.

'I managed to get away another day to go foraging. I'll always remember this because I found some *dulce de leche* [a milk-based sweet]. As soon as I saw it I went mad. I stuffed myself with it and then stuffed more into my pockets with three bars of cheese. Then I managed to get a small box of it and began to carry it back up the mountain. On the way I dropped the box and the glass jars broke, but I still took it with me and hid it. When I was ravenous again I went and got it and ate it despite the shards of broken glass. I just licked round them or spat the ones out that got in my mouth. I know it could have got into my stomach and killed me, but I was so desperate I didn't care. That is how hungry we were. Another time I got my hands on a box, but I didn't know what was in it, so I stopped to make sure it was food before I carried it all the way back up the mountain. It was full of tinned tomatoes, which I shared around. We had been up there four or five weeks and things were just getting worse and worse. I was so skinny my trousers were just hanging off me.

'As well as this, another major problem had arisen: with the constant radio checks my batteries were only lasting a week then I would have to change them. When the radio was shut down they sent me to relieve the guys in the gun positions so they could rest and sleep. Often, while they were asleep, I would clean the weapons in the best way I could.

'Lieutenant Nairotti wasn't a bad guy and he treated me reasonably well, but I must say the conditions generally were horrendous. We were badly prepared for war, our clothing was thin and soaked up the damp and rain and we were continually cold and wet. We were never taken off the mountain for a shower or a rest or a chance to dry our clothes and bedding. We had to use open pits for toilets. We were in the front line and we should have had the best of everything. We felt we had been abandoned, left up there all on our own to fend for ourselves as best we could instead of being part of a line of major defences around Port Stanley.

'The cold and wind and rain were making us look like tramps so that when we went into Stanley scavenging, the clean soldiers down there knew immediately we were out of the mountains. We stuck out like sore thumbs, and talking about sore thumbs – and sore fingers! In Stanley one day I came across a whole big sausage which had been thrown away. I couldn't believe it. I didn't have a knife or my bayonet with me, but I managed to find a piece of glass to cut away the skin used to seal the sausage. I hacked at it in desperation and, at the same time, I was cutting my own fingers, but I didn't realize it because they were so numb with cold. I was so ravenous I got my little improvised cooker out and cooked some of it right away. The smell... oh, what a smell! I hid the rest and got it back to my mates.

'On another occasion I managed to bluff my way into the "sanity nursery", a place reserved for the worst cases. They were given a night's rest in a clean bed. You could watch television and be warm for a while. But it was also to give me my worst scare. I met a kelper there and offered him money, making him understand that I wanted him to go to a shop and buy food for me to take back with me. The Military Police spotted me, grabbed me and took me off for questioning. I told them I had given the man money to get me food, but they weren't bothered about that. They were only really interested in why a soldier off the mountains was in Stanley. I said I had to see a government officer on behalf of my regiment. Deep down I could see the military prison looming closer and then, by chance, I spotted an officer I knew from my regiment. He saved me, but it had been a very close call.

'The weather was steadily worsening as the days passed. I spent a lot of time using a small can to bail out my trench. Once, the cold was so bad, I was boiling some milk in a pot without a handle and had to hold it steady. I watched my finger melt and never felt a thing.

'I always felt lonely on guard duty. I used to think a lot, particularly about my father and what he had been through in the Second World War. I used to wonder what he would have done in my position. I still didn't think in my heart we would have a war. I believed we would give the place up and go home.

'The first bombing attack on our position was in early May, a Harrier attack. That was how I knew the English were in the area. As soon as that happened things got even worse. We were given three biscuits and told to make them last for three days. It was so cold, too, we didn't feel like washing. One day I decided to wash my hair to try to cheer myself up. As soon as I wetted my hair I could feel my brain freezing.

'A latrine had been dug fifty metres from our position, but it should have been filled in and replaced long ago. People didn't use it any more. They just went wherever took their fancy. It was all over the place and the consequence was that whenever there was a raid you had to crawl through your own muck to get to shelter. Some were just covered in it all the time.'

2

KEVIN CONNERY woke on the hard, inhospitable floor of one of the corridors of the assault ship HMS *Intrepid*. The men had been lying head to toe all around the decks – anywhere, in fact, they could find a space to kip. The whole battalion was on board, plus Marines, pilots, Navy divers, stores, weapons and ammunition and even the SAS. The ship had never been built to carry this sort of load. Never mind, he told himself, we'll soon be away ashore. He expected the operation to get them ashore to run smoothly. But as soon as he stepped on deck with his machine-gun to begin the perilous descent into the little landing-craft he was quickly disabused of that idea. He began to realize things were not going his way. To his left he watched in amazement the battle for Fanning Head in the growing daylight.

Christ Almighty, this is all we need, he thought. Broad daylight and a battle raging and here am I stuck right up front of this thing. Whoa, boy, this is just not the right place to be. As soon as that ramp goes down I'm either the first to be shot or to step on a mine or something. Jesus.

There was nothing he could do. If it wasn't him it would be some other poor sod, so he braced himself, his eyes looking everywhere for a sign of the enemy. Kevin wasn't going to go cheaply, he'd see to that. He'd take some of the bastards with him. The gun was ready and he too was as ready as he'd ever be. He cleared his mind, looked at his gun again, then back at the approaching beach. The landing-craft grounded, and he tensed his muscles for a burst of speed as the ramp began to go down. He and Mike Bateman leapt out, shoulder to shoulder, side by side, all aggression and fire-power, just as they had been taught and just as they had seen in all the old war films.

They were ashore, nerves tingling, fingers on triggers, looking, looking, looking. For what? For nothing. It was a complete anti-climax. There was no enemy, not even a sign, no mines... nothing. Kevin laughed. It was not a bit like the old war movies. 'It was nothing like a Hollywood epic at all,' he says. 'It was an unopposed landing. In the films the stars storm ashore and get pampered between every shot. In reality it is bloody hard work. The kit we were carrying was horrendous. I could just about wobble, let alone run.'

His relief at surviving the beach landing soon turned to disappointment as the bitter South Atlantic wind drove the freezing rain into his face, his eyes and every other exposed part of his body. He hadn't a clue what was supposed to be happening now. He was only a tom. As he humped his kit off the beach and began the tab inland, an enemy aircraft appeared. This was what he had come for. This was more like it: a chance to have a go at the enemy. The twin-engined propeller-driven Pucara drew nearer, coming into range for his machine-gun. Instinct had taken over. Kevin was ready. With him was a sapper from 9 Squadron [9 Parachute Squadron, Royal Engineers, a unit which forms part of the Airborne Brigade and whose soldiers work closely with the Paras] and they both opened fire on the intruder.

The snooper flew off and Kevin and the sapper smiled. They hadn't knocked him down but he'd learned not to mess about with Paras. They both felt good. At last they were doing their bit. The warm glow was soon extinguished. No sooner had they finished congratulating themselves than a furious officer appeared.

'Who fired, who bloody well fired?' he demanded.

'I did, sir,' admitted Kevin. An instant bollocking followed. Kevin couldn't believe it. What the hell was going on, what was he here for? For fuck's sake, are we at war or not? He turned away furious, incredulous at what he had just experienced. Then, fuelled by anger that the bloody phoney war appeared to be continuing, he began tabbing up to a location called Windy Gap. He thought that once they got ashore and away from the Marines the fucking about would stop and they could get on and do what they came here to do.

At Windy Gap Kevin's machine-gun crew (Kevin, Skiddy and Johnny Crow) dug their trenches in the soggy peat as the pitiless rain lashed into them. Beside them was another crew: Vince, Ratch and Taff. Both locked their guns on their bases in the sustained-fire role, giving interlocking arcs of fire across a valley. Anything entering their area would be shot to shit within seconds.

Within an hour they were sploshing and sloshing around in their trenches. The positions had filled with water from the downpour, from seepage and from the peat walls, which drained into them. All around it was the same story. You couldn't expect anything else in this sort of terrain. They weren't happy, but they decided to make the most of it. Out came the hexamine stoves and on went the brews. Hot drinks – a lot of them – would help keep exposure at bay, and were also great morale-boosters.

Kevin was just savouring a brew when he saw another officer approach. The officer looked at the men, looked around the area and then back at the huddled crews. He stood posing just as Kevin imagined Wellington had done so long ago, then ordered the soaking gunners to move their positions a hundred yards to the right.

'Everyone was well pissed off,' says Kevin. 'What was the point of moving positions when our original one was perfectly OK? There was nothing wrong with it and this twat comes up and makes us move. We just couldn't understand the reasoning for it.'

The men moved to their new position and began digging again, setting up their precious guns and then trying to make themselves as comfortable as possible. Any notion that this was a temporary position vanished as the men survived against the elements and the lack of information for just over a week. As the days dragged by the men were incensed that nobody appeared to bother their arse to come and see them to tell them what was or was not happening. They just sat there like a bunch of frozen pricks. Surely someone knew where the enemy was, and shouldn't they be tabbing there to kick their arses off this soggy lump of British territory? For Christ's sake, what other reason was there for them being there other than to kick the Argies out and get back home?

Butterflies as big as bats were rumbling about in Denzil's belly as he clambered into the landing-craft. One slip and he was a goner. In addition to his normal kit he had the radio on his back and spare batteries and extra ammunition. If he missed the landing-craft and hit the water he would go straight to the bottom. He would sink like a bloody great stone, right down into Davy Jones's locker. Not the sort of ending a happy-go-lucky Welsh boy with a great singing voice wanted for himself. Denzil was extra careful.

Being Welsh, he had more culture in his soul than this English lot around him, Denzil told himself, even though they were good mates. Being Welsh was different: it meant being born with vision and great imagination. And his imagination was working overtime as the landing-craft approached the beach. He had a vision of the great Normandy landings of the last war, and his adrenalin was surging as he faced this great adventure. In the event, the unopposed landing was a great disappointment to a man with a sense of drama like him.

However, as he tabbed inland Denzil soon came face to face with the harsh reality of war. He watched quietly as other soldiers grimly but reverently placed the bodies of two aircrew from a British Gazelle helicopter into body bags, then carefully zipped them shut. They had been shot down by fleeing Argentinian soldiers then machine-gunned as they tried to swim to land. Despite the unopposed landing, Denzil realized there and then that this was not an exercise and maybe, just maybe, his luck would not hold out for ever.

Germán Chamorro had to wait for his date with destiny because his regiment was in a state of total confusion – and he hadn't had his hair cut. He caught up with them at Córdoba and walked into a camp where confusion fuelled chaos. Conscripts with only forty-five days' training were being drafted in to fill gaps. This was a Para-artillery unit and these raw recruits had done no parachute training and had never been near an artillery piece. He drew a weapon from the armoury and went in search of his old battery.

He had grown his hair again as he awaited his discharge and this did not go down well with the hard-line NCOs, who were running around flapping just as much as anyone else.

'Rivas, a commando, told me to get it cut and I told him

no way was that going to happen as it was going to be cold in the Malvinas. He marched me to the hairdressers and ordered the barber to "skin" me. All I had left was a bit on top of my head. When it was done he said to me: "You'll learn, motherfucker."

'That was it. I was furious. Here I was, about to be sent to war and I'm ordered to have a haircut. I can't tell you how angry I was and then the cheeky bastard says: "We're going to have a good time there!"

'At last they got round to giving us the order to move out. The first battery to go was the Commando Battery followed by A, then B and then C Batteries. They still hadn't told us officially we were going to the Malvinas, but that night before we moved we all wrote letters home. Morale was bad, very low.

'We flew from Córdoba to Comodoro Rivadavia in a 737 and were sent straight to the 8th Mechanized Regiment's camp. The huts were empty except for the rats scavenging on the floors for food. Nobody knew what was going on. Then they changed their minds and sent us all back to the airport to sleep. Every so often they would wake us up to load the planes with ammo. After that we were put on Fiat trucks for the ten-hour journey to Puerto Deseado. All they gave us to eat all day was bread and tinned corned beef. It was absolute crap and I've never eaten it since. We spent two days at the port loading mortars and howitzers on to ships. We loaded and loaded as fast as we could because there were rumours that English submarines had arrived near the Malvinas.

'At last they got round to moving us. We flew on 29 April and I fell asleep shortly after take-off. I awoke and could see a lighthouse as we circled waiting for clearance to land. We arrived at 2 p.m. and it was fucking freezing. The place was shrouded in mist and rain. I can remember saying: "Is it for this place we came?"

'It was a madhouse, a complete madhouse. Straight away we were looking for food. We nicked some from an Air Force officer and watched all the chaos going on around us. Heavy guns were being set up and rumours were sweeping the place about English infiltration. We seemed to have landed in the front line.

'They made us march into Stanley with all our kit and put us to work right away, digging defensive positions. We were gunners, but they had decided we should become infantry at this time. We put out our sentries at night, but it was with the morning that the cold really came. It really hit you. There was chaos everywhere. I had arrived a month after the islands were captured and there was still total confusion. The feeling of war was in the air, it was everywhere, and it made me wonder exactly how long we would be on these islands. We knew the British were coming... None of us knew anything about war. We didn't know it then, but in the next twenty-four hours we would find out.

'After breakfast, which wasn't too bad, they told us to move to a new position two kilometres away. Our howitzer had turned up and we set up a new position. I was on guard duty and saw 1 May break with the sound of explosions and booms and bangs. We were told the airport had been attacked by a British Navy ship. [It was in fact a bombing raid by an RAF Vulcan.] The anti-aircraft guns were firing rapidly and we could see smoke in the distance. Even where we were it was mayhem, with people running about all over the place. Nobody knew what was really happening. The whole thing only lasted seconds, but it really stirred things up. Afterwards we were standing about talking about it when someone yells: "Red alert!"

'"Red alert", we all said, looking at each other. "What does red alert mean?" You can see how raw we were. It means air attack and we found out quickly enough.

Suddenly British Harriers began attacking targets round Port Stanley and the anti-aircraft boys opened up. They were all firing like crazy and the area sounded like a firing range gone mad. We watched because there wasn't much else we could do. Can you imagine trying to fire a howitzer at a jet?

'We looked around and saw one of our corporals hiding in the bottom of our position shitting himself. "Get up, you motherfucker," we told him. Seconds later a Harrier flew so close to us I could see the pilot. It was 1 May – a day to remember... the day the war came.

'Later they told us two Harriers were shot down. [Neither was shot down. One, piloted by Flight Lieutenant David Morgan, was slightly damaged by 20mm cannon fire.] Next four of us were put on a truck with all our gear and a howitzer team from A Battery and a Commando team and sent to Mount Kent to set up a forward position. By the time we got sorted out and had driven through Stanley it was about 5 p.m. Another red alert was given and we all dived out of the trucks and tried to take cover behind the wheels.

'We could see a little black dot getting bigger and bigger as it came towards us. The anti-aircraft batteries opened up on it and it spiralled down out of control. A hit! Sadly it was an own goal. We had just downed one of our own Mirage jets. Garcia Cuevas became the first Argentinian pilot to die. And we saw it all.

'It was after dark when we got to Mount Kent. Our position was to be at the base of the mountain in support of the 4th Regiment from Corrientes. Because it was dark we decided to get some sleep, but alerts were being shouted all the time now. There was even a grey alert. Apparently it meant commando attack from the sea. Nothing happened. However, we faced a new enemy throughout the night: the rain. It rained and rained and in the morning we were soaked through. We had no shelter. For ten days we stayed in that position, making the best of it. Food was also a problem. The *rancho* only came out at night and then it only came as far as a valley two kilometres behind the mountain. We had to walk there and back through the rain and the mud. Morale was bad. Food was bad when we got it. We took to killing sheep and the odd cow. Things were so bad I went rooting about in the rubbish and one day I found a cow's ribs. The cold had preserved the remains, so they were in reasonably good condition. We collected some wood, made a fire, and cooked it barbecue-style. It was really great. But now, when I think back on it, it makes me feel sick.

'Another night, after a walk to the rancho in freezing rain, we found they had only a chocolate drink. That was it, a fucking chocolate drink to keep a front-line soldier going for a fucking day. We took two tins off them – we knew we could make thirty litres of drinks – and went back. We shared it out. We drank some and ate some and by 3 a.m. we all had the shits. But we had managed to get a tent and an old mattress. Luxury! However, we didn't know when we set up this bivouac that we had sited it on an old stream bed. Well, it rained so much during the night we were soon awash as the water followed its natural course.

'Around mid-May we received more orders to move, this time to the other side of Mount Kent. All the 120mm mortars and artillery pieces had to be moved and there were no helicopters to help us. We tried to tow them there using the Unimog trucks, but they got stuck in the boggy ground. Next we called up tractors. The same thing happened. So, what next? You've probably guessed: we had to dismantle the fucking things and hump anything that was transportable on our backs. Morale was through the floor. We were weak from hunger and wet to the skin. We were cold right through to the marrow of our bones. And it was pissing down with rain as usual. Each ammunition box alone weighed 53kg. For three days we slaved, carrying equipment through the mud and rain. It nearly killed us off, but we managed to set up our new position with all the artillery facing what the military geniuses regarded as the main threat area, Stanley Bay. On 20 May they decided to relieve us and fresh troops arrived to take over the position.

'We were making our way off the mountain when two British Harriers arrived, strafing and bombing the shit out of us. The bombs landed all over the place. It was an incredible sight, watching the Harriers spinning round and round, then diving at us. It all lasted about five minutes, I think, and by the time we had loaded our weapons and got into firing positions they had gone. Incredibly, no one was killed or wounded and we made it into Puerto Argentina [Port Stanley] by midday.

'The place was in total, absolute chaos because of the regular British raids. All the artillery had been repositioned together by the racecourse and right up to the old British barracks at Moody Brook. This, for some reason, was also the rest area where we did fuck all except clean the guns and do a two-hour sentry duty. Nobody came to bother us and we didn't bother anybody either. But I still didn't have a proper shelter from the weather.

'I bumped into my mate, Osvaldo, and he invited me into a hold. He had a steak in his pocket and that night we had it. It was beautiful. I never asked where it came from and he never offered to tell me, but it was so beautiful. In the area was a mixture of artillerymen, medics, conscript infantry and others. We formed groups sometimes to fetch water, food, ammunition and whatever else was needed.

'That same night we had the steak I experienced my first naval bombardment. It started about 1 a.m. with a single shell followed by salvo after salvo. The others were used to it, but I found it frightening. I was so frightened I lay against a rock shaking. The lads told me not to worry, but to keep my helmet on. The shells would land ten to twenty metres away and gradually creep away. It lasted about half an hour and someone always got hit, either killed or wounded. One guy was hit and his guts were all over the place. What made it even worse was the fact that he didn't die right away. He just lay there suffering.

'We knew the British had landed somewhere and we were sure they were watching us. [By this time units of the SAS and SBS had been landed by helicopter in advance of the main British landings and had set up OPs.] Every night the naval bombardment got more accurate. We had orders not to smoke or light fires after dark because, we were told, the English could pick them out in their sights. Nobody gave a fuck: soldiers smoked anyway.

'Even though we were so close to Stanley, food was a constant problem. One day a passing truck got stuck and we were ordered out to unload it so it could be freed. It was full of food so I nicked some boxes of cheese and hid them in our tent. A sergeant came over and started kicking up shit, but when I cut off a big slice for him he left. As he went he said: "Now, that's more like it: looking after a sergeant." Motherfucker! Things were becoming so bad we didn't think twice about stealing from our fellow-soldiers, either their food or their equipment to sell or barter for food. Everyone was doing it, honestly... We were doing things that were completely out of character. It was all about survival. I sold my binoculars for flour, jam and powdered milk. We auctioned off our Para berets and Para knives. I shot a duck with a rifle and it landed right in the middle of a minefield: I just couldn't believe my luck.

'The guys around me were going nuts, absolutely mad for food. Crazy. One guy called Toledo was sitting holding a plate over a fire, cooking it. There was nothing on it, but he was cooking. They took him away. Another guy managed to catch a rat to eat and I was looking in dustbins, gutters, anywhere I might find a scrap to eat. There was a corporal called Nancul, a right ugly black bastard, and someone stole his rifle and webbing and sold them to the 10th Engineers. He went mad. Everyone was bollocked the next day. So fucking what? We needed food. There was no logistical support and morale was so bad I even began thinking of ways of breaking a leg so I could be evacuated. Then I heard that casualties weren't being flown home any more, so that was that.

'Anyone caught going into Stanley or any out-of-bounds area was staked out. One guy was staked for three days. They put a tent over him, but nothing underneath. He lay there on the freezing ground deteriorating. When they cut him free he was in such a bad way with trench foot and frostbite they were considering amputating his feet at the hospital, but God was on his side and he survived. His toes were all black and swollen. We never saw him again.

'Morale was bad and getting worse all the time. Our officers didn't care. They were well fed and looked after, and the British were advancing all the while. They had recaptured Darwin. They were coming. Our mortars and artillery were repositioned again, this time facing the mountain ranges. Forward artillery observers were now stationed on Two Sisters and Longdon. Then Mount Kent fell. That was a serious blow to us. Every night the British Navy was still giving us our "stay awake" call. The loss of Mount Kent was like the beginning of the end for us. I heard we lost 200 killed in those hills around there. [In fact Mount Kent fell to D Squadron, 22 SAS, without a serious shot being fired. They were then replaced by 42 Commando, Royal Marines. Large amounts of bloodied shell dressings were found scattered over a wide area of Mount Estancia by a forward patrol of 3 Para's D Company, but no bodies were seen.] Reports of the British advance were filtering through to us. Guys coming off the mountains were saying our positions were useless.'

The great wave of euphoria, the orchestrated patriotism and the cheering and yelling and waving which saw Santiago Gauto off to war was replaced by the sullen stares of the Falkland Islanders as the men of the 7th Regiment struggled down the windswept airport road and into Port Stanley. They cursed, sweated, stumbled, gasped for air and ached on that cruel march, carrying their kit on their backs and clutched to their breasts with aching arms. There were forty men in 2 Section, B Company of the 7th Regiment, being buffeted by the freezing wind and drilled by the rain, the weather accurately reflecting the islanders' attitude to them.

'You could really feel the change in the weather compared with our homeland. We arrived in Stanley covered in sweat and exhausted. We were allowed to rest in some sort of shed. It was an uncomfortable first night, all of us cramped in there together. Next morning we began walking. We walked and walked, out of Stanley, past Moody Brook and up into the hills. We stopped eventually on a mountain. You really had to see this place to believe it. It was windswept, full of crags and covered in boulders. All around us was barren land, nothing, nothingness – just hills and barren land. It was an awful place. It was called Mount Longdon.

'The regiment was strung out all over Longdon and we, in B Company, had the western end. We faced mainly north and were to dominate the summit and bowl areas. We were the first line of defence. I tried to dig a hole, more of a shell scrape, and covered it with my poncho. The next guy was

200 metres away and the next 200 metres further on and so on. Within two weeks we concentrated ourselves in one position. The officers didn't like it but we needed the company for warmth and morale. Later, when the battle started, the guys in the positions on either side of mine were to die. Our number one enemy right from the start was the weather. Just trying to keep warm and dry was a full-time job, never mind sentry duties. Morale dropped very quickly. Then we were hit by constipation. Nobody could crap. My stomach ached with wanting to go. Even after five or six oranges I still couldn't go.

'Rust formed on your weapons in front of your very eyes. My officer, Captain López, gave me some stuff – it wasn't oil – to put on my rifle and it kept the working parts working. You may not believe this, but they only allowed us to test-fire our weapons once up there, and then we were only allowed to fire up in the air. Absolutely absurd.

'The cold also made us very hungry. It was like long, slow starvation. Within a week of our arrival the bread supply stopped. After twenty days there was no meat. The British hadn't even arrived then and here we were starving. When they started their bombardment we could forget about food altogether. The *rancho* used to come within 300 metres of our position, but all you got from that was a tin of water with a few grease or oil blobs floating in it. If you got a tinful with grease you counted yourself lucky.

'My hole, position, call it what you like, was little more than a puddle. I used to lie there freezing my nuts off. My chest was the only part of my body that was almost warm. The password changed three times a night and to move 100 metres took two hours.

'We cried. Yes, we cried with the cold. You cried with it biting into your cold, wet body. The temperature was -12 or -13 degrees most of the time and you even had to break the ice on puddles to get water to drink, maybe even break the ice on some of the puddles into which you'd pissed the day before. You got to the stage where you didn't give a fuck any more.

'I prayed with my rosary. I prayed and prayed. Some of the lads didn't know how to pray. I told them: "I'm praying for a bomb to land on me. No, that is bad. Just take a leg so I can get away from here." So they said they would pray with me.

'Our hunger was so bad we had to find ways of stealing food. I got into Stanley seven or eight times. We broke into a warehouse which was full of food. We got in through a hole in the roof. It drove us crazy seeing all this food stacked up to the roof, sitting there stacked so high, and we were on the hills starving. It didn't make sense. We filled our bags and got back up the hill as quickly as possible to share with our mates. Beto [Jorge Altieri] and Dario and I were good friends. Dario and I were particularly close. If he got anything, food, cigarettes, or whatever, he used to wait for me to share and I would do the same with him. The authorities didn't like us wandering around the positions so they stopped it. Dario and I would slip away to meet and share things. We are not soft or weak or anything like that, but we needed to meet and talk to each other to try to boost each other's morale to keep going. We would finish up crying, crying about our predicament, about the terrible hunger and asking why. What have we done wrong to be punished like this? We haven't done anything, so what is it all about?

'Once I found some chewing gum and we put toothpaste on it and chewed it for four days. Honestly, that's all we had for four days. My stomach became so small I doubt if I could have eaten a big meal without vomiting it all up again. By the time the British landed and started their bombardments we were eating potato skin, rotten onions or apples, or anything else we found lying around.

'I used to write letters home to my mother, to my girlfriend. I didn't tell my mother where I was because I didn't want her to worry. I never received any replies. Letters from our families should have gone to our base in Argentina and then been forwarded on to us from there. That was the procedure. But in all the time I was in the islands no mail reached me. In the end I was writing things like "If you don't love me, fine, but please send me some food." Drastic stuff, eh?

'The Military Police began to stop us soldiers from the mountains going into Stanley. We took to scavenging beside a river where all the left-over and wasted food was dumped. It was the sort of stuff you would normally throw to the pigs – but we ate it. Everyone in Stanley knew who we were. We were covered in mud, dirt and grime and had beards. They called us Jews and mountaineers and sneered at us. I remember a clean, well-fed sergeant telling me: "Soldier, shave – we are at war!" I wanted to kill that fucker. That bastard's attitude summed it all up for me. As far as I was concerned we had lost the war already and it hadn't even started. That smug, well-fed bastard telling me to shave, me who'd lost 19kg, me who'd spent two fucking months in a hole without being able to wash, me who'd had to steal food to stay alive. Motherfucker!

'This was supposed to be war. Was it? This was nothing like the movies, nothing like people believed war to be. There was no glory here, no firing guns and killing people. Here it was seeing a guy crying because he had to wipe his arse with a letter from his girlfriend or mother because he had no other paper. It was about seeing people collapse with cold, hunger and exhaustion. That was war as far as we had seen it.

'Then the raids started and I began to realize the real war was beginning. We could see the Harriers bombing around Stanley and the airport. At first it was like a movie, bombs exploding, a plane on the ground disintegrating before your very eyes, then it was our turn. As the planes came I grabbed my helmet and ran. A bomb landed to my front, so I ran back and then another one landed ten to fifteen metres away. I shouted: "I am at war. Santiago, this is war, what the fuck are you doing here?"

'We began to believe the Yanks were helping the English. We were sure they were using an illegal American bomb on us. I can see it now, an explosion in the air releasing twenty or twenty-five mines to float down among us and sink into the ground. You heard zuk, zzuuk, zzzuuuk, as they sank into the ground. [These were probably what are called Airfield Denial Weapons – more commonly known as cluster bombs. Designed to scatter "bomblets" along runways, approaches and roads, they deny the enemy use of them. They are particularly nasty but effective weapons which explode when disturbed. They are not illegal.] We couldn't leave our holes until the engineers came up to deal with them. Sometimes that took the best part of a day. You couldn't even go for a crap. Instead you did it in your helmet and threw it out to one side of your position.

'Then the psychological warfare began. The naval gunfire was designed to deprive us of sleep as much as it was meant to kill and frighten us. It worked. In the end you got used to it in such a way that you accepted you were waiting for it to land on top of you and that would be that. Every night they shelled us. They must have had bombs [shells] to give away, they threw so many at us. You used to try to put it out of your mind and curl up and try to sleep. It was hard. During one bombardment a shell from a frigate exploded ten metres from us, showering us with earth. This guy was shouting: "They'll kill me. They'll kill me." It had blown a crater two metres deep and a lot of the earth had landed on him, making it impossible for him to move. Some of the officers and senior NCOs ran over asking if it had landed near us. What a stupid question. There was a two-metre hole smoking right in front of us and these stupid fuckers were asking where the explosion was. We said: "No, that's just a garden we're digging."

'As I've said before, the mail situation was appalling, but one day one of the guys got a letter telling him he was the father of a baby boy. He was really proud and happy until this bastard corporal yells across to him: "See, I told you that your wife and I were going to make you a boy." The guy was really upset about it. He didn't like the corporal and he knew the bastard fancied his sister as well. Soon afterwards he came over giggling and told us: "He may fancy my sister, but he'll never have her. He's going to die. Look at how he is guzzling down his food over there. I cooked it for him – in my piss."

'We had some Marine infantry up near us and one was a particularly loathsome bastard. He was a real bully, but thought himself superior to everyone. This lot came from Chaco and they were manning a .50-cal. The others with him weren't much better. Some of them had had only twenty' days training... but they were Marines! Arseholes. Honestly, I have nothing against people from the province of Chaco even though they have brains the size of peas. One day I had a run-in and I was ordered by this sergeant to go down the mountain to the road by Moody Brook and look for a box of ammunition. Now, I was to do this on my own, find it and bring it back. A box of ammo weighs more than 50kg and at that time my weight was down to about 40kg. I knew it would take at least two of us to carry it. To make matters worse the English artillery had started and I would have to duck and dive and dodge that. When I tell him all this he just punches me so hard – and I'm only a little guy at the best of times – I roll fifty metres down the hill. Bastard. Anyway, another guy comes to help and we find the ammo. It was obvious the bastards had abandoned it because they were too lazy to carry it. It must have been five or six kilometres back up Longdon and I swore nearly every step of the way that I would kill this motherfucker. I swore I would kill him given just half a chance, but I couldn't get near him. He knew I was after him and that I meant it.

'But I did hear later that when the battle started he was running around without his boots or helmet, asking where I was, he was so frightened. That still gives me a lot of satisfaction. I heard, too, that after the war he was still suffering so badly from shock that he lost all his teeth and hair. Good. It is also possible that he has since died. If that is the case the human race has lost nothing.

'The medics, too, were a bunch of shithouses. You will always get guys who will try it on, try to work things so they get sent home. They were easy to spot, but our bastard medics treated even the genuinely ill as if they were malingerers. I got a bad infection and my face swelled up. I waited three days to see a medic and then the bastard just looked at me, grinned and said: "Come back when you've lost a finger, OK. Otherwise don't bother." Ten days later another guy actually did lose a finger in an accident. This same medic said to him: "Come back with no head, soldier." We hated them.'

Jerry Phillips was wary as he led his patrol back to 3 Para's lines in response to the radio summons. He didn't want another blue on blue. They had gone out from B Company's location – the guys with whom they had come ashore – and he was going back in to join them. 'We had just reached a big knoll near Windy Gap on our way back to Port San Carlos when this fucking big whoosh went over our heads. We got down immediately. I knew something else would follow it. We tensed and waited. The seconds seemed like minutes. But in reality it was only about three seconds before two Argentinian Skyhawk jets came over. I had the GPMG with me and just turned the gun to the vertical and fired fifty rounds into the belly of one of the jets which flew over me. It was only seventy-five feet above us and I could actually see my bullets and tracer going through the aircraft. Each of my lads fired a full magazine of twenty rounds into it from their rifles. The rocket which had whooshed over our heads was from an 84mm anti-tank weapon fired by one of our own lads whose lines we were approaching. We reported our contact over the radio and heard from John Graham, who had another patrol in an OP farther out, that the jet had crashed. We were never credited with that kill.

'We got back to our HQ at Port San Carlos OK and had just grabbed a quick brew when we were sent out again to set up another OP on Fanning Head. "It's only a quickie., twelve hours maximum. You can leave your bergens and doss-bags back here," they told us. Bollocks. As usual, things got stupid. Twenty-four hours passed, then forty-eight, and still no scoff, no sleeping bags, no relief, nothing. Three days we were up there, starving and cold, and the officer on the other end of the radio keeps on promising us a resupply. By this stage we are just about on our last legs with the cold and hunger. We kept sending messages by radio and Morse requesting our bergens – but nothing. Then, out of the blue, appears this chopper, a Scout. Brilliant, we think, here come the bergens. As the Scout landed, a big grey plastic box was dumped at our feet and this RAF sergeant tells me: "It's Twiggy."

"What's Twiggy?" I asked him, and he said: "It's a nightsight for you."

"Fuck Twiggy, where are our bergens?" I asked him.

"'Don't know," he says before flying off. We were left there fuming. We drop-kicked this box with £10,000 worth of kit in it. We kicked the shit out of it. Eventually we opened it up and it was like a DIY kit without any instructions. None of us knew how it worked because we hadn't seen one before. Anyway, a few hours later a chopper came back and picked up the box and told us to get on board as well. That was OK except for one thing: the Scout could take four or five men, but it already had two aircrew because it was wartime and it had the box with Twiggy in it and me and my three soldiers. There was no room for me. In the end I had to stand on the skid outside while it lifted off and flew us back. Here I am at 2,000 feet, hanging on to the outside. Jesus, this is something else. Jumping from planes with a parachute is one thing, but this... wow! When we got back we found the bulk of the battalion had broken out from the bridgehead and that 2 Para had taken Goose Green. Our battalion had tabbed it all the way to Teal Inlet, so we hung around waiting for new orders. We weren't hanging about long. We were flown forward in a Chinook and no sooner had we arrived than I was getting new orders. We had to tab another ten miles out to set another OP to watch an area where they thought an enemy threat could come from. We hadn't had a decent meal or any real sleep for four days and were off again. The tab nearly finished us off. By the time we got to the spot the snow was coming down thick and fast.

'Visibility was down to less than five feet and we were knackered. We just collapsed under one poncho and each of us took it in turn to do sentry while we all lay there. Soon we had four or five inches of snow on us and we vanished from sight. No one could have seen us. When you were not on stag you fell into a deep sleep. That was the best sleep I ever had!

'At first light we radioed in and were told to return as soon as possible. We broke cover and tabbed all day, arriving back near our own lines at last light. Remember, we had had a blue on blue and it was very much to the fore of my mind. I kept remembering the film *Cross of Iron,* when the soldiers were shot up trying to get back into their own lines. We had been listening in on the radio and there were no patrols coming back in. I knelt down and I could see a 3 Para sentry in my nightsight. We got a bit closer and my mind was trying to work out how I could tell this guy we were friendly forces without getting shot. Then he yells at us to halt and as soon as he opened his gob I recognized his voice: it was Geordie Nick. "It's me, Jerry," I tell him, but he yells halt again and demands the password. By this time he's aiming his GPMG and we're on tenterhooks. "For fuck sake, it's me, it's Jerry." Thankfully he recognized my voice and said: "All reet, man, come on in," in that Geordie accent of his. But he made me stay beside him and identify each member of my patrol as they were called in separately in case any enemy had tagged on at the end. We managed to get some sleep again that night before joining in with the rest of the battalion on the horrendous tab to Estancia.'

3

ALBERTO CARBONE was just like nearly every other Argentinian conscript arriving on the Falklands: confused. The place was nothing like he had imagined and to tell the truth he had not spent much of his young life thinking about those windswept islands. It was a strange, barren place to him. He joined a long snake of gasping, struggling soldiers on the hard, cold march into Port Stanley seemingly being mocked by the empty lorries driving past.

'You cannot possibly imagine the difficulty we had carrying our kit down that road. It was terrible. I had my rifle, a kitbag, three mortar bombs, a personal tent and two suitcases. We couldn't understand why the empty lorries couldn't be used to help us with our kit at least. Our rendezvous point was a school. We made it just before last light, put our kit in a pile and then we were shown sleeping quarters. Next morning I went to find my kit and it had disappeared, my sleeping bag, blanket, spare clothes, everything. Gone. It really pissed me off because I had to survive in what I was wearing for the next couple of months. All I had was what I stood up in and they refused to issue me with replacement clothing. I never ever had a sleeping bag or blanket again. Because of that I suffered and I mean I really did suffer. I stank as well.

'Lieutenant Baldini led us up this mountain the next day and he and Corporal Casio told us where our positions were to be. Although Baldini was the boss, Casio gave us most of our orders. I didn't like him much. Once up on the mountain they never told us anything. Every day became a test of endurance and survival for us conscripts. Our regular routine was to march down to the road near Moody Brook and hump boxes of ammunition back up the hill. I can only ever remember a helicopter dropping a load once and that was our kitbags. It was no use to me because my kit had vanished.

'At one stage someone, somehow, commandeered a white horse and it would be used to carry and pull ammo and stores up the hill. It was like a pet. The lads from the *rancho* also used it to pull their stores. It's funny having to use a horse in a modern war when you have helicopters which can fly about carrying so much more. In between humping stores we had to build bunkers. Build here one minute, then move a bit and build there. I still didn't expect the English to come, but the general idea was that our defensive positions faced north because that is where they expected a frontal attack to come from.

'There was a corporal called Orozco who had been a conscript like us in Class of 62 and had opted to make the army his career. Even though he was a regular we still saw him as one of us and this made it hard for him to make us obey his orders. He wasn't a bad lad, but he used to get upset at our attitude towards him.

'I was really suffering because of my lack of kit, and the

cold and hunger on top made it even worse. I had never suffered anything like it before and haven't since. I had to work out a way to get food and cigarettes. There was a detachment of Marines nearby who were there in support. Their supplies arrived separately from ours. And they were very well supplied compared with us. People like them were high on the list of priorities. We were at the very bottom. They had cold rations, chocolate, cigarettes, plenty of everything. I used to buy things from them for one peso and sell them on at two pesos. That way I could afford food and fags for myself. However, as it got colder and wetter there was less food to buy so I had to find a way to get to Puerto Argentino to find some. I went into a shed and found some rotting potato skin and orange skin on the floor. I ate it. Having a crap was always a problem. We had no paper. My aunt had sent me a letter with the Virgin of Lujan enclosed. I was adamant I wouldn't wipe my arse with it, so I used some papers with prayers on them. Mainly I had to wipe myself with grass.

'Our guard system was the two hours on, two hours off system and it meant we got no real solid sleep. That, combined with our starvation and the cold, made us like zombies. It was taking a terrible toll on us. I can remember one occasion as if it was yesterday. Snow had fallen, it was bitterly, bitterly cold, and it was my turn to relieve my mate on guard duty. I found him collapsed behind a rock. No sooner had I got him round than I, too, fainted. The next day they gave us chocolate. It was the only time I can ever recall being given anything sweet.

'There was a guy who had a position near Lieutenant Baldini and it was at Baldini's position where the supplies arrived. They were supposed to be dished out there, too. I was close by once and saw some nougat bars being handed round to the favoured few. I went for a bar and finished up with half of one, so I complained. Next thing I knew, this bastard was hitting me in the chest with a rifle butt, so I complained again and when he was questioned he said the rats had stolen the other half!

'The only place to steal or beg for food was Stanley, but the journey was so long and exhausting it wiped you out. You had to survive, but I began to ask myself if the journey was worth it. On my third trip I managed to get some food and struggle back to the mountain. Just before I got back to my position Baldini saw me. We had nicknamed him Wild Boar and he went straight into his wild boar act. Was he mad or was he mad? I was stripped of the food and kicked to the ground and then he made me crawl towards my position. He made me crawl like a dog and all the time he was screaming and shouting at me. He yelled at me to stop at a pile of rubbish and rotting sheep guts and intestines and ordered me to lie on my back. I was worried because I didn't know what he was going to do. He ordered me to be staked. I was spread-eagled and tied to four stakes, which were driven into the ground, and then he marched off.

'I lay there, cold, frightened and hungry. I could smell the rotting rubbish and sheep guts which were seeping into my clothes and the skin of my back. The cold was biting into me and then it began to rain again. I knew it was night when the *rancho* arrived to dish out the slops they called food. I could only just turn my head to try to see around me. I was delirious and there was nothing my mates could do to help me otherwise they would have finished up in the same predicament. I was fully expecting to die from the cold. After a time they came and released me. I had been there for eight hours but it seemed a lot longer. I just stumbled away and collapsed in my tent.

'I had already decided that was to be my last trip before I set out, so this punishment was particularly cruel as far as I was concerned. I decided to keep out of Baldini's way and to obey the rules up there even if it meant starvation. You see, the conscripts just couldn't win. There was a pecking order when it came to food distribution and we were way down at the bottom. I remember standing in the queue at the rancho and watching the discrimination with my own eyes. Officially, all the food came from the same pot – and it did. But the conscripts got a ladleful of crap from the top – greasy water – and the corporals' food was scooped from the bottom of the pot so they got a mess tin full of meat and potatoes and the like. When I asked the guy for a ladle from the bottom he told me to fuck off. Then the officer would arrive. He had cold rations to add to the pot and he got even better food.

'From early May we had known the English were coming, but we didn't think it would be possible for them to get here. It was a long, long way. Then their navy started shelling us. Jesus. It's weird being in a bombardment. At first you feel helpless and then you start being able to judge where they will land. You learn from the whistling how close they will come to you. It always followed a set pattern and we started to get used to it. Then, during one particular bombardment, our bosses ordered us to turn off a generator which powered the radar and charged our batteries. The shells always seemed to be zeroed in on this area, so we turned the machine off. Then the shells started going all over the place. We felt the English had managed to electrically pinpoint the generator. It didn't stop the shelling, but it meant we had no idea where they would land.

'Life was bad enough up there without the shelling. If it was meant to lower our morale ü did. If it was meant to be psychological it was. As I said, we now had no idea of where they were going to land. We heard one whistling in and knew it would be close. Bang! It explodes in the rocks right by us. There's shrapnel and pieces of rock flying everywhere. One of my mates, Garcia, was close to it and the shrapnel hit him. Poor Garcia, he was out of it. The shrapnel broke his arms and smashed his helmet. They casevac'd him away.'

Tony Gregory had tabbed across some country in his time, but he'd never encountered anywhere like the Falklands. It was a killer almost every step of the way to Teal Inlet. In addition to the wet, soggy ground they also had to contend with the vile Falklands weather and the scorching pace of the march. That, too, was a killer.

'We had about thirty-five kilometres to go to Teal and it was without doubt the worst terrain I have ever tabbed across. It was like a great big floating bog all the way. The speed of the tab was unbelievable. At first we thought it was just our OC trying to make a name for himself. He wasn't in any mood to slow down. Then we realized it wasn't just us in C Company, but the whole bloody battalion which was going at speed.

'The Marines were slogging along as well, heading for Douglas. They don't tab, they yomp. We were supposed to meet up with them somewhere further up the line, but I reckon it was the earlier frictions with them on the journey down which turned this into a race. Our brass seemed obsessed with doing the tab in record time. We were told if anyone dropped out they would be left behind. It all reminded me of the film *March or Die*. I wasn't the fittest of lads, but I could keep up when carrying weight. The ones who did fall out were left behind. It was as simple as that. We had very short rest periods before starting off all over again. After twelve hours we were knackered. Someone told the OC that if he didn't slow down he would only have a very small company left by the time he got to Teal. We got there OK, I think in just over thirty hours, beating the Marines by nearly a full day... But I still don't know how we managed it. Comradeship and working for each other along the way, helping each other, has to be what got us there.

'While we were settling in at Teal, organizing shelters, making brews and food, orders came down that at first light we would be advancing on Estancia House, another thirty-plus kilometres away. Jesus. What was this all about? I don't want to do that ever again. It was horrendous. By the time we got to Estancia I was on my chinstraps. We lost guys through exhaustion, trench foot, hunger – you name it. Jesus, people don't realize how much 3 Para suffered on that tab. I know the tab has gone down in regimental history, but I wouldn't wish it on anyone else. We lost an incredible amount of weight and some very good guys suffered.

'At Estancia the rifle companies were positioned in all-round defence and we were facing Stanley. We spent twenty-four hours settling in and then the name Longdon started doing the rounds. We were going to attack it virtually straight away. The plan was simple: the gunners would open up on the mountain to draw enemy fire and then the Milan missile crews would take out their heavy-fire positions such as mortars and .50-cals. It could have succeeded. C Company was actually in position when we were ordered back to Estancia.

'The brass back at brigade HQ wanted us to wait for the Marines and the rest of the hats to catch up so they could put in a brigade attack. We withdrew back to Estancia and got some rest for the next ten days. I was dug in on a windswept hill. At night, the only people who moved were sentries or patrols. We sat there watching and waiting. One night in the pitch black I was trying to peg down my poncho more securely in the wind and rain when there were four big bangs and the earth shook. Paul, my partner, asked what the hell it was. I thought it was artillery. In the morning we found the craters, which were close to us, and then we were told that Argentinian bombers had been over during the night. The bombs had gone into the ground before exploding and the soggy peat had absorbed most of the blast.

'The cold, the wind and the rain, coupled with the after-effects of our long marches, made our bodies demand more and more food. We scoffed everything in our ration packs and were still hungry. I was starving. We needed more food to keep the debilitating effects of the weather at bay. Trench foot, frostbite and hypothermia were beginning to creep through the ranks. All of our clothing and sleeping bags were soaked, but we had to keep morale up. We had to keep each other going, so we indulged in a lot of banter and slagging each other off. It worked. We had to look after each other to survive.

'It was comradeship which saved my life after a patrol. We had gone out at night and I fell into a river, right up to my neck. It was a fighting cum recce patrol and I was soaked right through and shaking and shivering. We also had to lie up somewhere and watch and wait, but by morning it was more than obvious that the cold had got me and I was going out of the game. The lads grabbed me and rushed me back to our own lines. They threw me into my sleeping bag and Paul got in beside me and used his body heat to revive me. If he hadn't I'd have been a goner.'

There was no hero's welcome for Jorge Altieri and his mates as they struggled, exhausted, into Port Stanley on or around 15 April, looking more like bedraggled pack mules than a conquering army of occupation. The place was a bit of a disappointment, dull and cold and the locals weren't exactly falling over themselves to make him feel welcome.

'I'll always remember the cold,' he says with an

involuntary shiver. 'I had never experienced a biting wind like the one in the Malvinas. I don't know what we had been expecting, but this certainly wasn't like anything we had ever thought about. It was a village. We thought the capital would be a city, but it was just a village.'

They marched into the chaos that passes for order when any army is securing a location and moving heavily laden men and equipment. Shouting, swearing NCOs were trying to drive sheep-like flocks of disgruntled men while the officers blamed them for their own lack of forward planning and inefficiency. Although they were in charge, the officers themselves didn't appear to know what the hell they were supposed to be doing or where they were going.

'I didn't know if I was coming or going with so many troops about,' Jorge recalls. 'Eventually we were allocated a shed or something like that. It was getting dark and we couldn't really make out what it was. But at least we had somewhere out of the wind to sleep for the night. Our officers then began to try to find out what we were supposed to be doing and where we were supposed to be going.'

Jorge slept fitfully in that crowded makeshift dormitory as men fidgeted, farted, snored and cursed one other. He was glad when morning came.

'At first light we started to walk again. We went past Moody Brook, which had been the British Marines' camp, and then the road stopped and it became a slow, hard slog up into the mountains. We were going over the roughest terrain you could possibly imagine. We got as far as the lower ridge of some mountain by nightfall and stayed there, and next morning we were ordered up on to the summit, up as far as we could go. One side sloped steeply down, facing west. On top was a bowl, a sort of huge crater which ran towards another ridge, and then another bigger bowl. This bigger bowl was to be our home for the next sixty days or so. It was called Mount Longdon. Next to us was Two Sisters and we nicknamed that Two Tits and if you ever saw it you'd know why!

'As soon as we got up there we were ordered to build positions. First we would pitch a tent, then build a bunker next to or around it. I had one with a friend between two big rocks. I was really pleased with it because it blended in perfectly with the rest of the mountain. We also spent many hours building positions for our superiors. The last from 1 Section had to build the positions for Lieutenant Baldini and his corporals and I helped build one for our company commander, Major Carrizo. Positions also had to be build for Lieutenants Nairotti and López and their people. Baldini was a tough guy, strict and military-green all the way through. As far as soldiering goes he was the soldier up on that mountain, but it was wise not to cross him. I was determined to stay out of his way as much as possible.

'Every day we had to add to and strengthen our bunkers, try to clean our weapons as best we could, then join the scramble for food from the *rancho*. This was normally watery soup. Really bad stuff. We never had one decent meal the whole time we were there. I know for a fact that Lieutenant Baldini complained about the food, but nothing happened. We never got a proper night's sleep because of the system of doing two hours on duty and two hours off. It was a very tiring routine. At first I shared a tent with guys called Garcia and Quintana, but Quintana was later moved to share with Corporal Orozco.

'Life was a daily struggle. Sanitation was non-existent... The officers told us to crap behind our positions, but not in front! Now hear this – their reasoning for this brilliant order was that if the enemy approached they would know where we were because of the smell of human crap coming from the front of our positions! We ignored it and crapped wherever.

'Mail was also a problem. We rarely received any. A couple of the guys managed to get a letter, but other than that we had no contact with the outside world. Our morale was suffering. Our world seemed to be this mountain and that was it. It wasn't until the latter stages of the war that we found letters piled up in a sergeant's position, many of them addressed: *Al Soldado Argentino* [To the Argentinian Soldier] from well-wishers back home.

'From 1 May the English began attacking us by air and from the sea. Every now and again we would come under attack by bombing or shells from the warships. That told us they were on their way. I remember one day an English Harrier was attacking targets and one of our planes came in to attack it from a different direction. We were given orders to fire at this jet with whatever weapons we could get our hands on. Just as we were about to open up Baldini cancelled the order. He also sent the cancellation down to the anti-aircraft gunners in the village [Port Stanley] but it was too late. They were engaging the jet and shot it down. It was one of our own.

'We heard that the English had landed on the other side of the island [East Falkland] and had taken positions at San Carlos. Our morale hit the floor. Our officers said we were now on red alert and we had to be careful. They told us nothing about the British movements or positions, I think because they feared we would get scared and leave. I don't know why they didn't tell us.

'The bombardments were also having a psychological effect on us. And we began to realize that a full-frontal battle could actually happen. There was a generator near the position I shared with Garcia and cables ran away from it. It hummed when it was turned on. I didn't honestly know what it was for. Eventually I found it powered the anti-personnel radar which was set up further along the mountain. A team of guys monitored the radar and the generator. We were convinced it was this which attracted the enemy shelling.

'During one bombardment this shell comes whizzing in and the air around us evaporates. The blast hurled a big rock down on to our tent, wrecking it. We weren't inside, luckily for us. Shrapnel ripped into Garcia. His arm was ripped and damaged. His helmet was hit and nearly blown off his head. He was on the ground screaming with pain. We left cover and ran to him. Lieutenant Baldini, who had been on the other side of the bowl, heard the screaming and ran over and examined Garcia. He told us to build a campaign stretcher using our jackets and rifles, and a corporal bandaged him. It was freezing and Garcia was stripped down to his white vest and we still had to carry him several kilometres down off the mountain to the first aid position at the edge of Stanley. The stretcher had been hastily made and Garcia was heavy and the journey down the mountain was a struggle. We were even attacked by a Harrier. Poor Garcia. We had to lay him down and I covered him with my body. We couldn't believe we had come under air attack as we tried to rescue a mate.

'I heard of another guy being killed by a shell on Longdon. They said it decapitated him. Morale was bad. Another guy simply froze to death one night. The officers told us nothing. It was as if we conscripts didn't matter. The fact that we had no stretchers and had to go all the way down the mountain to find medics sums it all up in my book.'

From the beach Dom had tabbed through Port San Carlos and up into Windy Gap. It didn't take long to figure out why the place had been given that name. Here B Company, 3 Para established a base, protecting the flank of the beachhead while landing-craft and helicopters worked round the clock offloading supplies, dodging enemy air raids during daylight. The impatient Paras sat it out, occasionally patrolling forward in case the enemy was trying to sneak up on them.

They were keen to be off, keen to make contact with the men they had come to fight. Sitting around in the cold and wet was doing no one any good and the Argies would be made to suffer because they were the cause of all this discomfort as far as the toms were concerned. Some of the officers were being a right pain in the arse and the sooner the order came to move out the less the chances would be of some prick with pips on his shoulder getting a well-deserved kick in the balls from a tom who would end up in the nick.

When the order to move did come it surprised some, but not the irrepressible Dom. They were told quite simply that they would have to tab with all the kit they could carry the full eighty-plus kilometres to Port Stanley, fighting as they went. That's what they were trained for, and why they were here. What was more, it was something they would take in their stride. Kicking ass all the way would be a bonus.

The reason they would have to endure this long march was that an Argentinian Super Etendard aircraft had sunk the chartered container ship *Atlantic Conveyor* with a French-built Exocet missile. The ship had been crammed with heavy-lift Chinook helicopters and other aircraft as well as winter-warfare supplies. The thoughtless bastard who'd failed to spread that ship's cargo through the fleet deserved to have his goolies cut off. His stupidity would cause a load of grief among the troops slogging across the ground.

The only thing that really annoyed Dom about the move-out order was that he didn't have time for a brew before setting off. He had just returned with his section from a night patrol when the order came. He desperately wanted a brew to recharge his batteries because he knew this was going to be a long, hard, debilitating march and they would all need every advantage they could get. They set off in a long snake, a great line of heavily burdened men, slipping, squelching, struggling across muscle-wrenching terrain which sucked at their legs and tried to unbalance them. Over hills and down through valleys they went, fording freezing rivers, skittering across treacherous scree slopes, pressing ever onwards towards their unseen goal: Port Stanley, the capital of the Falklands.

It was one of the hardest tabs Dom had ever done. Many of the men were hurting, their webbing digging into their flesh, chafing and blistering them, and their salty sweat ran into the raw flesh, irritating it still more. To Dom and some of the others the sheer speed of the tab was annoying because it seemed to them that those setting the pace were making little or no allowance for the loads the men were carrying or their tiredness. They should also have had the short-arses like Dom setting the pace with their little legs instead of some giant taking giant strides.

'We were pushed too bloody hard at times,' he says. But whenever spirits sagged they were saved by one of the greatest weapons the British soldier has ever possessed down the centuries: the wicked, warped sense of humour of Tommy Atkins. And then there was the perverse delight at watching some of the loud-mouths struggle and joy – oh, what joy! – when some PTIs (Physical Training Instructors) began to fall by the wayside. Only a short time before they had been beasting Dom and the rest of the lads round the decks of the *Canberra*, exhorting them to get fitter. But in soldiering, endurance is as important as fitness, particularly in Parachute Regiment soldiering.

Endurance and determination were just as important as what the gym-jockeys in their flash trainers preached. You could run all day round a track or a gym, but it was a different matter when it came to tabbing with weight. This was going to be some fucking march. It would sort out the real Paras from the pretenders. Seeing others drop out buoyed Dom. And when a craphat attached to B Company fell over and twisted his ankle Dom was delighted. Then, when the order came to leave the injured where they fell, he was ecstatic. He waved, then smiled at the injured man.

'Keep going, lads, keep going,' the NCOs told them.

That suited Dom. 'There was just no way we could carry anyone, let alone get rubber-dicked stopping for a hat,' he gleefully recalls, 'and it was four days before they were picked up by a chopper.'

B Company was in the lead, right out front, leading the battalion. But when word came back that their company commander, Major Mike Argue, was the man in front, Dom's spirits fell. Major Argue was a former SAS officer, but Dom was convinced that neither he nor any other officer had the navigating skills of the soldiers under them. His head dropped. 'We'll be lost,' he moaned. Shortly afterwards he was proved correct and they performed a U-turn. The irony of the situation really appealed to his sense of humour. As they retraced their footsteps they passed their mates in the other companies, who looked puzzled. Dom couldn't resist a spot of slagging. 'Hi, Jock, hi, Pete, you're going the wrong way.' Their replies were in language not used in the drawing-rooms at teatime in England's fine houses.

On they slogged, eating up the miles until they reached Mount Estancia, from where they could see Port Stanley in the distance when the mists and low cloud cleared. Now they were tantalizingly close, but still there were frustrations. They were in position, they could see the disorganized defenders of Stanley quite clearly, they were ready, but still no order came to advance.

Back at brigade HQ, as far as the Paras were concerned, the hats were fannying about trying to make up their minds. The Marines, with all their yomping, were forty-eight hours behind. Fucking boat people. Time was being wasted.

If the Paras could see the Argies, then the Argies knew the Paras were there, and Dom would bet a lot that they weren't letting the grass grow under their feet. They would be reinforcing their positions.

Kevin wasn't surprised, either, at the new orders to advance on foot. After all, tabbing was something the Paras had always prided themselves on. It was one of the basics of Parachute Regiment soldiering. He, too, joined the long line of swearing, muttering men and set off on the history-making march. It was the beginning of a fifty-mile advance to contact, something the modern British Army had never thought it would have to do on foot. The faceless generals, the heavy hats of Whitehall, who had for years been trying to water down the Parachute Regiment, trying to say it was obsolete, were now about to get their answer shoved right up them in spades.

The Paras would march to battle whether it was fifty miles or five hundred. The bastard hats would never make it without helicopters or armoured personnel carriers. But 3 Para would do it like soldiers.

For two days Kevin and his comrades tabbed across rivers, hills, bogs and anything else in their path. It wasn't easy and it hurt like hell, but pride and determination kept them going. As soon as he arrived at Teal Inlet, Kevin dug himself a full-scale trench for rest and sleep and began cooking a scoff. He expected to have a two- or three-day rest. As he stoked his tired and aching body with well-earned hot food two bits of news hit him.

The first was that 2 Para had captured Goose Green, though

there had been casualties. Men had been killed and others wounded, and Kevin wondered if any of his mates in that battalion were among them. Any illusions of a phoney war vanished. He heard, too, of the loss of the *Atlantic Conveyor* and was immediately aware of the impact that sinking would have on the war and on him. There was no doubt he would have to walk everywhere as the precious helicopters were somewhere on the bottom of the Atlantic Ocean. Food and rest were what he needed now. He would need every ounce of strength and endurance in the days to come. Rest and food, he told himself, as he went to sleep. But it was not to be.

At stand-to, just before first light, there were more orders, more tabbing, more sweating and swearing, another two days across the trackless terrain and then the loop round to Estancia House and up to Mount Estancia with its views of Longdon and Port Stanley beyond. Kevin was happy and they were still well ahead of the Marines and the logistical-support hats. He had marched his socks off. But it'll all be over soon, he told himself. Although the march was a killer it was in the nature of the beast: hard, fast, aggressive action. That was what had always been drilled into them from the earliest days of their training.

Kevin was content at first with the order from brigade HQ not to advance any further. They could rest here until the Marines caught up, but then he began to realize that if the enemy had any balls at all 3 Para could be in trouble. Here they were, way out in front, without any support. If the roles were reversed the enemy would be in bottomless shit. Have they got the salt to come and try us, he asked himself. The other soldiers were restless, too. They had come this far, so why not crack on and get it over and done with?

To this day Kevin still feels they should have carried on advancing. 'We may have lost a few more guys, but the war would have been over a lot sooner. I reckon if 16 Para

Brigade had still existed and been there we would have gone straight in and kicked the shit out of them straight away. Instead we had to wait for the Marines.'

That same rifle which Luis Leccese had only ever fired once was slung round his neck as he struggled through Port Stanley in the wind and rain. Even though he was sweating he was still chilled to the bone. The nineteen-year-old conscript looked at the local civilians and they stared back at him expressionlessly. What a place, he thought. He had never seen anything like it.

'They bedded us down for the night in some sort of school and in the morning we had a mug of *mate cosido* [tea] and some bread before setting out behind Lieutenant Baldini for the march up into the mountains. It was hard going across that boggy, marshy terrain. I was sweating like I had never sweated. Lieutenant Baldini never said anything to us – we just followed him up the hills. When we got on to this mountain called Longdon he pointed out our positions and told us to get on with digging in. We were positioned section by section and I was in Corporal Casio's section. Like most of the other corporals he was a lazy bastard, but another one, Corporal Rios, was the worst. They behaved as if they were a law unto themselves.

'You would be slaving away with your buddy, building a bunker, when he would appear, point out a spot and order you to dig a bunker for him. No "please", no help. He would just stand there like the lazy bastard he was, telling you the specifications he wanted and giving orders. Five or six days later he would come back and tell you it was no good because water was seeping in and send you to another spot to build him another one. We must have built him about ten bunkers. As far as I can recall Lieutenant Baldini was the only boss who didn't change his position.

'It was like living in hell on that hill. The weather, the wind, the rain, the fog and the cold just got into your bones. When you weren't improving your own bunker or building others for the lazy bastards then you had to flog up and down the hill humping ammunition. One helicopter could have lifted most of it, but the only one we saw was the one which dumped our kit two or three days after we arrived. That was our routine: build, slave, fetch. Morale was very poor. No one got proper sleep because after a day spent slaving, freezing and starving we had to do two-hour stints of guard duty throughout the night. None of our superiors showed the slightest concern for us.

'There were no trees or hedges around to act as windbreaks and the corporals were such lazy bastards that when they were cold they would send us out to find wood so they could have fires to warm themselves. If there are no trees and no hedges it stands to reason that there is going to be very little wood.

'Survival soon became our overriding priority. I was losing weight rapidly because of the slaving in all weather and because food was not reaching us. Trying to slip away to find food was very hard because that fucking Casio was always watching. When the *rancho* arrived we would join the queue for what was no more than dishwater. We were all supposed to get the same food, but you could stand there and watch the preferential treatment for officers and so-called superiors. I can quite clearly remember seeing big chunks of meat wrapped in nylon film put to one side. Your mouth just watered seeing that solid food, but when I asked the soldier in charge of the *rancho* for some he just shook his head and said it had to go to the officers. If he gave me any he would be in big trouble. No fucking superior ever lost weight like we conscripts did.

'As far as I can remember the days just passed in a blur of

trying to survive. The English started shelling us, first from the sea and then from the land, which told us they had arrived. One day we went back to the *rancho*, about 400 metres behind our position, to see if we could get some food from them. There were two of us and we had to go out through the side of the mountain to find it. No British soldiers had been seen around, although the artillery was coming in again. Baldini was up on the summit with his binoculars, trying to spot the artillery batteries. We were talking to the *rancho* soldier when his eyes widened and he said: "Look out, Baldini is coming up behind you."

'We turned round and came face to face with him. He seemed to have lost his head. He really went for me more than for the other soldier. He made us frogmarch and crawl on our hands and knees, kicking and screaming at us all the time. Then we had to crawl on our bellies all the way back up to our positions. I was frightened by the sheer temper, screaming, cursing and lack of control:

'At our position I tried to explain. It wasn't disobedience, but he flipped even more. Jesus. He pulled out his 9mm pistol, cocked it and rammed it to the back of my head. I could feel the pressure of the pistol pushing into me. I was crying and shaking with fright. Baldini was screaming: *"Te voy a matar, soldado!"* ["I'm going to kill you, soldier!"]. I was sobbing. I couldn't see me living any more. He was the type who would kill. Then just as suddenly as he had erupted he put the pistol away and sent me to my position. I was badly shaken. I thought he would really do it. I stayed out of his way after that.'

4

WHEN THE order was given for the soldiers of 3 Para to break out from the Port San Carlos beachhead, Denzil was bemused. At times he was even bewitched and when he wasn't either of those he was just plain bloody angry. He spent a lot of time pondering the wisdom, sanity even, of those who took the decision to order a tab like that in such awful conditions. There was only one word to describe the weather: diabolical. It wasn't just the weather; it was the torturous terrain the lads had to cross with all the weight they had to hump. He never had any doubt the men of his battalion could complete the marathon march, but he was anxious about the condition they would be in at the end of it. It was typical of the Army, and of the bosses, that they would tab till their bollocks dragged the ground.

Then there would be nothing. Just nothing. At the end of it they would just hang around and wait. He knew that would be the case because they had done it before on exercise. There must be better ways, he told himself, but if the men with all the rank said tab, then tab it would be. But it didn't stop him having a good moan to himself or joining in with the others as they slogged along.

It irritated him, angered him at times, that the *Atlantic Conveyor* had been zapped. They had seen it on the way down, a massive ship, and it was clear to anyone that it was a prime target. What stupid bastard, he asked himself, had let all the choppers be loaded on to just one ship? There were Harriers aboard as well and they had gone, too. Jesus, what a bloody mess.

A civilian tractor joined the trek. It dragged a pallet carrying the battalion's state-of-the-art Milan anti-tank missiles. Sometimes he joined a couple of the other footsore, weary soldiers and hitched a lift on the lurching vehicle. Being a radio operator had its perks! It was a little luxury in a harsh environment. Denzil's other luxury was dreaming, which took his mind off the agony of his wet and aching feet. He dreamed a simple dream of the delights served up by his favourite Chinese takeaway and of what a luxury it would be to crash out in a nice warm bed with clean sheets. He wasn't the only one suffering the discomforts of this gruelling march. And as the tab went on he knew they would not be going into battle immediately. They weren't in any condition to fight a full pitched battle. They needed to rest and recharge their batteries. They needed sleep and grub, and to dry out and to have time to tend to their aching feet and rest their straining muscles. On through Teal Inlet they slogged and up to Estancia House and the commanding heights of Mount Estancia with its views of their ultimate destination, Port Stanley, away in the distance cloaked by the mist and low cloud.

As they began settling into their new positions Denzil was pleasantly surprised at the condition of the battalion. Apart from tiredness and a few feet problems they were in comparatively good nick. After a little rest they would be right as rain, provided they didn't stop here too long in this poxy, freezing rain. At most a few days was all they needed, then on to do what they came here to do.

Too much hanging around would be just as harmful as being forced into battle at the end of an exhausting march. There was a happy medium and he just hoped to God the senior officers back at brigade HQ realized that. But they didn't, of course, and the longer they waited the more Denzil's fears grew. The lads were getting pissed off now with all the hanging about while the brass ponced around instead of getting on with it.

Just a few kilometres away the Argentinians, too, were sitting, wondering and waiting.

There was something about Mount Longdon Oscar Carrizo just didn't like. It was a funny shape as far as he was concerned and he didn't like it or the position he and his comrades occupied.

He was in the mortar platoon of Support Company and was sent with his two mortars and their crews to back up B Company. He was a regular soldier, a corporal, and his job was to fight for his country.

'As soon as the regiment reached Longdon the commanding officer spread his men along the whole summit, which was about a thousand metres long, and there were huge rocks everywhere. I was placed on the most western slope of the mountain, the steepest bit. The men were well spread out and as soon as we knew where we were to be positioned we began building our defences. I placed my two mortars on the western slope looking towards Estancia House. I built a big wall round my position: I didn't like my position, not at all. Something was wrong about it, I don't know what, but it didn't feel right. Perhaps you could call it a sixth sense.'

The giant corporal and his men spent the short, dull, grey Falklands days chatting and wondering if the British would come, before curling up for the night in their cold, sodden positions. They talked about home and what they were doing here and about the lack of information. They guessed what they thought was happening, then second-guessed each other, then asked each other for confirmation of what they hadn't a clue about in the first place. It was nothing new, but something soldiers had done for centuries to while away the long uncomfortable hours. All the same, it was new to these Argentinians.

Morale began to dip. It was the cold, the nagging cold, which bit deep into them. Then there was the rain, icy and misery-making. It became a wretched daily grind just to survive. It was an agonizing chore to keep the weapons serviceable in the awful climate, and to cap it all there was the appalling disregard the hierarchy had for the conditions of the soldiers struggling to survive on the exposed hills. The conscripts were being badly treated, neglected. Carrizo bickered and argued with Lieutenant Baldini in a vain attempt to improve the men's conditions and morale.

'He was a good soldier, but he didn't like the conscripts and he was a bit power-mad. He was always barking out orders. Orders, orders, all the time. And all the time everything was getting worse. Our food situation was terrible. We had weak tea in the morning then weak soup and a biscuit in the afternoon. I just couldn't understand what was happening, what was happening to me, what was happening to all of us. It was terrible. Everyone was cold, wet and hungry. Morale was sinking by the day. Silly things happened. You got silly orders, really stupid ones such as being told to shave in cold water. Imagine the mentality of someone telling soldiers who were cold, wet, miserable and hungry to shave in cold water.

'There was an atmosphere building up and you could feel it. Different units got different – and better – treatment. The Marines' Special Forces didn't like the conscripts or even regular soldiers like me. They thought very highly of themselves. I will never forget them or their arrogance. Their rations were much better than ours and so was their supply system. I can remember to this day how they used to sit in front of us eating very slowly just to tease us. They knew how hungry we were. They behaved like bastards, real bastards.'

As the misery grew so, too, did the arguments between the officers and the government officials, who refused to listen or acknowledge the evidence of their eyes. Morale began to nosedive and confusion reigned.

'One day I was called to a briefing and told: "Don't shoot at the English. Buenos Aires has ordered it."

'Maybe peace is in sight, I thought, and soon things might get better. You know, that order never changed, it was never revoked. When the shooting started the orders from the government were still in place. We sat around and wondered what to do if the British came. Did we shoot at all, or did we shoot above their heads? I'm still confused about it today.

'As well as that we weren't allowed to tell the men anything. Not that the British had landed or were advancing towards us. We were told we could tell the men that if anyone deserted his position he would be severely punished. I began to think the officers or government officials would start shooting us before the English did.

'I remember telling Lieutenant Baldini just a few days before the battle that the men just had to be told what was happening: that the British were coming. Eventually he agreed and told them. It was just as well he did because shortly afterwards their artillery opened up on us and one young lad had his arm torn off by an explosion.

'It was serious. Next thing they told us was that if anyone was thinking of deserting he would be shot. Anyone who retreated would also be shot. It was madness and the situation was getting worse. We had hardly any food. We had no medics. Baldini was fuming. The English artillery was shooting at us. We were only issued with one cigarette a day. We made herbal cigarettes with toilet paper. We were cold, wet, miserable and hungry. A couple of the lads were caught stealing food, a few biscuits. Their punishment was to be staked out on the ground in the rain. I really felt for them.'

Everything was combining to make life absolutely intolerable for Luis Leccese and his wretched fellow-conscripts.

'The artillery bombardments were increasing as the days went by. The land gunners would fire at us during the day and then the Navy would join them from the north in the evening and at night. It was very psychological. It seemed to us that every time the anti-personnel radar and its generator were turned on the bombardment started. The shells would land close to it in the bowl area near our positions, but when it was turned off the shells would deviate.

'I used to do my guard duties looking up at the sky. By day there was no sun, just fog and constant rain, but at night the sky cleared. I would look up and see the stars in the massive clear sky. They were clear, very cold nights and I would count the stars. By dawn a black line appeared and with it came the fog and rain.

'About a week before the battle began I was on guard one night and heard voices, strange voices. I popped my head up and strained to hear them. I couldn't make out what they were saying. It was like a whisper carried on the wind. I thought it was a bit peculiar but I never said anything. I thought perhaps I was hallucinating. This happened two or three times – really weird voices.

'One night there was a hellish wind. I heard the voices again. This time some of the other sentries heard them and screamed at an approaching soldier for the password. No reply came. It may be he never heard because of the wind, but shots were fired at him. The bullets whizzed off the slopes.'

Santiago Gauto, too, had grave misgivings about life on the mountain and in particular about being positioned close to the anti-personnel radar.

'We hated it. Fucking thing. We tried to keep as far away from it as possible because it appeared that the English, from the moment they arrived, knew it was there. The English shells and bombs always seemed to home in on it. I can still hear the humming it made every time it was turned on. By now it must have been about the end of the first week in June. We had no real notion of time up there. I didn't even know what day of the week it was half of the time. One night we were all in our positions on the summit. It was pitch-black, really dark, and the fucking radar gives out a scream – you know: "Look out, red alert, enemy in front" – and the guys behind me with big 12.7mm machine-guns start opening up. Now, the bullets they are firing are big fuckers. Really big. They knock big holes in people. These bastards are firing downwards right over our heads. For ten minutes there was this crazy firing with these big motherfuckers whizzing over our heads and then the order is given: "Halt. Stop firing. The target has stopped moving"... '

Jerry Phillips was, like the others in Patrol Company, a creature of the night. Darkness was his friend, his ally, and held no fears for him. It cloaked his stealth as he moved around and got into position to do his deadly work. He knew that as soon as he reached Estancia he would be on the move with his patrol. He was in good humour despite everything because they were getting closer to the enemy and this is what he had come for: to put his skills to the test.

As darkness fell he checked his lads and led them silently out through the 3 Para lines once more and up to the reverse slope of Estancia Mountain. The Argentinian conscript sentries, shivering in their positions, failed to detect them as they slipped ghostlike through the dark and quietly established an OP facing Mount Longdon before settling down to await the dawn.

'At first light all I could see around our position was shell dressings, bandages soaked in blood and spent cartridge cases. The stuff was everywhere. Something big had happened here and it had happened very recently. Longdon was about two kilometres away and I could see a smoking enemy chopper on the ground near there. To my front I had a panoramic view of Longdon, Two Sisters, Mount Tumbledown and Port Stanley itself in the distance. I started to report in by radio on the downed chopper and bloodied battlefield when the QM [quartermaster] cut in and told me to get off the air as he was awaiting a signal about a resupply of stores. I thought: You wanker. I want to tell HQ what I can see. The bloody stores can wait. That really pissed me off.

'I began to look down into Stanley and the bay with my scout telescope. This is a very high-powered piece of kit. There, right in Stanley Bay, is this ship smothered in red crosses, and it's unloading hundreds of Argie troops. They kept pouring out of it. This wasn't on. It was supposed to be a hospital ship, not a troop ship. Troop ships are legitimate targets and I'm excited and fuming. Every time I call in to report the fucking QM cuts in, moaning about his stores signals, and warns me off. I began calling for a Harrier strike to bomb the fucking thing, but the QM and the rest of the shiny-arsed officers didn't seem interested in anything I was reporting back. I'm still mad about it to this day.

'Next thing we saw was a patrol – I think it was Marines – coming under mortar bombardment from Mount Longdon. They were out in the open and I wanted to help, but I was helpless. I felt really sorry for them, but every time I wanted to call in a fire mission on Longdon to help them I kept getting butted off. I just said "fuck it" and didn't call them again for two days.

'We were later called back and given two days' rest. I talked to some of the other lads about what we had seen and I found out that the SAS had a major fire-fight on Estancia. It must have been some fight because all our rifle company patrols were reporting blood, bits of meat and bandages scattered all over the area. From the way things were scattered the SAS must have been up against at least seventy enemy. We spent the two days eating, sleeping and going over our kit. By this time the CO had started what he called CTRs, or close-target recces. One of our platoon sergeants, John Pettinger, had actually completed one and had found a way through enemy lines and established how to get up on to Longdon behind them. Now, from a soldiering point of view this was brilliant. Great news. He had got right up on top of Longdon, so close to them he was able to lie there next to their bunkers and sentries listening to them talking. He was so close he could have touched them.

'I stepped forward and asked the CO if I could go forward with one of these patrols and start harassing the enemy as a sniper to bring their morale down. I had been taught that if you sniped at them queuing for food or using the shit pit they would be really upset and stay in their holes. The CO gave the green light and we formed a team of four snipers: me, young Dickie Absolon, Bill Hayward and Kev Capon. But Kev's feet were in a mess. They were covered in blood and his boots were full of it. There was no way he could come.

'We set out to make contact with one of our forward OPs, which was going to act as a rear fire-base for us if we had to bug out in a hurry, and then we began to hear this humming noise. Next thing the world erupts around us. Argie Canberra bombers have come over at high level and dropped their lot all over the area. Jesus, a close one, but we were all OK. We tabbed on and got into position before first light, but instead of sniping we spent the time calling in artillery barrages on to Longdon. I was on the northern side and looking up into a bowl-like feature near the saddle of the mountain. I saw fifty or so Argies queuing for something – scoff, I think – and called up the artillery. I had a bit of trouble at first because I wasn't used to it and was bringing shells down all over the place. After half a dozen or so fire missions I got the knack of it and was calling down concentrated barrages on very small areas. We had the enemy running around all over the place. Once I had established a grid reference for them those artillery lads could go some. Jesus, could they perform. They seemed to be able to drop twelve rounds in a very small area, just like that.

'Through my telescope I spotted what I thought was a radar and I tried to get a round on top of that, but I think I failed. We moved back to our own lines under cover of darkness.

'Our next mission was three-pronged: we were to do a snipe, a close recce, and then try to snatch a prisoner and bring him back. He would be interrogated and we would have fresh, first-hand intelligence. With me were Dickie and Bill. Just as we were picking our way across some open ground on the approach to Longdon this great white horse comes trotting out of the dark towards us. It scared the shit out of me. Here we are trying to sneak up on the enemy and a white horse is trotting along beside us. Have you ever tried to tell a white horse to piss off while on a "sneaky beaky"? It's something different! Anyway, it eventually took the hint and pissed off and we carried on tabbing towards Longdon.

It was further than I expected, so I established an ERV [emergency rendezvous point] and moved out, with Bill covering our rear and Dickie in front. We carried on up the mountain and just as we approached a steep feature this Argie 120mm mortar starts firing. Boom. Boom. Boom. I could hear the rounds going down the tube. Now, we had gone much further than I realized. We were actually on top of them. Dickie was in front with a radio, I had a radio and Bill was fifty metres or so behind with another one, but he was dropping back. I was getting pissed off with him being so far behind and I turned to talk to Dickie and when I looked back I couldn't see Bill any more. Dickie and me carried on crawling upwards, very, very slowly and then stopped to set up our sniping weapons. I was looking through my nightsight for targets. I knew everything was zeroed because I was taking the heads off ducks and geese at 300 metres with it just before we set out.

'As I'm scanning round for targets I see this guy stood on the mountain 150 metres away. I couldn't resist it. He's a target – not a human being, just a target – and targets will fall when hit. I took up the first pressure on my trigger, and the green illuminator cross in my sight still had him standing there. I fired. He wasn't standing any more.

'Immediately a mortar began firing, but nothing came near us. Dickie and me looked at each other, nodded, and went to see if we could get the mortar position, take them out by the same method. We couldn't pick out anything with our scopes so we crawled further up towards the noise of their position. We crawled on and on and on and further in and in and in. I couldn't believe how close we were getting. We could hear them talking, chatting away, moving about. There was an opening in the rocks and we peeked in. There was everything in there: bunkers, sentries, heavy machine-guns, all sorts of things. A mist had come down by now and we were able to lie there, still undetected watching and listening. We were ten feet from the edge of this rock and there was a mortar on the other side and we could hear them reeling off numbers in Spanish.

'By this time I was on a real buzz. Now this was soldiering! We decided that there was no way we could take on such a large number by sniping, but we could take them out with grenades. I got a phos [phosphorus grenade] ready and Dickie produced an HE [high-explosive grenade] and we crept the ten feet to the rock. But, Jesus, it was one massive slab. We suddenly realized that if we tried to throw grenades over that they would roll back down on top of us. We could hear another mortar fifty metres further on so we decided that one would do and we would take it out with a "66" [66mm anti-tank rocket].

'I said to Dickie: "We'll blast the bastards, then piss off." I took his rifle while he unclipped and pulled the rocket casing into place. This is how you arm this particular weapon. Well, here we are sitting in the midst of the enemy in the dead of night, and the noise this fucker makes while arming. We look around but no one takes any notice. All we have to do now is go click, then there'll be a whoosh and a lovely big bang. But there is no click. Shit. It's still not armed. So Dickie repeats the arming procedure and, I tell you, I swear we felt everyone from Longdon to London could hear us. This time it did arm itself and Dickie fired it into this enemy position. Whoosh, bang – and I do mean bang – and we're up and running for our lives. We're going for the base of the hill. I look around and this bloody Argie is chasing us... stupid... this is war, not scrumping... we stop and kneel... he's still coming shouting his head off... we both whack Eve rounds into him... he's not there any more and we're up and running.

'By now things are starting to get hot. The world and his friends have opened up and the whole mountain erupts. It's going crazy with .50-cals, GPMGs on sustained fire, 81mm and 120mm mortars and even pistols. I wanted to stop and fire back, but Dickie grabbed me and told me to keep running. There was tracer and everything whipping round us. How we ever got out of there I'll never know, but we dived into the ERV and Bill called up the artillery to give the mountain a barrage so we could exit. Nothing happened so we legged it to the FRV [forward rendezvous point] and ten minutes later the barrage came in. What a brilliant barrage it was, around fifty shells exploding among the enemy. The gunners must have killed with that barrage.

'We got ourselves back and I handed in my report and crawled into my sleeping bag. My report stirred up a load of shit. The CO himself sent for me. Up until then all the reports spoke of small arms in the Argie defences, but there was no information about heavy weapons. Now I'm being questioned and grilled from all angles. I know what I saw and I know my weapons, I told them. I sat with the CO and marked the positions of everything I could remember. We made up a map of all the heavy kit I had seen firing.

'The CO believed me, I have no doubt about that, but some of the senior people thought I was bullshitting. Well, didn't they get a fucking big surprise when the battle started and even more .50-cals than I had seen started opening up... yeah.'

Santiago Gauto waited to see what the result of the night's shooting had been. 'The radar was always screaming and shots would follow. And then, of course, the British artillery would join in. We hated that thing, that radar. The superiors went off at first light for a look round to see what had made the radar scream. I saw them in a group, standing talking and pointing down below towards the River Murrell.

'A white horse lay there dead... with a thousand rounds in it.'

As the British stepped up their artillery harassment the Argentinian officers became daily more agitated. Their tenseness got through to the men and Alberto Carbone could smell war in the air. It was on the way, no doubt about that.

'You could feel it, feel it coming. Every night they told us the attack would come that night, but it didn't. We were still doing two hours on and two off. About 10 June I had just come off guard and crawled into my tent. My mate went out to his position. I wrapped myself in his blanket as I didn't have one of my own. I put my rifle inside the blanket with me... and bang, it went off. The barrel was pointing down towards my legs. The bullet went straight through my right calf. I didn't shoot myself deliberately – the thing just went off. The only thing I can think of is that the safety catch flicked off. I couldn't believe that I had shot myself. It was a stupid accident.

'It wasn't hurting, just throbbing. I could see blood on either side. An officer came over and put a tourniquet on my leg and then a group of lads carried me down off the hill to Stanley. At the hospital they tore my trousers away and cleaned the holes. They put a metal rod through to make sure there was nothing still in there and then they cut away the burned skin with a scalpel.

'They gave me an anaesthetic which killed the slight pain which was caused by the cold seeping in. Then they put me on a helicopter and flew me from Stanley to the hospital ship *Bahía Paraíso* in the bay. That's where I was when the battle started the next night.'

Felix Barreto still had his fabulous bunker – until 10 June.

'Then they ordered me to move position. I am still furious about it. I had to dismantle my machine-gun and take it over to the B Company positions and site it right in the farthest entrance of the bowl which runs along near the summit. For two months I had got to know every metre of the terrain of my old fire position and now I was being stuck out in an exposed position. I was madder than shit. Now I was setting up the gun facing north to north-east, facing the sea across from Stanley. Next thing they tell me is only to return fire at a distance of 900 metres. Nine hundred metres. What crap. I was really uneasy in this position. It was so exposed. I knew that the moment I opened fire they'd even see my position as far away as England.

'As the night of 11 June came I was overcome with hatred for the British. And I told myself that the worst thing that could happen to me would be to be taken prisoner. There was no way I was going to surrender, particularly after what our officers had told us about the treatment handed out by the English to our lads who had surrendered at Darwin and Goose Green. I was mad about it, mad about what we had been told the English had done to them. I hated them. I wasn't going to surrender to them, no way. There was no way in the world I was going to give them the chance to do to me what they had done to those poor guys: make them walk over all the ground to check if it had been mined. Would you do it? That's what they told us and I believed them.'

The grim realities of their situation began to eat into Antonio Belmonte. 'Eventually, as the bombardment increased, we realized the English had, in fact, not just landed, but were on their way. They had already taken Darwin, Goose Green, Mount William, Mount Kent and Estancia Mountain. We were slowly beginning to realize that the English were not just here to reclaim something they thought was theirs, they were coming to take back what belonged to them. By this time all my radio batteries had gone flat and I had no spares. That was all I needed. I knew that sooner or later the British would be on top of us, you could feel it in the air, the tension, it was all around. Night after night we had false alarms. Night after night we became more fed up with a wait that never seemed to end...

'Around 10 June they decided to move all our positions. They put 1, 2 and 3 Sections all in a line in the bowl area, facing north. Tumbledown was behind us and Wireless Ridge to our right. A and C Companies were positioned running along the mountain. So we started digging bunkers all over again. All day we slaved and that night I got into my shelter and slipped my boots off. I didn't like my new position: it felt precarious. We all faced north, all of us, and no one had seemed to be thinking about the west. The radar was manning that... '

For Tony Gregory the long, frustrating wait was over.

'Eventually Brigade and the rest of the hats got their act together and on 11 June we got our orders for the assault on Mount Longdon. A and B Companies were to attack, with C held back in reserve, then we would pass through them and secure Wireless Ridge. Simple. Rations were issued and we scoffed and brewed as much as we could because we were told it would probably be at least forty-eight hours before we got another meal. We began preparing our kit. Weapons were stripped, cleaned and oiled. Our webbing was firmly secured and then we jumped up and down wearing it to make sure there were no tell-tale noises like rattles. We even made sure there was nothing loose in our pockets which could make a noise. I checked every single bullet in the bands of link for my machine-gun for rust, mud and to make sure every one was in its proper place. The last thing I wanted was a jam or a misfire. Next I put on my cam cream nice and thick, then settled down to wait. Those three hours waiting for last light were a time for the lads of thinking of loved ones, and of home. I kept thinking: Will I be alive tomorrow? I didn't pray because I'm not religious.

'I also thought: If I'm going to go, then I'll go, but at least I'm going to die doing something I enjoy: being a Paratrooper. People would remember me as a Para who died in battle, I told myself. It sounds like a load of crap now, but at the time it gave me a lot of encouragement. I was totally prepared and that was one of the ways I readied myself for battle. I was completely tuned in to what I had to do.

'When we started the advance I passed my mate Pete Hedicker with one of the Milan crews. We wished each other luck. It was the last time I ever saw him. He died that night.

'We reached out company's start line at the base of Longdon. We were actually looking up at the western slope. B Company were formed up and ready in front of us. Paul and I put our GPMG on a secure position on a peat bank and began searching with our eyes for a good route up the mountain when our turn came. We whispered to each other identifying features and cover. We had our route ready. We were ready. There was about twenty minutes to go before I would see hell... '

The trickle of information about the advancing British forces became a flood. It began to panic some of the

Argentinian officers into a flurry of activity. As their orders to reposition the heavy weapons for a last stand around Port Stanley were translated into a frenzy, Germán Chamorro was caught up in it all.

'Mount Longdon became the next focus of our attention. We had orders to secure the heavy 120mm mortars on Longdon and all our artillery pieces were facing north-west towards the mountain. Observers went up the mountain and confidently predicted that the British could never attack us from any direction other than north because minefields had been laid to protect the other flank. Every night we would walk the four to five kilometres up to Longdon, humping 120mm mortar shells, and store them in protective pits. We had to pass through the lines of the 7th Regiment and the Marine Infantry, giving passwords all the way. It was hard work all night long. When we weren't doing that we were on sentry waiting for the English, waiting, waiting, knowing that sooner or later they were going to attack. By this time we had been moved back up the mountain. On 10 June I was lying in my position trying to catch up on some sleep when I was wakened at midday by screaming. I found three of my mates surrounding Corporal Alvárez, who was on the ground. I asked: "What the fuck is going on?" They said: "This motherfucker is a coward. He wants to leave us on our own and go into Stanley. He reckons he's got appendicitis."

'I told them to fetch Foresi, the doctor, and after a while he arrived at our position. He gave Alvárez a check-up, then said: "He's got fuck all. He just wants to go to Stanley. A coward." Ramé, one of my friends, heard the doctor say this. The corporal was still on the floor looking towards Stanley. Next thing we know Ramé walks towards him, puts the barrel of his rifle to his forehead and squeezes the trigger... Click!... nothing... the corporal's eyes went round and round, expecting death. I pushed the rifle away and the corporal ran away. The rifle was cocked and loaded, but it had misfired. Alvárez was lucky: his name wasn't on that bullet.

'On 11 June our forward observers – Lieutenant Tagle, Corporal Oliverio, Ramé and Bustos – were up in the crags on Longdon. I had a radio-telephone with an officer and some soldiers with the 120mm mortars on the southern slope. We had information that the English might attack tonight because it was a weekend. We were told they liked to attack at weekends because they were paid more money for weekends.'

Oscar Carrizo, too, was a victim of the confusion.

'Our anti-personnel radar was forever being messed about. We needed it. But one minute they would tell us to turn it on and the next to turn the bloody thing off. They didn't want the men to know the British were closing. It was the senior officers who were giving these orders. The night before the battle the sergeant in charge of the radar detected two men at between four and five hundred metres. He scanned further and picked up more men at 1500 metres and even more movement of men at 5000 metres.

'We called in our artillery and they fired at the Two Sisters hills. Then they fired at us. I couldn't believe it: our own artillery firing at us. I still had a deep foreboding about my position. I had had a sixth sense about it ever since I had been ordered to set it up. On 11 June, the eve of the battle, I had a big argument with Baldini about my mortar. He ordered me to test-fire it to prove I was wrong and he, the officer, was right, about its position. I fired two rounds and the English artillery zeroed straight on to me.

'That proved I was right. I was out in the open and the English were on to me. It should have been concealed in the bowl to my rear. 'At 18.00 hours that night we picked up a strong signal of men on the radar and reported it right away. They told us to turn it off until after midnight. At last light only five men knew about that strong signal. We had been told to keep our mouths shut. The position closed down for the night.'

Dominic Gray's chest filled with pride when he heard news that would turn most men's balls to blancmange: B Company's objective was Mount Longdon and they would be the first to go. Their Company Sergeant Major Johnny Weeks, a thoroughly professional and respected soldier, gave them a final pep talk in the way only he could. The lads liked their CSM and they knew the old stories about him. They knew that even though they had to call him 'sir' he wasn't much different from them. He'd knocked the shit out of many a craphat wherever he had the chance and wouldn't hesitate to do so again. Going into battle with a soldier like Johnny Weeks gave you confidence.

The soldiers returned to their trenches to write their last letters home, check their weapons and kit and have a brew and a scoff before putting on their cam cream and waiting for the 'green on'. There was an air of expectancy over the whole location. A sombre air, almost, as the men sat quietly, each man alone with his personal thoughts.

All the waiting was over and many were wondering who would still be alive tomorrow. Dom, too, was wondering and psyching himself up for the coming battle. Would he do OK? Would he let his mates down? Would he die? If he was to die, then he would die dressed like a Paratrooper. He rummaged in his bergen and pulled out a pair of damp OGs [olive-green cotton combat trousers favoured by Paratroopers over the camouflage trousers worn by most of the Army] and climbed into them. He had no intention of dying, but if he did at least he would look like an airborne soldier when they stuffed him into a body bag. Others watched, then followed his example.

'You'll find out soon enough,' he told himself as he checked his weapon and webbing for the last time and joined the others for the advance on Longdon as the night came down around them. They moved out, crossing a river where the soldiers of 9 Squadron had provided a ladder as a makeshift bridge to try to get them across without getting their feet wet. The aluminium ladder still had the Texas Homecare sticker plastered down the side. Some poor bastards fell off and got soaked, but despite the seriousness of it for them, Dom couldn't help but chuckle. He bumped into an old mate, Smudge from Patrol Company, on the other side and they wished each other luck. Then the night swallowed them up.

They walked quietly and purposefully to their start line at the bottom of the western slope. Dom's 5 Platoon was in the middle, 4 Platoon on the left and 6 Platoon on the right. As the minutes leading up to midnight ticked away Dom looked up at the mountain, trying to see what he could make out in the dark. He was ready, he was honoured, he was leading his battalion into battle.

As the foul weather and the frightening British artillery and naval bombardments sapped the morale of the young conscripts the rumour machine slipped into top gear. Santiago Gauto felt like an ant in the face of the Harrier jets screaming past on their way to their targets. What use was a rifle against such a thing?

'As the days of June passed, the stories about the English began. It was ironic they got double wages for fighting at weekends. Then we heard they would use crossbows and knives as well.

'On the morning of 11 June we had been desperately trying to get more ammo just in case the English came. We knew it was just a matter of time. You could smell battle coming in the air. That night I couldn't sleep, wondering if it would be my last night of life. That night we lay together in our holes, holding hands and praying, trying to give each other comfort and strength. I was scared and I am not ashamed to say it. I knew as darkness fell a battle was close. A sense of helplessness took over. We said to each other: "Why are we comforting each other? Nobody is going to save us."'

Part 3
Into Hell

1

THE MEN of B Company, 3 Para, all 120 of them, were lined out against a stretch of white mining tape which was their start line. Dom Gray was still quiet as he saw Sergeant Major Johnny Weeks come along the line. He was all sergeant major, from the scrim net on top of his helmet to the mud on the soles of his soaking-wet boots.

Dom knew the time was near. His heart was pounding, but it went into overdrive when he heard his sergeant major's words: 'OK, lads, fix bayonets.'

Fix bayonets! And they hadn't even taken a step yet. Jesus, this was going to be rough. Remember, Dom told himself, the weight of the bayonet makes the muzzle of the rifle drop, so when you're firing at a long target you could be shooting low. He slipped his bayonet from the scabbard on his belt and clicked it home. It was done as quietly as possible, not with the crash the Guards always managed when they were on public duties. But with 120 men all doing it at the same time it did make a noise.

Next came the order to advance. Dom's heart was

bursting, his mind in top gear, every sense in his body at its keenest. Deep down he talked to himself. 'Come on, you can do it. This is what we came for. Let's get it over with.'

He stepped across the start line and began climbing the dark mountain to close with the enemy, his rifle with its sharp, sinister bayonet extended in front of his small body, his finger on the trigger, his eyes everywhere, searching the darkness. The gas regulator on the rifle was set to a big fat zero. That meant malfunctions, such as stoppages, were unlikely. Dom had totally disregarded the standing instruction of only four magazines of ammunition per man. He had eight mags, each of twenty rounds, and a bandolier of 250 rounds wrapped across his chest. In the pockets of his Para smock lay eight HE grenades and two phosphorus grenades. On his back was a 66mm anti-tank rocket. On his belt was a Gurkha fighting knife, the dreaded kukri, with its razor-sharp, eighteen-inch curved blade.

'Just in case I run out of ammo,' he explained. 'It's a mean weapon.'

That was unlikely. In his webbing pouches he had stowed more rifle bullets still in their cardboard boxes. He had sacrificed his mess tins, spare socks and food to cram as much ammunition and water into his pouches.

Dom also knew that the military planners never told the soldiers on the ground the full story. He had spent much of his four years as a professional soldier devouring all the books on warfare he could get his hands on. He knew many of the lessons of history. They had been told they would be going up against about 150 enemy. Dom suspected there would be at least twice that number. Even he grossly underestimated! He was still 100 per cent prepared for the task ahead – even to die.

'My fear was not in going into battle or dying. A soldier

going into battle knows there are no more ifs and buts. It's the end of the line – the ultimate challenge. There's no point in whinging about it because that is why he is there. It's do or die, as simple as that. My fear was not of dying, but of mutilation. Losing an arm, a leg or my eyesight was what I dreaded. I had made up my mind that if I lost a part of my body I would top myself on the spot if I could.'

However, Dom had greater worries than mere survival.

'This may sound silly, but I hated puttees with a passion, those stupid fucking things we had to wrap around our ankles to support them because the crap DMS boots we had were too short. They were uncomfortable, embarrassing and old-fashioned, a shorter version of the ones the soldiers wore in the trenches in the First World War. I hated them then, I hate them now and I'll hate them for ever. Useless bloody things. They always soaked up water and you felt as if you had soggy wet rags wrapped round your ankles.'

His new lightweight helmet, replacing the old Second World War tin hats as worn by the Arnhem veterans, fitted perfectly, which was just as well because this would be the longest he would ever wear a helmet.

'It had a nice tight fit, like suction. Normally we only wore them for parachuting or small parts of exercises. We always preferred our red berets. That was our tradition. Chris Lovett, one of our medics, told me not to do up the chinstrap because if I got a head wound it would be difficult to remove it. He also said the impact of the bullet could break my neck. I suppose I looked like something out of the John Wayne movie *The Sands of Iwo Jima* with the straps hanging loose.'

They hadn't gone far when an explosion followed by a scream shattered the silence. Some poor bastard had stepped on a mine.

Jerry Phillips had already been up the mountain. Now he was at the foot of it again with the three section commanders – corporals – from 6 Platoon, B Company. He was there to point out the best ways for them to get up and to show them the enemy positions in their way. The corporals returned to their soldiers and briefed them. Jerry was to follow on behind, mopping up any enemy the sections left in their wake, then go forward as guide, pointing out more objectives. He was at the white tape waiting for the 'go' when the order to fix bayonets was given.

'Jesus, the fucking noise they made,' he still shudders. 'I told Lieutenant Shaw I could get his platoon further up the mountain and into a better position. We walked right up the western slope. We had actually bypassed the objective of one of the section commanders, Jock, in the dark. We were almost on the very top of the mountain, which was our main objective anyway. John Steggles's section was to get to the top and Jock's section dropped back a bit.

'Everyone says the battle started when someone stepped on a mine. As far as I'm concerned it started when John Steggles threw a grenade at some Argies.'

Oscar Carrizo was about to crawl into his bunker to sleep. He had just made sure the sentries had changed over when he heard voices.

'I stood and looked down towards the western slope. Then I heard a clank-click, then many clank-clicks. I knew that sound. It was bayonets being fixed. Panic surged through my body. I ran to the other bunkers to rouse the men. Many were sound asleep. "Get up, get up, the English are coming," I told them.

'Just then there was a loud bang followed by a scream. Men were scrambling out of their bunkers. Within seconds the whole place was alive with tracer bullets. They whizzed past my head and whacked into the rocks and the ground. Everyone was in a panic. I ran for cover and crawled into a bunker with a sergeant. It was impossible to fire my mortar now.

'Outside, the English were running past, screaming to each other and firing into tents and bunkers. I could hear my men being killed. They had only just woken up and now they were dying. I could hear muffled explosions followed by cries, helpless cries. I knew grenades were being thrown into bunkers in the follow-up. The sergeant and I discussed surrendering, but decided we'd wait until it was over. All we could do was wait. The English were all around us. They had arrived within seconds, like lightning. I prayed and prayed a grenade wouldn't come into our bunker. The sheer mental pressure exhausted me. I hated it.'

Kevin Connery had gone about 200 metres up the mountain when the mine exploded. In his hands was a GPMG in the light role. This meant he could fire it from the hip in instant reaction to any target or lie down behind it with the barrel resting on a bipod. Around his shoulders and across his chest were 1000 rounds of linked ammunition for the hungry weapon. He had a further 200 rounds in one of those silly little bandoliers which all machine-gunners were convinced had been designed to make it harder to withdraw the ammunition in a hurry.

In his smock pocket were four HE grenades and one 'Willie Peter' (white-phosphorus grenade). His whole body seemed to be weighed down with ammunition and his webbing fitted him like a glove. His only complaint, shared with most of the others, was about the bloody awful boots.

He looked around, then up at the mountain, and finally up at the brilliant southern sky. The stars appeared to be rocketing down at him.

'It was tracer, one-on-one tracer, and it was zipping round us like nothing I had ever seen or experienced before. I dived behind a rock for cover and a .50-cal opened up. When the bullets started hitting the other side of the rock it just seemed to begin disintegrating. It was being chopped into pebbles. I was hugging the ground, getting as close into it as I could. Then it switched direction. Then I could hear some of our lads storming it. That was a relief.'

He drew a few deep breaths, tightened his grip on his machine-gun, and looked around. He looked back at the gun and thought hard. What the hell was going on, what the hell was he doing here lying behind this shattered rock? He was now in his fourth different job since setting off for the Falklands. He had sailed as a number two on the Wombat anti-tank gun, but these had been left behind because the bosses could see no role for them in the mountains. Next he was a sustained-fire machine-gunner before switching to the role of lead scout on patrols. Then someone changed their mind again and here he was with a light machine-gun on a sling round his neck.

'Being on the Wombat or in the SF machine-gun role were not bad jobs, just being back that little bit from the nitty-gritty of hand-to-hand combat. Now I was right in the middle of it. Someone up above was obviously determined I would be in at the sharp end. That's my luck, always. Anyway, I would soon find out whether I was a coward or not.

'I can't tell you how fucking shocked and surprised I was when we were at the base of Longdon waiting for the order to advance and they told us to get into an extended line. I couldn't help thinking some bastard was on drugs and that they had turned back the clock and we should be lined out in red tunics. And when I heard "Fix bayonets" that was it. I knew we were in a lunatic asylum.'

Gerntán Chamorro was cold, hungry and very, very nervous. His imagination was running riot as he sat with a sergeant on that cold, dark night.

'There was something in the air, an eerie, cold silence. I was nervous, scared, shit-scared even. We were very near the front and we had heard all sorts of stories about what the English and the Gurkhas would do to us if we were caught. Even the officers appeared to be nervous. They kept telling us: "Watch out with the English. They are very silent, they can pass through the lines without being seen, then knife you." That was all we needed. We were static in a defence line. It was all getting on my nerves. I was getting to the stage of saying to myself: "Fuck it, I don't care any more, let them come once and for all and then it's over. I'll either be dead or alive."

'Suddenly we heard screaming, piercing screams in the night. The noise made my hair stand up. That scream! It was about midnight. Then all hell broke loose: shots, flares, more screams, chaos. Everything was coming from B Company's area in the bowl. In those same few seconds my landline telephone began clanging. We scrambled to our fire positions round the mortar. "Fire mission! Fire mission!" the voice screamed at us.

'I couldn't fire because my mortar was facing the wrong way. The British were attacking from the very flank the military geniuses had told us they wouldn't come from. We wasted valuable time getting the mortar resited.'

Santiago Gauto, too, was tasting fear.

'It is a subject some people are reluctant to discuss, something they confuse with adrenalin. The two are different. I know. It was cold, very cold, and the darkness on the ground was pitch-black. Yet above us, high above us, the stars were an outstanding sight. They were clear, crystal-clear. I must have been staring up at the stars again when everything erupted.

'I heard a scream, a piercing scream. I think it came at the same time as I heard a mine go off. Everyone grabbed their weapons. My eyes were as big as saucers as I stared into the dark, trying to see where the screaming was coming from.

'Then we opened fire. Everyone, all of us, desperate shooting into the dark. We couldn't see anything. We were shooting at nothing, but we were shooting. Tracer bullets started coming back at us, the air was thick with them, they were everywhere, whacking into the ground all around us.

'It is hard to describe that first moment under fire other than to say that fear was overtaken by sheer terror.'

Felix Barreto was huddled in a bunker with three other soldiers from B Company, sharing a cigarette and trying to get warm, when he heard the scream. Their eyes widened as they stared into the total darkness.

'I knew something wasn't right. I was disoriented because I had just moved to a new position and had spent the day trying to improve it to get me out of the weather. I got my boots on and grabbed my rifle and spare ammunition and we crawled into the dark. I crawled fifty metres or so in the direction of some voices... They were weird voices, not normal at all. I got closer and closer to where I thought the noise had been coming from. At first I thought it was some Cordobezes – lads from another province who had been brought up as reinforcements and who were always joking and larking about.

'It wasn't. It was the British. The slope erupted. I fired two or three rounds in their direction, then ran back to the hole where we had been sharing that cigarette. I saw a corporal in the hole and told him: "*Loco, los ingleses están aquí*" ["The English are here, you nutcase"] and he told me to fuck off.

We got out of the hole again and it was like going into hell...
rifle fire poured into us.'

Morale was low as Luis Leccese awaited the battle he knew
had to come. Reinforcements had arrived to work on the
accursed radar and the general atmosphere of anticipation
only heightened his anxiety. He was cold and miserable,
having spent the entire day labouring in the unforgiving
Falklands weather. As night fell he moved to a bunker
overlooking a path that ran down towards the north-west
side of the mountain. His abandoned tent lay empty in the
middle of the bowl.

The nightly artillery barrage had relented after they turned
the radar off and a little relief flowed through Luis's tense
body. He began to wonder if tonight would now be a night
like all the others, where the British didn't attack after all. He
began to relax a little and lay down in the bunker. Then he
heard those bloody voices again, the ones he had heard
before but never mentioned. Another soldier was beside him
and Luis sensed that he, too, had heard something.

'I strained my ears to try to hear better. I wanted to know
if they were real. Then we heard screaming, then screaming
and shouting. It appeared to be coming from the bowl
which was behind and to our left. Next thing all hell broke
loose around us. It was like a movie in slow motion,
grenades exploding, machine-guns bursting into rapid fire,
rifle fire blasting away. But it was the screaming which
chilled me. I knew then they had come.'

Antonio Belmonte was in his bunker trying to get warm. His
rifle with its twenty-round magazine was close at hand. He
had given his pistol away the day before to a soldier who
had injured his hand and found it difficult to handle a rifle
because of the injury.

Then he heard the cry of alarm: *'Ingleses... ingleses...'*

'I grabbed my rifle and got out of the position. Lieutenant Nairotti came out, too. When he saw the British storming into the bowl he dashed for the command post, but he was hit and went down. I think he was hit in the leg. He was dragged away and this left us in 3 Section without a commander. We had been expecting a full-frontal assault from the north, but the British didn't come that way.

'Lieutenant Baldini's section, 1 Section, had been destroyed on the spot. The soldiers on guard were killed where they stood. The others were killed as they slept. Many had taken to sleeping in tents because the bunkers were waterlogged and the British simply raked them with machine-gun and rifle fire as they moved through. The section was wiped out, totally destroyed. Many never knew what happened as they were shot while they slept. Within minutes I could see the soldiers who had attacked from the west forming a circle round us. Our only defended position was to my right. My location was under intense fire. Bullets were raining in all over us. I could see some of them coming towards me like little red stars. They seemed to be landing around me with no strength in them, as if they were throwing stones, But I knew if I stuck my hand out I would lose it.

'Our password that night was *"llanura verde"* ["green plateau"]. But the British attacked so swiftly our sentries never had a chance to ask for it. We were in trouble, big trouble, and I didn't know if I was going to live or die. There were bullets, screaming and death all around, but I suddenly realized I wasn't afraid. Strange, isn't it? I don't think that at that stage I valued my life at all. I had to be there and that was it. I could see British and Argentinian soldiers falling dead and wounded in front of me, just thirty metres away. It was that close. The British were walking about shooting or dashing from rock to rock, calling to each other.

'They seemed incredibly brave, very professional, very cool. Bang-bang, move, bang-bang, move. They were talking, but I couldn't understand. Sometimes they were talking to each other and at others to us, insults maybe or warnings that we should surrender or they would kill us. They had come storming in full of hype, bravery and determination. They were going for it in a big way.

'I could hear the horrible sounds of the wounded crying for help, English mainly. I think at that time most of our lads who were hit had been killed outright. Perhaps that is why I could hear the English voices more plainly. Bullets were whacking into the rocks around me and thudding into the earth. One hit a rock beside me and a splinter smashed into my head above my left eye. I could feel blood running down my head and face and my eye begin to swell.

'Flares were lighting up the area. They made it so clear. You could see a pin on the ground. All around was chaos, absolute chaos. I threw a small hand flare, but it landed only a metre from my position. That was suicidal, lighting up my position like that. I didn't throw another one!'

As Jerry Phillips surveyed the mayhem all around him his frustration grew.

'The rifle company lads were going in, going for it and coming under fire and we guides were being held back. I calmed down a bit and told myself we would be needed soon enough. Then the Argies began opening fire from our rear, from the area we had come through. We were in the bowl and it was absolute bloody murder. There were bodies everywhere, many of them screaming in pain.

'There was screaming and shouting coming from every direction. Jock's section had all but been wiped out within five minutes. The wounded were lying out in the open. Bullets were hitting rocks and spinning off in all directions. Someone went back to sort out the bastards shooting at us from behind and I went to try to help the wounded. Trev Wilson, from 6 Platoon, was trying to sort out morphine for them.

'Four of us got to one of our lads who had been hit. He was still conscious. We picked him up, each one of us grabbing a limb. Their snipers were zeroing in on us very quickly. I suppose it was a suicide mission, but you can't leave your own guys lying there. We were running up a bank towards our own positions with him when a burst of fire hit him. His hips and body just flew up in the air. The bullets missed us, but he died. We tried everything to revive him.

'By now it was bedlam. Their snipers were blasting into us. They had killed about six of our guys. I say they, but there could have been only one at that stage. I didn't know. Lieutenant Shaw told me to try to take them out. I really felt like telling him to fuck off because of the position – a reverse slope – he wanted me to engage them from. It really would have left me in a bad position, stuck out like a dog's bollocks. Steve Wright was my partner for that night. Every sniper has a partner and tonight was Steve's turn. It was agreed I would link up with Steve and go for it. I started calling out and shouting for Steve. Then I found him crawling about. He had been hit in the arm by a bloody sniper. The adjutant was out there, crawling around trying to help the wounded. He was giving out shell dressings and bullets were whacking all over the place around him. They had very good nightsights and it was very hard to move without being shot at.

'I got Steve and helped him down to the FAP [first aid post] and left him with the medics and started off back up the hill. I spent the next couple of hours going up and down the mountain, helping with the wounded, getting them back, making sure they were all right. I knew my chance to have a go at the snipers would come round soon enough.'

Jorge Altieri froze with fear. His heart was pounding. He could hear it. He was lying under a collapsed tent absolutely rigid and barely daring to breathe. The slightest sound, the merest movement, would bring brutal, instant death. Two British Paratroopers were standing on the tent unaware that Jorge and his bunker mate, Sánchez, were there. Only yards away their friends were dying from rifle, grenade and bayonet wounds as they lay there swaddled against the cold in almost every stitch of clothing they possessed. But the cold was as nothing compared with the chill terror eating at them now.

'I could hear them talking to each other. I could hear their radio. I could even see the outline of their boots through the fabric of the tent. We had just been about to get out of the tent to go on sentry duty when we heard a bang, like a grenade or a distant English bombardment. We had balaclavas, ear flaps from our caps and our jacket hoods up, so the sound was muffled. Then we heard voices, strange voices, English voices. We thought perhaps the wind was playing tricks again. Then we heard the screaming, piercing screams, awful screams, and we knew it was no trick. The English soldiers were talking to each other calmly. They appeared to be chatting to each other. I couldn't understand how they hadn't realized we were there. We were right beneath them. Maybe they thought the tent was empty because it was collapsed. Sánchez and I knew the slightest movement or sound would have them on us with their bayonets. We heard more Englishmen nearby and these two were calling to them. We could hear our friends dying.

'I heard Quintana's voice. His position was close and he was shouting something. The English opened fire: bang, bang, and Quintana went down. They were right above us. Then Corporal Orozco went down. It was horrible. The frustration of it was awful. I heard Orozco screaming: "Lieutenant Baldini... Lieutenant Baldini... " then a shuffling noise, some shuffling, and he never spoke again.'

A feeling of uneasiness began to swell in the pit of Dom's stomach as he prowled up the mountain. The jagged features of the terrain meant his platoon was being forced in small groups on to the well-worn pathways which the Argentinians had been using. And any soldier worthy of the name knew that these tracks would lead straight to enemy concentrations and killing grounds covered by vicious machine-guns. Yet there was really nothing else they could do but note the danger and be prepared to act when it presented itself. They were operating a buddy-buddy system: each man had a partner and they covered each other.

Dom had teamed up with Ben. He could see in the gloom the outlines of three or four tents, US Army-style two-man pup tents very similar to the ones he had seen in his dad's military collection. It was quiet and still.

'We all stood there looking at them and at each other. No one knew what to do. It was as if we were still in a Northern Ireland situation "Don't fire unless you're fired on first." I remember saying to myself: "Well, someone's got to start this fucking war."

'So I zapped half a dozen rounds into them. I don't know if anyone was in them, but I clearly heard the bullets whacking and thunking into the tents and the ground. My platoon sergeant, John Ross, looked at me and we both realized in that split second that there was no going back now. It all happened so quickly, so naturally: bang... bang... bang...

'Some of the other lads looked at me as if I was mad. They didn't look for long because all hell was let loose as the Argies opened up on us from all angles.

'Within seconds I was battling with an Argie. Hand-to-hand stuff. I rifle-butted him to the ground, then sat on him. He was resigned to his fate either as a prisoner or execution. I shouted for someone to take him down to our company HQ. I remember hearing an NCO shouting something like "Don't take prisoners" or "Forget about prisoners", but it was too late. This guy was no threat to anybody now and there was no reason to kill him. He was dragged off to the rear, but he wasn't very happy about it because he had to duck and dive through the bullets. Ungrateful bastard. At least he was still alive.'

Prisoners were always going to be a problem. They simply didn't have the men to leave behind to guard them. Their orders were to move on, to keep up the momentum. But what would happen if prisoners rearmed themselves and rejoined the battle at their backs? Luckily for Dom the problem didn't arise. In this sort of close-quarter hand-to-hand fighting there was no dividing line. It was simply kill or be killed. If you didn't react instantly and get in first you died.

In the bedlam they had to duck as green tracer from a .50-cal machine-gun searched the darkness for them. They spotted it above them and Dom and Ben decided to storm the position and its occupants. They crawled under its arc of fire towards the bunker. Very slowly and carefully, they got to the bottom of the bunker. It was only twenty metres away and they could hear the Argentinians shouting excitedly. They decided to 'frag' the position: take it out with grenades. Dom carefully set aside his rifle, pulled some grenades from his pocket and he and Ben started to pull out the pins. They wouldn't budge. The ends of the cotter-type pins which have to be withdrawn to arm the grenades had splayed apart. Some fucker had forgotten to crimp them for easy withdrawal. Jesus, this never happened in war films. They began to argue about what to do next as they struggled frantically with the pins.

'Have you got any pliers?'

'No, haven't you?'

Dom was sure the enemy knew he was close. Eventually they stood on the grenades, managed to free two pins and lobbed two grenades in among the machine-gunners and grabbed their rifles again. As soon as they heard the two explosions they scrambled up and over into the position. Their impetus carried them into the stunned and frightened enemy with their bayonets. The machine-gunners who had been trying to wipe out 5 Platoon a moment or so before were no longer a threat.

It was the only way. Everything around was bedlam and confusion. On the landing-craft he had warned himself that things could turn ratshit. In the confusion of battle the soldiers automatically paired up together and carried on fighting. It was nasty, hard fighting as 5 Platoon doggedly, methodically, wiped out their enemy. Dom and Ben stayed together, clearing bunker after bunker with grenade and bayonet, killing clinically, unfeelingly, killing to stay alive.

Each position seemed to have three or four enemy in it. They all died.

This was their first experience of this type of warfare. Nothing they had ever done before remotely resembled what they were doing now.

'Three Argies were shooting down at us from behind a defensive wall and shouting at each other at the same time. Ben and I decided to go for it again together. I felt as if we were doing it in slow motion. The adrenalin was pumping so fast I felt I was floating between life and death. My brain was telling me very rapidly to "Go, go, go" and at the same time I knew in the pit of my stomach I could be dead in the next few seconds. As we ran towards the position everything was registering in my mind as if it was a computer. We were out in the open, completely exposed yet our feet never missed a step, moving in perfect harmony to the ledge leading to the position.

'The Argies fell back in total surprise as I appeared over the wall. I was aware of my finger squeezing the trigger, but the bangs from my rifle seemed like far-away sounds. I was so hyped up nothing in the world could have stopped me. My eyes were staring into one of the Argies' eyes as he screamed "No! No! No!" He knew he was about to die. The whites of his eyes were quite clear to me, showing fear and the certain knowledge he was going to be killed. My bayonet plunged into him with an almost obscene ease.

'Killing in battle seemed easy, but the overwhelming memory was the smell. It was overpowering, so overpowering I could taste it. It was so strong I had to breathe through my mouth to rid myself of it. It was like rotten onions, damp and smelly clothing, human shit and blood all mixed together in one big bag. Add that to the smell of fear and the stench of body sweat coming from your enemy in his last seconds of life and it is nauseating.

'The power surging within me was taking over. I was keen to get on, to take out more positions, to kill more enemy, to carry on without even taking cover. Ben and I stalked the place in search of prey. I think some of the Argies thought we were Gurkhas because we were so short. A lot of Paras are small, but most people think in terms of the six-foot Americans that they see in the movies. We weren't six-foot movie stars. We were real fighting Paratroopers.'

They stopped for breath and Dom could see 6 Platoon reach the right side of the summit to be met by a maelstrom of tracer fire. He heard screams from their position and knew that over there all wasn't well.

Luis Leccese crawled out of his bunker and lay flat on the cold, damp ground. He was clutching that same rifle he last fired a year before on the training ranges. He could see soldiers, silhouettes, coming up the path towards him. [This was 5 Platoon, 3 Para.] He lay still and watched as they darted from rock to rock. He could hear other English voices calling to each other from the direction of the bowl behind. The machine-gun and rifle fire and grenade blasts swept over him. Nearby a silhouetted soldier fired.

'I saw him because the muzzle flash gave him away. I was sure he was firing at one of our .50-cal positions. I was above him and he hadn't seen me. I lay there undetected. No bullets were coming towards me, so I knew I hadn't been seen. I aimed at him and fired two or three bullets and he stopped firing. I know I hit him, but I don't know if I killed him or wounded him. I'll never know. But he did stop shooting.

'I moved over a bit and my partner came to join me. He had a machine-gun. Some figures were moving towards us and he took aim at them. He squeezed the trigger, but only one round was fired instead of a burst. The gun packed up. He looked at me as if to say "What do I do now?" and I told him to carry on. I told him just to fire as much as he could. He re-cocked the weapon and tried again. Another single shot. We couldn't believe it. No bursts – just a single shot every time he re-cocked it.

'We were a few metres from our bunker so I told him we should move back to it, but he wouldn't come. Then I said we should go up to the bowl to see what we could do there. He looked at me again and said: "No. No way, not there, there's a real mess in there. We'll get blown to fuck."

'We were in a dangerously open spot and really had to

move. The bowl – with the eruption of fighting and screaming – would be a suicidal place to be. So we crawled back up on our hands and knees to another position in the rocks with a small path below. There was one guy there on his own in this cave-like recess in the rock, watching the battle raging around him. We could have stayed there unseen, but we got into fire positions and started firing down on the British as they came into view. This time they spotted us and started blasting back. The return fire was horrendous.'

Enemy fire rained down on the advancing Paras of B Company like a hail of death. Kevin Connery darted from cover to cover, moving relentlessly onwards. As he breasted a knoll he could just make out a huddle of two or three Argentinian tents neatly pegged out.

'I was pointing my GPMG towards them when I heard a voice, out of all the bedlam and screaming, shout: "Clear those fucking tents quickly, will you."

'I let a long burst go into each of them. The tents were shaking under the impact of the bullets. As I fired I was half registering the screams from inside the tents. Screams of sheer terror as my actions killed them. Inside, in those two or three seconds, they knew they were about to die. All around me guys were being killed. I felt nothing – only the sensation of movement from my trigger finger caused by the vibration of the gun. It was as if it wasn't me killing them. I felt nothing. No personal feeling existed.'

He hosed each one before slipping back into the cover of some rocks. Behind him was a small rockface and he looked towards the skyline. He could make out the crouched, dashing figures of 6 Platoon moving across the western slope. Then, silhouetted perfectly against the skyline, a figure appeared twenty-five metres in front of him. 'Halt!' he yelled.

The man roared back at him in Spanish. It was the last

sound he ever made. Kevin fired a three-round burst into his chest, killing him before he ever touched the ground. He had hardly fallen when another took his place. Kevin challenged him, too, and gave him time to respond, then opened fire again. The man went down. As Kevin watched in amazement the man rose to his feet again. This time both he and Johnny opened fire. And again the man got up, this time to his knees. Johnny threw a grenade, which hit the man and bounced nearby.

'It was all happening in slow motion. Then the Argie actually crawled towards the grenade. Just as I thought he was about to throw it back it exploded, killing him. I began to think that if the rest of them fought like that we would be in for a very long night.'

He got ready to move forward again, when a missile exploded in the rocks behind him, bowling him over and enveloping him in a sheet of flame. Incredibly he survived it and managed to crawl to another position. The blast had illuminated their position long enough for Sergeant John Ross to locate them. He was trying to pull the platoon back together into some sort of formation. They moved out and got into another fire position at the summit.

As Kevin looked around he saw Sergeant Ian McKay and a section of men storm a bunker with rifles and grenades.

'Everyone seemed to go down like ninepins, the Argentinian arcs of fire were covering the bowl very professionally.'

(Sergeant McKay was killed taking out that bunker. For his gallantry he was posthumously decorated with Britain's highest award, the Victoria Cross. Killed with him was Private Jason Burt, just seventeen and one of two seventeen-year-olds killed in that battle. The other was Private Ian Scrivens. Another youngster, Private Neil Grose, turned eighteen as the battle began.)

Kevin now teamed up with Dickie Absolon. The young sniper fired single tracer rounds from his rifle at targets he could see through his nightsight, then Kevin followed the tracer with bursts from his machine-gun. It was a desperate measure which had to be taken to dampen the blistering Argentinian machine-gun fire. They poured about 3000 rounds into the stubborn enemy, but their muzzle flashes were soon located and resulted in their coming under desperate return fire. They moved and shot, moved and shot, until Kevin's machine-gun packed up. No matter what he did it resolutely refused to fire.

'It had decided it didn't want to play any more. I got in behind a boulder which gave me some protection from incoming rounds. My feet were aching in the useless DMS boots. I could see an Argentinian bunker, so I crawled into it. Straight away I found a pair of Argie boots and they were near enough my size. I cut my boot laces and discarded the worst piece of British Army equipment I ever had. My OGs were ripped to shreds. I must have looked like a tramp. Amazingly I found a pair of Argie denims lying amongst the abandoned kit in the bunker. I squeezed into them. With my new trousers and new boots I felt much more comfortable. I threw away the useless puttees as well. The boots were perfect. They had a sewn-in tongue and were high-leg combat boots.

'I felt my way around in the darkness, seeking more spoils. I found an Argie FN rifle, much to my delight. I worked the cocking handle and checked over the working parts. Perfect. I set the gas regulator to zero then found eight fully loaded magazines. As I got out I clipped on a magazine, cocked the weapon and fitted the bayonet. I felt like a new man with my new boots, trousers and weapon as I rejoined the chaos and bedlam around me.'

Kevin moved back to the main body of what was left of 5

Platoon, who were now regrouping and moving out again on a path leading to the bowl. Dickie went off in search of more targets. It was the last time Kevin ever saw him.

'I saw another Argentinian position. I could see a head pop up and then down again. In a couple of seconds I made my mind up to take him out. I found myself running in long strides towards him. I was in another world. It was as if it wasn't me. The only way I can describe it is to say that I had departed from myself completely in thoughts and actions, if that makes sense. The Argie was completely taken aback with shock as I leapt into his position. He was cornered... he didn't have time to point his rifle at me... his eyes had a look of complete resignation mingled with shock... it was all happening in slow motion.

'He screamed in English: "I like the pop group Queen... I want to see my grandmother... I want my grandmother... " It must have been the only English he knew. He was screaming it as my bayonet struck him in the throat and chest. I stabbed two, three times... I was in a rage, doing my job, knowing that if I didn't kill him it would be me dead. I was reacting to my military training to kill. I was fighting for my own life and that is one of the basic instincts of mankind: survival. Kill or be killed. The Argentinian slumped back dead.

'All around there was killing and death. There was the acrid smell of battle and the awful smell of death. I was getting closer and closer to it. I was awash with adrenalin, floating, not the same guy at all. All the training was taking over, it was becoming instinctive. The smell of battle and death was being absorbed into my body. My sense of smell was thick with sweat, blood and human shit, the odour of dirty clothes, damp kit and stink and mould. I was so hyped up I was alert to the slightest sound, the merest flicker of something. The smell was becoming a taste. I could taste death now, I could taste it around me. It was as if my body was aware it was near to death. I was resigned to fate.

'The lads were organizing themselves into small fighting groups. I found myself lying next to Lieutenant Mark Cox. He was the son of a Parachute Regiment officer. Just across the bowl from us was an enemy position which looked quite strong. We thought there must be about four or five enemy in it. We looked at each other and agreed to take it out. Some of the lads withdrew a bit to cover us and I got out a 66mm anti-tank rocket. I blasted the position with it, then Lieutenant Cox and I threw some grenades into it. As soon as the explosions went off we leapt in and thrust our bayonets into the enemy, firing quick double-tap rounds into them. All were dead. It had taken only seconds. We had done it quickly.

'We were about to consolidate the position when enemy fire started coming in round us. It whacked around our feet and buzzed past our heads. We decided to conduct a fighting withdrawal. We didn't even talk about it – we just did it automatically, naturally. We were headed back to our original position on the other side of the bowl. I would cover Mark Cox and then he would cover me. We were in the open and they should have killed us. I'll never know how they didn't get us. But that was when I became convinced I wouldn't die. I didn't seem to be worried any more. I honestly began to feel I had some sort of spiritual guide helping me. It's weird, really, the amount of confidence I felt inside. It was so powerful.

'It was a case of listen, look, shoot, move, keep moving and shooting and get the objective. That was all that mattered: keeping going until the mountain was captured. Prisoners were not high on our list of priorities. At all times the objective was our priority. We weren't even sure if there was a system for dealing with prisoners. All we knew was we had to keep the momentum going. Anything looking like an enemy shooting was killed. It wasn't personal – just our job. We had to capture that mountain.'

Luis Leccese and his mates were learning the hard way just how dangerous it is to shoot at British soldiers. They had stirred up a hornets' nest.

'We couldn't even put our heads up to see where they were. When we shot down at them we had thought our fire pretty accurate, but their return fire... their bullets thudded and pinged all round us. Then they stopped. Perhaps they were waiting for us to show so they could nail us more accurately. Maybe they thought they had killed us. We waited. Nothing. We waited. Again nothing. We popped up and fired and again all hell broke loose on to our position. I don't know how long it went on. It seemed like years. We couldn't see them. We decided not to fire again. We lay there for about half an hour, I think. It quietened down. Maybe they would now look elsewhere. We looked out. Nothing. We crept out. Nothing. We watched and waited. The fighting seemed to have died down a little. We didn't know if our forces had repulsed the English attack or if they had won. The fighting in the bowl appeared to have died down. Some artillery was landing. There were still some rifle shots and shouting, but the shouting was much more controlled now.

'What to do next? It was still dark. We decided to head towards the bowl. That was our command area. We crawled and slithered through some rocks and stopped to listen. I heard some English voices. I looked over the top and saw some of our guys in a line like prisoners. There were a couple of British and one of them had one of our rifles and he was pulling and tugging at the cocking handle and moaning. He threw the weapon to the ground. We could have shot them there and then. I began to wonder: perhaps the British had taken Longdon and were collecting prisoners. We decided to lie up quietly where we were. I was certainly afraid of being taken prisoner at night in battle. You never knew what your enemy's intentions were if you appeared in front of him. We moved back a little bit into the rocks to a better hiding place.

'We crawled slowly and very carefully. No sooner had we stopped in what we thought was good cover than some British soldiers came right up to us. They stopped right on top of us. I broke out in a sweat. One soldier was talking into his radio. I was lying there, just a metre away. I couldn't move, hardly breathe, the slightest movement, the slightest noise, would have meant death for sure. Still they didn't see us. They moved on into some crags. Oh, the relief.'

2

THE SUDDENNESS and ferocity of B Company's assault on Mount Longdon caused chaos in the Argentinian ranks. Felix Barreto heard a sergeant shout: 'Hold your fire, you're killing yourselves.' The position of 1 Section had been overrun and 2 and 3 Sections were firing on each other as they turned to face the oncoming Paras. Felix heard a scream, a terrible scream.

'It was Corporal Orozco. He was found later with a bayonet in his stomach. I had heard him die. It wasn't very pleasant. I went up to the command post and started fighting. Major Carrizo [no relation of Corporal Oscar Carrizo] was there and gave me a nightsight. Bullets were pouring into our position. I could see the British darting about and firing at us. I began spotting targets and relaying the position to a soldier called Cáceres and a corporal and they would fire at them. The British had a machine-gun nearby and every time we fired it opened up on us. I couldn't spot its position. Some shells started landing; I don't know if they were mortars or artillery, but I just nailed myself to the ground. I didn't want to be killed by shellfire. There had to be better ways to die.

'Cáceres then stood up. Crazy. Four or five shells landed within fifty metres and I heard him groan. Aaaah. Just like that. He fell beside me, covering his face with his hands. I grabbed him and dragged him across to me. He was covered in blood. He was not a nice sight. His eyes had popped out. I had to leave him there as he was. There was nothing I could do. I never saw him again.

'The British fire was becoming more and more accurate. They were obviously desperate to get us because we were holding them up. About an hour or so had passed when Major Carrizo tied something white to a stick, like a flag, and began considering a surrender. Now he was no coward, but I think what was uppermost in his mind was preserving his soldiers' lives and the lives of those who had been captured. He was also in a very difficult position because it was nearly impossible to organize a counter-attack to try to drive the British back.

'We had all got it into our heads that we would be killed anyway if we surrendered. We told him that for this reason we were not pre pared to give up. He lowered his flag and we carried on fighting.'

Tony Gregory was at the start line as the battle erupted into a firework display from hell. He could hear the crack of rifle fire, the tell-tale double-tap of soldiers going about their business, see the red and green tracer criss-crossing the night sky and see and hear the explosions of grenades. He wanted to be up there, supporting the lads of B Company. The yells of command and the screams of the wounded drifted back to him. His frustration grew. At last they were told to move, then just as suddenly to go back again. His temper was fraying. He should be up on that hill helping, not sitting down here doing nothing.

Then out of the dark a sniper started firing at them. He took cover behind a bank in a line of moaning, frustrated soldiers. They took up firing positions in the slim hope that the sniper would do something to betray his position. Out of the darkness came the indistinct shapes of men. Friend or foe? Each man picked out a target and aimed his weapon. Tony flicked off his safety-catch and prepared to fire. A shout rang out: 'Hold your fire, it's friendly forces.' Tony breathed out and watched the men come closer.

'It was B Company coming back down a bit to reorganize. They had taken a lot of casualties up there. We hoped we could go back up with them, filling the gaps left by the casualties they had taken. They dived in among us. Some were distraught. They were in a different world. We asked how it was up there and they just muttered. Sergeant Major Weeks gathered his lads together and off they went up the hill again under a hail of bullets. I really felt for them. I'll never forget the sight of them disappearing into that battle again.

'We stayed put, dodging snipers who were able to pick us out with their nightsights. Then they called in artillery to keep us pinned down and to stop us joining the battle. We ended up digging into a peat bank with bullets whizzing round us and into the ground above our heads. We stayed like that until first light.'

Sergeant Major Weeks gathered the remains of 5 Platoon around him. He knew how to talk to young soldiers, how to inspire them, how to lead them. He was one of the old school, a senior NCO who had come up the hard way and revelled in it. Their company commander, he told them, was being hassled because their advance had been slowed by the dogged defence fire of the Argentinians in their bunkers. They needed to get to the other side of the bowl to create a diversion and deal with the defenders there.

Dom and Ben volunteered to go. It was only fifty metres, but the longest fifty metres Dom ever went. Snipers and every rifleman in the area seemed to open up on them as they dashed – under covering fire from their comrades' machine-guns – to the shelter of a jumble of rocks. They made their way upwards again and once more were way out front, alone and virtually unsupported.

They got so close to an enemy mortar position they could clearly hear the soldiers talking to each other. The Argentinians were reeling off numbers, obviously target locations, so they decided to take them out. Dom and Ben began discussing the best way to do it, when the ground around them erupted as British artillery and mortar fire began raining down all around them. They were so far forward they were in danger of being vaporized by their own side.

'We legged it and dived into a crater. It was an Argentinian shit pit. I was covered in the stuff. The stink was overpowering, but we couldn't move out again because of the shelling.'

During lulls in the shelling Dom yelled to his comrades that they were pulling out, but was told to stay put as help was on the way. Shortly afterwards the FOO [forward observation officer], Captain Willie McCracken, and his party arrived to spot targets for the British artillery gunners.

'They just piled into the crater full of shit beside us. They were all covered in it. You had to laugh.'

Dom's laughter was brief. Captain McCracken's party included radio operators whose long aerials drew enemy sniper fire on to them. One aerial was sliced in two by a sniper's bullet. The signallers and the artillery spotters were stirring the mess in the crater so much the stench was becoming even more unbearable. As soon as Dom heard Captain McCracken call in the British artillery fire missions he and Ben decided to make a break for their own lines.

But as Dom stood up a sniper's bullet cracked between his legs. He began to run. A British machine-gunner spotted a sniper shooting at the pair and opened up on him. As they ran they were passing through a hail of both British and Argentinian fire. They dived into cover beside the rest of their platoon as shells from the British artillery and Royal Navy ships crashed into the area they had just crossed.

Within seconds of the last British shell exploding his mates were trying to kick him away from them because of the smell.

Major Carrizo was buoyed by his men's refusal to contemplate surrender. He began organizing a counter-attack. Felix Barreto was one of the twenty volunteers who joined him in a jumble of rocks to hear his plan, then set out from the bowl to the crags to try to recapture one of their overrun .50-cal machine-gun positions.

'Once this had been achieved we would try to free some of our lads taken prisoner by the British. We were greatly concerned for them and had to help them somehow. It was rough getting to the crags. The British machine-gun fire was good and they seemed to be able to land their artillery right where it mattered.

'Two British appeared out of the rocks and began firing at us. Two of our guys were mortally wounded immediately. I tried to dive for cover. The guy next to me was hit. He grabbed hold of me as he fell. Really tight. I couldn't move, couldn't get him off and I was still being shot at. I fell over with him, but I couldn't relax his grip. He was dead, I'm sure of that. He fell on top of me and he wasn't breathing. I could smell the faeces from him. It was horrible. He had mortar bombs on his back, which made him heavy, and it was a struggle to get him off.

'The British had halted our counter-attack there and then. I was seeing death all around me. A shell landed right in my friend Araujo's hole. He was a good mate, but he died right away. There were wounded everywhere. A bomb – it could have been a grenade – exploded in a sergeant's face.

'We regrouped back at our positions and tried to decide what to do about rescuing our prisoners. With all the mayhem we didn't know if there were any or if they were still alive. We were still wondering when we found out some had managed to escape. Corporal Pedemonte threw himself into our position. He had escaped. He was worn out, bleeding from shrapnel wounds, and had lost his boots. He said it was impossible to rescue the prisoners. We started shooting at the English again when we could see them. I don't know how long we had been fighting at this stage – easily more than four hours, maybe even longer.

'From time to time I watched two of our lads who had been running about all over the place with an 81mm mortar. I was worried about them because they were always moving about in the open. A burst of about five shells landed all around them. They disappeared. I began shouting and shouting to them. They just popped up again, grabbed their mortar and carried on. Cool as you like.'

Santiago Gauto was less than 100 metres from his command post, but had no idea how the battle was going. He was surrounded and running low on ammunition.

'We were firing like mad, but as the ammo started getting low we had to revert to a more controlled rate of fire. Tracer rounds from the British were whacking all around us. I had visions of them storming all over the top of us. There was a poncho roof on our trench and I began to wonder if we would still be lying here, out of ammunition, when the British came to rip off the roof and bayonet and shoot us without a chance of surrender.

'One of the guys began to cry and that made it worse. The air was filled by shouting and screaming and the noise of grenade explosions and rifle fire. We decided to hold our fire for a time to try to conserve what little ammunition we had left. The British stopped by us, then moved on in a different direction. We lay there hidden, watching, waiting...

Jerry Phillips had laid down his deadly accurate sniper rifle and his webbing and was trying to comfort the wounded. They needed help and reassurance. He knew that shock was one of the biggest killers of wounded men on the battlefield. A little tender loving care calmed them down and helped them survive. Jerry Phillips, the man whose job was to strike from the dark in a sudden snuffing out of life, was doing his damnedest to save it.

The wounded had been gathered in a dip on a slope, which gave them some cover. Suddenly it was all lit up as a screaming enemy soldier burned to death.

'The Argie had taken the full force of a phosphorus grenade and was on fire. He was stumbling about screaming. He was stumbling about all over the place. Next thing another Argie appears, running to get away from him. I was underneath them. The one who's running suddenly appears to be in mid-air and then he lands right on top of me.

'Now I'm in some sort of shit. He's on top of me, I've no weapon or webbing, and all our wounded are lying there helpless. I grabbed hold of him and started punching him. There's at least a dozen wounded lying there watching and I'm shouting at them to pass me my rifle. I knew I had to kill him. I didn't want to kill him by hand but no one was in a position to help me. I kept on punching. Then he says in broken English: "I surrender."

'Bingo! That was it. I had a plan. I dragged him over to where someone had another prisoner. I told my prisoner I wanted the sniper to stop and surrender. It was a long shot, but one worth trying as we had so many wounded lying out in the open and every time lads went to help they were being shot.

'My prisoner explained my plan to the other one. Well, this guy just nodded and walked off up the slope into the battle. No tactics, nothing, just as if he was walking down the street to go shopping. He was shouting as he went. We sat there with our mouths open. The sniping seemed to ease off a little. I still had a grip of my prisoner, but I don't for sure know what happened to the other one. We didn't see him again.

'But he obviously hadn't persuaded the sniper to give up. The man was good. He was holding everything up. We couldn't illuminate his position so we could take him out. I told my prisoner: "Take me to your friends." I meant him to take me near the sniper. He nodded and stood up. Great, I'm thinking, I can either get him as a prisoner or pinpoint his position and deal with him. Oh, no! My man trots off down the slope away from the main battle area. I was shocked. I'm thinking, what the fuck's this guy on, when he stops and starts talking to holes in the ground. Then the hole started talking back to him. A couple of the rifle company lads stood with me, watching my prisoner talking to the ground and getting answers.

'We got to one side and watched. Our prisoner moved and sat among some rocks. I don't know what happened next other than all hell breaking loose. We moved in on one hole and cleared it with grenades. The next one we cleared with our bayonets. These positions were behind us. The situation wasn't good. There could be a whole platoon of enemy lying up behind us and only the three of us to deal with them. Earlier I had asked for assistance and wasn't given it. Our prisoner shouted that if the rest of them didn't come out we'd do them with grenades. Our next target was a sangar. We were just about to take it when a guy appeared, then another, then another... then three more. Six in one position. We collected another ten. My hair was standing on end. Three of us with sixteen prisoners. If they decided to go for it we were brown bread. I decided to march them back to our HQ area near the FAP as soon as possible to get rid of them. They knew we meant business at the bunkers, but they could get brave again and that would be that for us.

'I saw a group of our officers near the FAP and asked them to take the prisoners off my hands as I had to get back up to the summit. They looked at me as if I was stupid. They didn't want to know. The impression they gave was that they were too busy to think about prisoners and didn't give a fuck for them anyway. So what was I supposed to do: shoot them? I've got a bolt-action rifle with ten rounds for sniping, so how the fucking hell am I supposed to dispatch sixteen guys? Line them up one in front of the other and say: "Hang on a minute while I reload"?

'I stood there. There was no way I was going to shoot them. Fuck that. But it was as if I was meant to. I could be wrong about that, with all the chaos and confusion, but there was no way in the world I was going to top them. Eventually I moved them to one side and searched them. I got some help. I will always remember one thing: all of them had knives, mostly six-inch Bowie knives.

'We left them there and the three of us and our prisoner went back off up the mountain. I knew he would still be of great help. We told him we wanted him to do the same again and he led us to the southern slope, which, so far, had escaped the battle. He took us into thick rocks. Lots and lots of cover. We came to a huge rock and got him to shout round the corner to his comrades to surrender. No one answered. I had a sixth sense. So did he. We felt they were waiting round the corner for us to show ourselves. We could feel an eerie presence there. It was a stalemate. I know that if we had shown ourselves round that corner they would have had us all. It wasn't worth getting into a huge fire-fight so far from our own lines. I took the decision to bug out and we withdrew. It was the right thing to do at that particular moment. Anyway, it would soon be daylight and their position would be exposed to the Marines on Two Sisters.

'It was time to see how the battle was progressing. We moved back towards the summit to see if our Argie could get more of his mates to surrender, but everything seemed under control there. This left us with our prisoner and the problem of what to do with him. One of the lads knelt him down and put a pistol to the back of his head, ready to eliminate him. The Argie was in total acceptance of his fate. He just looked up at us as if to say: "Do your worst." It was as if it was the most natural thing to do, a well-rehearsed act. Death was all around us. You could smell it.

'The rifle company guy looked to me to give the order to shoot. I could see it all happening in my mind. The one thing I will remember for the rest of my life is the power of the word "No"! It was the strongest word I have ever spoken in my life. The Argie was stood up. He was smiling, a big grin. We told him to get off to the POW area. Off he went, skipping, waving his hands. He never said anything, nor did we. All of us knew it was right to let him live. He was running now, down the hill. I remember saying to myself: "Good luck, you bastard, you owe me!"

'I saw the soldier who knelt him down a couple of years ago and we chatted about that incident. He told me: "I'm glad it ended up like it did. I'm married with kids myself, now. At least I can live with myself."

'I feel good about it, too. It's at times like that when you can look back and realize you're not a bad person.'

The phone in Germán Chamorro's mortar pit rang non-stop with fire missions as Argentinian commanders desperately tried to stem the British advance.

'Every time our forward observers saw a group of two or three English they gave fire orders for time mortars instead of instantaneous. The *preparador* would change the fuse with tweezers and that meant the bomb would explode in the air instead of on impact with the ground. When the bomb explodes in the air the shrapnel sweeps a wider area, hitting more enemy soldiers.

'From my position I could see shadows running about, both Argentinian and British. The rifle and machine-gun fire was mad. It was always followed by screams. It was incredible watching our machine-guns and the British machine-guns firing tracer at each other.

'The British artillery started firing on to us and we tried to return the fire. Then the British Navy guns started a bombardment. One shell landed twenty metres from us. Our observers kept ringing. They kept telling us we had to get the British machine-guns on the summit. They were doing untold damage to our battle control. Again and again we tried to get them. Again and again they kept on firing.'

Denzil Connick knew this would be different, a world away from the actions he had fought in Northern Ireland: He had seen the battle erupt, watched the angry tracer hissing and floating through the night sky, then ricochet off rocks and men's bodies. Denzil could hear the awful screams of wounded and frightened men. He was advancing now, his legs like lead, fear gnawing at him as he realized those screams could be coming from his friends in the rifle companies. In the next few hours some of his friends would be dead, never to join him again in a sing-song and a good piss-up. Denzil realized that he, too, could be dead before long. It wasn't a thought that made this normally philosophical soldier want to jump for joy.

His ears were tuned to a fine pitch as he listened to the radio traffic waiting for his call-sign and the ensuing demand for either mortar, machine-gun or anti-tank support for the lads of the rifle companies. His Sterling sub-machine-gun, an ugly little black weapon, was in his hand, the working parts still forward. He didn't want to cock it, then stumble and have it go off blasting thirty-odd rounds up the arse of someone in front. It would only be useful close to and when the time came to use it he would be fighting for his life.

They were heading for a position from which they could view the battle and give more support to B Company as they fell upon the Argentinian defenders in their bunkers. The fire support team consisted of two other radio operators, Lance-Corporal Cripps, an expert from the Royal Signals, 'Errol' Flynn, and their company commander Major Peter Dennison and Company Sergeant Major Thor Caithness. As they reached their prearranged rendezvous they realized that B Company had swept on further than anticipated, so they headed off for the summit.

Dread began to well up in Denzil Connick for the soldiers of B Company, outnumbered and outgunned, but still fighting like tigers. On his left were 5 Platoon and on his right 6 Platoon, shooting, shouting, fighting and, in some cases, falling. Sergeant Graham Colbeck, the man in charge of the Milan missiles and the British Army's top Milan expert, was on the radio screaming for permission to open up.

Permission denied. The sergeant major had other priorities, trying to direct the machine-gunners on to the deadly snipers he was spotting with a nightsight. But the machine-gunners were up shit creek because they began to pack up, one by one, until only Vince Bramley's weapon was still firing.

Sergeant Colbeck was still giving everyone with a radio headset grief when a great whizz, then BANG! set his ears ringing. Denzil was groggy from the impact. Everyone was dazed. Then he heard the calls for a medic.

This was definitely different from everything before...

Jorge Altieri was still lying deathly still under the collapsed tent.

'I don't know how long we were there. A minute, an hour – it was a lifetime. They moved off, but we didn't know how far or in what direction. In our immediate area it was quiet. Perhaps we would be lucky. Perhaps we would survive. We slowly crawled out and looked all around us. In the bowl it was bad. A mass of tracer was flying all over the place. We could hear screaming and the shouted orders of the advancing English. I saw them on a path. Then I saw a grenade explode near one of our .50-cals and the British took the position. They began advancing again...

'Near us it was quiet. We heard voices again, our ones this time. It was Guerra and Pedraza and they were calling names. About six or seven were left and we got into a group. They told us: "The British have really fucked up Lieutenant Baldini's position. They've fucked up everything. They have prisoners, too."

'I said we should see if we could attack them, but the others said the British had overrun all the positions in the bowl. Our first line of defence had been smashed. Some guys were still holding out up in the crags, but we didn't know what to do. We would try to withdraw somehow. We found Quintana. He was still alive although very badly wounded. The guys told him to take it easy and they'd return for him, but he died.

'We were all whispering in case we were heard. We didn't even like being together as a group in case the English machine-gunners saw us. We were afraid a machine-gun could get us all in one burst. We began to cover each other and went towards some rocks near the bowl. That was when I lost sight of Sanchez and Pedraza. We had a machine-gun and our rifles. We moved slowly over the summit, crawling across the flat top ridge and then down the south side. We found some telegraph poles and crawled down the valley. Mount Tumbledown was behind us. We set up the machine-gun and watched the British.

'I could see them silhouetted against the sky. An artillery sergeant crawled in beside us. He had a nightsight, infragreen. I could see the English more clearly now and our guys and them shooting at each other. Bullets were going in every direction. We were on the British flank and when they came close enough we engaged them with rifles, the machine-gun and grenades. I had just fired off my third magazine of twenty rounds, hitting the English flank, when they pinpointed us. Next thing a shell landed right among us. I remember falling or rolling to my side. I got up, holding my head. My helmet was still on, but I knew everything wasn't right. I knew I was dazed and stumbling about and then I collapsed. The sergeant was dead: he had taken the main force of the blast. Another guy was screaming with a leg wound. I was lying on the ground groaning. Everything was very weird. Someone said: "You're wounded, Jorge, take it easy, we'll get you to the village." I don't know what happened after that... I passed out.'

Jerry Phillips had given the troublesome snipers every chance to surrender. Now it was 'game on' as he stalked the mountain again. He had seen the results of their handiwork back at the first aid post and it was time to give them a taste of their own medicine. The vicious .50-cal machine-gunners also needed to be neutralized.

'I fired 100 rounds at targets over a two-hour period. My shooting was accurate. If something moved and I fired it didn't move again. I don't know if I killed and I don't want to know. But the shooting from those positions stopped. At the end of it there were two particular snipers I was after: They were diehards just like us.

'One of them had an infrared beam coming from his scope. We shot him and his beam suddenly pointed upwards towards the sky. That's how it stayed: a small red beam pointing upwards and doing no more damage to us. The other one I never got.

'By now the sustained-fire machine-guns were in position, so I slithered back to 6 Platoon's first aid post. There were more casualties.'

Dom and Ben still stank to high heaven as 5 Platoon regrouped yet again. The 'Nine Mile Snipers' of the Royal Artillery were pounding the Argentinian defenders mercilessly and every time they eased off 3 Para's machine-gunners hosed them. They may be hats, thought Dom, but thank Christ they're our hats and on our side. Not the sort of guys to fall foul of if you're anywhere within range of their 105mm howitzers.

The mood was sombre because dead and wounded comrades were lying beside them. As usual Johnny Weeks was up front with them, talking, giving orders, explaining. Bullets were cracking past his head, but the sergeant major chose not to notice.

'This geezer is something else,' Dom muttered to himself. 'He just doesn't give a fuck. He's all balls.'

The commanding officer and B Company's OC had arrived on the scene to get a clearer picture of the difficulties facing the men. They moved out again, Lieutenant Cox in the lead, followed by his radio operator Steve Phillips and then the rest of the platoon. Again they were on a path and heading upwards, back towards the bowl. Despite the artillery bombardment and the machine-guns, the area was still deadly, Dom warned anyone who would listen. Within minutes Cox was confronted by two Argentinians, who stepped out in front of him firing as they came. He dived aside, yelling a warning as the bullets blazed towards his platoon.

Dom hit the ground, thinking Cox and Phillips had been hit. 'Shit,' he said to himself. Frank Reagan and Lennie Carver were down. So, too, was Johnny Crow. Dom crawled to Johnny's side, but he was dead. Frank and Lennie were wounded, but the rest of them were OK. From the rear came orders to press on. Those behind would care for the wounded. Dom, Ben, Kev Connery and Skiddy and a couple of others formed up and began moving again. They reached the entrance to the bowl. Dom's finger had taken up the second pressure on his trigger. He was ready. He quickly poked his head round the corner for a glance and saw a large enemy bunker. Strange, he thought: he couldn't see or hear anything from it. Every time they had come across a bunker before all hell had been let loose. Something wasn't quite right. The Argies must be keeping their heads down, waiting.

It was decided they would take as few chances as possible. First they would zap the position with 66mm rockets. Three rockets were fired and all three failed to explode.

'Maybe the warheads killed them without exploding,' Dom told himself reassuringly.

It was the false dawn, that confusing period of time when things are still indistinct and don't quite look what they are. Santiago Gauto was moving, crawling, making himself as small as possible. He didn't want those machine-guns chattering in his direction again. He was one of a group of half a dozen Argentinians strung out near the bowl, determined to get off this accursed mountain. With them was 'Grandad', a soldier of only twenty-five but old compared with the teenage conscripts.

'He didn't want to know. He just wanted to go home. To be honest, so did the rest of us, but we were in a battle. We knew things were bad and we were losing ground. We were near the entrance to the bowl and almost out of ammunition. I found a rifle lying there and an automatic pistol. I picked them up and flicked the firing mechanism of the rifle to automatic. The only way out for us, the only way to safety, was to run across the bowl, over the summit and down into the valley below.

'It was eerie. The battle had died down and it was almost as if there was nobody around. You could hear the silence, then you could hear eerie voices whispering in the dark almost as if they were miles away. They weren't. Your instincts told you eyes were nearby, watching, waiting for the slightest movement. In between the voices was the silence again, a dreadful silence. We couldn't stay here. We had to move. We had to get out of this place.

'I decided I would give my comrades covering fire as they ran across the bowl one by one. I fired a couple of quick bursts and then it was my turn. The others had made it. I saw their helmets disappear over a rise. I just hoped they would be there to give me covering fire. Just as I was about to run for my life tracer rounds began to hit around me. Zuss-ck... zuss-ck... zuss-ck... In the middle of this I had the stupidest thought of my entire life: I told myself these little bits of light can't kill me. Impossible. I could touch them and be unharmed. The thought didn't last long as the other bullets being fired with the tracer started banging off the rocks beside me. These ones would harm me all right. No mistake about that. I dived into cover by two rocks at the very entrance of the bowl.

'I couldn't stay here. How was I going to get out to join the others? Suddenly English soldiers appeared right in front of me. Instinctively I fired a burst at them. They were no distance from me, only metres. Two of them went down. One seemed to be hit in the chest, the other in the middle. I ran immediately, and kept on running up the rise and on towards the valley.

'I had made it. I began to head towards Moody Brook. Shells began to fall on Longdon now. I could hear them exploding up there behind me. Now others were suffering up there on that terrible place where I had suffered.'

Kevin Connery was heading into the bowl. With him were Dom and Ben. A couple of other soldiers appeared out of the gloom and joined them as they stormed in, firing as they went, to keep the Argentinians' heads down.

Kevin spotted another bunker. He approached it with great caution.

'An Argie leaped out with a pistol. I couldn't believe it. I was face to face with him and when I pulled the trigger my rifle just clicked. I had forgotten to change magazines. Shit. I punched him in the face and we both fell to the ground fighting. It was like a pub fight. If he had been quicker he would have got me. I was lying across him holding his gun hand and punching him. There was shooting going on. Out of the corner of my eye I could see the other lads diving for cover. I saw one of our lads hit. This spurred me on.

'We were punching and gouging and kicking each other.

There was a bandage. I grabbed it and managed to wrap it round his neck. I began to strangle him. It was becoming a personal killing and I didn't like it. I didn't want to kill him like that, but if I didn't he would do me. I could smell his breath, his sweat, his clothing. His tongue swelled up and his eyes stared into me. He gave one last struggle, a grunt and then died. I could see he had died from his eyes. I didn't like it.'

Kevin looked over to where he had last seen his comrades. Dom was lying there, to one side of the entrance of the bowl. He knew immediately that it was little Dom he had seen being hit.

As soon as they disposed of the bunker, fire erupted all around them. Dom knew he would have to get to cover. As he dashed across the soggy ground he could see Kevin fighting with an Argie on the ground.

Then he felt as if he was being lifted off his feet. He felt himself being thrown over a bunker, then falling... falling down a hill. He hit the ground with a bump and sat for a time gathering his thoughts.

His head was swirling. Ben had fallen, too. There was something wrong with Dom's head. He began to ease off his helmet.

Ben watched. Dom could tell from his face something had happened. Ben looked incredulously at Dom's head, then his helmet and then his head again. A bullet had hit the side of Dom's helmet, run across his skull and smashed its way back out again through the other side of the helmet. Dom's mind had been racing all the way through the battle; now it appeared to be going in slow motion. Suddenly he realized he had been shot – shot in the head. With the realization came the confirmation: blood poured down his face and neck. He stood up and put his helmet back on.

'Well, I'm not dead, then,' he told himself. 'How can I be wounded? I can't be. It's only a scrape. Fuck it. Let's go.'

He set off to join the others. The adrenalin was pumping again. Everything was OK. He was a soldier, for fuck's sake. And so was Johnny Weeks. The sergeant major overruled his protests and sent him off to the first aid post. Dom snarled and headed for the rear area.

'The first aid post area looked like something straight out of hell. There were wounded Paras and Argies lying all over the place. The moaning and groaning, their suffering, was something I will never forget. There were prisoners sitting staring at me. I stared straight back at them.

'Chris Lovett, the man who had told me not to do up my chinstrap, dressed my wounds. I reckon he was right. I think my neck would have been broken if I had done up the strap. Chris was a good medic. Shortly after seeing to me he was killed trying to save some other wounded.'

Dom had done his bit. And in the face of B Company's onslaught, the accuracy of the artillery and naval gunfire, and the backup of Support Company, the Argentinians were beginning to withdraw. A Company had joined the fray from a different direction and were pushing home their attacks with the same deadly determination as B Company further along the summit.

Kevin felt a surge of relief as he watched Dom's rapidly disappearing back. At least he's alive and not too badly wounded, he told himself. It was about time for a breather.

Orders came to dig in and get some overhead cover. As if to reinforce the orders a 155mm shell exploded behind Kevin and Skiddy, picking them up and throwing them about ten feet from where they had been standing. They landed side by side.

Kevin could feel a red-hot sensation all over him: his face, his clothes, his whole body was tingling and burning hot. His ears were ringing. He shouted to Skiddy, who then started screaming with shock.

'I got to Skiddy. My hands were drenched in sweat. It was difficult looking for Skiddy's wound. Eventually I found a hole in his smock. I put my finger in it and it went right on through all his layers of clothing. I felt a lump of shrapnel in his back. I ripped his clothes to get a better look at the wound and he started complaining: he didn't want his smock ruined. I got a shell dressing and applied it to the wound and Skiddy was OK. I got him to his feet and he was sent off for treatment. It was only later we found out he had been hit in the leg as well.

'I was now the only one left of my gun team. Johnny had been killed and now Skiddy was wounded. I began to feel a little lost until more artillery came in and more of our guys were hit. I was treating Corporal Stewart McLaughlin, who had been fighting like a hero all night. He was saying "My time is up", but he was OK. He would survive this wound. We put him with another guy to go to the FAP. On the way back he was killed by another shell. It was as if he had a sixth sense about it all.

'It was getting light by now. I saw two Argies lying to one side of me. They had been riddled with bullets. Suddenly one started moving and waving his hands. I couldn't believe he was still alive. A few of us started treating him, but next thing he let out a gasp and fell back dead. He really did try, but death just beat him. Poor bugger.'

The Argentinian artillery began to pound the Paras. Shells were coming in thick and fast as Kevin awaited fresh orders. Then he was hit. Shrapnel hit him on the leg, numbing it. He looked and could see the shrapnel. He picked it up and burnt his fingers. It was his only injury of the entire night.

Sergeant Colbeck was still champing at the bit, desperate to join in, to blast the enemy bunkers with his deadly Milan missiles. Sergeant Major Caithness was determined he would wait until he had found the Milan crews proper targets. Piggy in the middle during these exchanges was Denzil, relaying the irate sergeant's requests to the cool sergeant major and repeating the latter's refusals. Jesus, who'd want to be a Lance-Corporal radio op sandwiched between these two?

Caithness, using his nightsight, gradually talked the machine gunners on to the positions he wanted. Then he rapped out his orders to Denzil: 'Milan – stand by. Fire!'

As Denzil relayed the order he could feel the relief in Colbeck. The missile flew down the line of tracer and smack into its target. Bingo! From beyond the mountain Argentinian artillery opened up again and another shell came close. Major Dennison was convinced that the enemy were desperate to knock out Bramley's machine-gun and Sergeant Colbeck's Milan teams.

Denzil was just amazed none of them had been killed yet. He had no sooner thought about it than the air around the position evaporated in a deafening explosion. Cries of 'Medic! Medic!' could be heard through the ringing in their ears.

In that instant Dennison's fears were confirmed. Privates Pete Hedicker and Phillip West lay dead on the ground. Their commander on the Milan, Corporal Keith McCarthy, was mortally wounded. Other members of the company were wounded by the shrapnel.

The fire support teams were now finding it increasingly difficult to back up the advancing riflemen of A and B Companies as they fell upon the remaining bunkers. The danger was that they would be firing too close to their own troops. As dawn broke they watched and waited. Argentinian resistance was crumbling.

Jerry Phillips was back up the mountain yet again. All night he had been climbing it then returning with the wounded. Now he was at the entrance to the bowl gazing in, the bunkers and the features blacker than the night which concealed him.

'It was eerie. I felt as if eyes were watching me. I sensed something and turned and saw about 150 guys in formation. I dropped to one knee, rifle at the ready, and shouted, "Halt!" They marched right past me without so much as a blink. It was A Company and no one had told me they were even in the area. They were moving through our lines to assault the far end of Longdon. I knelt there absolutely still with my mouth open as they passed. They were so intent on where they were going, so psyched up for battle, they never even noticed me.

'I decided "bollocks to it" and went back down to the FAP and had a brew-up with some of the lads from 9 Squadron. I was knackered and decided to rest until first light then go up and try to get that troublesome sniper again. When I went back up the battle for that area was over and some of the lads said his position had been overrun. They thought he had been taken out. Bollocks, I wanted him.'

Major Carrizo had decided to rescue as many of his men as possible then conduct a fighting withdrawal. Felix Barreto was one of the riflemen providing covering fire in that hell-hole of a bowl.

'I could see some of our soldiers crawling back under our covering fire into relative safety. They would be safe from close-quarter battle, but the machine-gun and artillery fire from the English was becoming more and more accurate. Lizcarra and I were the last to pull out, threading our way through the rocks while British artillery landed all around. We were going to head for Stanley. The guys we had got out were from 2 and 3 Sections. We knew 1 Section had borne the brunt of the attack and that Lieutenant Baldini and Corporals Carrizo, Diaz and Rios were inside the English-held positions.

'Lizcarra then started going mad. He was shouting: "*Vengan Inglish. Vengan Inglish.*" ["Come on, English."] Then he was laughing and laughing and laughing all the time. Next thing this captain stops me and says I have to go back. I had no ammunition. So he trots off to get me some and as soon as he is out of sight I rejoin Major Carrizo. Artillery was coming in all over the place. As far as I was concerned the British had taken the mountain.'

Germán Chamorro had a mixed sense of relief when his supply of bombs for his mortar ran out.

'You see, our troops were so close to the English our bombs were falling on them. They were fighting hand to hand and we were trying to support them, but it was impossible at times. By the time we ran out of ammunition the position was unsustainable. I had been firing all night and all night the English were firing at us. I had hit the floor so often I was aching all over. Incredibly none of us was killed or wounded. My head was empty of everything, even fear. I had a gut feeling we had lost the battle.

'The soldiers of the 7th Regiment were withdrawing, taking their chances running, walking, even crawling away. They were in confusion, with no direct orders to guide them, and as far as I could see no officers or NCOs to control things. There was fuck all from above. It was the soldiers who took the decisions to keep on fighting. I heard that some soldiers shot their officers because they thought they were cowards. Others shot them for different reasons, but I didn't see any of this. It was just stories going round.

'The British soldiers were all over the place and there were smells in the air, gunpowder, blood and death, smells that never leave you, but smells you cannot describe to anyone who has not been in battle. It was time for us to pull out, to crawl away. Yes, I crawled. The shells, tracer, bullets and all the rest of the English bombardment made you crawl. During each lull we got up and ran, but soon came the clatter of machine-gun fire and we dived down again. Once I dived in someone's crap and had to crawl through it.

'All around me soldiers were withdrawing along the summit, guys I didn't know. Explosions followed us. I could hear guys scream as they were hit. All around I could hear guys shouting in pain things like: "My leg, I can't feel it" or "They've blown my arm off." The hardest part was not being able to help. The enemy fire was so intense guys who went to help were hit themselves. I could see the shapes of soldiers falling. It hurt, it hurt deep inside, the frustration, the helplessness of seeing your own people go down, dead or wounded, and not being able to do anything to help them. I'll never know who those guys were, but that doesn't make it any easier.

'The withdrawal took us about two hours, two hours of ducking, diving and crawling into different types of cover. I reached my original artillery position just as it was getting light. Ramé and Bustos, my mates from the forward observation team, arrived as well. Ramé had the English shooting at him all night long. As he withdrew a shell exploded right next to him, covering him in rocks and earth, but he survived unscathed. Bustos said: "There's a lot of bodies up there, an awful lot of people have been killed."

'I had seen bodies myself, but I neither touched nor counted them. No sooner had we got to Moody Brook than some guys were boasting about how many they had killed. Others were sad, saying their mates had died. Others were looking for friends. Many had carried wounded mates all the way back rather than leave them to the English. We didn't talk to any officers: we just talked among ourselves. Some of our officers began organizing a counter-attack. Ramé and Bustos were detailed to go back to set up another OP for the artillery. The 7th Regiment guys began pinpointing positions. As daylight strengthened we launched a heavy and concentrated barrage on to the bunkers which had once been ours and the ones the English would now be using for cover.'

A cloak of depression brought on by deep frustration had settled on the men of C Company. B Company had fought and A Company were now fighting. Their sister battalion, 2 Para, had arrived in reserve. Tony Gregory and others began to feel as if they were going to be mere spectators. But as daylight arrived they were ordered to advance at last, to clear the western and southern slopes.

'We got to the top in extended line, the weirdest sight you can imagine. We all walked bowed over in a half crouch, making ourselves as small a target as possible. We could hear rifle shots up the far end where A Company were operating, but around us it was quiet. Our area was really quiet, deserted, except for the bodies of the dead. The bodies didn't shock me because I was expecting to see bodies. It seemed natural to see bodies. We moved from the southern slope to the top and then on to the western slope to clear more bunkers. We had just begun on the western slope when the Argies started bombarding us with their artillery so we had to withdraw again.

'We were all very sombre, the frustrations of not being involved, of spending the night under sniper and artillery fire, were getting to us. Rumours were flying about. We knew B Company had a hard time. I knew we had casualties, but the reality of seven teen dead was a shocker.

All the normal joking and slagging off was gone. We felt for the lads of B Company and we felt sad and shocked at the loss of so many good men, so many good friends.

'As the shelling went on another rumour spread that a counter attack was on the way. They said the Argies were trying to mount a heli-borne attack. That boosted morale and brought us right back to a state of full alert. We waited and waited, but it never materialized. Our expectations and our nerves were going up and down like yo-yos. One minute we were going to get action and the next nothing. The frustration was getting unbearable.'

3

DENZIL WATCHED the new day dawn, a sight seventeen of his friends and many more Argentinians had not lived to see. He looked round and discovered that Lance-Corporal Cripps, the expert from the Royal Signals, had been wounded by shrapnel. The Argentinian artillery was bombarding the position.

Major Dennison's suspicion that the enemy regarded the machine gunners and anti-tank teams of Support Company as prime targets was being confirmed by the shells falling thick and fast around them. 'Take cover,' he told them. Dennison had been under fire before, winning his spurs as a young officer with the SAS in the secret war in Oman. Denzil crawled into an alcove-type piece of cover with Mark Hammill as the enemy shells straddled his company's position.

'The lads just hid as best they could. I crawled out during a lull and the OC decided to move us out of this area as quickly as possible before we were all wiped out. John Pettinger from patrol company arrived and led us into the bowl where B Company had spent most of the night fighting. It was a shocking sight, yet unreal. I was shocked by the sight of our lads lying there dead. I looked at some of the enemy and they seemed to have a wax-type complexion about them almost as if they were dummies.'

In the bowl they piled into abandoned enemy bunkers and took up defensive positions in case the artillery heralded a counter-attack.

It had been a long, long night for Oscar Carrizo. The screams of the wounded and the dying were ringing in the corporal's ears. He had heard his comrades die and the British, too. Burned deep in his memory were the words of a wounded Argentinian: 'Lieutenant Baldini, I'm wounded, please kill me, please kill me.'

'To my front I could clearly the English shout "Tommy, Tommy" and then Tommy would shoot. I'll always remember that name. [Tommy was Tommo, one of our machine-gunners, firing his GPMG in sustained-fire role. Oscar Carrizo was only ten metres from us without knowing it.]

'As it started to get light I crawled out of my new hiding-place in the rocks. I remember standing up. Suddenly I was confronted by two English soldiers. I was shot in the head as I tried to surrender. I passed out, thinking I was dead.'

Kevin waited for the piece of shrapnel to cool before carefully putting it away in a smock pocket. Then he massaged his numb leg and congratulated himself on escaping. The machine-gunners from Support Company were nearby when he heard a shout from Vince Bramley, who was sitting at his gun.

'Vince waved me over for a brew he was making. I was on the way over when I heard another barrage on the way and I dived in beside him. He started yelling at me:

"Watch my mess tin – this is my last water. Don't spill the bloody thing."

'Did I laugh? What else could you do? That bloody brew was more important to us than the artillery. We lay there side by side with our hands over the mess tin to stop the dirt from the shell explosions landing in the water. I teamed up with Vince and some of the others and during lulls we were detailed to clear the area of dead Argentinians. We took them for temporary burial on the reverse slope. We all found it a bit emotional... but placing our own lads in body bags was something I didn't like at all.'

Kevin then restocked his weapon and ammunition supplies from discarded equipment on the battlefield and settled down to await the threatened counter-attack.

Dom Gray got bored easily and the little game of staring out the prisoners soon became flatter than the crap beer they sold at exorbitant prices in some of the Aldershot pubs. He went to sit with Stewart Gray, who knew a bit more about his mates and what had happened to them than Dom.

The two wounded soldiers were chatting away when Stewart brought Dom up short with his tale of what had happened to him. 'They thought I was dead,' he said, 'so they zipped me into a body bag and that's where I woke up.'

Dom couldn't help but burst out laughing. It appealed to his sense of humour. 'What did they do?' he asked. 'Must have scared them shitless, a body yelling at them!'

His laughter soon subsided when he heard of the deaths of his corporal, Stewart McLaughlin, of Sergeant Ian McKay, Lance-Corporal James Murdoch and other brave comrades. He started to realize just how lucky he had been, and fell into a pensive mood.

But the crashing Argentinian artillery barrage soon shattered Dom's thoughts, as he searched for cover. The prisoners, too, were shepherded to safety. Dom began to feel helpless for the first time since landing.

The wounded had to be got to safety and the prisoners back to a more secure area before they all escaped, rearmed themselves and started fighting again. 'Shirley' Bassey arrived with a tracked all-terrain vehicle to take some wounded back to a helicopter pick-up point for evacuation. Dom piled in with Lieutenant Andy Bickerdike, Bill Metcalf, Pete Hindmarsh and Jim O'Connell. Pete was badly wounded, but it was Jim who was causing Dom concern.

'Jim was very distressed. He had lost his right eye and the wound was still open. He rested his head on my shoulder and all I could do was reassure him. I told him everything would be OK. The bloody vehicle was bouncing and lurching all over the shop and the smell inside was terrible, blood, sweat, shit and the atmosphere of death. "Shirley" dropped us off in the middle of nowhere and went back for more casualties. What a fucking place. There were no medics, no markers, nothing. The cold and damp were beginning to hit the badly wounded guys, particularly Pete and Jim. We were there for two hours. Pete and Jim and the rest of us were slagging each other off to keep going. Next thing, this helicopter arrives. Captain Sam Drennan was flying it and he was as surprised to see us as we were relieved to see him. We got Pete and Jim on first and he took off with them. Although he was in the Army Air Corps we knew him and he promised he would return for the rest of us. Sam was true to his word: he came back and got us and flew us to Teal Inlet.'

At the field hospital Dom discovered he had phosphorus burns as well as the gunshot wound. As he lay on an operating table he watched a Royal Engineer having his foot amputated. His head was feeling like a brick had hit it. They dressed his wounds and sent him off to rest. Dom found a hut where Captain Nobby Menzies, the 3 Para Quartermaster, was chewing over a casualty sheet. Jesus, he's got a bed in there with nice clean sheets and pillows! The QM looked at Dom and the former RSM in him took over. He handed Dom a disposable razor and ordered him to get a shave!

Shave! Fucking shave! Bollocks. Stitched up, bandaged up, worn out and knackered from fighting all night, Army bullshit was the last thing he needed. Dom went off and decided to keep out of the QM's way until he was moved. The Hutchins family lived here at Teal Inlet and they invited Dom to stay in their home until he was flown out to the hospital ship *Uganda*. There was no bullshit there – just warmth and appreciation of what the soldiers had done. The family's affection was as good as a cure.

Oscar Carrizo returned to consciousness to find he wasn't dead after all. He was totally confused and had no idea how long he had been lying there. He struggled to his feet and began stumbling along.

'I staggered down into the bowl. I was dizzy, like a drunk. I kept falling against the rocks and falling over. It was hard to stand and I couldn't see properly or focus on anything. I managed to stagger a bit further, then sank to my knees.

'I was dying... I could feel it.'

Denzil was resting against a rock, surveying the battlefield, watching the work parties, his sub-machine-gun beside him. Suddenly a lone Argentinian appeared, lurching from the rocks nearby. Denzil was on his feet in an instant, cocking the weapon and flicking off the safety-catch. He put the Sterling to his shoulder and aimed at the Argie. Hang on... hang on... there's something not quite right... He took his finger off the trigger.

The soldier, a big man, was lumbering about. He was bumping into the rocks and boulders. The man was swaying and looking at the ground. What's he looking for, a weapon? The Sterling was back on his shoulder. Discarded weapons lay all around. Finger back on trigger... don't touch... don't touch a weapon or you're dead.

Denzil framed the soldier in his sight as he stooped for something. Don't... you don't want to die... don't for Christ's sake touch a weapon... Then the soldier sank to his knees and collapsed.

Two toms were close by and Denzil sent them over to the man.

Oscar Carrizo's head was burning. Hot, so hot, yet the rest of his body was trembling with cold, a cold which had eaten deep into him. He opened his eyes and blinked.

'I saw feet standing by me and I looked up and saw two Englishmen with reddish berets. They beckoned me to stand up. I tried, but I couldn't. They helped me up, talking to me, but I couldn't understand. Their voices were calm. I felt at ease, almost relieved now it was over. The last thing I remember was being helped down off the mountain by the two English soldiers.'

Denzil was glad he hadn't squeezed the trigger as he watched the two toms approach the Argentinian. The man was clearly wounded and in a bad way. They got him to his feet and began to take him to the rear. Denzil was listening to his radio when he heard a resupply of ammo was on the way. He also heard, just as important, that a resupply of cigarettes was awaiting collection at the base of Longdon, along with maps and details of his company's next objectives. Everyone needed cigarettes – even the non-smokers had started puffing. He volunteered to go back for the resup.

Antonio Belmonte knew it was not just suicidal to throw flares, but to even show himself, such was the ferocity of the British assault. But he knew he had to do something. Gradually he was being surrounded. He popped up, fired a couple of rounds in the direction of the British to keep their heads down, then headed for a machine-gun post. It was abandoned, so he moved on. He was also very bitter at the decision to make him and the rest of his section change their positions the night before. It had left them flat-footed when 3 Para attacked.

'Some of the guys had withdrawn, but I didn't want to do that. I had only twenty rounds of ammunition and I decided to use them. It was kill or be killed. Our position was bad. I kept firing until I used all my ammo, then found a hollow in the rocks and crawled into it. I lay there. It was tense. I could feel the English soldiers passing me. I felt they could see me. I felt that if I looked up I'd see a rifle pointing at me. I knew if I moved I would be a dead man.

'I don't know what orders they had been given, but it seemed to me as if they had been told to kill all of us, every last one of us. I knew I was trapped. I stayed in hiding, waiting for daylight to see if they would accept my surrender. I put my rifle down and waited. At daybreak I could see there had been a massacre on the mountain.'

Luis Leccese survived the night. At dawn all he could hear was the odd shot and British voices. The new day brought a new fear for Luis. Now he had to stand up in broad daylight and surrender – and hope to survive. He could see the British all around now, taking prisoners and marching them off. He had no alternative, but his nerves were fraying, as he didn't know what would happen when he showed himself.

'An English soldier was standing nearby. He had his back to us. My partner and I nodded to each other and stood up together. The soldier must have had eyes in his back because he spun round the instant we stood and fired at us, two or three rapid rounds. Everything I had feared was happening. I flung myself to the ground, but my mate froze. The bullets missed. I was on the ground, waiting for him to fire again, and my mate was scrabbling around. Then he grabbed a bit of paper and started waving it. More English soldiers joined the first one. They acknowledged us then and called us towards them to surrender.

'I didn't look around at the mess of the battle. I didn't acknowledge anything, dead bodies, anything, I just concentrated on the men calling me forward. I tried to obey every instruction. I didn't know what was going to happen, what they were going to do to me. I stared and walked with my hands up towards them.

'As soon as I reached them I was kicked and pushed to the ground and made to lie face down. My duvet jacket was stripped off me immediately and my bootlaces removed. They gave me a few more kicks then began frisking me for weapons. It all seemed to take ages, but it only lasted seconds. Then they put me in a line with other prisoners.

'They marched us off in single file. The British guarding us were on one side, not on both, and I began to think they were looking for a place to shoot us and leave us lying there dead. I imagined it was a line-up for execution, a line-up for the firing squad. My heart was racing.

'We were marched on down the western slope. They hadn't shot us. We got to a piece of ground and they made us sit there in a group. All day we sat there watching them. A photographer [Tom Smith of the *Daily Express*] came up and took pictures of us huddled together. As evening approached helicopters began moving some of the prisoners but we were left there. We were told we had to walk about two kilometres because no helicopters were available any more. It's dark now and we're marching in single file and the English are on one side of us. I was convinced that this was it, my last night on earth. I was absolutely convinced they were going to line us up in front of a firing squad in the dark. Nobody would ever know. We had gone about two kilometres when they stopped us and made us get together in a circle and told us to sleep. We found out they had moved us for our own safety because our own artillery was firing on the mountain.

'Nights are always cold in the Malvinas and this one was no different. We were huddled together for warmth and so the British could watch us. There were a few blankets, but I didn't have one. They had given me my duvet jacket back and that helped. During the night it started to snow. I was freezing and my feet started to go numb. I began to move my body to try to get my circulation going when an English soldier asked what I thought I was doing. Another prisoner who spoke English explained and the soldier told me to start walking around the circle of prisoners. I spent the night walking round the other prisoners while they tried to sleep. The soldier was OK after all: he didn't point his rifle at me. Then he told me to start jogging and that helped warm me up.

'Next day helicopters arrived and flew us to Fitzroy. As soon as we arrived we were given three biscuits and a piece of cheese each. It was the best food I have ever tasted; it will remain with me for ever. We were taken to a sheep farm with a big shed divided up into sheep pens inside and they put us there. We were there for a few days and they fed us regularly. I was very happy. I was being fed and I was in shelter. We were then moved to San Carlos, where the British had landed and where they had a POW centre. About 100 of us were put in a big prisoner cage and their officers arrived and said if any of us were wounded they were to tell them and the wounds would be treated. I said I couldn't walk any more and they put me to one side with some others and examined my feet. They let me wash them with some special soap. The reason for my pain was the first stages of frostbite.

'About two days later I hobbled on to a landing-craft and was taken to a huge white ship in the bay. It was the *Canberra*, the ship most of the British had used to get here.'

Santiago Gauto was determined to run all the way to Moody Brook if he had to. It was English-speaking voices dominating the airwaves now, not Argentinian.

'On my way I caught up with a wounded guy. Three of his fingers were missing but he still had his bandage stuck to his helmet. He honestly didn't know it was a field dressing and for his own use. Another guy had one of his hands blown away. I bandaged them and then we came across a deserted bunker. There was food in it and the three of us ate it like pigs. We whoofed it down. As we got to Moody Brook they were trying to move a 105mm artillery gun which was stuck in the mud. This artillery officer shouts at me: "Hey, you fucking little orphan, come here and help get this out." I couldn't believe him. I looked at him and told him: "Go fuck yourself."

'I walked on with the two wounded. A truck was collecting the wounded so I loaded these two guys on to it. I walked on across the little bridge through the confusion. There was confusion all over the place. I was in a daze. Nothing was as bad as where I had just escaped. I began to feel mad then when I saw all these clean guys shouting and screaming at everyone coming off the mountain. Bastards.

'I headed on towards the church and found some of my mates there. The joy when I met up with Dario again! We hugged each other. We were overjoyed each of us had survived that hell-hole. The relief was indescribable.

'Father Fernández was there and he was going to give us a sermon. A fucking sermon! To me Fernández was a "red priest", a communist. He stood there and told us: "You've got to get together and go and kill those motherfucking English." Hang on a minute, I thought, is this guy supposed to be a Christian? What sort of stuff is he coming out with? The least he could have said was we were going to go out and kill another human being or something more fitting. He was the motherfucker and always will be one.

'Outside the church they gave us a magazine each for our rifles and told us to gather at the artillery positions on the edge of Stanley. Major Carrizo was organizing a group to counter-attack. I met Felix Barreto and we watched and listened to what was going on. There had been other attacks and they had failed. Major Carrizo asked a colonel for a radio and was refused. We stood watching them arguing. Carrizo told him: "We'll never win a war like this." He was right.

'Then he turned to us and said: "Those who've got balls, follow me."

'We advanced. Around me guys had tears running down their faces. Inside we knew we were not going to get very far, we were going to die, we were marching to death. The British were firing down on to us with machine-guns, mortars, artillery. It was like advancing through the gates of hell itself. We had gone about 300 metres when our own artillery started landing on us as well. We were in a no-man's-land. Everything collapsed then: communications, organization, everything. Both sides were firing at us and we had nowhere to go. I was totally disoriented and when we withdrew towards Port Stanley again I found the British were already there. I couldn't understand it. I must have been in a time warp.'

Daybreak came and with it the cold, a painful, penetrating cold which crept through Antonio Belmonte's fear-racked body and soul. There had been a dusting of snow overnight which was crystallized by the frost. The light mist in the distance was lifting and all around him it was quiet, eerily quiet, punctuated by the occasional rifle shot. Antonio could feel the presence of enemy soldiers.

'They were near, they were passing, they were talking to each other. I couldn't understand what they were saying. I was convinced they were Gurkhas. There was a group of seven or eight of them and their features were dark and they were small, not big men like I expected the English to be. As they got closer I could see blond hair and blue eyes on some of them beneath the camouflage cream and realized they were probably not Gurkhas after all. They were kicking tin cans about and I wasn't sure if they were still looking for us or looking for food.

'The time had come. I had to surrender. I had nowhere to hide and I had nowhere to run. My brain was awash with uncertainty. They passed me so it was now or never. I stood up with my arms raised and one of them immediately spun into a firing position, aiming his rifle at me. I was looking straight at him. Another pulled me out and I saw more Argentinian prisoners. He pushed me towards them. We looked at each other but didn't speak. They took off my jacket, threw me to the ground face down and began searching me. They took any papers which looked important, including a telegram I had. They found the little money I had and took that, too. They found a flare in my pocket and began asking what it was. I tried to explain. I wanted to help, I wanted my life, I wanted to survive. They found some ammo on me and one of them took it and loaded it into his weapon. By this time all of us were lying on the ground. They made me turn over on to my back and shut my eyes. My bootlaces were cut and I began to think: This is it, Antonio, they are going to shoot you.

'I could hear them talking about us. They were talking in a very low tone. I don't know how long I was lying there but the cold was horrible. We were ordered to our feet and marched out of the bowl on to a path. I was first in line. We weren't really marching, just shuffling, because they had cut our laces. I was cold, weak, tired and afraid and the terrain was very difficult to walk across. One of the English whacked me on the back of the neck and said something like "Scum" and then another one came and started hitting me on the back with his rifle. We were all in a line, with rocks to our side and back and the English all on one side. They were looking at us in a way which made me think we were being lined up to be shot. One of my friends, Delgado, was lying on an English stretcher with shrapnel wounds in his legs.

'Even as the artillery started they were still talking quietly. Then they split us up and took our group back into the bowl. I was back in what had been our sector, the place where I had lived and survived for so many days. I cannot tell you what I felt when I went back. I didn't know the place any longer. I couldn't take it in, I couldn't comprehend what had gone on here even though the evidence was there before my very eyes. It looked different. Our friends' bodies were lying there. Some I could recognize; others were totally unrecognizable because of the way in which they had died. English dead lay among ours. The bowl seemed to be just dead bodies, the British ones covered with blankets.

'They wanted us to start collecting up our dead. Lieutenant Baldini was lying face down still holding a 9mm pistol. It was gripped tightly in his hand. He must have died instantly. He had been shot many times, probably hit by a burst of machine-gun fire. He had no boots on, so I assumed he had been killed coming out of his bunker as the English swept over his position. He had been dead for some time. Next to him was Corporal Rios with a horrific head wound. He must have been hit by shrapnel. They had died side by side.

'A little further on was Corporal Orozco with his stomach lying open. A bayonet was still embedded in him. We couldn't tell if he had been bayoneted or had died in a hand-to-hand knife fight. Gramisci, another soldier, was there with bayonet marks in his stomach. To the side lay Massad, a good lad who came from Bandfield, my area of Buenos Aires. He was Major Carrizo's assistant and he had fallen close to the radar monitor.

'This was my first experience of dead bodies. I had never seen anyone dead before. They looked like rubber dummies which had been inflated. Most still had their eyes open. I couldn't understand that. The English stood by and watched as we began to move our dead.

'We were tired and weak and I was trying to carry Lieutenant Baldini. He was a heavy man. I tried to detach myself from this painful task. I tried to tell myself it wasn't real. Half carrying and sometimes dragging, we got Baldini and Corporal Rios to a shell hole. The others carried Massad and Corporal Orozco. We put all four in the hole. Quintana was lying dead up on the path with a gunshot wound to the head. He had been wounded and died after the surrender. I gestured to the English about him and they told me to leave him. I looked at my friends lying there in that mass grave and then they told us to make it wider to fit them in better. All the time an English soldier stood over us with a 9mm pistol. As I felt him there I began to feel real fear. I was absolutely convinced he was going to shoot us as well. It would be easy, no problem, and no one would ever know. I was scared. I just wanted to survive, I just wanted to go home. After all I had been through I didn't need this.

'At the same time our own artillery was firing heavily on to the mountain, especially around the bowl. The English took cover as the shells landed, but we had to carry on digging. Sometimes we clung to the ground to avoid the shrapnel, but they ordered us to carry on burying our friends. I was in a bad way with the cold, particularly as they had taken my jacket. The fear was nagging away and I was starving and exhausted. I didn't know whether I just wanted it to be over, to die, or what. I asked myself: Why am I here, why has this happened to me? Now I'm going to be killed.

'I wanted to put blankets over our dead, to wrap them up. I couldn't register that they really were dead, that their lives had been lost for ever. Eventually we covered them with earth, hiding them from this madness which surrounded the rest of us. I asked the soldier if I could put a cross there but he shook his head. I wished I had ignored him and put a cross there for them. They were my comrades and they deserved one. I started talking to God. I stood and asked Him to do the best for them, to let them have lots of light, to keep them in glory. "Let them rest now. Let them rest in peace... " '

Some of the shells landing round Antonio Belmonte and his grim-faced comrades in the burial party were being fired by Germán Chamorro. At times he fired at targets on Two Sisters, but Longdon was his main killing ground. His crew had fired so many that the barrel of their gun was glowing red-hot. It was the only way, he knew, to keep the advancing British at bay. A deadly game of cat and mouse developed as British artillery spotters guided their guns on to the Argentinian fire-bases.

'Around midday I broke away from the position and went to fetch some water. I was parched. I was kneeling by a big puddle and breaking the ice on top when I heard the whistle of an incoming shell. I dived down, covering my head. Bang! Less than ten metres away. Seconds later the screaming started. Five lads had been hit, two in the legs, one in the arm, another in the hand and the fifth had shrapnel in his stomach. I went to one and he wasn't too bad at first. He was cursing "those motherfucker English". I ripped his boot off and his trousers and found blood, then a hole as big as a tennis ball. Then the shock set in and he began screaming: "I'm burning, I'm burning."

'Next this captain from the War School arrives and tells us to dismantle and disable our artillery pieces because the English were about to descend on to us. By the time it was discovered that this information was wrong we had removed the breeches. We settled down for the night armed only with rifles, waiting for them to arrive. All night we waited and they didn't come. Before first light we were ordered back to the guns and had to spend the next hour putting them together again. Then we started firing an early-morning call back on to Longdon.'

Denzil was on his way to the base of the mountain to collect the precious cigarette resupply when he saw Corporal Alex Shaw and Private Craig Jones, two of the REME armourers attached to 3 Para. Just as they stopped to chat he heard an almighty whoosh and they began diving for cover as the shell exploded in their midst.

He landed on his stomach with all the wind knocked out of him. His helmet had been blown off and his mouth was full of dirt. For a second he began to panic. 'That was close,' he told himself. But he had barely uttered the thought when he felt a burning sensation surging through his entire body. He turned over and sat up to see what the problem was. His left leg was hanging off and his right was riddled with shrapnel. The shock of it made him scream.

Comrades dashed from cover and he was rushed back to the FAP and into the care of Colour Sergeant Brian Faulkner, who, along with the unit doctor, started working to save his life. Brian Faulkner's homespun approach and broad Yorkshire accent soon convinced Denzil the man wasn't as bad as he feared. Reassurance was a very important ingredient in the treatment of shock, a condition which killed many a soldier who could have survived his wounds. Brian kept reassuring Denzil as he and the doctor worked on his wounds.

'Hang in there, Denzil, mate, a chopper's on the way. Hang in, you have to, we still need you to run the rugby club bar. You're not getting out of it this easily.'

(Brian Faulkner had risked his life from the time the first shot was fired, leading his team of medics to snatch wounded Paras to safety. His gallantry was recognized with the award of the Distinguished Conduct Medal.)

Denzil smiled briefly. He knew he was weakening fast, and felt he was dying, as he lay on a stretcher to one side of the FAP, waiting for the helicopter. He thought nobody expected him to live. Corporal Shaw and Private Jones had died instantly and maybe now they thought he would go, too. He was hovering on the brink of consciousness.

'Don't go to sleep, don't go to sleep otherwise you'll die,' he told himself.

The lads of B Company were knackered. It was daylight and Jerry Phillips could see the exhaustion in their faces. He was with the remnants of 6 Platoon when the Argentinians started their artillery bombardment.

'The world seemed to crumble around us. Shells were

landing among us in thick salvoes. I dived into a hole with Lieutenant Cox. Every time I looked up I was pulled back down again into cover. During a lull we got out and I met my platoon sergeant, John Pettinger. We were both from D Company and I briefed him on what D Company casualties I knew about and we moved off the mountain. Conditions up there with the shelling were horrendous. We found a fairly safe haven and stopped to rest. We were there for twelve hours and we really did need the rest. All day the shells fell.

'We maintained a radio sentry in case we were needed. Next day, 13 June, we got a call to report to HQ for a mission and we started tabbing back. On the way I bumped into more D Company lads, Dickie and Mark Brown. It was nice to see familiar faces again and to see that they were alive and kicking. Standing there talking in a group was a bloody silly thing to do. Next thing I know there was a big bang. It got the lot of us: me, Mark, Dickie, Jock and a few others. It took us all. I remember being thrown through the air. When the shell landed I had been wearing my bergen. When I landed it was gone. There were arms and legs all over the place. I saw an arm across my face. Fucking hell, what's this? I grabbed it and tried to chuck it away. I knew it wasn't mine – but it came back to me, flopping down beside me. It was mine and it was still attached to me. I couldn't feel it, then the shock hit me and I screamed. I began to feel I was on fire, like a Chinese burn. Then came the pain. I knew I was in the shit. Harry Gannon pounced on me and started working on me.

'I was taken to the FAP and given morphine. I still had my wits about me, but I was in pain now. I was hurting. I only relaxed when the doctor came and put a huge needle into me and pumped some kit into me which made me feel as if I was floating. As I lay there I saw Harry, one of our signallers.

'I called him and said: "Harry, give me a fag, I'm

gagging." He looked down at me and said: "Only one, because I know I won't get it back." I thought, you tight bastard, but he gave me about six in the end. They put me in the steel coffin, the box which is attached to the skids of the helicopter, and I was flown to a clearing station where all my ammo was taken off me. Most of it by that time was Argentinian. I was able to walk by this time and actually walked into the hospital in Ajax Bay. Old Doc Jolly [Surgeon Commander Rick Jolly RN] was there to meet me. He operated on my arm there and then and I don't remember another thing until I woke on the hospital ship *Uganda*.

'When the war was all over and I was back in England I met Harry... and he asked for his fags back!'

Even on the helicopter flying him to the emergency medical centre at Ajax Bay Denzil knew his time was just about up. There was no great mystery about it: he was dying. He was afraid, but what could he do?

'I felt like I just wanted to go to sleep. I knew if I did that I would die. As I closed my eyes I saw my mother. I knew if I died it would cause her no end of grief. I doubted if she would survive herself if I died. I didn't want that to happen to her, I wanted to see her again. It was that will-power, the will to see her again, that kept me awake.' At Ajax Bay he was rushed into the emergency centre still struggling to stay awake. A medic from the Paras began preparing him for his operation. Denzil relaxed then. 'One of our own,' he told himself. 'He won't let anything happen to me.' There was a feeling of warmth, of cosiness, from the paraffin heaters that he could smell quite clearly. He whispered to the medic cutting away his clothes: 'I want to sleep, but I don't want to die. Can I sleep?'

The medic assured him all would be OK and Denzil closed his eyes and went to sleep.

Death claimed him.

But the medic had a crash team around him in seconds and they resuscitated him.

The next day Denzil came to aboard the hospital ship *Uganda*, still in deep trauma. His right leg was still in a dreadful condition and the surgeons feared they would have to amputate that, too, to save his life. They advised him to have it amputated and he signed the paper giving permission. As he was wheeled to the operating theatre he began to wonder if he would survive again.

As he recovered from the anaesthetic he found that his right leg was still there. The surgeons had decided to try to save it rather than remove it. They told him they wanted to leave it for a week or two to see if there was any improvement. He also had the reassurance of the *Uganda* doctors: 'Anyone who gets here alive leaves here alive.' For Doc Jolly had promised every soldier that he was part of the finest medical team Britain had ever sent to war and that every man who reached him alive would go home alive. He kept his word.

The spirit of the wounded soldiers, their common will to make light of their injuries and recover buoyed Denzil. Lying beside him was Mushrooms – Mick Bateman – who could no longer speak because of a throat wound. He communicated to the other patients by writing little notes.

'Jesus, if Mushrooms can get on with life without a voice I can get on without a leg,' he told himself. All around him were guys suffering from a variety of wounds and injuries, sailors who had been burned, amputees and soldiers who had been 'gut-shot'. Many of them, he told himself, were worse off than him.

Denzil was going to get better. He may not be able to play rugby again, but he would certainly be able to go fishing, boozing and singing. He could still get married, still father children. No bloody point in moping, the bloody leg's gone now, so let's get on with life.

That was the common view on that hospital ship. One day the staff put on a video of the Monty Python movie *Life of Brian* for the patients. The film ends with a mass crucifixion and the victims singing 'Always Look on the Bright Side of Life'.

'Before you knew it everyone – all 100 of us – was singing it. All those guys, with wounds that would change their lives for ever, singing at the top of their voices. It is something I will never forget. It brought a lump to my throat. The medical staff stood watching us and there were tears in the eyes of the nurses and medics. The spirit of the Parachute Regiment that was in those of us from 2 and 3 Para as we convalesced together spread to the others and helped them recover as well.'

Felix Barreto awoke on the morning of 13 June, having slept on some sacks near the old Royal Marines barracks at Moody Brook. He had survived the suicidal counter-attack of the night before. The British definitely had Mount Longdon, but Wireless Ridge was still holding out.

He was pleasantly surprised that he had lived this long. The more so because his best friend Araujo had been killed.

'We had to crawl towards the mountain to try that counter-attack. I mean crawl up the slopes. The shellfire and sniper fire were so accurate... I knew we were going to die. Then everyone around me started to withdraw and that was that.

'Parts of our A Company and some commando units were under attack on Wireless Ridge [by men of 2 Para] and I was told one of our officers, a lieutenant colonel, had been wounded. Major Carrizo told me to go up there and get him. I was to avoid the fighting and get him back to Moody

Brook. We made our way up, but the battle was everywhere. The gorse was on fire and we had to fight our way to the command post. When we got there and found the officer he said he had no intention of withdrawing to Moody Brook with us, so we turned round and went back.

'It was then decided we would counter-attack to help the guys on Wireless Ridge, but a lot of people threw their weapons down. That was that. I didn't and I wish the others had not done what they did. I wish we'd stayed united and then things could have possibly been different. They split us up and formed us into guard units, some to guard the withdrawal of the artillery, others to guard the road to Stanley. I was mega-tired by now, but I still had another job. Twelve of us were resupplied with ammo and Major Carrizo sent us to guard Government House, where General Menéndez had his headquarters. He told us it was not to fall into English hands.

'Artillery was being positioned in Stanley and it looked as if there was going to be a fight. I waited at Government House for the English to arrive.'

Britain's artillery gunners had the scent of victory in their nostrils. Never since the Korean war had gunners on the land or at sea had such a plentiful supply of ammunition to fire and they were making the most of it. Their bombardments were unrelenting and deadly.

German Chamorro and his crew were doing their best to answer back, to get their forces a breathing space. It was the night of 13 June, a cold night, but the gunners could feel the heat radiating from their red-hot barrels.

'We were firing, firing... bang... bang... bang... and then this officer shouts that we are low on ammo. We had to get more. Our reserve stocks were exactly 100 metres away, but shells from the British guns across the mountains and the ships off the coast were screaming in. It was raining shells.

How the hell were we supposed to get the resupply? We had no alternative but to go: the lads on the hills facing the British needed us. We dashed ten or fifteen metres, got into cover, up... dash again... down into cover... and so on. There was a wall near the supply dump and we headed for that only to find about fifty guys in there already cowering from the incoming shells. Our rate of fire slowed down because it was so hard to get through the bombardment to get the shells back. It was like that all night long.

'By 5 a.m. two of our five guns were out of action. One of our guys was hit in the hand by shrapnel, but he stayed at his post helping one-handed. The only time he stopped was to put his hand on to the frosty grass to relieve the pain. Eventually they ordered us to stop firing. A sergeant was shouting for the ten men manning the second piece in our battery. They had deserted during the night and to make matters worse they had abandoned the unit's colours at their gun.

'At 6 a.m. I was desperate for a crap. Now I couldn't go and knock on somebody's door and ask permission to use their toilet, so I just went where I was. I was in the middle of it when the battery chief comes over and starts laughing at me. Then he said we were to abandon the artillery, dismantle the guns and make our way to the airport to act as infantry support to the gun batteries there. We set about destroying everything that could be of use to the British. I threw a grenade into what had been our position. We moved across a field towards the road and a shell landed among us. Toledo, the radio operator, had the radio blown completely off his back, yet none of us was injured. We're just moving off again when we discover we're right in the middle of a fucking minefield. Castro, the sergeant, yells that we are to follow in his footsteps and we got out OK. Nobody told us the bloody minefield was there.

'It was still dark, but the road to Stanley was full of soldiers, some going up front as reinforcements, others heading into Stanley, others going... just going. We passed the Monument and Government House and stopped for a rest at the post office. We could hear the shelling. It was as if we were surrounded. I sat there and had a cigarette and watched the madness, the chaos, the street full of soldiers, some lost, some dazed, some on trucks rushing nowhere. I asked myself if this was just a bad dream. It couldn't be real.

'Then I got new orders. I was to take up a new position in a garden and get ready for urban fighting. We were going to make them fight for every street. That was it – enough. I took the lad from our gun team with the hand injury to hospital. We waited patiently for his turn for treatment and I waited outside. He was screaming as they removed the shrapnel without anaesthetic.

'Back outside the hospital it was daylight. There was total disorder in the streets. It was also silent, no gunfire, nothing. It was unreal. What the fuck was going on?

'We met our boss, Lieutenant Colonel Quevedo, and the rest of our unit. He formed us up and with tears in his eyes told us the war was over. We had lost. A helicopter then flew past with a white flag. [This was the SAS helicopter carrying Lieutenant Colonel Mike Rose, CO of 22 SAS, who had carried out the ceasefire negotiations with General Menéndez by radio and was now arriving to finalize the arrangements for the British entry into Port Stanley and the Argentinian surrender.] Lieutenant Suárez got hold of a radio and contacted an amateur radio operator in the south of Argentina and told him that both he and I were well and asked the man to contact his sister. She passed on the message to my family.

'That night we slept in a building beside the town cemetery and in the morning the door opened and a massive man, two metres tall with a moustache, face covered in camouflage and wearing a maroon beret looked at us. It was my first contact with the enemy. He looked at us and we looked at him and then he motioned for us to go outside. We were put to work in the cemetery digging a mass grave for our dead. The bodies arrived on a truck. Two of us picked up a stretcher with a body on it. There was a blanket over the body. One of the arms fell out and the blanket moved and I could see the face of the guy we were about to bury. He was a young kid, younger than me, and his eyes were open. Those eyes still haunt me even now as we speak.

'After that the English brought us food and allowed us to find blankets in the old positions. Some of the English were very aggressive. Next day they woke us early and marched 300 of us out of Stanley towards the airport. On the way we had to stop and throw our personal weapons on to a pile that was gradually getting higher. I found the surrender of my weapon hard because the English laughed as each weapon went on the pile. I watched the English inspecting the 9mm and .45 pistols, putting the best to one side. One of our soldiers and an officer who spoke English were with them. They told us: "We are going to the airport. Don't take any food. We may have lost the battle, but not the war! March there with a high profile."

'On the way to the airport we were stopped and searched at two separate checkpoints before getting there at midday. Hundreds of troops were milling around. No sooner had we got there than we were ordered to turn round and march back to Stanley, to the port this time. We got there at four o'clock and the *Canberra* was anchored there. It was a huge ship, the first time I had seen a transatlantic liner. I was very impressed by the size of it.

'I joined a queue waiting to be searched before going on

board. I watched the British driving around in vehicles and on motorbikes. They were back to driving on the left side of the road, the wrong side... and they attacked the wrong side!'

Part 4
After The Battle

1

THE FRUSTRATIONS which had dogged C Company, 3 Para, since the fighting began appeared to be nearing an end. Tony Gregory finished his sentry duty and watched in amazement the display of rockets, tracer, mortar and artillery fire which accompanied 2 Para's attack on Wireless Ridge. He watched until the early hours, then crawled into his sleeping bag. This time, he could feel it, it would be C Company's turn.

'At first light we were told that 2 Para had captured and secured Wireless Ridge. Now it was C Company's turn for battle. We were given orders to take out Moody Brook, the old Royal Marine barracks, and the racecourse. The previous day, 13 June, we had been told the plan and now, on the 14th, it was all running through my head over and over again. We talked among ourselves and rehearsed it over and over again. We were ready. Today belonged to C Company. At last we would get into action.

'We were the lead company, out in front, leading the entire brigade assault into Port Stanley. We moved up and through 2 Para's lines and into point position. We passed the SAS and our own D (Patrol) Company guys, who had recced our route to our start line for the attack. H hour was to be last light on 14 June. We were within a mile of Moody Brook, all the platoons and sections lined out in their positions, and looking down on our objectives. We settled down to wait for H hour. We could see the Argentinians running down off the mountains on to the only road in East Falkland. Many were retreating, but others were milling around unsure of whether to stand and fight or retreat. Then things became tricky for us: we had assembled in a minefield. It was only later that a story went round that the detonators in the mines had frozen.

'For a couple of hours we lay there, watching, waiting, ready - then a shout went up to make safe our weapons. We looked at each other. It seemed a stupid order. Then we heard the Argies were surrendering. We couldn't believe it. The lads began to moan. You have to understand our position. Of course we were relieved and happy and smiling that it was over. The tension within us just floated away. We had survived, but we had endured the worst mental torture a soldier could experience, not just once but twice at least. We had been all psyched up, butterflies flapping, nerves jangling, everything on go, ready for action, and twice we were stopped. Think about it. We would never know how we would have performed in battle. It still eats away at me to this very day. Some of the lads who did fight said we were lucky because it was a bloody nightmare. Technically, I suppose they are right, but as far as I'm concerned it's a case of the unknown.

'Next thing a company of 2 Para appears and starts to head down towards Moody Brook and Stanley. That gave us the urge to join in. Everyone was shouting: "Get into Stanley before the Marines. We deserve it." Some thought it could be a ploy by the Argies to get us out into the open, but nobody gave a toss. It was Stanley or bust. You had to laugh because even though the Argies were the enemy throughout the campaign it was the Marines we were always eager to beat. All the way through there was a rift between us which I believe the brass created. They had been in charge of the whole operation on the land, but it was the Parachute Regiment which did the real dirty work. It was us in C Company and B Company of 2 Para who entered Stanley first.

'I can remember it as if it was yesterday. We were marching on tarmac for the first time in weeks and it made our legs wobble. My body just flopped, the energy evaporated from my body with the release of the tension. On this last small but famous tab, I began to fall back. It was weird. We were marching alongside Argies who were still armed. No one spoke or smiled or anything. We all, British and Argentinians, marched into Stanley together. An air of silence hung over the town and I stopped at a house and sat with some mates. We followed the best British tradition and made a brew. Mates we hadn't seen for a while began arriving and we all started to chat. We began to hear who had been killed and wounded and that was a real spoiler knowing those lads and knowing that they wouldn't be with us any more or here to see the end of it all. Serving in both 2 and 3 Para were ten of us who all came from within five miles of Ilford and not one of us was killed or wounded. Even though we were talking about who was killed and wounded we didn't realize the numbers at the time: almost fifty killed and more than a hundred wounded.

'Next we turned our minds to spoils of war: souvenirs to take home. The funniest thing was an Argie chopper landing on the racecourse and the crew getting out with their hands up to surrender to us. They were wearing shades, smart flying jackets and pearl-handled pistols – real John Wayne stuff. Within minutes the Paras had left them nearly naked. Even their boots were taken. Everyone took Argie boots: they were far superior to ours.

'Orders came down the line to break into empty houses. We smashed windows and clambered inside. This would be our first decent shelter for more than a month. All our clothing was going to be written off. At this stage our uniforms were just lumps of dirty, ripped junk. We stank to high heaven. We all washed, shaved and scoffed. I was surprised that on that first night we didn't have to stag on sentry duty, what with 10,000 armed Argies still wandering around. There was a curfew in place, but we managed to sneak out for a look around. Some of the lads found hidden whisky and weapons for souvenirs. The whole town was a big playground for us. Eventually the military police chased us off. Those first days of liberation were good fun in Stanley.

For Antonio Belmonte the war was over. So was life for the comrades he had been burying in the cold and soggy Falklands peat. At least they couldn't feel the cold which gnawed its way through Antonio's tired and hungry body. The fear that the soldier with the pistol would still shoot him nagged deep inside as the burial party was marched to the western slope and ordered to sit in a huddle on the cold, damp ground.

'I was worried and I was cold. The cold was horrendous. I sat there watching the English soldiers. I watched their every move. They were very well organized and relaxed with each other, even with their officers. Their officers seemed to be friendly with them, to actually listen to them, what they had to say and their point of view. I learned from that. Then one of our guards produced a quilted uniform.

To my amazement I discovered it was part of his uniform. He just zipped it up his legs and it formed a pair of trousers and he had a jacket, too, and thick leather gloves. They were better equipped than I had ever imagined.

'I was still worried about being shot, but then a helicopter arrived. I had never been on one before. When I came to the Malvinas it was by plane and that was my first time in the air. Now I was going on a helicopter for the first time. What an experience that was! The pilot flew so low I kept feeling we were going to crash. He flew so low he appeared to be hugging the ground. I never knew a helicopter could manoeuvre so quickly.

'We landed at a sheep farm and joined a line of prisoners. We were searched again and an interpreter asked us our names, ranks and where we had come from. We were each given a number. Then they gave us food. I was so hungry... but the spoonfuls of soup hurt my stomach because it had shrunk so much. It was nearly impossible for me to eat. We were all put in a big sheep shed with armed guards outside. I was still wary, still very tense. They watched our every move.

'I only began to wind down a bit, to relax, when they flew us to Port Stanley and held us there for a time in a cold-storage shed. I began talking to the other lads there and realized that it was over. The war had ended and I was alive. I began to relax. Our treatment was improving all the time and the English, too, seemed to be relaxed. I volunteered to join a work party fetching water to an English field kitchen. I watched them all the time. I saw the food they had: tins of ham, beans, meat. It was incredible. I watched an English soldier and one of their officers sitting together talking and eating. They were eating the same food. I had never seen anything like it. They smiled at me and offered me some. I was ashamed, but I ate with my hands, which were filthy. When I finished they washed up with soap and a sponge and rag. We had to clean our mess tins with grass. It was just another example of their professionalism, their spirit. They had come to take back what was theirs and they did it with their professional preparation and training. They had come mentally and militarily prepared. We had no experience in war.

'Next they put us on a landing-craft and took us out to the *Canberra*. They were filming us and taking pictures and I began to think: Oh, how shameful, not just for myself, but for all of us. We had gone there representing Argentina...

'As soon as I stepped on board the *Canberra* I was searched again, then given a cabin. I was a prisoner, but the treatment was great. I was dizzy with comfort. I fell asleep almost immediately. That was all I wanted: sleep and a bath. My clothes were so filthy and rotten they could walk on their own. Even my underpants were stiff. We were only allowed showers, but I yearned for a bath. Once our guard fell asleep and I slipped past him and into the bathroom. He caught me, but instead of punishing me he let it go. He was only concerned about numbers and as long as I hadn't escaped he didn't seem to mind. The food on board was hot, tasty and filling and they gave us cigarettes like Marlboro, L&M and Jockey after meals. Those who didn't smoke traded their fags for more food, but some managed to slip back into the queue for second helpings. They even allowed us up on to the deck to walk round in the fresh air.

'We docked at Puerto Madryn, where army lorries were lined up on the quayside for us. There were some officers and a few locals who had gathered to watch. They took us to Trelew for a flight to El Palomar and we finished up at Escuela General Lemos, where we had showers, shaves and haircuts and new uniforms were issued, and then it was on to our regiment. A radio message had announced our arrival home and all the relatives descended on the main gate. It was there, for the first time, that mothers and fathers found out that their sons weren't there – and that some weren't coming home. My sister was there even though she was told I had been wounded and was in the infirmary. She found me after slipping past the guards. There were thousands of people around the camp, some joyful, some just standing in a trance of sadness.'

Luis Leccese, too, was searched, processed and documented on boarding the *Canberra*, then sent to the medical centre for treatment to his feet.

'An Argentinian officer was on a bed and had just come round from an anaesthetic. I don't remember what unit he was from but he was a commando. He looked at me and said: "Soldier, have we won or lost the war?" He wasn't too happy when I told him the result. We chatted for a while and it was clear he had had a rough time. He had been infiltrated behind the British lines and his target was their helicopters. For twelve days he had lived in a ditch, observing and reporting back. Every time he asked for action he was ignored. Eventually he had enough and when escaping back from his observation post he was hit in the back by a burst of machine-gun fire. I left him lying there shaking his head in total disbelief.

'I was taken to a cabin and it all seemed to be too good to be true. The one thing I was desperate for was a shower. I was so dirty and smelly after two and a half months of living in grime. I opened a few doors in the corridor and found a big shower room. I just had to get in right away and clean myself. I stripped off and dived straight in under the hot water. The luxury of it!

'It was only when I stripped off my clothes that I realized what a sorry state I was in. I was actually scared at the sight of my naked body. As I ran the soap over my chest it was bumping on my ribs. I could see bones sticking out, hips, ribs, everything, I was like a skeleton. When I got back to my cabin carrying my clothes the others burst out laughing and called me *Fosforito* [little match] because I was all head.

'The treatment from the English was good. Even before we were put on the *Canberra* they gave us more food than our own people did while we were on Longdon. On the ship we got good cigarettes after every meal. They even let us up on deck for fresh air. I can't complain about the treatment. One of our guards was a really great guy and I hope he doesn't get in trouble even though this happened twelve years ago. He used to sit in the cabin and talk to us. Sometimes he would smuggle some extra chocolate bars in for us and he used to allow us to smoke in the cabins which was against the rules. Once he gave us a real surprise when he produced some beer for us. I had to laugh and I still do when I think that only a few days before we had been trying to kill each other and then I thought they were going to execute me and now we were sat chatting and laughing over a few beers. I hope that guard, whoever he was, reads this. If he does – I owe him a beer!

'We said our farewells to the guards when we arrived in Argentina. As I stepped on to our own soil again it was a relief to be home. There were rows and rows of trucks waiting for us and this officer shook my hand and said: "I congratulate you, soldier. Next one, please." Ha!

'Trucks and planes and then some regimental barracks. We were all so thin they said they wanted to keep us for a week to fatten us all up before we were seen. They gave us food with lots of potatoes in it. We were still desperately hungry and any food that went into my mouth went straight down without being chewed. Lots of the guys had no intention of staying there a week and trouble soon started between the conscripts and the officials. They quickly sent us on to our respective regiments. I arrived at our camp on a Sunday and on Monday they sent me on leave. I remember walking out of the camp, hobbling rather than walking, thin, but alive.

'I got on a train to Avellaneda with Gonzales, a friend from training days, and then I got on a bus for Bandfield. I was in a bad way and I had no money in my pocket. I said to the bus driver: "Look, I've just returned from the Malvinas. I have no money. These are my blood-group medals. Can I have a lift home?"

'He laughed and allowed me on to sit at the back. I was looking at the lights in the streets and the people walking about. After such a long time without seeing civilization it was hard to take it all in. Then I realized I was alone, alone at the back of a bus with no money and my friends gone, either dead, wounded or home, too. I was alone and crying, going home, alone and crying... '

Felix Barreto had spent the night outside Government House in Port Stanley, making sure it didn't fall into British hands. In the morning the Argentinian governor in the Falklands, General Mario Menéndez, appeared with a staff officer, who told Felix and the other soldiers in the grounds: 'It's all over. Our position is untenable.'

Menéndez watched as the officer ordered the soldiers to withdraw further into the capital and then they went back inside.

'I hung around while the other guards walked away. I wanted to see what would happen. Then I saw the English calmly walking down the road. One had a beard and was wearing a beret. They walked into Government House. It was clear to me then that the fighting was all finished. The British were walking down the road and soon seemed to be all over the place. Within half an hour they were everywhere. I walked down the road side by side with them, all of us armed, like brothers or something, all talking to each other – yes, actually talking and still armed.

'I let the British know I was starving and that I wanted to break into a container for food. They weren't bothered and let me get on with it. I began to lose all sense of time after this. I didn't know what day or month it was.

'The next thing I remember is joining the queue to give up our weapons. I began to get angry because a group of kelpers – islanders – placed a British flag over a wall right in front of where we had to hand in our weapons. They were laughing at us, laughing out loud. I reloaded my weapon, saying I would kill them, but a mate stopped me and told me to be cool otherwise we would all be killed. I cried as I handed my rifle on to the pile. I cried because of the anger that I was unable to do anything to them and because we had lost.

'I had dismantled my pistol and hidden it in the lining of my helmet. When we queued on the pier for embarkation on to the *Canberra* we were searched, but I got past that. But when we were searched again on the *Canberra* they found it. I was stripped and they began punching and beating me. They also took my Swiss Army knife, pictures of my missus, a religious stamp and a set of keys. I was left with nothing, absolutely nothing. I was beaten again for telling someone to "eat his *tuco*" [soup, but which the British thought meant something else]. I was so hot-tempered. A Red Cross official told me to take it easy and no one would touch me. But then they took my last cigarettes and that was the final straw. I exploded and then the English boot came down. They kicked and beat me all the way to my cabin, then they threw in my clothes and a card with a number on it. There was no mattress on the bunk.

'I was sharing with a guy from Lanus who was looking at

all these buttons on the cabin wall. He turned one and music came out of a speaker. Then he starts to dance around the cabin. I asked him: "What are you celebrating? We've just lost a war." And he says: "Bygones are bygones."

'Well, with that I just started punching him. They had to separate us and put us in different cabins. Next I came out of my cabin and said to the guard: "What am I, a dog, you motherfucker? I want a bath." He shoved me straight back into the cabin. Eventually I was allowed a bath and it was only when I lay in it that I began to calm down. I felt better for being clean and didn't cause any more problems after that. The rest of the trip was OK and I was well treated. We arrived at Puerto Madryn and I was very, very calm. If it hadn't been for my personal and patriotic pride I could actually have shaken hands with the English saying goodbye at the gangplank. They had treated me better than some of our own officers did.'

Kevin Connery was proud as he marched along the road into Port Stanley in his Argentinian boots and carrying his Argentinian rifle. His red beret sat proudly on his head. The enemy were fleeing through the town and he felt good as he stepped out on the first metalled road he had walked along for six weeks.

He marched past dead enemy and shattered enemy gun positions, taking it all in, but he drew in his breath sharply when he passed the former barracks of the Royal Marines Naval Party 8901 at Moody Brook. It was riddled with gunfire.

'If the Marines had been in that barracks on the night of the Argentinian invasion they would all have been killed. It was all shot up and gutted. There is no doubt they were all out to kill the Marines.'

A short distance into Stanley the Paras were ordered to

halt. Brigade told them to go no further. Even though they were first into the capital they had to watch as Royal Marines hoisted the Union Jack so that the press and TV could get their pictures. Kevin went into a bungalow and heard the telephone ringing. He picked it up to hear a screaming Argentinian voice.

'It was like somebody's missus bellowing at him for being naughty. So I told him to shut up and listen and it went quiet. Then I said: "We're coming to get you." Then an officer grabbed the phone and said: "Shut up, you prat, we're coming to get you." Then the pair of us stood there and just laughed and laughed.

'We settled into the bungalow and went to sleep and then I heard a shout and we all began cocking our weapons until we realized the lad who had been shouting was having a nightmare. Next thing we hear is another voice saying: "I can't find it... I can't find it" and when we put the light on we could see a guy sitting there holding a grenade. He'd lost the pin so we had to search round and find a pin to secure the grenade.

'Eventually the *Canberra* returned to the Falklands after delivering the prisoners home to Argentina. The Marines began to board. We were going home with 2 Para on the *Norland*, the ship which had brought them. Sending us home separately was one of the wisest decisions of the whole campaign. We had not been getting on with each other.'

Dominic Gray just couldn't believe the high morale of his wounded comrades in 3 Para during his four days on the hospital ship *Uganda*. He was impressed, considering many of them had lost limbs. If they were on a high what had he to worry about? He was transferred to another ship for the voyage to Uruguay and a flight home from Montevideo by RAF VC10 to Brize Norton.

The world's press had gathered to watch the British Ambassador greet the walking wounded with cucumber sandwiches as they boarded a fleet of ambulances at the quayside for the short journey to the airfield. Armed guards provided a grim warning that they were just across the River Plate from Argentina.

Once aboard the aircraft Dom popped a few sleeping tablets and slept throughout the twenty-hour journey. As he walked down the aircraft steps to British soil once more the top brass were there shaking hands. Crowds of relatives and photographers were corralled in the terminal building as Dom and the other wounded were ferried straight to an RAF hospital. No one saw their relatives that day, but staff at the hospital treated them like kings.

After check-ups Dom was released into the bright English summer sunshine. His father, Peter, was waiting for him, to take him home. They chattered throughout the journey and when Peter produced a big bowl of succulent strawberries and cream Dom wept... he wept with relief that he had survived and for his dead and wounded comrades.

Jerry Phillips regained consciousness in the recovery ward of the hospital ship *Uganda*. He opened his eyes, blinked, and looked again. Sure enough there was an Argie lying in the next bed. Then he saw Mark Brown to whom he had been chatting when the shell blast hit them all.

'I felt good. I was in a warm bed with clean sheets and had a lot of 3 Para lads around me. I felt really hungry and could smell roast dinners. The aroma was magnificent and I couldn't resist it – what a mistake. I was sick everywhere. I tried to eat again and was sick again.

'However, my morale was good. In those first few days on the *Uganda* it seemed to me as if everyone who went up that hill was either dead or sat here with me. They moved me down to another ward where I didn't have to be monitored so much, a ward with three-tier bunk beds, and I didn't think that was fair because I had to watch lads with leg injuries struggle up and down to the top bunks. When the nurses came round to do the penicillin jabs we all took great delight in laughing at each other being injected in the arse. They really hurt and we all had big black bruises. The nurses were really good to us, but the civvy merchant navy guys were pig-ignorant. Those of us who weren't bedridden queued for our meals and then struggled to the tables to eat. Those bastards would just sit there watching us struggling without even offering to help. There was only one – he was an Indian or Pakistani – and he was a real gentleman who always got up to help. The others, mostly Scots, well, I wouldn't piss on them if they were on fire. My arm was useless and I had had some skin grafts as well.

'After a time I was moved to another ship and there we had the best of everything. The crew couldn't do enough for us and even made us welcome in their own bar. We sailed to Montevideo on the River Plate where the *Graf Spee* was sunk during the Second World War. When we docked there were troops and armoured vehicles surrounding us. I could see Argentina across the river. I was on a bus being escorted through the city to the airport and on the way a car pulled out of a side street. Within seconds the driver was spread-eagled on the road with guns pointing at him from all directions.

'We had a straight flight home and then things began to become pretty emotional. As soon as we saw the green, green grass of home many an eye had a tear. It was the end of a long, long chapter for us. The nurses gave us welcome-home hugs and little badges from their own uniforms. It was very touching; they were brilliant people. As we stepped from the plane people were shaking our hands and saying words of encouragement. My father met me and just to see a relative was a huge help. He gave me a big hug. Both our eyes were full of tears.

'I was taken to the hospital at RAF Wroughton and spent a month there. My family and mates visited me a lot, so did the CO, Colonel Pike, as often as he could. It was good to see them all, particularly my family. My mother had found out I was wounded when an Army officer turned up at her work and casually told her I was injured. She fainted on the spot with shock. The hospital staff let me out with my family for a few hours and I got blasted in the first pub we saw.

'A senior doctor on the *Uganda* had told me that my arm may still have to be amputated. In those first few days that wouldn't have worried me a great deal because I was in an environment where lots of guys had lost limbs. Once I got back home, however, it was a different story. I felt different: now I wanted it to stay on. By the time I left Wroughton I had undergone five operations to save it. The last time they inserted metal framework to hold the bone together to try to get it to mould properly. Pieces of metal were also sticking out like a Meccano set. It was not a pleasant sight and not a pleasant thing to have to walk around with. It was bloody painful, too.

'I went on leave to my sister's house in Aldershot and was also close to the military hospital, where they regularly monitored me. I could relax and visit all our pubs.'

Tony Gregory heard all about the bullshit of the Royal Marines raising the flag at Government House for the press and television. What a load of crap. The Parachute Regiment's flag was the first to fly over Port Stanley – before the Marines even arrived. It was all good propaganda.

He had spent three days guarding work parties of

prisoners who had been detailed to clear the rubbish and mess with which they had littered the streets before they were transferred to the *Canberra* for their journey home. C Company would accompany them as guards on the ship.

'When I boarded the *Canberra* Paul Read and I were allocated a cabin on A deck. When we walked through the door our mouths dropped open as we tried to take it all in, a luxury apartment with carpets, its own bath and shower, sheets on proper beds... remember, I had travelled down in a poxy four-berth cabin below the water-line, and now this. I was well shocked. What luxury. The *Canberra* crew laid on a big five-course meal for us. It was magnificent – but a mistake. Our systems weren't ready for such rich fare and we all got the shits. We bathed and showered and bathed and showered to try to get rid of the grime which was embedded in us. I crawled between those white sheets and slept solid for twelve hours. In the morning the sheets were black despite all the bathing and showering. This gives an idea of just how dirty we were. I got up and washed my uniform before the POWs came aboard.

'Later in the day about 4000 prisoners began boarding. Half of us in C Company would guard while the other half rested. All our GPMGs were locked away and we carried rifles and SMGs [sub-machine-guns] on guard. About 500 prisoners were allocated to each deck to be guarded by a company of soldiers from each of the units which had taken part in the battles. The prisoners were searched as soon as they came aboard and then searched again by whichever unit was guarding the deck they were living on.

'Some poor Argie tried to smuggle his dead brother on board in a kitbag. I don't even want to think about what he must have been feeling. Other prisoners were caught with pistols and other weapons. I was on the first guard duty. We put them into their cabins and that was where they were to stay for the four-day journey to Argentina except for meal times and exercise. Everyone had to be told that if they needed medical treatment they would get it. Some still had bloody bandages on wounds. We then had to make sure every single one of them had a shower in case of a breakout of lice or dysentery.

'Language was a problem, so we went to every cabin to see if any of our prisoners spoke English, then they could translate for the others. They always seemed to be sitting quietly in their cabins staring at us. I went into one cabin and asked if anyone spoke English.

'"I do, mate," came the reply.

'It was a real cockney accent. "Do what, mate?" I asked incredulously. "I said I speak English," he told me. And when I asked him where he learned to speak it just like us he said he had lived in Tottenham, north London, and was studying there before the war broke out. He said his name was something like Mike Savage. We took him out into the corridor and I said to him: "What the fuck are you doing fighting in the war?" and he said he had what he called dual parents and had been studying in London up until December 1981, when he had returned to Argentina for the Christmas holidays and had been called up for conscription. We got on well with him, friendly. We looked after him with showers, fags and sweets in return for help communicating with the other prisoners. The World Cup was still on and he had to go and tell his mates Argentina had been knocked out... 1982 was a real bad year for Argentina! We didn't regard him as an enemy soldier, but as someone unfortunate enough to have been in the wrong place at the wrong time.

'Things settled down quite quickly and with Mike Savage we were able to talk to the prisoners. We talked to them a lot and the ones we had were a good bunch. We had a few laughs with them. We organized arm-wrestling contests in the cabins and the winners got free fags. There was a mutual respect for each other. Soldiers don't hate each other as most civilians think. Soldiering and fighting are a profession, killing people is part of soldiering, part of battle, but afterwards you can become friends. This happened on our deck on *Canberra*. The only Argies who gave off bad vibes were their special forces, who had a real big chip on the shoulder about losing.

'We made sure they had an hour a day exercise out on the decks. They hated going out there for their walks because of the bad weather, but it was unhygienic for them to stay cooped up in their cabins all the time. It was a very educational duty escorting the prisoners.

'We used to have a real laugh at mealtimes. We'd escort them to the galley for their scoff. After their meals they were all given one fag each whether they smoked or not. Even the non-smokers smoked their fag. Jesus, the coughing and spluttering round the tables!

'On the fourth day we were in Argentinian waters. We were expecting to see the Royal Navy escorting us, but it was the Argie Navy round us in a show of force. When we docked some lads went up to one of the upper decks and hung out a Union Jack and started to give two fingers to the Argie brass ashore. This was quickly stopped and we had to stay out of sight. The place was deserted: no families, mothers, wives, there to meet the ship, just a few high-ranking officers with a convoy of coaches for the officers and things that looked like cattle trucks for the troops. No press, TV, nothing. I thought that was bad. I know they lost the war... but cattle trucks.

'Then there was a loudspeaker broadcast through the ship warning us that if we went outside we would be severely reprimanded. Apparently someone had tried to piss overboard on to their officers. We went back to our deck and told Mike Savage to tell them they would be going ashore within the hour. It was incredible the number of them who shook our hands and waved as they went to the trucks. I know some of them exchanged addresses with some of our lads. There was one thing, however, which stuck in my craw and has annoyed me over the years: the attitude of some of the Marines and some of the hats towards the prisoners. These were probably ones who never got near a real battle but they treated the Argies with total contempt, kicking them up the arse and bullying them. It was totally unprofessional behaviour.

'As we sailed out of Argentinian waters the captain announced that we were heading back to the Falklands to pick up the rest of the Task Force and sail for home. Everyone cheered.'

Alberto Carbone was travelling home on the hospital ship *Bahía Paraíso* when he learned his country had lost the war. He had heard through the grapevine that a battle had taken place on Mount Longdon, a big battle, in which many of his mates had been killed.

'If I had not shot myself accidentally I would have been there. Would I have been killed there? I'll never know. Sometimes I feel depressed that I wasn't there at the battle. Was I lucky or unlucky? Even if we had won it would have made no difference to me not knowing how I would have fared in battle. It's something I have to live with. The hospital ship stopped once on the way home to collect more wounded from another ship and then we arrived in Comodoro Rivadavia. From there we flew to the military hospital at Bahia Blanca and the army flew my parents there to see me. After two weeks I was moved to another military hospital in Buenos Aires and two weeks after that I went to

Campo de Mayo and was discharged. I will always remember my discharge, hobbling out of the camp with my leg in plaster and on to a bus. That was it, simple as that.

'When I arrived home all my neighbours had a party for me and then it happened... remember that girl I mentioned, the one who was too young to look at? In the eighteen months since I had last seen her she had blossomed, blossomed into a stunner. She had grown up. Her name is Sandra. We started courting – and we've been together ever since.

'I was a bit lazy when I first came home. I needed a rest. I also needed work, a job. I began applying and applying until eventually the Post Office and Telephone Company took me on. I was finding life tough after the Malvinas. If I'm unexpectedly frightened, like a firecracker going off behind me or a car backfiring, I jump. In the beginning thunder frightened me even though I could watch it and know what it was. Then some people would suggest I wasn't even there simply because I missed the final four days of the campaign. I was there, but it doesn't seem to matter to them that I had to endure all the English bombardments from 1 May until 10 June. I still get depressed about that bombardment.

'I was also suffering from the treatment I endured at the hands of my own superiors. When I was staked out on that hill it completely knocked the stuffing out of me mentally and physically. We lost a war and the treatment we endured is the last thing anyone wants to hear about. Some people might think I am just trying to make excuses, but what chance did we ever have if our own superiors treated us in the way they did? Physically and mentally we had lost before the first shot was fired.

'Compared with some of the Malvinas veterans I'm very well off. I've seen a lot of them on the streets still in their uniforms, begging for a living. It's sad no one helps them or even really cares. I suffer from depression at times and it is something I have to live with. It's like an individual war within me. But I have matured. Before the war I was a young kid who was a walking disaster, drinking a lot and doing fuck all. Two years ago the government gave us a small war pension. It's small, so small it's an embarrassment, about 90 pesos [US$90] a month, which in today's market in Argentina buys nothing.'

However, life is not all gloom for Alberto. He is happily married to Sandra and they live in the area in which they both grew up and are surrounded by friends. They also have a sparkling six-year-old daughter.

After our interview I had just shaken hands with Alberto, and with Luis, who was standing beside him, grinning, when I noticed a horse and cart coming down the road. 'Alberto, Luis, look,' I shouted, 'that fucking white horse is still following you!' And that's how I left them: doubled up with laughter at the memory of an event that had seemed so serious at the time. Because otherwise you'd cry for ever.

Antonio Belmonte's family were delighted to see him home safe and almost well. He, too, was relieved to be back among them. But his problems were about to start: bouts of depression and four months in bed with pulmonary problems brought about by the cold and wet of the Falklands and the abysmal living conditions.

'I'm OK now, a peaceful person. But during the early days of my return I would stare at the sky when it thundered or when it rained. There is a calm within me, like a candle not even flickering, but I don't understand what happens to me sometimes, a nervousness, something I can't put a finger on. Sometimes I get so nervous that I can't do things I normally do, sometimes it takes me three or four attempts. Maybe part of the problem stems from the fact that when I returned I had no one I could really talk to about it. I don't know.

'Despite the outcome of the war I don't think all has been lost. I still believe Argentina still has some claim on the islands apart from the geographical one. I am not sure if we were up to the task we were given. It's done now, but I would do it again. That is something which is still inside me.

'I don't think Argentina has ever really acknowledged us properly as veterans. The bureaucrats are not interested in whether we are psychologically sound after what we went through. The military attitude is: if you can walk you are all right.

'If anyone asked me if I ever had dreams, nightmares, about the Malvinas I would certainly say no... but my wife, Alicia, says I do. She says I wake up in a sort of dream seeing the guys I buried as if they have come back to life. I don't realize I dream about it. My workmates support me, they always have done, because they know what I have been through. My real strength is my family; my wife is an excellent person. I have two sons now as well as a wife: Pablito and Esteban. Pablito is a Down's syndrome child. He has intestinal problems as well and is due an operation soon. Esteban has heart problems. Pablito's problems affected me a lot, as if there was a knife being twisted in my back, but I know both of them will be fine.

'I lost my mother to cancer in October 1993. She was only sixty five, but at least she managed to visit Italy, her homeland, before she died. My father is seventy-two and was so alone, so depressed after mother died. We took him to find another companion. He's found her now, a Spanish lady, and they are together and all the family accept her, which is important. He's just been back to Italy for the first time in forty years to see his brothers.'

Today Antonio Belmonte is happily married, living for his wife and adored sons. Five months after returning from the Falklands he began working for the state telephone company and is still there. Throughout our interviews he was helpful and sincere. I showed him a photograph of the Argentinian war cemetery in the settlement of Darwin and he looked at the rows of white crosses realizing one of them could so easily have had his name on it. He looked at me and said: 'I never knew that, never knew they had a proper resting-place. I now know my friends didn't stay in that common grave. I feel at ease now knowing they have been buried properly.' Every Argentinian I interviewed shared the same simple wish: to be allowed to return to Darwin, to the cemetery, to lay a wreath to their friends. Is this not a wish that should be granted?

Grievously injured Britons like Denzil Connick were taken to the Woolwich Military Hospital in south London. Denzil's time there was painful both physically and mentally as he struggled with the knowledge that only four inches of his left leg remained and his right was badly damaged, the consequences of which were that his robust physical life and front-line soldiering were almost certainly over. These would be devastating blows to the morale of any normal man, but even worse for a fully active soldier. The family who had turned out in force all those years ago to wave him off when he went to Aldershot to become a soldier gathered in strength at his bedside, led by his mum Carol. The size of his 'family' had increased over the years to embrace his friends and comrades of the Parachute Regiment. And then there was a girl, a nurse called Theresa, a fiery Scots lass who travelled all the way from Wales on her days off to visit.

'Not a day went by without someone from the regiment, an officer or one of my mates, coming to visit. Someone always arrived for a chat and with a beer hidden somewhere. Even during the long leave period after the war the lads always turned up instead of spending their time in their own homes and pubs. I never tired of their visits.

'With Theresa it was different. I was a bit reserved with her. I don't know what it was. I thought she liked me, but courting... It was only when my best friend, Benny Bental, said: "Look, Taff, that girl thinks an awful lot of you" that I began to think. But I was in pretty poor condition physically and was depressed and feeling sorry for myself. I couldn't imagine any girl looking at me twice. There I was, looking and feeling like a man crippled for life. Anyway Benny gave me a good talking-to more than once and Theresa and I got together. She, my mother and the lads nursed me through a rough time in my life.

'Eventually I was allowed home to Chepstow for a week. The whole street was out to welcome me. Going home was like a breath of fresh air. But that first week also gave me an insight into the difficulties I was going to encounter. Things most people take for granted, like upstairs bathrooms, were to prove an obstacle for me. I had to move about the house on my backside, pulling and pushing myself. I couldn't walk. If I wanted to go out I had to be pushed in a wheelchair. My right leg was far too weak to hold me. I had to have doors opened and held open for me. Gradually my stays in hospital became shorter and my periods of leave at home longer. At this stage I wasn't too worried about my career in the Army because even though I knew what my injuries were I didn't accept that I was disabled. As well as that our CO, Lieutenant Colonel Hew Pike, stuck his neck right out for all the wounded guys and said he would find a place in the regiment for us. That was a brave attitude for him to adopt, considering the attitude of the rest of the Army towards soldiers and Paras in particular. But the colonel was going to stick by his men like he had always done. The Paras are an élite and if you fail to attain the correct standard you are out, but here was an opportunity for all us physically disabled guys to stay in.

'I thought this was wonderful because the last thing I wanted to do was leave. Just before the Falklands I put my name down for a course as a helicopter pilot with the Army Air Corps. Flying is my second love after the Paras. Three of us had been due to be considered for this: Johnny Crow, David Scott and me. Of the three, two were killed and I was missing a leg. Ironic, isn't it?

'As I started to think seriously about staying in, the doubts began to nag at me. I just couldn't see myself stuck in a storeroom or behind a mess bar while the lads went off on exercises and jobs around the world. It wasn't me. I could see myself becoming bitter and eventually unwanted in the regiment as personalities changed. I had to leave so I could get on with my life and so the regiment could carry on with its duty. I reckon I had made my mind up before my treatment was finished.

'Considering my injuries, which were among the worst in the Paras, I recovered quite quickly compared with the injured hats. All of us injured Paras with our more positive mental attitude to life, our get-up-and-go, had got up and gone... whizzing about in our wheelchairs and bunking off to pubs before the hats had even sat up in bed!

'During the last stages of my hospital treatment a good mate, Tom Pollock, came to visit me. Now, old Tom was an amazing character. He was a fully qualified doctor and had been an officer in the TA Paras in the north of England, but he joined 3 Para as a private soldier. He spoke very well, just like the officers, but he had wanted to experience soldiering as a tom. So they made him a medic in Patrol Company and the lads there couldn't have been in better hands.

'Anyway Tom was off to some far-away land, so he turned up before he went and gave me the keys to his car. Now there's a mate. It was a nice big automatic job, sitting there in the hospital car park. As soon as I sat in it I realized I had freedom and mobility. I nearly crashed it on my first spin. I just discovered in the nick of time that my right leg was too weak to put proper pressure on the brake.

'Another visitor was Lieutenant Colonel Simon Brewis, an officer and a gentleman and a real unsung hero if ever there was one. He was the commanding officer of the Para Depot and was always visiting the lads and watching over our welfare. I cannot praise him enough. Having a man like Simon Brewis there when you need help is rare indeed. He was a major help to everyone and if ever anyone deserved a knighthood it is him.'

(Colonel Brewis went on to administer the South Atlantic Fund, which was made up from money donated by the people of Britain – not the British government – to help the dependants of those killed in the Falklands campaign, as well as the wounded and their families. He spent countless hours making sure the funds were properly and fairly distributed and throughout my research every soldier I have come across who has had dealings with him cannot praise him highly enough. Long after their careers are over and Colonel Brewis has retired from the Army, he still keeps in contact, helping men who would be forgotten by the military system. He has saved many an ex-soldier from the pit of deep despair.)

'Eventually I was on permanent sick leave and I knew it was only a matter of time before I became a civilian. I had Tom's car and could get around to visit my mates in the battalion. I was missing the comradeship. We had all been through a war together and they were really the only people I could talk to. I felt they were the only ones who understood. The battalion, too, was changing. Colonel Pike had gone and a new CO, Lieutenant Colonel Rupert Smith, had taken over. I got the feeling he hadn't got off on the right foot with the soldiers and it was not a happy place to be. His attitude was different and many felt he wanted rid of the Falklands men who remained. Morale was not good, in my opinion. It got worse when lads going on courses found the instructors were insisting on teaching out-of-date tactics – tactics which had been proved to be impractical during the Falklands. Other guys thinking about transfers or buying themselves out were allowed to go immediately – no chat or even attempted persuasion to keep them and put their experience to use to benefit the new soldiers filtering into the ranks. It was a crying shame to see good experienced soldiers going. New officers were coming in, too, and I got the impression that the soldiers were unhappy, disillusioned and demoralized by the attitude of the new command structure.

'I knew it was time to go, but I didn't know what I was going to do or what I could do. Little help was coming my way in terms of resettlement from the Army. The regiment was helpful, but the Army... Damn near half my body was missing or unusable and my prospects of employment were limited. I was in a wheelchair, I was disabled, but I still could not accept it. I felt like crap, a horrible feeling which brought on depression, but it is the only way to describe how I felt: like a lump of crap.

'The Army didn't help much. I had an interview with a hat officer whose heart was in the right place, but he wasn't qualified or experienced in dealing with problems affecting people like me. Neither he nor the Army could offer any practical guidance. I knew the South Atlantic Fund was going to help me, but when, how or how much was unknown at that stage. I started thinking about employment, but what the hell was I going to do? I knew I would have to be self-employed, but at what? I did a course in business studies.

'Exactly a year after the Longdon battle, on 11 June 1983, I married Theresa. It was a brilliant achievement for me. I had vowed to walk down the aisle on crutches and I did it. I had a girl beside me who had been and still is a tower of strength, a tigress in her support of me. All the lads turned up and we had a great day. Simon Brewis was there, too.

'A few months later I received a cheque from the South Atlantic Fund. I was amazed at the amount. Incredible: about ten years' salary. Theresa said: "It's yours". She said it was nothing to do with her. I was to put it in my own bank account in my own name. She insisted. Her sole aim was to support me in anything I chose to do. That tells you what a great girl she is. I put down £30,000 to buy into a franchise selling cookies and snacks to corner shops and garages. I had a 1920s-style van and a uniform from the period. My dad, Ernie, gave up all his free time to help me, to try to help me make the business a success. I needed him because my injuries made it extremely difficult for me to carry the goods into the shops. Dad worked hard and wouldn't accept a penny. I felt I was actually achieving something, doing what the regiment had drilled into me – going for it. But I was green, a chicken ripe for the plucking. Remember, I had joined the Army straight from school and knew little of the perils of Civvy Street. I lived in a background of comradeship and loyalty, not a cesspit where people were just queuing up to pick me off, to fleece me. I had also, by this time, been persuaded by a so-called friend from Civvy Street to invest heavily in a garage business. I was like a lamb being led to the slaughter. Both businesses crashed and I lost so much money, thousands, that even my house was under threat. We had to sell our home and buy a smaller, cheaper one to survive.

'Everything began to crowd in on me and I began to feel a total failure even though I still maintain it wasn't all my fault. I was ill advised by the bank and ripped off by so-called friends. Then the miners' strike didn't exactly help the local economy. On top of it all Benny Bental, my best friend, was shot dead in Belize. I was awash with depression and grief and began drinking far too much. The way I started treating my family was bad, like dirt. I feel awful about that now. The only people who could make me see sense or tell me I was out of order were my mates from the regiment. On top of my moods and depression I started having nightmares. It was hard to console me, to calm me. I went from the always happy-go-lucky Denzil to a guy who was not a nice guy to know. I would barely say a word to anyone and would sit locked into my own dark world of utter depression.

'By this time I had two brilliant young sons and my marriage was going through shaky periods. I was locked into a spiral of self-destruction. I still could not accept my disability and the fact that we had moved yet again, this time to a terrace house on the side of a mountain with fourteen bloody awful steep steps up to the front door, didn't help. I could not accept the impossible, that my dearest wish to be the old fit Denzil I was before the Falklands was never going to come true. It was an awful time.

'Then, when all seemed total gloom, I got a lucky break, another chance. I landed a job as a consultant in life assurance on a commission basis. It gave me new horizons and my contacts in Aldershot saw me back with the regiment giving advice and selling insurance. At first it went well, but soldiers being soldiers, they would soon cancel their standing orders at the bank so they could have a few more beers instead of paying my insurance premiums. My commission was always being clawed back out of my wages and, believe it or not, I ended up paying my employers! Nevertheless I stuck at this line of work for a few years and built up quite a reputation. I enjoyed it and I was out and about seeing people and doing something useful. Eventually I got the feeling I was being used by the people above me for their own ends and the time had come for a change. I had to try something else... but what?

'Late in the 1980s I landed a flying scholarship. Flying was something I had always wanted to do, a chance to prove to myself I could have made it as a pilot in the Air Corps if only I had not been wounded. I passed with flying colours and my results would have got me through to be a helicopter pilot if I had not been injured. Life is full of "if onlys" but at least now I knew the answer to one of them. Flying has always been a great love of mine, a passion, and I know that despite everything I am capable of flying a plane. That's a great feeling, a great morale-booster.

'But as we sit here talking in the summer of 1994, twelve years after the Falklands, I can't help but reflect. I get angry, very angry at times. You know, it has only been in the last eighteen months that I have accepted my injuries and recognized that they have prevented me from working in any proper capacity at all. Now that is a very hard thing for a man like me to have to accept. We are talking twelve years and the loss of all the money that was meant to help me before I finally find out I can't work. Christ, that hurts, but it's true: with my disabilities I'm unemployable in a proper job. My right leg, the so-called good one, is still giving me terrible gyp and is still under threat from the surgeon's saw. That's the truth and reality of the situation.

'Do you know that I've just discovered that I'm entitled to an unemployability supplement to my pension and nobody ever got round to telling me. For most of the last twelve years I have struggled and suffered bouts of depression, not knowing what benefits were available to me or what benefits I was entitled to. The government doesn't tell you and doesn't seem to bloody care.

'For years I didn't know what was really wrong with me. I do now and so does the government and the Army, but it is a condition they didn't acknowledge until 1987 and still try to turn their backs on. It is post-traumatic stress disorder, first diagnosed in American Vietnam veterans, but it has been around much longer than that. I have had two counselling sessions for it and I suspect that if the government and Army had recognized the problem long ago instead of sticking their heads in the sand I would have been able to solve many of my earlier problems, keep my money and be in far better condition than I am now. Many other soldiers have similar problems. I feel betrayed over this by the government, I feel that my family has suffered because of this, that the treatment I dished out to them was brought on by my condition. Here is a government which slaps you on the back and says well done, wins a landslide majority at the next election with the "Falklands factor" – the blood and sacrifice of our comrades – then kicks you up the arse as soon as your time is done. You're no use to them any more.

'The Army is not the same as it was twelve years ago because of the policies of this back-stabbing government and the penny-pinching money-grubbers at the Ministry of Defence. They have done more damage to morale and standards than the Red Army could ever have achieved. Look at the situation with the armed forces today, where front-line soldiers risk their lives with inadequate resources. How's that for loyalty? Training standards are suffering, too.

'Although I'm out now I still keep in touch with my mates. This government has failed to realize that wars and killing will never stop. Switch on your television and you see rabble armies slaughtering innocents by the score and everyone standing by, wringing their hands, instead of doing something like sending in well-trained, disciplined troops. Soon, with the cutbacks, we won't have the ability to do that even if we at last get a government with backbone.'

Denzil and Theresa's marriage is on rock-solid foundations and his two lively boys, Matthew and Stephen, fully understand their dad's disability. They know why he can't chase after them or play football with them. But his adoration of them more than makes up for any of those disappointments. Denzil takes them fishing and gets about as much as he can on his crutches. His right leg still causes him terrible discomfort and pain, but he is determined to keep it as long as he can. The family has at last moved to a bungalow in south Wales, which makes things easier for him. He has taken on a voluntary position with SSAFA (Soldiers', Sailors', and Airmen's Families Association) helping other servicemen overcome their difficulties.

Denzil's mother, Carol, whose face he saw as he lay close to death, and the rest of his family, are nearby. Earlier we learned how he was afraid to close his eyes in case he died. Well, he did die – and the medical crash team in Ajax Bay brought him back to life. Denzil never knew this until after he left the Army and managed to get a glimpse at his medical records. Sadly, as this book was being compiled, Ernie Connick died suddenly. It is Denzil's wish that his contribution be dedicated to his father.

2

MOST OF OSCAR Carrizo's friends thought he was dead. Two bullets were removed from his skull by surgeons aboard the *Uganda*.

'I didn't know at the time I had two bullets in me. I soon came to terms with the fact that I had lost the sight in my left eye, but at least I was alive and would be able to see my new-born son. I cannot thank those doctors enough for saving my life. I also thank God.

'I was repatriated home and spent many months in a military hospital in Buenos Aires. It was a long, slow recovery. I was relieved the war was over.'

Oscar left the army in 1988 and lives with his wife and three children near Buenos Aires. His son knows what happened to his father and how close he came to never seeing him. But Oscar maintains his wife suffered more than he himself.

'They have the mental stress to cope with, the not knowing. We are now closer than ever.'

Oscar is now a guard with a security company, working

long hours for poor pay. His grateful government gave him $140 for his injury.

As I left him after our meeting in June 1993, Oscar said: 'I often wonder about the radar, Vince... If it had been allowed to stay on and do its job properly maybe the battle for Longdon would have been different. We'll never know now.'

German Chamorro had fought and fought hard. Losing was a bitter pill to swallow, but his humiliation was far from over as he was searched again and again, then documented and processed aboard the *Canberra*. His bootlaces, scarf and belt were taken from him and then he was put before a medical panel.

'I was full of crab lice, crabs – not pleasant. We had not been able to wash and this was the consequence. I was moved into a room and a woman comes in dressed in white. I'm absolutely filthy and I'm told to undress in front of her. I haven't been this close to a woman in two months and now she's close and fiddling about with me. I keep thinking I'm going to get a hard-on! Anyway, she confirms I've got crabs and I'm taken to another room. This bastard guard keeps prodding me with his rifle and I'm told to undress again and then a nurse starts painting me all over with some liquid. All the British in the room burst out laughing at me. I was not amused in the slightest.

'I moved on to the dining hall and had some soup which I'm convinced must have been drugged because as soon as I lay down in my cabin I was out like a light. When I woke the ship was moving and we were well away from the islands. We were well treated and well fed and given cigarettes. They let us listen to the World Cup, but 1982 wasn't a good year for us.

'I couldn't get over seeing Englishwomen on the ship.

TWO SIDES OF HELL

One day we were in this piano bar on board when a guy comes in with a video camera and starts filming us, a real queer, one of the seamen. He didn't stay thirty seconds because of all the abuse and queer gestures we made at him. On the last day we saw some of our own frigates escorting us and we knew then we were in our own waters. Some of the guys smashed open a bar and stole the beer, whisky and champagne. The British guards just turned a blind eye.

'We were happy and excited as we docked at Puerto Madryn, but as we disembarked it all fell flat. We had expected family and friends to be waiting for us but instead we walked down the gangplank to be greeted with a handshake from a senior officer and then were put on trucks and had the canvas pulled down to hide us. There was nobody about. They were obviously keeping people off the streets and they were deliberately hiding us. It was the start of the long process of brushing us under the carpet. Eventually some people came on to the streets and clapped and waved and threw flowers.

'We eventually arrived at some depot and the processing began all over again – what unit, what combat role, etc. – and then on to another depot and another depot within this base before boarding more buses around 5 p.m. for the airport. No planes. We just changed buses for another journey to a naval airbase where we were greeted with a hug and lamb stew. We didn't have time to eat it because they began to cram us on to Boeings without seats for the flight to El Palomar. Then we had to run to more rows of buses for another drive through empty streets to Campo de Mayo. We were herded into a gym and the doors were locked, and more officials with more questions. They told us relatives would arrive in the morning and at 2 a.m. we were shown to beds with clean clothes piled on top. Then they said we were going to be fed and when we saw the food we couldn't believe it: so much. We still had a mind to steal it, but were told to be calm: there was plenty more. There was a captain in charge and he kept ordering more food for us. So we stuffed ourselves stupid before getting back to the sleeping huts at 4 a.m. He said reveille would be 6 a.m. and we told him to piss off. He woke us at 9 a.m.

'Outside, by the perimeter fence, people were gathering and we managed to get them to send messages to our families. On 21 June I was in the canteen talking to Amalita Fortabat, a nice lady who was listening to our problems, and then went for a walk. I saw one of my neighbours, who hugged me and then, suddenly, I was grabbed from the back and it was my mother, crying. My dad was there as well, hugging me and crying. It was the first time in twenty years I had ever seen him cry. We went and sat on some grass and I spent two hours telling them everything that had happened. I talked about 50,000 things non-stop. I discovered that on 1 May, when the British started bombing us in Stanley, my mother hid underneath a wardrobe crying and had to be prised out by the rest of the family still screaming and crying. She had to be sedated. I suppose no one thinks of the families suffering like that.

'But the hardest thing to witness in that camp was mothers and fathers wandering lost round the place, asking soldiers: "Have you seen my son?" Nobody could bring themselves to tell them their son was dead. You had to lie, you couldn't break it to them just like that. How could you possibly tell relatives that their boy was lying dead over there in some hole and you were here alive? How could you make them understand that?

'My family had to leave the camp after a few hours still not knowing when I would be able to come home, but they were more relaxed. For two more days we did fuck all and even disobeyed orders until they paraded us to say goodbye.

On the parade were soldiers who deserted their artillery piece on 14 June and we totally rejected them. These were the ones who left the regimental flag in their position. You don't do that: it's a big war trophy. Lieutenant Suárez said goodbye to me personally while our lieutenant colonel forgave the deserters. He said: "What am I to do? It's over. Do I court-martial them, put them against a wall to be shot?" Maybe he was letting them off because there were officers there who did the same as them.

'We left that camp and returned to La Calera, where our regiment was stationed. People greeted us in the streets, shouting and waving, and inside the camp soldiers were lined up at attention like a guard of honour. Almost immediately we were given four days' leave. The barracks must have emptied in an hour. I finally arrived home in Adrogue in the early hours. One guy gave me a lift and even thanked me for going to the war. I knocked on the door and our dogs wakened everyone in the house. At 4 a. m. we had hugs, kisses and lots of tears. I slept until 10 and everything was quiet, nobody about, nobody in the street. I went down to my local bar and the people there all wanted to know what happened after 14 June. There had been no news about us after that.

'I spent the four days resting and on 30 June at our barracks in Córdoba we had a parade and I walked out a civilian. At the time I wasn't worried about my future. I was just happy to be a civilian again and going home for good. Fifteen days after that I went back to my old job, which had been kept open for me, and my workmates held a welcome-back party for me. It was good.

'But within a short time the atmosphere in the office made me feel ill. I couldn't handle having so many people so close around me. I started missing work, only going in one or two days a week. The rest of the time I was out of it.

Even when I went to work I would sleep all the way there. I just longed to be back in bed. My boss didn't know about my experiences in the Malvinas and eventually my mother went to see him and updated him. Through July, August and September I went downhill. I saw a doctor, but he didn't really know what was wrong with me. I was having nightmares and then I was scared to go to sleep. I could see explosions, bombs flashing in my dreams. My mother would wake me and I would be covered in sweat. Psychologically I deteriorated. At one stage, for no reason, I leapt up from the dining table, grabbed my mother from behind and held a knife to her throat, shouting: "This is how the English killed." Another time I even grabbed my sister and was squeezing her throat ready to punch her. I couldn't rest, I couldn't sleep, I couldn't go to work and I was getting violent. It wasn't nice. I wasn't in control any more. I was losing myself, but I didn't understand what was happening to me.

'One day I was called into the boss's office and basically I was asked to resign. I knew deep down that it had to come. He offered me a deal amounting to nearly five years' wages, which I accepted on the spot. He was worried because under our laws I could sue him. But what was the point? I went and blew the money so quickly I have no idea where it went.

'My father arranged for me to see a private psychiatrist. She came to the conclusion that my problems were rooted in the way I had killed people, hidden, impersonal killing, and the face of the young Argentinian I had buried in Stanley. After two months of counselling I was in a position to face the world again. I started to feel better and was beginning to relax a little, but I still couldn't communicate properly with my family. I was more at home talking to other veterans. I was still locked in a private war civilians would not understand.

'I grew a beard and went off to Paraguay for a while, then came back and went to San Clemente on the coast. On the first anniversary of the war I met up with my mates from Córdoba and then I got a job at a stockbrokers dealing in dollars and shares. Things were looking better until, suddenly, my psychological problems returned. I became a zombie. Deep inside where I was still locked, like many others, in my own private war, I knew the time had come for me to try to beat this problem once and for all.

'I realized I was marginalized, that all the Malvinas veterans seemed to be marginalized. No one in authority seemed to want to know. We were having difficulties getting jobs, difficulties with the attitude of the government, difficulties with officialdom. Everything was against us. We didn't expect to be put on a pedestal, but some acknowledgement of what we had endured would have helped. Instead it was as if we didn't exist. It still is. It's all fucked. Even the archives are hidden from public examination. By 1984 many veterans had had enough and held a big demonstration at the English Tower on the second anniversary and burned it down in protest at government treatment.

'On 14 June two years after our surrender, my father died. My mother had a breakdown, the family was in bits. I had to be strong and I was until my father's coffin went into the grave. It was then I cried as I remembered all the good things about him. Then I began to remember the soldiers I had buried and that was what broke me. For a while I seemed to be permanently drunk. In 1988 I went back to school because the law said that any Malvinas veteran who passed his course would receive 6000 pesos. By this time I had a girlfriend. I had been working but Menem had frozen everything, so this was good. I passed and I went to Paraguay and Cristina and I got married. But things didn't work out there, so we returned home and rented an apartment. I got occasional work as a security guard and Cristina worked in a shop. Then she had a miscarriage and I found myself arguing with my in-laws, who thought I was lazy.

'Eventually I applied for a job at the airport and they said it would take fifteen days. That fifteen days lasted seven months until I went to the base and saw an officer, who found out that as a veteran I had priority status and started bollocking those who had delayed my appointment.

'I am settling again, recovering a lot of what I lost. I lost a lot of mates in the war and a lot more since who have committed suicide – more than 400 since 1982 – and, of course, my father.'

Things are looking brighter for Germán Chamorro. He and Cristina have succeeded in having a baby and they have managed to buy a house. He still has his job and is progressing. He said as I left: 'It's the soldiers who suffer, isn't it?'

The journey back to the Falklands after delivering the prisoners to Argentina was four days of lazing and relaxing aboard the cruise ship *Canberra* for Tony Gregory and the lads of C Company.

However, anger set in when he was told to cross-deck to the North Sea ferry *Norland* for the journey home to Britain. The Marines, he thought, would sail home in glory, grabbing all the headlines as they had done throughout the campaign, but at least the two Para battalions would be together. Airborne Forces Day, the most important day of the year, would be celebrated at sea. The powers that be decided the toms would be rationed to four cans of beer a man, an order that outraged men who had just fought a war and were now being treated like children. The order was ignored and Wendy – a homosexual member of the *Norland*'s crew – played all the old favourites on the piano as the Paras sang their heads off.

'Wendy was thumping out all the sing-along tunes and the atmosphere was brilliant. Then the senior NCOs arrived in the toms' bar to try to control the drinking and a full-scale battle broke out. It all ended in a free-for-all with everyone fighting everyone else. In the end it was a good thing because it got all the pent-up aggression out of our systems. Next morning everything was forgotten, as if nothing had happened, even though there were guys sitting around all over the place with black eyes and fat lips.'

At Ascension Island the Paras bade farewell to the *Norland* and the crew who had brought 2 Para to the Falklands. Then they boarded flights home to Brize Norton and their waiting families and an initial ten days' leave.

'I can remember seeing England again as we flew out of the clouds. Jesus, it was so good to see good old Blighty. When I got into the terminal I saw my mother and stepfather, both wearing Union Jack hats and carrying flags. I was quite shocked to see them there considering the way I had been brought up. Suddenly, in their eyes, I was the best thing since sliced bread. I did give her a kiss, but asked why she was there. She kept trying to cuddle me, something she had never done before, and it niggled me. I didn't respond to her. I walked over to my best mate, Mark Sains, and his parents, Jenny and Del, the people with whom I had spent a lot of weekends in East Ham. I had more in common with them and they invited me home to their place, where they were having an organized street party, but because my mother was there with my stepfather I felt obliged to travel home with them.

'I had third-degree questioning all the way about what I had done, but I sat quietly in the car until we arrived at her place about midnight. I was still in uniform, I had no civilian clothes with me and I felt I should be somewhere else. I told her I really wanted to be with my friends and promptly left to catch a Tube. I reached my old local in Ilford, and some of my civvy friends were still there and a little party started. My brother was there, too. But do you know, the landlord only offered me a pint after everyone moaned at him. The bar staff didn't want to know. I ended up at Lawrie Wales's house and we watched all the news videos he had saved for me. Because he was an ex-Para I was able to relax and talk to him.

'We were given eight weeks' leave and Mark and I went to Ibiza for a holiday. The other holidaymakers found out about us and held a party for us, but the Spanish barmen nearly caused a riot by trying to refuse to serve us.

'When I returned from Ibiza the full implications of the war started to hit me – that was when I realized how many had been killed. I lost nine good friends. Then my mother contacted me and asked me to meet her for lunch. She asked me to dress smartly. I turned up in jeans, desert boots and a T-shirt, normal Para walking-out clothes. I met her outside the City bank where she was working and it was only then I discovered they had laid on a meal specially for me and that I was the guest of honour. I got some strange looks as I stood around with the City suits sipping white wine and then the big boss says to me: "Well, son, what's it like to kill someone?"

'I said: "Do you know how many friends I've had killed?" The place went deadly quiet. I put my glass down and walked out. My mother rang me later and said I had embarrassed her.

'People are only interested in how many people you have killed or what it is like to kill, not in how many friends you lost. They're only interested in the glory of it all. Anyone can pull a trigger. You don't have to be a hard man to kill somebody. A bank robber who shoots someone and kills them is a coward as far as I'm concerned.

'Battalion life after that long leave was never the same again. Colonel Pike, who was a great CO, disappeared off on his next posting. In fact, all our bosses from officers to senior NCOs seemed to go very quickly to other postings. I can still remember the new CO's speech on the parade square. I felt he insulted us. I don't wish to repeat what he said. It infuriated me. I've never forgotten it. To me it summed up the Army's attitude. I feel he said it because people up top wanted us out, but if he said it off his own bat then it is unforgivable. You can just imagine the shiny-arses sitting back and saying: "Let's get rid of the experience now. We don't want this sort of soldier in peacetime." Hats have always hated the Parachute Regiment because of our professionalism. They have been trying for years to destroy the Paras and if they ever succeed then God forbid what will happen if there is another war. There will always be wars where people like Paras are best at dealing with the situation. We are the best at clearing up the dirt for the shiny-arses, but afterwards the government and the MoD always nip in quickly to stab us in the back. Morale was sinking as the new thinking and attitude towards us took over.

'We showed everybody else the way home in the Falklands, but the Guards and the hats and the shiny-arses run the Army. They know we are the best fighting force they've got and they don't like it. But if you look at the higher echelons they are all Guardsmen or ex-Guardsmen, gubbinses, craphats and shiny-arses running the place. The same among the politicians. There's big snobbery at that level, people from what they call the right background who make the rules and decide policy. I thought all that was supposed to have been kicked into touch, but it hasn't. They won't be happy until the Paras are gone.

'They're still at it, watering down our standards, trying to make us "normal" like the hats. They've even taken our depot away and our recruits have to train alongside the Guards, people with whom they have nothing whatsoever in common, in a joint depot. Guardsmen are good at what they do, standing outside Buckingham Palace stamping their feet and parading up and down Whitehall, but Paratroopers are 100 per cent fighting soldiers, not parade-ground automatons.

'I stayed in for another three years after the Falklands and tried to fit in with the new order of things, but it all got steadily worse. In 1985, after our tour in Belize I had had enough and decided to buy myself out. It cost me £700, which was all I had in the world. I was still young and had time to start over again. I loved the regiment and my mates. The Paras had given me a purpose in life, had educated me and matured me. I had settled down with my girlfriend, Sonia, and it was time to go.

'I had no job lined up and no real idea what I wanted to do. I went and sat at home and began to think. Next day, my first as a civilian, I went to the employment office, signed on and was told to go to the DHSS and tell them I had just got out of the Army. I had no money as I had used my savings to buy myself out. They said I had made myself unemployed and that I wasn't entitled to anything for at least six weeks. I was gobsmacked. Talk about thanks for serving your country. I got a job with a plant-hire firm, delivering equipment to building sites, and within a year got on a course learning to operate a JCB excavator. Sonia and I saved hard and managed to get enough together to buy a house. Then I got a job working for an insulation firm and at times I undertake security jobs such as close protection.'

Tony and Sonia are now married and have two children, Jamie and Michelle, and he feels secure. He feels the Army saved him from a life of drifting and petty crime. He is still working in the building trade and is surrounded by firm friends. He openly admits he dotes on his wife and children.

'I never had a family upbringing myself, but as God is my witness my kids will. I love my family more than anything else; they are the most important thing in my life. My mother has not seen my children, her grandchildren, for five years. Is history repeating itself?'

Tony Gregory, like all the others in this book, has one ambition: to visit Mount Longdon once more to lay his own wreath in memory of the friends he lost there.

The lady in the pizza shop knew exactly where Luis Leccese had been as he hobbled off the bus on his frostbitten feet. She handed the emaciated conscript a free pizza.

Still, he had made it home. His mother knew he was alive, but not what state he was in. She was shocked when she saw him. Throughout the campaign she had been distraught, not knowing what was happening to him or even if he was alive. She only found out he had survived when she was told by another soldier who arrived home before her son. It was an emotional homecoming, with neighbours coming out of their houses to shake Luis's hand and welcome him back.

'I couldn't walk properly for two weeks. Then there was a radio announcement that the state-owned utilities were to employ Malvinas veterans. I hobbled off and put my name down for a job with every one of them. I had to wait until October, more than four months, before something cropped up: a phone call from the gas company. It was a relief to have a job and start doing something constructive. I was paired up with another vet and our job was to cut off the supplies to the people who had not paid their bills. This other vet and I got on well together and we fitted in with the other members of the crew and even the bosses. But I wanted to better myself, I wanted promotion, and every time I applied for a better job within the company someone else would get it because they had a relative who had influence or was friendly with the bosses. I stayed there for a few years, but I wasn't getting anywhere.

'By this time I had joined the Comisión de Enlace, a group of veterans campaigning for changes in the law to benefit veterans. We lobbied and lobbied but the government never acknowledged us. It made me angry, our own people ignoring us and at the same time making sure everything that happened in the Malvinas stayed quiet. It hurt. Also, the people from whom we were seeking support could only ask silly questions like did I kill anyone, the sort of thing I didn't want to discuss.

'The vet groups tried and tried to get the government to give us some concessions and eventually a small pension was granted. Then we get a call to say the government want us to parade on 10 June because they are going to give a fucking annual medal. Well, they can stick that one right up their arse. A nice little ceremony and then you go back to being another piece of shit in Argentinian life. There are a lot of guys out there on the streets without a job or even a home. You'd think the government would want to help them. Medals won't feed them or put a roof over their heads. It does make me so angry. I'm not seeking special status, just recognition of what we tried to achieve and some sympathy for a lot of guys who are far worse off than I am.

'I eventually left the gas company and started delivering wine with a friend, but that didn't work out. Next I got an upholstery shop and that failed and then I tried a video club, but that went under, too. I've had a few jobs since the war and I'll keep on trying to make a go of it.

'I lived with my parents for most of this time and then I met Alejandra, who worked in a local disco. We got on great and ten years after the war we marred. My father helped me buy a half-finished house, which we did up, but because it was some distance from our own neighbourhood we sold up and moved back here to Bandfield and now we live in a flat above Alejandra's parents' house. We don't have any children yet, but when we do I will be very happy.

'I never had nightmares like some of the others, but I did feel resentment towards the British. That has faded now. I'm sitting here with you, my former enemy, giving you my life story. I have a dream, even stronger now that I have met you. Before we met I always wanted to go back, even to fight if I had to, but a compulsion to go back. Now as we sit here I'd still love to go back but not to kill, because that will achieve nothing. No, I would like to go back with you and your friends from Britain and we could all walk across Longdon again in friendship and talk about it all. That would be much better than fighting again. It has been good talking with my former enemy because it has helped me see that you and your guys were just like us... young soldiers doing a job.'

As I took my leave of Luis he said: 'You know, Vince, I've been with you on and off for a fortnight now, and although we can only communicate through Diego we understand each other. Yesterday I was telling my cousin about you and your visit, but he was more interested in the football on TV.'

'Luis,' I said, 'civilians will never understand soldiers. They can't relate to us. That's why this project is important. If people in each of our countries understand what I'm saying in this book, we will have achieved our aims.'

A solid handshake and the look we exchanged said: 'I hope I meet you again someday.'

As Felix Barreto arrived back in Argentina families were gathering at his regimental headquarters to see if their sons had survived. There was no one looking for Felix because he had not told his family he was there. The letters he had written from that windswept mountain had never reached his girlfriend, Mirtha, or his mother. They were all handed back to him shortly after he arrived back at camp.

He went to his mother's shack to collect the belongings he had stored there before going off to war. His brother begged him to try living at home again instead of the bedsit where he had spent his life before conscription.

'We agreed we would build our own house – a common practice in Argentina – and try to live together. My mother would live downstairs and Mirtha and I upstairs when we were married. But they didn't get on and the living-together plan was doomed to failure from the start. Instead I went to Mirtha's, where she lived with her parents, then went back to my job at the Delgado shoe factory. Everyone welcomed me back and the boss told me to have a month's rest and when I came back he gave me another fifteen days and then a further fifteen days, saying I deserved it. They were really good to me – and I was being paid!

'When I eventually started work properly I began to notice I was nervous, the noise of the machines really disturbed me. Even earplugs didn't help. One day I was late and was suspended. I was drifting between Mirtha's and my mother's and things began to get difficult. She had a new life and I had friends coming round to chat all the time. One day I just told her: "I've been on the Malvinas, mum." She was surprised. I don't know why I said it. I can only think it was because I was troubled inside. I was all over the place. My sister was also getting worried about me. Apparently when I stayed there I was having nightmares and shouting in my sleep: "Red alert... get down, you motherfucker."

'By this time she was cooking for a colonel and she spoke to him about me and he recommended I should see his brother, a medic. 'Things were getting worse. I had worries and problems trying to settle down and people just weren't interested. At discos the police would arrive and take veterans out and search us for weapons. I felt we were being singled out. If I heard loud noises or planes flying overhead I would dive to the ground. Then I started going to a psychiatrist, Dr Irrazabal. I went to him every day for six months and for the next nine months I visited him once a week.

'At one stage I went back to Resistencia to find my father, whom I had not seen for many, many years. I had never really known him. I don't know why, perhaps I was searching for something, but we met and shook hands and there was nothing there, no father-son feeling. Nothing. I've never been back to my birthplace.

'I still get hot-tempered, frustrated, about the Malvinas. It hurts, hurts that people don't care, that they are more interested in things like football than in the lads who were killed. I used to think that one day I would be able to go back, go back and fight for the Malvinas again, because deep down I thought we could win. I think of people like Lieutenant Baldini, who died where he had to die. Would he have been able to cope with coming home alive knowing he had lost the war? He was very military. However, over the last couple of years the thoughts about going back and fighting have faded. And I certainly would not go back with most of the officers we had at that time. I would be far more demanding of the officers if it were to happen again. I still regret the fact that my friends are still in the cemetery there – it doesn't torture me, but it does upset me.'

Felix is married now, to Mirtha, the girl he has known since he was fourteen, and they have two children. She has been a tower of strength for him. They live in a home Felix built in the area where they grew up and he is working again, for the telephone company.

Although he has had his difficulties after the war, Felix is a strong character and I am sure he will succeed. One of his dearest wishes, in common with all of the Argentinian veterans I have interviewed, is to return to the Falklands in peace to visit the battlefield and the Argentinian war cemetery.

Despite his wounds Dominic Gray had wanted to carry on fighting. He had to be ordered off the mountain – and it still rankles with him today.

'I feel I should have been allowed to carry on to Port Stanley, to see it, to see what I had been fighting for.'

In truth Dom should not be here at all. He had a truly miraculous escape. The bullet smashed through his helmet, ran across his skull and went out through his helmet again. He has a groove where you can trace the bullet's path across his skull. The tiniest deviation would have caused it to shatter his skull and blow his brain across the mountain.

After the Falklands the men of 3 Para went on a long period of leave – 'outrageously long', in Dom's view.

'I had thirteen weeks and deep down I was just yearning to get back to my battalion. The summer of '82 was a great summer to be a Paratrooper, a superb summer to be airborne. I was telling people I couldn't wait to get back because we were going to be the best fighting unit around. Us and 2 Para had put the regiment back on the map. I felt we were the masters of the universe, the best in the British Army. I knew a lot of the guys, because of their injuries, would not be able to continue as soldiers, but there were enough of us left to go on to further glory for our regiment and for them.

'We were posted from Tidworth back to Aldershot and I remember arriving back on my motorbike. I walked across the parade square dressed in jeans, sweatshirt and desert boots and with my long hair and sideburns, feeling ten feet tall. I strolled towards my barracks block and I couldn't give a shit for anyone or anything. I was back, back where I belonged. I saw B Company's block and thought: Brilliant, I'm home.

'I made my way to the company office, where a mate said: "Lucky, lucky bastard." I thought he meant my escape from death until he told me I was being posted. Within minutes our sergeant major, Johnny Weeks, bellowed my name. I marched into his office and stood to attention. It was great to see old John again, a marvellous sergeant major. I was gobsmacked when he said: 'Dom, I've screwed the nut for you, I've got you a little trip. It is in the way of compensation... you were put forward for a Military Medal and the powers that be have decreed it will not happen. Instead you will go round the world with a presentation team, lecturing on the Falklands. You will be the only private soldier, but you will be treated the same as the officers."

'I was distraught. We had a brilliant RSM in Lawrie Ashbridge, Colonel Pike was a superb CO and Johnny Weeks was just the dog's bollocks as a company sergeant major as far as we were concerned. All I wanted was to get back to soldiering, I was hungry for it and this trip meant I would not be soldiering for three months. There was no appeal. I was handed my documents and packed off within the hour.

'Just before I flew from Brize Norton the list of Falklands decorations was published. I read through the medals and was horrified to see some of the names there, but I was utterly disgusted to see who was not, particularly Stewart McLaughlin, my section corporal, who had been killed. His name wasn't anywhere. I couldn't believe it. As far as I was concerned then, and still am now, he was robbed. They robbed a dead man of his rightful recognition.

'Anyway I did the tour and I did enjoy it. I arrived back at 3 Para just before Christmas ready to get back to soldiering at last.

'It was the biggest downer of my life. The CO had gone, the RSM had gone, many others had gone. I had come back to a totally demoralized battalion. In B Company we had fresh faces, people in charge we didn't know and who didn't know us and didn't care. It was virtually impossible to take in the changes, to begin to comprehend them. The new soldiers seemed to be a bunch of moaners, always whinging. The experienced guys' morale was shattered. Guys were transferring out – even going craphat – and buying themselves out. Good guys, but no attempt was being made to keep them and their experience. The new CO, I was told, had slagged off the whole battalion on the square. The lads felt he had no respect for Falklands veterans or what they had achieved. I felt I had been shat upon from a great height. It was time to start thinking about getting out.

'The new CO seemed to have a thing about us Falklands guys. I don't know if it was just him or if he was having his strings pulled by some arsehole above, in the Ministry of Defence, or somewhere like that. He never stopped any guys leaving, just stamped their records without so much as a thank you. It was soul-destroying to see wave after wave of seasoned experienced soldiers disappear, the cream of the British Army utterly destroyed within six months of a glorious victory.

'Some of us felt it was a deliberate ploy to deflate us because we knew the Army system, run by craphats, hated elitism and us in the Parachute Regiment in particular. For years the shiny-arses in the Ministry of Defence had starved us of the proper equipment we needed for our role. Time and time again we held together and did our job despite them, but as soon as a war appeared we had all the kit delivered within hours, equipment the hypocritical bastards had been telling us for years was impossible. They wanted elitism and professionalism then all right. I could see these legions of faceless bastards who had starved us in the past plotting against us. 2 Para were getting the same shitty treatment. Suddenly after all the glory, all the bullshit, the Army didn't want us any more. The REMFs [rear-echelon motherfuckers], the peacetime career creeps, the shiny-arses who had been left out, were back in charge. Well, fuck them, they wouldn't drive me out. I decided to stay in and fight and maybe in a couple of years things would improve.

'Next thing is the big furore over the American Cruise missiles in Britain and the peace women protesting at Greenham Common. Before you know it we're there. Now, I have nothing against peace protesters; they are perfectly entitled to disagree. After all, that is what you have an army for in this country: to fight to preserve democracy so people have the right to protest against what they think is wrong. But to put front-line Paratroopers, hard-fighting soldiers, up against a bunch of protesting women is misuse and mismanagement of the highest order. Here we are facing down a bunch of women and guarding Yank missiles, I ask you. The seeds were sown for me to get out.

'At the same time I was seriously looking at the idiots commanding us. The good guys had gone and we were given utterly stupid tasks. We became a battalion wasted as far as I was concerned. As far as I could see all the good work done by our old CO and his team was being poured down the drain instead of being built upon. We were deployed on craphat tasks instead of the duties Paratroopers should be performing. We went to Belize for six months, which was a total waste of time. And it was after that, seeing even more good guys leave, that I decided to go as well.

'It hurts me to say this, but I was glad to be leaving, glad to be getting out before I was thrown out. We had a brilliant unit, a bonding among the guys which must have been the envy of virtually every other unit, something I had never experienced before or since and am never likely to again. But it was gone. I had done seven years and was by now a corporal and the lads gave me a brilliant send-off in the pubs in Aldershot. That is how I want to remember it – a brilliant night out with the lads.

'I left Aldershot and went to London and lived in a hostel for about a month until I found a job and new accommodation. I worked with the Wellcome Institute for a couple of years and then went to work for a stockbroker in the City of London. Two years on and I changed again to be a property maintenance manager for a very rich businessman and after three years of that I decided I wanted to study law. I've just finished my second-year exams.'

Today Dom is still studying and living with his girlfriend Karon and Harry, their enormously affectionate Doberman pinscher, in a riverside cottage in rural Suffolk. He plans to do an extra year's study to take in military law so he can appear at courts martial should any Paratrooper need his help. 'I'll even defend a craphat against the system,' he vows.

Dom still has problems associated with the trauma he experienced on Mount Longdon and has been counselled for post-traumatic stress disorder, a condition he is not embarrassed to discuss, unlike many other ex-soldiers. After the Falklands many of his friends ended up drifting and living on the streets in total bewilderment, branded loose in the head. They weren't – they were suffering from PTSD, a subject he feels strongly about and one which he absolutely believes the British government should begin addressing as the Americans have done.

Dominic Gray, for his gallantry on Mount Longdon, was mentioned in dispatches.

Jorge Altieri regained consciousness in a military hospital in Comodora Rivadavia, having been flown from the Falklands on the last flight before the surrender. He awoke to find his father, face etched with worry, at his bedside.

'How are you, Papa?' he whispered.

He had survived his horrific shrapnel wounds and the heart attack brought on by them in the hospital in Port Stanley. He had survived the callousness of the officer who didn't want the grievously wounded conscript on his truck for the ride to the hospital. Shrapnel was dug from his head and brain and he was paralysed down the right side. He had survived the battle of Mount Longdon, but his biggest battles were yet to come.

'There were things I couldn't remember. A medical officer told me that when I was in the hospital in the Malvinas I was shouting: "Go and fight, you motherfuckers. Get up and fight, you cowards." The only thing I could remember after waking up was meeting my grandmother. I told my father about it.

'She told me: "Go, Jorge, you shouldn't be here. Go." You see, my grandmother had died in 1981, the year before.

'The medical staff did physio on me for about half an hour a day to try to get my arm and leg working. My parents were at my bedside all the time and took over from them. They had to shave me, wash me and feed me, just like looking after a little child. I had a bandage round my head, covering half my face and something, I could feel, wasn't quite right. I suppose I looked a bit like something out of Frankenstein. They were always very secretive when changing this bandage which covered my left eye.

'At the end of June they said they were going to fly me to another hospital at Campo de Mayo in Buenos Aires province. I was put on a stretcher and taken in a van with my father to the airport. They took me from the van and left me there on the ground beside a Fokker aircraft. It was fucking freezing and my father was going mad. At Garnpo de Mayo I was taken to see a neurosurgeon and an ophthalmologist, Dr Nano, one of the best in the country. He removed my bandages and prised open my left eye. He made me look into a machine with lights. I could see OK with my right eye, but nothing with my left. What was going on? It was only then I found I had lost the sight in my left eye as well as my other injuries. I was very upset. Why couldn't they have told me earlier? I sat there shocked in a wheelchair, paralysed down one side and blind in one eye. Half paralysed and half blind... what could be worse? I asked myself. Death. I had to carry on, to live life with dignity. It would be hard, but I would do it.

'There were five or six other wounded guys in the ward and one of them was Corporal Carrizo. He was able to walk about a bit and we spent many hours talking to each other, about our lives and how we were wounded. It was good to have someone else from Longdon to talk to. My parents visited me every day and my friends from the judo club were able to come to see me and give me their support. My rehabilitation was under way. For an hour a day I was taken to a gym to learn to walk again. It was damned hard work. Slowly, very slowly and gradually, I started to walk, dragging my right leg. I still have a distinct limp and my arm is well nigh useless.

'At times I was very angry and frustrated at it all and at the treatment. One day all our family visits were delayed, so a bunch of do-gooders ushered a group of people and kids past our beds saying: "Look, children, this is a Malvinas hero who fought for you," as if we were attractions in the local zoo. We didn't need that.

'Then there was a fight in the next ward and one guy threw his crutches through the glass partition separating us. Glass showered all over my bed.

'We had arrived at the hospital thin and underweight. The food was good in the beginning: steak, chicken, potatoes. But once we started getting back to normal weight it changed to rancho-style crap: beans and pasta which tasted horrendous. Our complaints fell on deaf ears and my parents would take me to the canteen in my wheelchair and buy me a decent meal. I think we should have been treated better than that.

'At the end of September I was transferred to another military hospital in the centre of Buenos Aires. No sooner had I arrived than I was taken to the Gymnasia y Esgrima for a medals presentation hosted by the 10th Brigade. Many of the guys were there and it was great to see them again, but the whole thing was overshadowed by clashes with the police. Our relatives were chanting at the police and they flew a helicopter overhead.

'My treatment in this hospital amounted to half an hour's physiotherapy a day and half an hour's vocal therapy. For the other twenty-three hours I did fuck all. I heard about the League of Wives, an organization of powerful and wealthy women who took guys out for picnics in the country every Wednesday, so I applied to go on one. Next thing I heard General Menéndez was due to go on the picnic, so I cancelled my application to go because I didn't want to see Menéndez. I had deep feelings about the way he surrendered.

'Next day I was taken to an office and told to wait. The door opened and in walked the general. The hospital staff knew my reasons for withdrawing and somehow Menéndez got to hear of my decision. I must say that when we met he was very polite and we sat there, just him and me, having a heart-to-heart chat. I told him I disagreed with his surrender and he said: "Jorge, I surrendered because the English had just about surrounded us. They were on top of us. I surrendered chiefly to save life. To waste life in that situation was unthinkable, perhaps 400 or more soldiers would have been killed." He felt it was more honourable to save life than waste it. It wasn't until after he explained that I understood. Since that day he has been a friend both to myself and my family.

'Eventually I left hospital, able to walk, able to talk, able to see... wanting to see if I could survive in the outside world. Things had changed in Argentina. Democracy had arrived, but for us veterans this wasn't a great help. When the military ruled, the state-owned companies were obliged to employ veterans.

'President Alfonsin's government changed that policy. The present government has carried on where they left off in that respect. Once you go for a job and give your date of birth, 1962, they immediately know you are a-veteran because Class of 62 went to war. Some companies send veterans for psychological or psychiatric tests and even then they don't get the jobs. Until the Malvinas Argentina had not been at war since 1800 and in our country there is no experience in dealing with war veterans. There have been many cases of suicide. Some politicians are beginning to address our problems, but most of them only take an interest for their own reasons.

'Although I have not suffered from nightmares I did have a lot of resentment against the British for a long time. I would lie in bed thinking of ways to turn back the clock so I could do more in the battle, more to save my friends, more to secure our position on Longdon.

'Now that I have met British soldiers I realize we are the same in many ways and it has helped. I can still remember the rumours about what the Gurkhas would do to us and that the more of us they killed the bigger bounty they got. I remember them telling us that the English got more money for attacking by night and that if they did it on Saturday or Sunday they got even more pay. It was as if they killed for money whereas we did it for patriotism. Lies, all lies. I know that now, but for a long time I believed those lies. On Longdon we had a radar and on the night of the battle signals appeared on it – advancing troops – and it was reported, but it was turned off. The officers didn't have the decency to alert us. Instead we were allowed to sleep. Some of my friends died without even getting a chance to defend themselves.

'Things like that are hard to come to terms with. Life wasn't easy. The Army gave me a pension, a small pension, and only then because I was more than sixty-six per cent disabled. I started visiting centres for disabled people and joined the veterans' association. I met some guys who introduced me to selling bin liners on the streets. I would have to buy them and sell them on at a profit, standing there in the street yelling: "Bin liners, bin liners, help a Malvinas vet." I found this hard, very hard. Street selling in my condition affected me deeply because I felt people only bought from me out of pity. It wasn't a very dignified way to earn a living.

'Our vets' group in Lanus tried different ventures, like making calendars and running a newspaper for vets, both of which failed. We had a small success with self-adhesive labels and stickers which I sold on buses. I would stand behind the driver's seat, give a short speech, then try to sell the stickers. At least I tried.

'Around this time I met a girl, Miriam, and we started

courting. A year later we married. I also joined a veterans' group which takes part in sports events for the disabled and has been to Austria and England. Ten of us went to England in 1993 as guests of the British Legion. Meeting British soldiers like you and Dom and Denzil and other veterans in England has helped. We can meet and we can talk. That is good, the main thing.'

Jorge and Miriam have a five-year-old daughter and as this book was being finished added a baby boy to their family. Jorge is working on the lobby desk of a pensioners' association and is president of his local veterans' group. He regularly campaigns for better treatment for his fellow-veterans and, after twelve years of struggle, is able to support his family.

T HE RODS which had been holding Jerry Phillips's shattered arm together were removed and he returned to battalion life doing, in his own words, menial jobs. But tragedy was to strike again.

'In mid-1983 I fell over and the bone shattered again. I ended up in the Cambridge Military Hospital again for half a dozen operations, with them trying all sorts to fix it. After one operation I got an infection and was kept in hospital for ages. There was internal pinning, external pinning, internal and external pinning. Nothing seemed to work. I was pissed off. I felt like a guinea pig. Operation after operation failed. I couldn't believe what was happening. Nobody seemed to have a clue what to do. It was my hardest time. Eventually the Army surgeons handed me over to a civilian surgeon in Woking, Surrey, and he performed an operation and then I went to hospital in Bristol. For seven or eight months it was more operations, bone grafts, all of which failed.

'Finally I had an electric box fitted to my arm and for sixteen hours a day it buzzed away as it tried to get the circulation going correctly around the wound and the damaged bone to get it to fuse together. This, too, failed. After all this the doctor took me into his office and quietly told me I would have to have the arm amputated. I was in total shock. This would mean the end of my Army career. I drove back to Aldershot nearly in tears. I went straight into the HQ office and applied for discharge. They didn't want to see me go, but in the end I was discharged within two weeks.

'Looking back now I feel 3 Para was in a mood for change. I felt it was a fighting unit and I was in the way of its restructure. I had to do the right thing and release myself from 3 Para so it could continue without a hanger-on like me. The Para regiment treated me right as far as my rehabilitation was concerned, but the Army was a waste of time. I had absolutely no advice whatsoever. It took nearly six years for me to find out about my claims and entitlements for my disability. Six years and the bastards only pay you from the date on your claim form, not from the date of your discharge. You get no advice or backdated pension. There are hundreds of lads out there from all over the Army who are being ripped off. Recently I worked out I was £32,000 adrift, which they'll never pay. All I get is the cold shoulder and letters full of bullshit and regulations. The government did fuck all to help me and the rest of us.

'It was the Great British Public who bailed all of us out with their donations to the South Atlantic Fund. I was told my basic Army pension rights, but nobody told me anything about disability claims and other claims I am entitled to.

'No, it was the South Atlantic Fund which the ordinary British people supported, which gave me something to tide me over. What little savings I had went on supporting my family, my wife and two sons. The helping hand from the

South Atlantic Fund – an interim payment – enabled me to put a down payment on a run-down house in my home town and friends rallied round to make it habitable. You find who your mates are at times like that.

'Because the treatment was ongoing the Fund administrators could not assess my level of compensation. We would all have to wait to see how things progressed. But at least they gave me something. I had to make a living and the only thing I really knew about other than soldiering was fishing, so when my payment eventually came through I bought a small trawler. I knew I would have to work for myself because the local job centre basically told me to piss off because of my injury. I started lobster potting, probably one of the worst jobs someone with my injury should attempt, but it was always something I had dreamed of doing and right up to 1986 I was doing OK. I bought another old boat, did it up, and started trawling.

'By this time a hospital in Bristol had taken over my case and with all the trips to and fro my business was beginning to suffer. I couldn't maintain it and things went from bad to worse. My wife and I split up and she took the kids. Eventually I lost the house to her in the divorce negotiations. I had to sell one boat to pay bills and the other got engine trouble. It just lay there tied up. I had nothing left: no home, no family and no money. Then the recession hit as I was trying to scrape a living. From paying £300 a month my payments rose to £800-£1000 – more than I was earning. I was working seventeen hours a day running a video shop and with a road gang. Every time I started to make ends meet I would be called for another operation and this would put me behind with my payments. I lived above the video shop, fished at weekends, working seven days a week. The pressure was enormous. I handed all my paperwork over to my solicitor, gave my sister power of attorney, packed my bags, sold my car to raise enough for a flight to New Zealand and tried to get away before I cracked up.

'As I arrived in New Zealand I told myself I had to sort myself out. I walked and hitched for two months, working in the fields and on small farms. I kept in touch with my sister and I knew I would have to go back to sort things out. New Zealand freshened me and I returned home to face debts of £8000. I worked and worked and managed to clear those debts.

'It was about this time I was referred to the Northern General Hospital, in Sheffield, for more specialized treatment. For the last four years I have been regularly making the long journey from the West Country to Sheffield for operations.

'Now I'm having problems with some of the other local fishermen, who seem to feel that because I wasn't born down here in the West Country I shouldn't be allowed to fish here. Others say that because of my disability it is against regulations for me to be allowed to be a fisherman. Others claim I can fish only because the South Atlantic Fund bought me a boat. Let me tell you something: I would rather have a good healthy arm than any money. These guys think they own the sea. Well, I fought for this country and its democratic system. The government has never helped me. All I've ever enjoyed was soldiering and fishing. I've lost one trade and now some of the locals would like to see me lose the other. What a sad outlook on life some people have. Even now I don't think I'll settle to civilian life, where there is nothing fulfilling. You only seem to work to pay bills.

'I know if I hadn't been wounded so badly I would definitely have tried for the SAS. Soldiering in the peacetime Army was never going to be the same after the Falklands.

Now I only feel satisfied if I can do a good, hard day's work. The Parachute Regiment taught me that and made me what I am today. I won't lie down and die – never.'

Jerry Phillips is settling down. He Lives in the West Country with Denise and they have a bright and rumbustious two-year-old daughter, Sheryden. Again Colonel Simon Brewis has stepped in to help and Jerry is on a five-year course in marine science. He is able to fit his studies around his constant hospital treatment. Jerry had his nineteenth operation on his arm at the end of 1993. As I write he is in a body cast and his arm is immovable. It will be like that for three to six months. This will not be the end of his ordeal. He lives with the constant threat of losing his arm. Maybe not this year or next year. Maybe in five years or ten. Jerry will carry the legacy of the Falklands with him to his grave.

Says Denise: 'We have to keep praying that eventually his arm will mend. He doesn't deserve this.'

Jerry Phillips was without doubt one of the finest soldiers in the ranks of 3 Para in the South Atlantic. For his actions on Mount Longdon on 11-12 June 1982 he was mentioned in dispatches.

Kevin Connery arrived back at RAF Brize Norton to find Michele, his bride of four months, waiting for him. He had spent three and a half of those months at war. They had an Army house in Aldershot and now was the time to settle down.

'We were on leave for eight to ten weeks and it was boring and frustrating because we were all still hyped up inside. There was no counselling or debriefing, no wind-down system. I went on the piss with the lads. I took my wife with me – a lot of the married lads did – but it all ended with the wives standing in a group watching while we got drunk. I know some people will say we're professional soldiers and dealing with things is what we are paid for, but we are human beings, too. The sights we saw were a shock to our systems – the training only tells you ~it is not pretty. I was grieving for my mates who had been killed. Getting drunk seemed the easy way to escape the grief. I don't think the wives understood, but there again it wasn't their fault either. We had changed, we were all different people.

'Four months earlier my wife had married a young Para. The guy who came back was totally different to the one she had married. The divorce rate of guys who served in the Falklands rose alarmingly over the next three to five years. On the military side I could see straight away that the Army did not want experienced troops. Everything changed overnight. I didn't feel that our new CO was the most understanding of officers. Within a year about sixty per cent of the guys who served in the Falklands had gone from the battalion. Today, as I understand it, there are only about twenty-five guys there who served. Incredible, isn't it? From 600 down to twenty-five in twelve years. All those men gone on the wind.

'It saddened me to see the new mentality. It swept into other units as well, including the Marines and the Navy. Someone up top should have said: "Hang on, let's talk to the boys. After all they're the ones who do the donkey work for us." Personally I don't think 3 Para has ever recovered from the MoD mentality which took over after the Falklands. Now they've got their dirty paws on our training. They want hats. Now, hats are very good in their own field and doing what they are trained for, but they are not élite shock troops.

'I hit the bottle and it got to the stage where I had to go to hospital to dry out. I was surprised to see how many lads were there with problems related to the war. My wife stuck by me for about a year. During this time she became pregnant and we had a son. I was discharged about a year after the Falklands and at the same time my marriage foundered. I was on the street with no one. Some friends stuck by me and they are still my friends today.

'So what does a professional soldier do when he leaves a professional army? I decided to do the one thing I knew best: I departed Aldershot and England and went to France and joined the French Foreign Legion. If my own country didn't want me perhaps the Legion did. Straight away I felt at home. I came top in my training and mastered my new language, French. If you didn't the Legion gave you a pretty tough time. I joined the 2ème REP [2nd Foreign Parachute Regiment], a battalion with a long history of campaigns, including flying to the rescue after hundreds of Europeans and Africans were massacred by Katangese rebels in Zaïre in 1978. I joined their Premier Company, which is a night Para-commando unit. I passed top in that course, too.

'The French liked my professional outlook. I teamed up with various other British guys who came from all sorts of backgrounds; most of them were ex-soldiers. My main friend was John Willard and we became inseparable. We were posted to Chad where the Chadians were fighting the invading Libyans. We saw action, lots of it. After Chad both John and I were promoted to corporal and I went to Djibouti, back to Chad, Corsica, central Africa, etc. The Legion was good to me and for me, but nothing I experienced in the Legion will ever compare with the battle on Mount Longdon.

'People say the Falklands was a conflict. It wasn't: it was out-and-out war. I don't know what the legal definition is for conflict or war, but the Falklands to me was a war. We used every piece of ordnance that could be found other than nuclear weapons. If somebody tells me we have to use nuclear weapons to turn a conflict into a war then that person needs his head examined. Surely a conflict is the job the Army is involved in over in Northern Ireland, where – whenever possible – the rules require me to issue a warning to my enemy before I squeeze the trigger. In the Falklands I just squeezed the trigger as soon as I saw the enemy. In Northern Ireland I never used my bayonet, I was never required to even fix my bayonet and I never carried my bayonet on my belt. In the Falklands I carried my bayonet, I fixed my bayonet and I bayoneted somebody. That is the difference, in any soldier's book, between a conflict and a war.

'I served my five years in the Legion and returned to England. My little son Michael had died a cot death. My father's first son, my brother Noel, had also died of a cot death and my other brother's first son died a cot death, too. All first sons. That period immediately after the Falklands didn't bring me any good fortune at all.

'However, on my return from the Legion I landed a job I enjoyed as an Outward Bound instructor, teaching sailing, canoeing, diving and all the rest at Poole, Dorset. It was run by an ex-PT sergeant called Peter Cunningham. He was an amazing character and I enjoyed the work, but the money wasn't very good so I had to move on. I had changed: I had basically grown up. I had more respect for other people and their point of view. A few years earlier I would have settled an argument by thumping the other person, but now my communications skills have grown. Look at us now, in our mid-thirties, we have grown up. We can communicate with people so much better now. Remember when we were just eighteen... we ruled the world, or at least we thought we did. We were the future as we saw it. Growing up is a difficult process, isn't it?

'After all these years I can count my true friends on the

fingers of one hand, people to whom I never have to say "I love you" or "You are my best friend" because they know and I know and it doesn't need to be said. However, my relationship with my girlfriend is different as is any relationship with the person with whom you plan to live the rest of your life. In that domestic environment you constantly say "I love you" and reassure the other party. With my special friends a phone call now and again, a week, a month, a year on, is enough to rekindle that special friendship. That alone is the tale of combat soldiers who have fought together, who have a common bond, and if that type of friendship ended it would be like losing a limb to me.

'Every morning when I wake up I take a sharp breath. I'm alive. Johnny Crow isn't, neither is Georgie Laing and so many of my other friends.'

Kevin is now based in London, where he lives with his girlfriend of five years – 'the girl with whom I will spend my life' – and works in security. Occasionally he flies to various parts of the world on business. Hong Kong, Africa, Kuwait and Bosnia are regular ports of call as he continues to risk his life to protect others. This time, however, those for whom he is prepared to lay himself on the line reward him well. Despite his globe-trotting there is one place he wishes to visit: Mount Longdon, where he can pay a last tribute to his friends.

Kevin Connery, the man who wondered if he would be a coward on that long journey to the Falklands found his answer on Mount Longdon. And for his gallantry in that battle he was mentioned in dispatches.

Santiago Gauto threw the working parts of his rifle into the cold, grey water, then joined the queue to add his weapon to the growing pile. Surrender had a nasty taste. He tossed two grenades on to the pile and was immediately thrown to the ground, punched and found himself staring into the muzzle of a British rifle. The powers that be might have surrendered, but Santiago's spirit burned as fiercely as ever. Soon he was on the *Canberra* and sailing for home. On the landing-craft taking him to the big white liner he had a last moral victory: he stared down a British Royal Marine guard who had been grinning at him.

He remembers seeing the officers who had treated them so abysmally and led them so incompetently walking the decks as he took his exercise. It filled him with delight.

'We watched them walking about like dogs. We had cabins and we had heard they were held in the holds. I hope it is true. The British gave us what our own people didn't: food. We had their round white bread, their soup and their round potatoes. Where the fuck do they get such round potatoes? After food they even gave us a cigarette. The treatment shocked a lot of us because it was good.

'After arrival at Puerto Madryn – we were still dirty and stank despite showers on *Canberra* – we waited for nineteen hours before three hundred of us were squeezed on to a plane designed to carry just ninety passengers. We stood shoulder to shoulder all the way to El Palomar and if somebody threw up over your shoulder it was tough. You couldn't move or even fall over. From there we went to the 7th Regiment's base at La Plata. The streets all around were crowded, but it was different from when we had left. Then it was all cheering; now the streets were full of anxious people looking for their sons, mothers milling around wailing. Someone asked me about Corporal Carrizo and I said he was on another bus. I couldn't bring myself to say he was dead. Now I know he survived in the end. At that time we all thought he had died. Massad's father was waiting for him with a Peugeot 405 he had bought specially for his homecoming. When he found his boy had died he took it away and set fire to it. Sad, so sad.

'I was discharged virtually right away so I rang my mother and headed for home. A guy gave me a lift. I was in such a state he even offered to buy me new clothes, but all I had in my head was getting home. The man was an estate agent and he said if I needed anything to ring him. I was very emotional as I walked to my mother's back door. I knelt to pray and then knocked on the door. She opened it and hugged me. My father was there, too, and that was a great joy to me. He had begun visiting mother again, asking for news about me. After fifteen years apart they were back together. Brilliant.

'I visited my girlfriend, Cristina, and we just hugged each other and cried. We had a very close relationship and she understood me. I said to her father: "Give me two years and we will marry." He was so shocked and emotional he almost died crying.

'Throughout July and August 1982 I locked myself away at home, refusing to venture out. I walked around the house in a trance. I lost everything. My family thought I was mad. I would just sit there and stare at them round the table. Only Cristina understood me. I was also upset to learn that my family had sent me parcels of food and not one of them reached me.

'Finding work was another battle, one which is still going on for many of us today. It is the war of the "Malvinas Argentinas" – if you have been there they don't want to know you. It is as if we are all mentally deficient. I put my name down with Entel Telephones, then the gas company, YPF, Banco Nación and all the big companies in many places. No work, sorry, Malvinas vet. I eventually found a job at the same factory as Cristina. But now I work for the borough council. I'm the cashier doing the wages for 4000 people. Now some other vets have jobs there as well.

'Cristina and I married in April 1984 and we paid for everything, even buying our own presents. I set about doing up our house and a year later our daughter Mayra was born. To be at her birth was spectacular, a beautiful thing. I was actually shaking with emotion.

'After the war I had a couple of hard years psychologically. People don't realize or even begin to understand war and the effect it has on soldiers. Perhaps they think we are robots without feelings. Even now I don't like the noise of engines or even the sound of our washing machine at home. It reminds me of that radar which attracted all the bombardment on Longdon. It brings nothing but horrible memories and I have to tell my wife to turn it off. In those early days I would always dive for cover when a plane whizzed overhead.

'There was no help with employment to get us earning, to get us integrated back into society again. The state companies took on about fifty guys each and it was made to look as if they had employed 1000 apiece. I couldn't even get my job at the printer's back and neither I nor my mother received a penny despite the fact that the law said conscripts' jobs were to be kept open and their wages paid. I joined one of the many veterans' associations and became vice-president of our local branch. My friend Beto [Jorge Altieri] is now the president, but I broke away when it all started to become political.

'I've kept many things bottled up inside. When I think back to when I was starving to death on Longdon and couldn't get into Stanley to beg for food and how I cried... I still felt a man even though I cried to myself... When I think of how hard my mother, my brothers and Cristina toiled I couldn't tell them how I lived up there.

'When we got back we saw flags flying and thought they were for us. It made us happy. Then we discovered they were for the World Cup. We went into a bar one day and the owner didn't charge us because he said we were heroes. I couldn't accept that, that we were heroes. The heroes were the dead. We stood there and supported Brazil because after that we didn't give a fuck for Argentina.

'The people back here at home were lied to and so were we. I was on a mountain freezing and starving and crying. Here in Argentina the people were told we were winning the war, sinking four or five British frigates. Afterwards some people would thank me for going and then spoil it by asking: "How many did you kill? Were they blond, tall?" I would tell them to piss off.

'Today I'm sitting here talking to you, an Englishman, my former enemy, who didn't aim where I was and I didn't aim where you were. We could have killed each other, but we didn't. It's an incredibly weird feeling. Here we are talking, and you may have killed one or even ten of my friends and I may have done the same to some of your friends, but at least we sit here understanding each other.'

Santiago is still a cashier, still married and now has a son, Demis, in addition to his daughter Mayra. He is a strong character and I respect him and understand him. When we first met he regretted not being able to speak English and my not being able to understand Spanish. Two months later, when I read the transcripts of our meeting, I understood fully why. He was right because it would have been a much more fulfilling meeting for both of us. My final question to him through my interpreter was: 'Have you anything else to say?'

His reply: 'Send my good wishes to the boys in England.'

The soldier on the battlefield is aware of what is going on around him. His parents back home have no such comfort. They are the ones who wait, who worry, who wonder how their son will return. Will he survive unscathed? Will he be horrifically wounded, crippled, a mental wreck? Will he even come home alive? The parents' war is even worse in many ways than that of the front-line soldier, but they are sidelined, forgotten, even ignored by the authorities. Let's now look at their story.

Peter Gray knew something of war. He had lived through the German occupation of the Channel Islands and still clearly recalls the day the Nazis bombed St Helier. He had watched in horror as Russian and Allied prisoners of war were herded into forced labour gangs to build underground hospitals, bunkers and sea defences. He was old enough to know what was right, but too young to be a soldier. He joined the Resistance, stealing, hiding, damaging German equipment, anything to hinder them. He was thrown into jail at the age of fifteen after being caught daubing walls with anti-Nazi slogans. Peter shared a cell with a Russian major and a friendship was formed which lasted long after the war. He made friends, too, with a German soldier from the occupying force. After the war Peter worked and worked and is now a successful businessman.

'In April 1982 Diana, Dom's stepmother, and I travelled to Southampton docks. We had no idea if we would be able to see him or even see the *Canberra* sailing, but it was a chance I had to take. Not only were we allowed within touching distance of the ship, but a message was passed to Dom on board. He came to the departure lounge with some of his mates. When I saw them all I was surprised they weren't all great big six-footers. They were all of average height, but their morale was amazing. You could feel it, cut it with a knife. They were off into the unknown, but with their morale so strong and their mental attitude I felt nothing could go wrong.

'When the time came for him to go back on board we had difficulty expressing our feelings in words. Both of us knew, however, what was in the other's mind. We comforted each other with hugs, but how can you say to your son "I may never see you again"? You don't. You say: "See you when you get back, son." When a parent is faced with this situation it is a strain, a terrible strain. As the ship sailed and the military bands played and the relatives waved I could just see Dom waving. That was when the tears appeared.

'On the way home I said to my wife: "Will we ever see him again?" We had to keep telling each other he would be OK. I kept telling myself I would see him again. I kept saying: "It will never happen to us – maybe some other poor lad will get killed or wounded, but not our Dom." But it did happen to us.

'I received letters from him fairly regularly. My morning routine was always the same, checking for the postman and absorbing all the news on BBC Radio Four. That is all any parent can do, listen and wait. It is slow and frustrating. Towards the end of May we heard ground troops had secured a bridgehead at Port San Carlos and I knew then that mail and information from him would slow down. All I could do was wait and pray.

'That was how I spent the time right up to the victory. A couple of days after that, when Diana and I were just beginning to relax knowing Dom would be OK and would soon be on his way home, I returned about ten o'clock one evening and found Diana on the sofa crying. I knew immediately it was Dorn. She said the local police had been round with bad news. A piece of paper said: "Your son, Dominic, has received a wound to the head." It was rather vague to say the least. I rang the police, but that was all the information they had.

'We passed an awful night. All I kept thinking was: Jesus, a head wound. Has he lost his mental capacity, might he be a human vegetable? I made my mind up there and then that we would care for him. It was such a vague description of his injury, anyone receiving it was bound to think the worst. As soon as possible the next morning I was on the phone and for the next four or five days I rang and rang every military establishment I thought might be able to help, to tell me more, the Ministry of Defence, the Paras in Aldershot and Tidworth, anyone I thought could give me some information about my boy. Nobody could tell us a thing. It was frustrating trying to find what had happened and what his condition was. I eventually discovered he was aboard a hospital ship and I sent a telegram to the ship. As a result of that the Para Depot in Aldershot called me and said he had a head wound, was not serious and was on his way home. They said he would fly into Brize Norton and then be transferred to the hospital at RAF Wroughton. We eventually received another message saying he had arrived.

'We jumped in the car with a huge bowl of fresh strawberries and a carton of cream and headed for the hospital. I walked what seemed miles of hospital corridors, dreading what I would find – a mentally retarded son, perhaps? As soon as I saw him I was relieved. He was standing there patiently waiting for us to take him home. The joy of travelling home with him and eating strawberries and cream on that beautiful sunny day was overwhelming.

'After some time at home I took Dom back to Tidworth to collect his motorbike, which had been left with all the others securely, they believed, in the transport compound. We arrived to find that many of the motorbikes and cars had been vandalized. Even today I find it hard to believe people could stoop so low as to do this when the boys were away fighting a war. It was one of the meanest things I have ever had to witness and then, when they wanted compensation, well, what a waste of time! It wasn't a nice welcome home.

'Today, when I look back, I realize how lucky we were to get him home in one piece. So many didn't come home at all. I do feel it was a war which had to be fought. Sending troops over such a vast distance was an enormous achievement. It is only recently, however, that I have been told how terrible the fighting was. Nobody realized just how fierce the hand-to-hand fighting was. Maybe, in time, the Argentinians will have some control over the islands but in 1982 we had to fight that war. I know my son has become wiser for his experiences.

'I still thank God that Dom came out of it in a better physical condition than so many of his mates who were severely wounded. We must also never forget the others who died there.'

Jorge Altieri was of great help to me in researching this book. He welcomed me and took me to meet his parents, Victorio 'Cholo' Altieri and Hazel. I thank them and respect them for their honesty and openness and for reliving their nightmare for me, their son's former enemy.

'My son, Jorge,' says Cholo, 'went to war, a war his mother and I didn't want him to go to. Being a father, a parent, I could see things differently from eighteen- to twenty-year-old kids. Hazel would have done anything to stop him going. He left saying he'd rather die in the Malvinas than be shot on our own doorstep. Once he had reported to his barracks, that was it – no stopping. We all travelled down to the barracks the day he left. I can still see it all now, the madhouse atmosphere. Outside, mothers, fathers, girlfriends and wives all crying. No celebrations. The only ones celebrating were the soldiers shouting "Argentina, Argentina" as they left the camp on buses. It was only after the war I was told they had been ordered to shout like that to pretend they were happy.

'Only a few told the truth about their true feelings before they left. One was Santiago Gauto, who gave us a letter for his mother, who lives in our area. When I saw the weapons leaving on the trucks behind the buses I wouldn't believe it. I was shocked. I said to my other son: "Look what we are going to fight a war with: old Mausers."

'My neighbours would say to me: "Look, Cholo, we've taken the Malvinas. Be happy." I would say: "What do we want to go to the Malvinas for if we can't even build a school for our own children?" There was going to be a school in our street which was never built. People behaved as if it was a football game, as if war was a game. All the kids knew about war was what they had seen in American films on TV.

'We only received two letters from Jorge, both containing requests for food, any food, chocolate, salami, food, food, food. We sent him food in parcels. One weighed about sixteen kilos. He never received anything. Where did the food go?

'As the war escalated all we heard on the news was lies. Everyone lied to us. We were always winning on the battle front. We had sunk the *Invincible.* Then... peace. It was surrender. I went to the camp for news of Jorge. All day I waited outside his barracks. They told me: 'Go home. He is fine.'

'Soon after, the phone rang. It was a local policeman, not a military policeman. "Mr Altieri, don't panic now, but your son is here in Comodoro Rivadavia. He's being checked over, OK?"

'I asked: "Is he wounded?"

'"No, it's just a routine check-up on all the soldiers."

'I thanked him. We were all relieved.

'I grabbed some things and told my wife I was going to fetch Jorge personally. I went to the airport and bought myself a ticket, but there weren't any seats. I sat in the airport all night waiting and got the first flight next morning. I arrived in Comodoro and got a taxi. The driver said to me: "Your son, eh? My sister Petrona is nursing him and he's OK. Bruised shoulder, that's all."

'My wife had phoned the hospital and told them I was on my way. A surgeon met me and took me to one side and started a lecture that I wasn't really interested in.

'I said to him: "Look, doctor, we are both adults. Tell me the truth."

'He said: "You can see him, but don't behave as if you are shocked. Behave as if nothing has happened. Don't cry. Nothing. If you want to cry go to a corner somewhere and cry as much as you want. Your son has been wounded in the head. He is paralysed down the right side and he has lost his left eye."

'I couldn't believe what I was hearing. I immediately said: "Doctor, please, can't we transplant my eye for him?" He said it was impossible. When I entered the ward it was full of wounded guys. They were everywhere: feet missing from the cold, shrapnel amputations, stuff you only see in the movies. Jorge was at the far end, out of intensive care, but still unconscious. I sat for ages holding his hand, talking to him. Eventually he looked at me. He could only say: "How lucky that you came, Papa." He lapsed into unconsciousness again.

'For four nights and days I stayed beside him, talking, feeding and cleaning him. The staff were so busy I had to help. He was so hungry he nearly bit one of my fingers off. He had gone to war weighing about seventy kilos and now he was just about thirty kilos of skin and bone. After four days a man invited me to his home to rest, to wash and shave and even borrow his clean underwear. He ran me to and from the hospital in his car. I cannot thank him enough for his kindness.

'By the time Jorge was ready to move to Campo de Mayo

hospital I was feeding and helping other wounded kids in the ward. I knew my son had a feeling, a suspicion, about his left eye. Many a time he had tried to reach a mirror to look at himself.

'The day he was transferred I went with him, carrying his stretcher. At the airport there was a biting wind, freezing. We had to unload them on to the runway beside the plane. All they had was trousers and a blanket. Imagine it: all those poor lads lying there on the runway in that freezing wind. An old Fokker was standing there waiting and two of the military personnel were standing there arguing. I went over to them and said: "Do you know why we lost the war? We lost because of what you're doing now, arguing. Instead of talking nonsense do something. Do you want these kids to die here on this runway? My son didn't die in the Malvinas and he's not going to die here on this runway." They were arguing about how to get them on to the plane. I pointed to a forklift truck nearby and told them to use it to lift those boys on their stretchers into the plane. You should have seen the inside of that plane. I spent the whole flight holding blood and plasma up in the air because they didn't even have the hooks for the drips. Nothing was organized.

'At Campo de Mayo hospital my wife and I helped every day. We helped Jorge and the other wounded lads, boys with no parents to visit them because they came from far away at the ends of our country. They had no one to visit them or help them.

'The neurosurgeon gave us a lecture on the brain. He said the first thing to move would be his leg because it was part of the thickest part of the cerebral command. Every day my wife and I copied what the physiotherapist taught us. Imagine our happiness when, one day, Jorge showed us he could move his toes. All the rubbing and massaging started to pay off. It was the start of a long rehabilitation programme which would eventually see him walk again. Not properly – but enough for him to get about unaided.

'It is only now, twelve years on, that I am beginning to settle, that my nerves are calming down. To hear all those kids screaming in pain in those wards does something to you. People should respect those who were wounded and the suffering they went through. We suffered, too, my wife and I. It was our son, our son who left fit and healthy and returned the way he is, suffering. That is a word we know the full meaning of and it hurts, it hurts deeply. Even now if my wife heard of a witch-doctor in China or somewhere who could cure him she would take him there tomorrow.

'I'll always remember how we found out. In his unconsciousness he was mumbling his name and address. At first they thought he thought he was General Galtieri. Then a woman told a constable to check the phone number for the address and that was how they found his true identity, otherwise it would have been a long time before we knew where he was or what had happened to him.

'It is twelve years on and people forget. They forget within a week. They don't want to know. There was more interest in people returning from the World Cup than there was in the wounded coming home from the war. Yes, people forget too quickly.

'The pain and suffering is for ever... '

'As soon as I saw Jorge in Comodoro,' recalls Hazel Altieri, 'I wanted to cry or scream. I was in pain. Oh, the pain at seeing my son like that. I talked to him, trying to hide my pain. I didn't want him to see it. After a while I went to the other kids in the ward who were crying for their mothers. My tears were falling. I was crying for Jorge and for those other kids in the ward.

'I arrived at Campo de Mayo hospital one morning to find his bed empty. I was scared until I found he was with Dr Nano, the eye specialist. When he was brought back he said: "Mama, Mama, my eye is missing."

'I kept talking to him. I stayed with him, talking. I knew if I left he would cry. When I did leave him I went into the corridor and leaned against the wall and cried and cried. My heart was aching.

'Some people had no idea what we were going through. You would get stupid comments like: "Why don't you buy him a nice new wheelchair?" I had no time for them. My son was going to walk. He and I were going to walk together. We would fight this thing together.

'Cholo was suffering too because he knew I have heart problems and he was worried about the stress on me as well. The pressure on him was intense. Quite often I would lie in bed at night and see him just standing there too worried to sleep. It is only when you have been through what we have been through that you realize the suffering and the pain of parents of soldiers.

'I cried inside. I cried outside. I cried until I couldn't cry any more.'

War didn't seem a possibility to Carol Connick as her son Denzil was recalled for the move to the Falklands. She would rather he went there than back to Northern Ireland.

'I started worrying after the *Belgrano* and *Sheffield* were sunk. Until then it was all speculation. Now it was real. When the news was on I would pace up and down the living-room, wearing holes in the carpet. I wanted to watch the news and I didn't want to watch it. If I could have gone to sleep until it was all over I would have been happy. I wanted to be an ostrich and bury my head in the sand. I began to realize this was no Northern Ireland when 2 Para fought at Goose Green.

I knew then it was much more serious than I had anticipated. Lads were being killed down there.

'Our only relief came from his letters, always full of cheer and happiness, his usual confident manner, and telling us about the practical jokes they pulled on each other. We would laugh at them. They cheered us up no end.

'I had this horrible feeling deep down, almost psychic, that something was going to happen. I had it throughout the war, not one good day. On 14 June I was in a terrible state all day. It was a Monday, I believe. We didn't even know what was going on but I knew something had happened. About nine o'clock that night a neighbour came running down the hill to our house and said the war was over. By that stage we were not watching TV: we just couldn't bear it. We were all relieved, almost happy, but my husband, Ernie, refused to open the champagne until we knew Denzil was OK.

'I went to work next day thinking maybe we could have a few drinks in the evening but as I got off the bus on the way home Ernie was there waiting for me. I knew, I just knew as soon as I saw his face, that what I had felt had come true. I ran away crying. I didn't want to hear my Denzil's fate. Ernie had only heard half an hour before. They told us Denzil had lost a leg four inches below the knee. The doctor came and gave me Valium and I slept. Next morning I told Ernie Denzil had lost his left leg. He couldn't figure out how I knew. It was because my own left leg was numb.

'I got a telegram from Denzil on the Thursday and I knew then that he would survive. Then nothing. I rang the Paras, the Ministry of Defence, Army manning and records, everyone I could think of to try to find out what had happened to him and what was happening to him and when he was coming home and where he was arriving home. Nobody could help. Then I got a letter from the Army which utterly disgusted me. Well, it wasn't really a letter, just an impersonal formatted sheet of paper with things like "Son is dead/fatally wounded/seriously wounded/" etc. pencilled through. I couldn't believe it. The people who dreamt up this type of impersonal communication and sent it to relatives are totally out of touch with reality. Today I am still disgusted about it.

'Denzil phoned me himself from the hospital on Ascension Island. He sounded shaky. He said he would be arriving at Brize Norton the next day. When I phoned the Paras to say I would be meeting him they said I would not be allowed near him. I told them I would wreck the place if anyone tried to stop me getting to him.

'I had been told his flight landed at 10.30, but we set off so early to beat the traffic that we got there at 9 a.m. We had only just got there when his flight arrived. I am convinced I was deliberately given the wrong time because they didn't want relatives there when the wounded arrived home. When you are in the Army you are just a number, you're never a mother's son. All the Army and the military wanted us to celebrate on the tarmac with no injured in sight. Ernie and I and our other three sons, Kevin, Michael and Neil, waited in the lounge. We watched as families were reunited and hugged each other. Next thing, we noticed a big canvas screen being placed around the doorway so nobody could see who was coming off. I was fuming. I saw some Air Force men popping champagne and went over to them and told them this was not a place for a party while wounded men were still on the plane.

'My name was broadcast and a young Air Force officer began to take me to the plane. We were stopped by some high-ranking officer, looking all high and mighty, who said it wasn't allowed. He didn't stop me.

'When I saw Denzil I didn't recognize him. I went pale. I had a son who went off weighing thirteen stone and came home weighing six stone. The Army told me he had lost his leg four inches below the knee. He only had four inches of leg left and his other was badly shattered. I held his hand as his stretcher was placed on the ambulance bus. All around us were soldiers with missing limbs, arms, legs, feet. I was the only parent on the bus as it set off for RAF Wroughton hospital. As we arrived the matron said: "You have broken all the rules. This is not allowed. Civilians are not permitted."

"'So what," I snarled back at her.

'Denzil was too ill to talk. He was terribly weak. I just wanted to be by his side, holding his hand. Tears flowed from both of us. I stayed with him all night and next day they transferred him to the Woolwich Military Hospital in London. I went home, packed a bag and headed for the Woolwich. They flew Denzil to Woolwich by helicopter and I was given accommodation nearby. I stayed with him for the next five weeks. Ernie managed a week but we couldn't afford to have both of us away from work and in London. My bosses were marvellous. They told me to take as much time as I needed and not to worry about the job. He improved all through the five weeks. When his mates came to see him he put on a brave face, but that's all it was, a front.

'After I had returned home I was phoned and told he would be coming home for a week and would be arriving in a couple of hours. Within an hour our street was covered in flags. Denzil's community welcomed him home. It was emotional for us all and it was hard to watch as Ernie carried him out of the car and into the house. We went up to the rugby club for a party and the Caldicot Male Voice Choir sang for him. There wasn't a dry eye in the place that night.

'We now had a situation where we had to learn about Denzil's disability and the best ways of helping him. He had to have a bed downstairs, but the lavatory was upstairs.

Watching my son moving around the house by dragging himself on his behind hurt me. Even today, when I think of it, I hurt. Family, friends and the people in this community banded together to show us their support and that they cared for Denzil and for us.

'Inwardly I am bitter. Why my son? I sometimes ask. I have never said it to Denzil and Ernie and I never discussed it because we didn't need to. Each of us knew how the other felt. Ernie and I could read each other's mind.

'Looking back, I think it was a pointless war, a war that should never have happened. Look at what it is costing to keep a garrison down there when it would be cheaper to give every Islander who wants to leave a million pounds and let the Argentinians have the place.

'I know my son was doing his job as a soldier. But it hurts when people say it was his job.

'I am not political but I blame Margaret Thatcher's government. The Argentinians were wrong to invade, but the Islanders, too, should carry some of the blame for the war. The Islanders and the Falkland Islands Company traded with Argentina. They all knew what Argentina was up to, what its ambitions were. As far as I'm concerned they all encouraged them. Another thing which infuriated me was that two months or so after the war the local pubs and shops wouldn't accept cheques from the soldiers. They took pesos from the Argentinians.

'Our military authorities at home do not keep in touch with the wounded. Only Simon Brewis has ever bothered, keeping up his wonderful work with them.

'If there is ever another war the military should learn that the soldiers are our sons and that relatives are not just numbers. Relatives should be treated with respect and consideration with a more personal touch shown when bringing bad news.'

Afterword

M Y STOMACH was in knots, but it was not because I'd
just met Argentinian veterans of Mount Longdon. It
was the sight of the young sentry that made me so nervous.
Twelve years had passed, but seeing him standing there at
the gates of the 7th Mechanized Regiment's barracks was
like stepping back to June 1982.

In the car with me were Diego and Jorge Altieri. Jorge
explained the purpose of our visit to the sentry, who
pointed to the guardroom. There a corporal issued us with
a pass, as young soldiers peered round the corner out of
curiosity. I was curious about them, too. After all, I had
never expected to find myself in the nerve centre of my
subject of research: the 7th Regiment's training camp. Jorge
had set it up as a surprise for me, though I must admit I had
dropped a few hints.

As we climbed back into our car another conscript got in
with us to act as our guide. We drove to the HQ building,
where I was glad to find some relief from the hot sun. Jorge
went off to find the officers in charge, so that we could visit

the military museum, while I had the slightly uncomfortable feeling of being scrutinized by three or four young officers standing in the lobby talking. I understood nothing of what they said, of course, but the atmosphere was not hostile.

Then Diego and I were shown into the office of what I took to be the regiment's second in command. Through Diego I explained that I was honoured to be there and grateful that he understood the purpose of my visit. The officer gave me a firm handshake and said: 'If I'd known before this morning I would have seen to it that you could have had the use of everything here. I know my men and officers would like to meet you, but, so be it, a quiet affair it will be. My only request is: no photos, for security reasons.' It was a request that is all too familiar in Britain too.

We went outside and I inspected the new Baldini parade square. It was explained to me that Lieutenant Baldini was the only Argentinian officer in that regiment killed in the war. 'He was a brave soldier,' said the young officer accompanying us. 'We even have a tank named after him, and since we're a mechanized unit it seems appropriate. Some of the camp roads are named after Longdon vets. Those who failed to come home are the heroes.'

His English was limited but what he did speak was good. There was no mistaking the enthusiasm and dedication of this well-turned out young platoon officer. He was very much like a young Sandhurst officer newly assigned to his company.

Next we visited the regimental museum, with its trophies and battle honours dating from 1813 to the present day, along with photographs and uniforms displayed proudly in glass cabinets. Within ten minutes about four officers in track suits had tagged on to our guided tour, and Diego was soon busily turning back and forth between them and me.

Much of what they had to say was fascinating, and their manners were impeccable. I only wished some of my mates and officers from 3 Para could have been there.

I stood looking at a photograph of Lieutenant Baldini in his number one uniform. Smart and typically military, I thought as I looked into his eyes. He was very hard on his men, but he held his ground on Longdon. Just like the Argentinians, we too name roads and places after dead heroes. And Lieutenant Baldini is a hero in the eyes of the 7th Mechanized Regiment. It is not for anyone to pass judgement on him now, for he is no longer here to defend himself. All the same, perhaps there are lessons to be learned for the future.

Beside the tribute to Lieutenant Baldini was the regimental flag, beautifully displayed in its glass case. A young officer laughed as he stood watching me looking at the flag. Whispering in my ear, Diego conveyed to me what the officer went on to say. 'There is a good story behind that flag, Vincent. You see, when our regiment was in full withdrawal from your army we had to rescue our pride. That flag was brought back off the hills [Mount Longdon and Wireless Ridge]; then, after the surrender, each battle honour was unpicked from the flag and hidden inside the collar of the uniform of one of our men. But we had one problem during your searches. To get this flag home without you having it as a war prize, we chose one man you wouldn't search to bring it home.'

'Who?' I asked.

The officer smiled as he said: 'The padre, the man of the cloth. So, you see not everything was left behind.'

As a result of this brilliant stunt these battle honours were to remain safe for many years. At the time I really laughed. But, looking back now, I remember many a man who has died trying to save his regimental colours.

Maria, the museum keeper, looked through my photographs of the war, for the one thing the place didn't have, apart from a solitary British mess tin, was a Falklands stand. It is only when you see the situation from the Argentinians' side that you really understand what happened. For they lost not only a war and their pride, but also every personal belonging. It's obvious why they have no photographs to display.

As I chatted with the officers, some of them senior, I was presented with a plate by the second in command. In return I presented them with a plaque from 3 Para which I hope will prove to be a symbol of peace. Then an older soldier walked in and the senior officers smiled, and one of them said: 'He was on Mount Longdon.' The soldier squeezed me in a bear hug and shook my hand warmly. 'It's an honour to meet you,' he said. 'You were fine soldiers, fine soldiers, professional.'

A young officer shouted: 'I'm trying to get Vince to tell us about their training, but he just grins at me and winks.' Then I, Diego and the Longdon vet sat down together. 'Pedro López', as I must call him, was the man I'd been trying to track down for four months, and now, by pure chance, he suddenly turned up. Sadly, I was coming to the end of my stay and it was late to arrange a proper interview.

On 11 June 1982 Pedro López was the sergeant attached to B Company, controlling the 120mm mortar in the bowl on Mount Longdon. He was the very same guy Jerry Phillips and Dickie Absolon tried to take out just before the battle. And the same man that Dom and Ben tried to grenade during it. Pedro grinned and said: 'I knew the English wanted me badly, so I moved back ten or fifteen metres. All your tracer rounds hit my old position. God was on my side.'

Pedro is still serving with the 7th Mechanized Regiment,

and as I write he is in Bosnia with the UN, working alongside British troops. Ironic, isn't it?

While Diego and Jorge spoke with Maria and the young officers about future contact between us, I wandered over to a wall covered with framed photographs. Each photo in the regimental lobby is of a soldier they lost, and every one of them is there – nearly all young men barely out of their teens. As I stared at the pictures I could see all my friends in 3 Para who had died on Longdon. My mind flashed back to the summer of 1982, when as a nation we basked in the glorious sunlight of victory.

That summer I attended the Falklands memorial service in St Paul's Cathedral, in London, which TV crews were filming for national posterity. Sitting just across the aisle from me was Margaret Thatcher and a clutch of important MPs, as well as the Queen and other members of the royal family.

The Archbishop of Canterbury stood up and, with a few simple words, angered many people, including some national newspapers. As we all bowed our heads in prayer, he said: 'Let us also pray for the young Argentinian soldiers who died.'

Afterwards I, along with a coachload of soldiers from 3 and 2 Para, was invited to the terrace of the House of Commons, overlooking the Thames. None of us enjoyed the warm beer and curled-up cucumber sandwiches very much. One of the MPs came up to us. Well done, chaps, good show, but it was easy, eh? All young conscripts, seventeen years old. No match for us pros! That was his message to us.

What a prick, I thought. They were young, but so were our boys: seventeen, eighteen or nineteen mainly – the same as the Argentinians. Twelve years on I was looking at the Argentinians' faces on the wall of their regimental lobby. Their faces, our boys' faces – there was no difference at all really. I realized that the Archbishop had been right in 1982, but I didn't think so at the time.

It was time to go. I didn't want to overstay my welcome. But just then, as I was about to leave, I could see both sides. I saw the need to put aside questions of race, colour, religion or politics. Forget whose side you're on. It's the soldier and his loved ones who suffer. So next time you feel an old soldier is boring you with his wounds and his stories, remember this book and think of Hazel Altieri, who speaks for all mothers whose sons have been to war, then perhaps you'll understand the 'two sides of hell'.

'I cried inside. I cried outside. I cried until I could cry no more.'

Appendix

BRITISH LOSSES ON MOUNT LONGDON:
3RD BATTALION, PARACHUTE REGIMENT

Sergeant Ian McKay, VC
Corporal Stephen Hope
Corporal Keith McCarthy
Corporal Stewart McLaughlin
Corporal Alex Shaw
Corporal Scott Wilson
Lance-Corporal Peter Higgs
Lance-Corporal Christopher Lovett
Lance-Corporal James Murdoch
Lance-Corporal David Scott
Private Richard Absolon, MM
Private Gerald Bull
Private Jason Burt
Private John Crow
Private Mark Dodsworth
Private Anthony Greenwood

Private Neil Grose
Private Peter Hedicker
Private Timothy Jenkins
Private Craig Jones
Private Stewart Laing
Private Ian Scrivens
Private Phillip West

47 wounded

ARGENTINIAN LOSSES ON MOUNT LONGDON AND WIRELESS RIDGE: 7TH MECHANIZED REGIMENT

Lieutenant Juan Domingo Baldini
Corporal Pedro Alberto Orozco
Corporal Dario Rolando Rios
Private Elbio Eduardo Araujo
Private Miguel A. Arrascaeta
Private Angel Benítez
Private Omár Aníbal Brito
Private Sergio A. Carballido
Private Alfredo Cattoni
Private José Luis Del Hierro
Private Luis Alberto Díaz
Private Miguel Falcón
Private Aldo Omár Ferreyra
Private Miguel A. González
Private Nestor M. González
Private Donato M. Gramisci
Private Guillermo E. Granado
Private Ricardo Herrera
Private Carlos A. Hornos
Private Manuel A. Juárez

Private Julio Hector Maidana
Private Marcello D. Massad
Private Rolando Pacholczuk
Private Miguel Angel Pascual
Private Dante Luis S. Pereira
Private Alberto D. Petrucelli
Private Ramón O. Quintana
Private Isaac Erasmo Rocha
Private Jose Luis Rodríguez
Private Macedonio Rodríguez
Private Victor Rodríguez
Private Julio Romero
Private Enrique H. Ronconi
Private Alejandro P. Vargas
Private Pedro Voskovic
Private Manuel A. Zelarayán

At least 80 wounded

Leabharlanna Poibli Chathair Bhaile Átha Cliath
Dublin City Public Libraries